THE POLITICIAN'S DAUGHTER

Marion Leigh

Rudling House

Rudling House

Rudling House Publishing Limited
Suite 11480 145-157 St John Street
London EC1V 4PY

Published in the UK in 2011 by Rudling House

A CIP catalogue record for this book is available from the British Library

ISBN 978 0 9562760 3 2
Copyright © Marion Leigh 2011

Printed and bound in Great Britain by
CPI Antony Rowe, Chippenham and Eastbourne

ABOUT THE AUTHOR

Marion Leigh was born in Birmingham, England. After receiving her M.A. in Modern Languages from the University of Oxford, she worked for a year as a volunteer in Indonesia, then moved to Canada where she enjoyed a successful career as a financial and legal translator.

Marion now lives on the Costa del Sol. She and her husband spend the summer in North America, cruising aboard their 20-metre powerboat. To date, they have covered over 15,000 nautical miles exploring the Great Lakes and the Eastern Seaboard of the United States and Canada.

This is Marion's first novel featuring RCMP Marine Unit Sergeant Petra Minx.

ACKNOWLEDGEMENTS

There are many people who have encouraged, helped and inspired me while I was writing this book and I am extremely grateful to them all. In particular, I would like to thank my editor and publisher Peter Brookes of Rudling House, Ole Dammegard for the cover design, Isabelle Crail, Professor Brian Ellis, Loveday Ellis, Dr. Jim Haight, Lynn Haight and Raquel Sánchez Mesa for their assistance and advice. Any errors and inconsistencies are my responsibility. Above all, I thank my husband Peter for his unconditional support. Without him, this book would not have been possible.

(

PROLOGUE

For the first time in her short adult life, she felt out of control. It was a sensation she did not relish. Could she finally have pushed the envelope too far, to a point of no return? Always she had known where the edges were and relied on an unerring instinct to steer her away from the brink of disaster. Now it seemed she had crossed a boundary into savage, uncharted territory. Had she been too engrossed to see the warning signs or had there been none?

Lying on her back, she focussed her eyes on the ceiling and wondered where she had gone wrong. A shiver ran up her spine, despite the itching and burning of her skin. The slightest shift in position increased the agony and caused her wounds to suppurate. She wished she could relieve the pressure on her hips, but the leather restraints held her firmly in place. At least she couldn't tear herself to pieces.

With the hollow mirth of the near-delirious, she gave a silent laugh then shivered again as the gravity of the situation struck her. If she had been less insistent on doing things her way, she might not now be fighting for her life.

She was, to borrow Shakespeare's words, hoist by her own petard. Hoist, moist, foist, joist, the words jangled in her brain. Her eyes rolled backwards as pain shot through her and she slipped into semi-consciousness.

Something roused her: the feeling of someone bending over her, not touching, but very close.

'Too clever for your own good this time, eh?' The smell of garlic and hot breath. 'Thought you were better than the others, didn't you?' pursued the rough male voice. 'Well I can still teach you a thing or two.'

She glued her eyelids shut and tried to block out his presence. Petard, retard, leotard, discard. Go away! Leave me alone! She hoped he wouldn't see the tiny beads of sweat forming on her brow.

'I know you're awake. You can't fool me.' His voice was harsh and insistent. 'I've had enough of your kind. This is the end of your games.'

The sickly-sweet smell of his breath began to turn her stomach. If he touched her, she was powerless to protect herself. She fought to suppress a rising panic and found herself reciting a long-discarded bedtime prayer.

'Look at me...' His hand shot out and grabbed her chin. In desperation, she gathered her saliva and spat in his face.

'Stay away from her, you fool! Let her go!' The door closed with a bang and footsteps hurried across the room. 'What in God's name have you done?' The woman's tone was accusatory.

'Nothing she didn't ask for.'

He was right, of course, in a way. Hot tears of relief and regret welled up under her lashes and she stifled a gasp as the pain hit her again. She had to stay quiet and keep her breathing shallow. If she lost her resolve and the last shreds of strength and determination, hysteria would overwhelm her.

'Don't bullshit me. This time you've gone too far!' A hand touched her forehead. 'She's as hot as hell.'

'That's not my fault.' The whine of the hard-done-by. 'Whatever happens, we're in this together. You'll pay too!'

'You and your lousy threats! Just get rid of her.'

CHAPTER ONE

The A34 was one long snarl of traffic. With mounting irritation, Petra checked the clock on the dashboard of her rented VW Golf. There was no way she could be in Oxford by two o'clock.

Her day was not going to plan. If it were, she would be sitting with a cup of coffee in her sister's conservatory after sailing on Southampton Water; she would be enjoying the unusually mild October weather and recharging her batteries before returning to Canada at the end of the following week. For the first time in five years, she had requested enough leave to make the trip worthwhile. Instead, she was stuck in a hot, manual-shift car with no lunch and sore ankles.

By the time Petra reached the outskirts of Oxford, she was ready to scream. The beneficial effects of ten days' R&R had vanished without trace, along with her newfound resolve to allow more time for herself. With relief, she turned into the Botley Park-and-Ride, found a parking spot close to the bus stop, locked the Golf and jumped onto the waiting bus.

Twenty minutes later, she stepped into an oasis of tranquillity. Beyond the stout oak door guarding the College lay a different world. The roar of the city was a barely perceptible hum. Through the archway ahead, the grey stone quadrangle basked in the afternoon sun, the mullioned windows in its ancient walls glinting like polished brass.

Petra scanned her surroundings with interest. It was over a dozen years since her last visit to Oxford as a summer student at the impressionable age of sixteen. To her right, in the porter's lodge, a man in a sober black suit sat at a counter behind a cashier's window, squinting at banks of CCTV screens. He looked up as she approached and swivelled his chair towards the window.

'Sorry, Miss. No visitors allowed. It's after two o'clock. You'll have to come back tomorrow morning.'

Petra gave a slight shake of her head and placed both hands on the window ledge. 'I've come to see the Dean. I was told he'd be expecting me. Will you let him know I'm here?'

Several seconds passed while the porter made a show of examining his screens. Finally he said: 'What name shall I say?'

'Minx, Petra Minx.'

With a small sigh, he picked up the telephone. She waited until he dialled before turning her attention to the College notice board. It was thick with announcements and posters urging students to take part in a host of activities, from a lecture on medieval numerology to a sleep-in on the front lawn to raise funds for the homeless. The choice was mind-numbing.

'Dr. Stevenson? I have a Miss Minx here at the lodge. Says she's come to see you. What do you want me to do?' The porter paused. Petra could feel his eyes boring into her back. 'Right then, Sir, I'll send her over.'

As the porter finished giving her directions, Petra flicked her wrist at the array of monitors. 'What a shame you have to spend your day watching those things,' she said.

The porter shrugged, impervious to her sarcasm. 'CCTV's a fact of life. You wouldn't believe the riffraff we see nowadays. Hardly human, some of them, with their piercings and tattoos.'

'I'm sure you'll rise to the challenge!' Petra threw him a warm victory smile. She had made her point and could afford to be magnanimous.

She heard the porter grunt as she left the lodge and latched the door behind her. Halfway across the quadrangle, she raised a hand to push a wing of black hair away from her face then turned it into an ironic wave. No doubt he was following her progress on his screens.

A faint vibration of the phone in her pocket alerted Petra before it rang. She pulled it out and flipped it open. There was only one person it could be: her boss A.K.

His first call had come in at 9.30 that morning just as she was preparing to cast off from the dock in her brother-in-law's Nonsuch. The inventive Canadian design made sailing single-handed a delight.

As soon as she had heard the urgent tone of her Ottawa-based boss, she had known something was up. And for him to be calling at 4.30 a.m. Canadian time, it had to be something important. Now he was on the line again.

'Have you interviewed her yet?' A.K.'s voice was, as usual, full of impatience. Not so much as a "sorry" for cutting into her vacation.

'I'm on my way to see the Dean right now. I made the best time I could, Sir. The traffic …'

'I don't care what your problems are! I'm getting a lot of flak from high up. My orders are to get someone in there ASAP, but to keep it low-key. No police, no media. Donald Mortlake's vying for party leadership. He doesn't want anything to foul his chances. Call me back as soon as you've finished.'

Petra dropped the phone into her jacket pocket with a quiet curse. Her holiday had been interrupted, the pressure was already building and still she had no idea of the circumstances surrounding Emily Mortlake's apparent disappearance. The girl's father was clearly more interested in his own success than his daughter's whereabouts.

She passed beneath a pair of smirking gargoyles and through an arched passageway worn smooth by the feet of generations. The scent of learning seemed to hang in the air, pervasive and sweet. At the far end of the flagstone corridor, she paused outside a door marked Office of the Dean, raised the brass knocker and gave a sharp double rap.

'Come in!'

Petra opened the door and walked into a panelled study dominated by a massive refectory table, behind which sat a rather rumpled man. The room smelled faintly of tobacco smoke. There must be a pipe somewhere, she thought, as her eyes roamed the room. Yes, there it was, on the bookcase.

The Dean rose and extended his hand. 'Miss Minx? How do you do? Please take a seat.' He indicated an upright wooden chair on Petra's side of the table. She shook his hand and took her place without comment.

The Dean leaned forward and studied her with such undisguised curiosity that she began to feel like an alien species in a cage. 'I understand you want to speak to Emily Mortlake's former roommate Amy Shire,' he said. 'I've arranged for her to come over shortly. Before she arrives, I'd like to know something about you and your organization. Frankly, I was expecting someone more – ah – mature.'

Petra bristled. There were times when she wished she looked her age. 'You should be the last person to judge a book by its cover, Dr. Stevenson,' she said. 'It might help you to know that I'm a Sergeant with the RCMP, that's the Royal Canadian Mounted Police. I have over ten years' service in the Marine Unit and Special Investigations. I was enjoying a well earned vacation in the South of England when my boss called and asked me to get here as quickly as possible.'

'Forgive me, but you hardly look as old as our third years.' The Dean cleared his throat. 'I know that I speak not just for College, but for the whole University when I say that we appreciate your prompt response. This couldn't have come at a worse time. We are already in the media spotlight over increased fees and the whole question of access to Oxford. If the press get wind of it, you can imagine the headlines: "Oxford student missing after jet-set summer".' He stood up and began to pace up and down the study, a frown creasing his forehead.

'For the time being, Sir, this is not an official investigation,' Petra said. 'I've been sent by the Canadian High Commission to find out from Amy what actually happened and why she's so certain that her friend has disappeared. Emily might simply have been delayed.'

'It's possible, but I fear not. Amy was close to breaking point when she came to see me yesterday. She's normally a well balanced girl, so I suspect there is something behind all this.'

'Why was she distressed, Dr. Stevenson?'

'Emily had arranged to meet Amy in Geneva on September 23rd. She failed to keep the appointment and hasn't returned to College. Amy's worried that the summer vacation job Emily obtained on board a motor yacht was some sort of scam. She was so distraught that I thought it best to contact Emily's parents in Toronto.'

'What was their reaction?' Petra asked.

'I spoke to Donald Mortlake, Emily's father. He's adamant that there's a simple explanation for her absence.'

'Have you had much contact with him since Emily came to College?'

'No. There's been no need, everything's paid on time. Emily's a bright student, a bit casual in her approach sometimes, and she has a tendency to be arrogant, but there hasn't been any real trouble.'

'But there has been some trouble?'

'She wanted to switch courses, which is not generally allowed as it is in North America. When I explained the situation to her, she let the matter drop – after calling us backward and out of date.' The Dean smiled. 'Miss Mortlake holds a high opinion of herself and of her ability to do what she wants. We, on the other hand, have centuries of tradition to maintain.'

'I understand, Sir.'

'I hope you do, because I'm relying on you, Miss Minx, to conduct your enquiries with the utmost discretion and to keep me informed.'

He gave Petra a piercing look that belied his casual exterior. She held his gaze and nodded. She was beginning to form a picture of Emily and was anxious to talk to Amy.

A timid knock sounded at the door. 'That'll be Amy now,' the Dean said. He pulled open the door and greeted a petite, wan-faced girl with dark circles under her eyes. Shoulder-length fair hair hung limply about her face. 'How are you, Amy? This is Miss Minx from Canada. She's going to help us find out why Emily didn't meet you as planned. I'll leave you to talk. I have a meeting to attend. Make yourselves comfortable.'

Petra closed the door firmly behind the Dean and placed a hand on Amy's arm. 'You look exhausted. Come and sit down, and please call me Petra.'

Amy acknowledged Petra's solicitude with a slow nod. 'I'm trying to focus on a paper that I have to write by the end of this week,' she said. 'It's really difficult with Emily missing…' She shook her head as if to stem a rush of tears. 'I'm sorry, I don't want to cry.'

'I know how difficult it must be for you,' Petra said. 'Let's begin at the beginning. I don't know any of the details – only that Emily didn't meet you as planned and there may be cause for concern.' She steered the young girl to a padded window seat overlooking the quadrangle. 'What can you tell me about Emily's summer job?'

Amy took a deep breath. 'It wasn't just Emily. It was both of us. We wanted to spend the summer working together. Emily didn't want to go to Canada, so we began to look at options here and in Europe.'

'How did you go about that? Did you use the University placement service?'

'No. We wanted something different and exciting, preferably outdoors. Emily said it would be a good idea to advertise on the Internet.'

Petra drew in a silent breath. The naivety of young women, even the educated and highly intelligent ones, never ceased to amaze her. The Internet was the perfect vehicle for fraudsters, perverts and loonies of all kinds.

Before Petra could voice her misgivings, Amy bent down to the rucksack she had placed on the floor by her feet and took out a laptop. 'I brought my computer,' she said. 'I can show you our ad and the response we received.' Amy typed in her password and opened a file. 'Here it is,' she said, passing the computer to Petra.

Petra sat back on the window seat and read the advertisement in silence. "2 blonde undergrads seek job in the sun June-Sept. Hotel, resort, villa or similar. Can cook, drive, swim, sail – and belly dance."

'Why did you mention belly dancing?' she asked, handing the computer back to Amy. 'Can you belly dance?'

'Not really. I tried it once, but Emily was very good. She said it would make us stand out from the crowd. And it must have done because we had a reply straightaway.' Amy scrolled upwards. 'Here it is.'

Petra noticed that the email response had come from MY *Titania*. The text was straightforward enough. "Megayacht lying Monte Carlo requires summer help. Light duties include silver service and relief bartending. Uniforms and training provided. Send name, age and photo in first instance. If selected, interviews will be held London, May 10th."

'I assume you sent photos as instructed,' Petra said. 'Do you have a copy?'

Amy nodded and clicked on another file. 'That's Emily,' she said.

Petra examined the picture closely and was not surprised by what she saw. Emily radiated confidence. She was standing with her right hand on her hip, looking directly at the camera, a slight smile on her face. Her long flaxen hair fell in soft curls over her bare shoulders. Her lipstick was the same shade of red as her strapless cocktail dress. She wore nothing round her neck so that the eye was drawn to her chest, but each wrist was enclosed in a chunky silver bracelet. A wide black and silver belt accentuated her waist and black spike-heel shoes gave her additional height.

'When was this taken?' Petra asked Amy.

'Last April, at a charity fashion show, just before we placed our ad on the Internet.' Amy minimized the picture of Emily, opened another file and showed Petra the photograph of herself. 'This was taken after the show. It was Emily's idea for me to pose with my legs crossed on that velvet sofa, smoking a cigarette in a holder. More sophisticated, she said, a bit Agatha Christie.'

Petra had to admit that with make-up and a little manipulation Emily had turned the pallid Amy into a much more appealing prospect for a megayacht owner seeking decorative crew. There was colour in her cheeks and her fair hair shone with health, picking up the gold of her deep V-necked blouse. Her black wrap-around skirt had been carefully parted to reveal slim legs and delicate ankles. One gold stiletto sandal had been kicked off and lay on the floor.

'Very sexy,' Petra said. 'Did it occur to you that the reply to your ad might just be a ploy to obtain hundreds of photographs of attractive young women?'

Amy refused to meet Petra's eyes, turning instead to stare through the window into the quadrangle. 'Not at that stage,' she whispered. 'We assumed they just wanted to know what we looked like. Emily said they wouldn't want dogs on a beautiful yacht.'

Emily the controller again, Petra thought, with Amy the typical follower. Yet it seemed that Amy had had the sense not to follow Emily blindly all the way. 'What happened after you sent the photographs?' she asked.

'Emily received another email confirming that they wanted to see us on May 10th. They told us which hotel to go to and how to get there. I can't show it to you because Emily didn't send me a copy. All the communication was done from her computer.'

'And where's her computer now?'

'I assume it's in storage with the rest of her stuff. Only the international students are allowed to store things here in College during vacations. I do know Emily didn't take it with her. She was instructed to take as little as possible.'

Petra steered the conversation back to the job interview. 'So you both went up to London. What happened when you arrived at the hotel?'

Amy turned again to the window, a faraway look in her pale grey eyes. She began to speak quietly, but without hesitation, as if every detail was etched in her mind. Her account was so vivid that Petra was able to visualize the scene as clearly as if she had been a gecko on the wall.

Emily and Amy walked along the carpeted corridor and stopped outside the door to the Ducal Suite. Amy hung back as Emily pressed the bell. After a few seconds' delay, the door opened and they walked into a marble-tiled lobby with a coffered ceiling. A tall girl with short, platinum blonde hair cut square across her forehead greeted them with a wide smile. Amy looked askance at the girl's tautly stretched Lycra top, leather mini-skirt and high boots. She could have been a character in a Bond movie. Emily was unperturbed by the girl's appearance. In heavily accented English, the girl asked them their names and ticked them off on a clipboard. 'Go right on through the lounge to the bedroom,' she said.

Emily walked through the lounge without a glance at the ornate Louis XV furnishings. Reluctantly, Amy followed. She plucked at Emily's sleeve as they entered the bedroom, but Emily shook her off. In front of them, on a king-size bed, lay an assortment of bikinis.

Amy was about to ask Emily what was going on when a stocky, grey-haired woman confronted them. Amy recoiled as the woman leered, revealing stained teeth, and ordered them to get changed into a bikini. 'I'll call you one by one,' she said, and disappeared through a door on the far side of the room.

'I don't mind going in first,' Emily said. 'What's the matter, Amy? You're not going to chicken out on me, are you?'

'This isn't an interview, it's a beauty contest,' Amy muttered.

'So? You know we'll have to wear swimsuits if we're on board a yacht.'

The short, mannish woman reappeared, calling Amy's name. When Emily tried to take Amy's place, she wouldn't let her. 'I'll keep the best for last,' she said, and prodded Amy through the door and into the adjoining room.

Amy found herself in another sitting room, smaller and more intimate, like a boudoir. Two middle-aged men in dark suits and ties were sitting on a sofa. The white of their shirts contrasted sharply with their olive skins. The one on the left, whose pointed chin was softened by a close-cropped beard, made a remark in a language Amy didn't understand. She fancied he could have been from India or the Middle East, even North Africa. Both the men were staring at her. Then she noticed a young man in the corner taking photographs with a camera on a tripod. The grey-haired woman was standing right behind her. She spun Amy round to face the camera and instructed her to take off the bikini top.

Petra could see the distress on Amy's face as she relived the experience. The implications were clear and Petra knew the answer to her question before she asked Amy: 'And did you?'

'Of course not! I turned and ran back into the bedroom. As soon as Emily saw me, she knew something was wrong. I didn't have time to warn her before the fat woman came and hustled her away.'

'Was Emily's reaction the same as yours?'

'Not at all. It was at least ten minutes before she came back, smiling and saying she thought they liked her and would give her the job. She was used to sunbathing topless in the Caribbean, so it didn't bother her one iota. There was even the possibility of doing some modelling, she said. She seemed to revel in the attention and didn't see anything wrong with their demands. I just wanted to get out of there as quickly as possible, I felt so stupid and unclean.'

With a little coaxing, Petra gleaned the rest of the story from Amy, who couldn't stop berating herself for being taken in by something on the Internet. The two girls heard nothing for several weeks after their visit to London. Even Emily started to put it out of her mind and apply for other jobs. Amy accepted a position with a firm of accountants in her hometown so that she could live with her parents and save her earnings.

Close to the end of term, Emily received an email advising her that she had been selected to join the summer crew of motor yacht *Titania*, leaving from Monte Carlo on June 25th. A return air ticket would be provided if she confirmed her acceptance of the job within two days.

Emily telephoned her mother to tell her what she was doing and fired off a positive response. Her mother's only stipulation was that Emily should visit her uncle in Geneva before returning to Oxford at the beginning of October. Chronically ill and childless, he took an intense interest in his sister's only daughter and she returned his love unconditionally.

Shortly after the end of the summer term, Emily took a plane from Gatwick to Nice, having persuaded Amy to join her in Switzerland at the end of the third week of September, all expenses paid.

Amy immersed herself in work and might have forgone her holiday if Emily had not already given her a full-fare ticket to Geneva. She was debating whether to use it or simply call Emily's uncle and cancel when, at the end of August, she received an exuberant postcard mailed from Cannes. The careless handwriting and hyperbolic style were typical of Emily: "Yacht awesome. Boss amazing, great job…mostly! Lots to tell. Must run. See you in 3 weeks – be there! xxx Emily". So Amy flew to Geneva and spent an anxious time with Emily's uncle, waiting for her friend to arrive. Emily's parents were unconcerned and insisted that she would turn up.

'How long did you stay in Switzerland?' Petra asked.

'Until the end of September,' Amy answered. 'I couldn't stay any longer; I had to get back here to prepare for the new academic year. I kept hoping Emily would just walk into my room.'

'And she hasn't telephoned or emailed you?'

'No.'

'What about Facebook and the other social networking sites? She could have contacted you that way,' Petra said.

Amy hesitated for a moment before shaking her head. 'Emily isn't on any of them. Her parents forbade it. Her father said he would disinherit her if she disobeyed him. Her mother was petrified she would meet some undesirable and run off somewhere.'

'Do you think that's what has happened?'

'I don't know, but I'm sure something's wrong. Emily and I are very close, even though we're so different. She was supposed to be mentoring one of the Freshers this week. When she didn't show up, I just had to go to the

Dean. Now you know everything.' Amy dropped her head into her hands and began to shake.

Petra laid a comforting hand on her back. 'You did the right thing, Amy,' she said. 'I'll do my best to find out what has happened to Emily.'

'But she's been gone so long! Anything could have happened. The last time I saw her was the day she left Oxford to begin her summer job.'

Petra heard a distant clock strike six as she made her way back across the quadrangle to the porter's lodge. He looked up as she poked her face round the door. She flashed him a conspiratorial smile and watched the sag go out of his shoulders.

'Thanks for your help. I'm leaving now,' she said.

'No problem, Miss.'

'By the way,' Petra added, 'what do you call that little pedestrian gate in the big door?'

'That's the late gate,' he replied. 'There used to be a curfew. Now the students can come and go all night, but the big door is kept closed for security reasons all the time. I've also heard it called a Judas gate, after some Victorian painting.'

'I'll take the late gate! Thanks again.' Petra pulled the door closed and exited into the street just ahead of a group of students. Alarm bells were already ringing in her head. If Amy's tale was true, and she had no reason to doubt her honesty, time could be of the essence. And A.K. would be waiting for news.

CHAPTER TWO

Cornmarket was awash with people. Students, keen to take advantage of the October warmth after an unremarkable summer, mingled with shop and office workers making their way home at the end of a wearying day. Petra threaded through a mass of oriental tourists gawking at the squat medieval tower of St. Michael's, turned into the calm of Market Street and pulled out her phone. The signal strength was poor. She pressed a speed dial button and waited until A.K.'s acerbic voice crackled through the earpiece.

'You took your time. What have you got?'

Frosty bastard, thought Petra. Never one to waste time on a greeting.

'Sir, I talked to the girl. It seems that her friend's disappearance may be linked to an Internet job offer. The job interview was a farce and obviously a way to recruit young women – for what I don't know. I've got a copy of emails sent and received and I'd like to try and make contact myself.'

'That's more like it! Now get yourself to London – Dolphin House, keys at the front desk. Our London liaison will contact you there. Remember, I need results.'

'Right, Sir, I should be there in a couple of hours.'

'Fine. Do it. Just be careful.'

Petra shook her head ruefully as the line went dead. Her boss, whom everyone called A.K. because of his staccato manner, was short to the point of being rude, yet she never doubted his concern for the safety of his staff. Their comfort was another matter.

Water cascaded over Petra's head and down her back in a torrent of heat and sensation. No one had contacted her on Wednesday evening though she had stayed up till midnight expecting a call. Her sleep had been troubled and she had woken early. The pulsating shower made her skin tingle and glow. For as long as she could remember, she had loved water. It was her element and held no fear for her. As a toddler, she had screamed and struggled violently whenever the time came to get out of the bath. Later, after learning to swim and snorkel, she progressed quite naturally to boating and scuba diving.

One of her mother's favourite books had been The Water Babies by Charles Kingsley. She recalled her mother telling her how she had stumbled across a dilapidated copy of the book in a flea market and been struck by the quality of the images, both pictorial and verbal. Throughout her childhood, Petra clamoured for the story to be read to her over and over again.

Rotating her head so that the water massaged her scalp and neck, Petra let her thoughts return to the previous day's interview with Amy Shire. There was no doubt that Amy had been thoroughly shaken by the episode at the hotel, and it was obvious that neither the blonde who had opened the door to let them in nor her domineering companion subscribed to Mrs. Doasyouwouldbedoneby's philosophy. From what the Dean had said, Emily was an arrogant young woman, an assessment confirmed by the slightly supercilious smile on her face in the photograph.

Petra's instinct told her that Emily had probably got herself into something much more sinister than she had expected. Teens and twenty-somethings were not known for their sense of self-preservation, according to Petra's Polish father. When his words resonated in her head, as they often did, she felt as if he were still with her.

The sense of human presence was so strong that Petra turned involuntarily to look behind her. The bathroom door was ajar, but the small room was empty. Petra turned off the shower, opened the sliding glass door and climbed with care out of the bath. English baths were so high and slippery compared to North American ones. She wondered how someone older and less agile would manage as she put one foot up on the edge of the bath to dry between her toes. Suddenly, she froze and gripped the towel tightly. She was sure she had heard a noise. Without looking round, she whirled to the right and slammed the door shut with her foot. There was an agonized shout as it bounced off the shoulder of a stranger whose spectacles, one earpiece detached from the frame, went skittering across the tiles.

'Who the hell are you and what are you doing in my bathroom?' Petra shouted, clutching the towel with one hand to cover her nakedness. 'Stay away from me! Get out of here!' She looked round for some sort of weapon and grabbed her nail scissors from the side of the washbasin. 'One step closer and I'll use these!'

'Woah! Easy there, Miss Minx! Slow down! I'm from the High Commission. My apologies if I gave you a fright.'

'A fright! That's an understatement!' Petra sized up her opponent. 'What are you, some kind of pervert? You obviously know who I am, so why didn't you announce yourself? I could have done you real harm!' Even in her adrenalin-fuelled rage, she had to admit that the intruder didn't appear to constitute much of a threat. His mild manner and salt-and-pepper hair suggested a computer nerd rather than a dangerous criminal or lunatic.

'There's certainly nothing wrong with your reflexes,' the man commented. 'A good job I chose those plastic frames; they're easy to replace.' He bent to retrieve the two sections from the floor and Petra tensed, ready to defend herself if necessary. 'I didn't think you'd be here yet,' he continued. 'I heard water running and came to investigate. Look, why don't you go and get dressed. I'll make coffee, then we can talk.'

'What a good idea,' Petra replied in her most sarcastic voice. She wasn't sure whether to believe him or not. His story was flimsy at best. If he had come to investigate running water, why the hell hadn't he knocked on the bathroom door first? Then she realized that she might not have given him time to do so before smashing the door shut in his face.

Still angry at being caught unawares, she let the bedroom door slam behind her. It was a form of protest she knew was futile. Nerds never noticed anything.

He proved her wrong as soon as she reentered the lounge. 'That crucifix you're wearing, Miss Minx, it's 18th century Italian, if I'm not mistaken.'

Petra looked at him curiously. A lot of people remarked on her necklace, but few had any idea of its age or provenance. 'Actually, you're right. It's a family heirloom. My mother's family came from Northern Italy. Its first owner was a priest. I wear it all the time – instead of a wedding ring.' His eyes lit up with surprise. 'Don't worry; my joke.' She fingered the heavy silver inlaid with black stones. Dressed now in a blue jogging suit, she felt more at ease though still wary. 'You'd better explain what

25

you're doing here and why you were watching me in the bathroom.'

'I wasn't watching you, though I could have enjoyed a few more minutes of voyeurism if you hadn't flattened me with the door. As I told you, the High Commission sent me to greet you.' He stood up from the sofa, drew himself upright and extended his hand. 'Sorry the formal introduction was overtaken by events. I'm Tom Gilmore, Political Officer, with a few additional responsibilities.'

Petra shook his hand briefly. 'I suppose I'm one of those.'

'Indeed. As acting RCMP Liaison Officer, I've been asked to give you whatever assistance I can. But first, let me atone for my sins.' He picked up a mug from the coffee table and handed it to her with a short, stiff Japanese-style bow. 'Please accept this as a peace offering.'

Petra could not help smiling. His meekness was deceptive and he had a self-deprecating sense of humour. 'Do you have more information for me? As I understand it, Donald Mortlake's pulling strings at the highest level, but doesn't want to go public. It doesn't make sense.'

'Do you know him?' Tom asked.

'Only by reputation. He's a high flyer and wants to take over the party leadership this year.'

'Right, and he's scared to death that the media will get wind of his daughter Emily's disappearance and scupper his chances. Apparently, a similar incident occurred four years ago. She went missing during her high school graduation trip to Mexico. He and his wife flew down there to help the police and found her living on the beach with some guy. Said she'd been conned into taking drugs and forced to stay against her will. Mortlake downplayed the whole story, but the scandal hit him hard. That's why he doesn't want an official investigation.'

'I suspect the press will dig up all the dirt they can anyway,' Petra said. 'Unless, of course, I can find her and bring her back before the leadership race heats up.'

'And how will you do that?' Tom asked, scepticism in his voice.

'I plan to do exactly what Emily and her friend Amy did: put out a "Job wanted" ad on the Internet. I have the details. With luck, it'll be enough of a lure to attract a response from motor yacht *Titania*.'

'And then what?'

'I'll join the crew, just like Emily. Follow in her footsteps and find out where she is.'

'You're crazy! If you do succeed in getting aboard, you could be exposing yourself to significant risk.'

'I have no illusions on that score, Tom,' Petra replied. 'I've been involved in undercover operations before.'

'It's still a hazardous undertaking. I don't like the idea, but I'll do what I can to give you a better than even chance. At least your hearing's good. Unusual nowadays,' he added. 'So many young people have been deafened by loud music.'

'In the Marine Unit you need sharp eyes and ears – to navigate in fog, for example – so I'm used to reacting instantly to the slightest sign or sound.'

Tom held up his broken glasses. 'There's no doubt whatsoever about that!'

Throughout that Thursday afternoon, Petra worked to establish her cover. She decided to portray herself as a disenchanted Canadian graduate student wanting to take an immediate six-month break from her thesis. After some discussion with Tom, she decided to keep her own name. She telephoned the Dean and asked him to enter her into the University records so that any background check would corroborate her story. Then she sat down to compose the crucial "Job wanted" ad. In it, she professed a desire to travel, an eagerness for new experiences and a love of the water. It was always best to stick close to the truth.

The bait laid, Petra prepared to sit back and wait.

At breakfast on Friday, she checked her messages and was astonished to find there was already an email response from *Titania*. It read: "Unexpected vacancy within household staff of ship's crew. Light duties. Please send photograph and indicate earliest start date if selected for position". From her computer, she chose a picture of herself on the beach at Hilton Head wearing a low-cut, high-legged, red and white striped bikini. Her hair hung like a glossy black curtain framing her face. Looking with satisfaction at her Pilates-maintained flat stomach and tapered legs, she felt certain she could pass herself off as a young student.

Petra glanced at the clock. She was due to meet Tom in the gym at Dolphin House at nine-thirty for her first training session. His additional responsibilities, as he had delighted in telling her, included a mandate to ensure that she was as well prepared as possible to defend herself without the use of conventional weapons.

When she entered the gym at the appointed time, there was no sign of her mentor. The adjacent swimming pool, visible through a glass wall, was also empty. Miffed, she knelt on an exercise mat on all fours, drew in her stomach muscles and arched her back like a cat. In a single fluid movement, she flattened her spine and extended her left leg and right arm, reaching without straining. As she bent her knee to tuck it under her chest, she felt resistance. A few seconds later, she was on her back.

Tom, minus his glasses, released his grip on her foot and stood looking down at her. His expression was hard to read. 'Whatever you do, you must never let your guard down, and never ever make assumptions. When you came in, you decided no one was in the gym and you didn't stop to verify that before turning your back on the door.' Tom offered Petra his hand to pull her up as she started to protest. 'End of homily. I know from our first encounter that you're quick and inventive, and you've probably taken some self-defence courses in the past.'

Petra ignored his hand and pushed herself up from the floor. 'That's not important, Tom! I had a reply to my ad and they requested a photograph, which I sent.'

'A flattering one, I trust. So let's get down to business. I may have less time than I anticipated to add to your arsenal.' He ran his eyes slowly over her body until she began to feel self-conscious. 'The method I use I call "fifo", like the inventory accounting method – first in, first out, which is what you want to be every time,' he said. 'The element of surprise is essential for you to keep an edge, particularly as the lighter combatant. Some of the principles I'm sure you'll recognize – best practices from a variety of martial arts plus some common sense and a few down-and-dirty tactics of last resort.' He paused. 'Those shouldn't be a problem for you!'

Unsure how to respond to his half patronizing, half bantering tone, Petra chose to ignore it. She needed to hone her survival skills if her instincts about the Mortlake case were correct, and Tom was a good instructor. He kept her working and the time passed quickly.

On Saturday morning, a second email arrived offering her a job on board *Titania*. Petra confirmed her acceptance immediately. By return, she received an e-ticket to Nice and a terse reply that reminded her of A.K.'s telegraphic style: "Uniforms and training provided, including silver service. Bring minimal personal items. Ship's personnel will meet you on arrival. Look for MY *Titania* greeting board".

Tom seemed to delight in keeping her off balance. 'They must be hard up for choice this late in the year,' he said when she told him the news. 'No in-the-flesh interview, no nothing.' He went through her valise scrutinizing every item. He discarded anything that might invite questions or arouse suspicions and substituted High Street brand name underwear and jeans for her more unusual designer labels. He exchanged her Canadian phone for a European Siemens that would raise fewer eyebrows and programmed it with various fake friends' phone numbers all leading back to his own blue Ericsson. Then he began giving her advice. 'Remember you're an impoverished student, a little older perhaps, but still poor. You just want to get away from academia for a while, take some time out …'

'Tom,' she interrupted, 'I can do this. I'm not a neophyte.'

'Well you look …'

'What?'

'Delicate.'

'That's my mother's paleness. In reality, I'm tough as nails, like my father was.'

'Let's hope so,' he said. 'What's the boat of your dreams?'

'A Lazzara Eighty Four motor yacht, hardtop, walk-around side-decks, 1,150-hp MTUs…' she replied without hesitation.

'Spare me the detail! Lazzara is all I need. That'll be your code name. Use it whenever you text me and I'll know it's you. If you call me and use it, I'll know you're under duress.'

'And if you don't hear from me?'

'I'll worry.'

The plane banked to the right over the Baie des Anges and lined up to make its approach to Nice Airport. Petra looked down at the star-spangled waters of the bay coming gradually closer as the plane began its descent. A light wind ruffled the crest of the waves, but lacked the force to turn them into whitecaps. She caught sight of the familiar bulk of the Parc du Château off to the right and followed with her eye the line of majestic palms that still gave cachet and shade to the Promenade des Anglais.

It was a place she knew well. The summers spent on the shores of the Mediterranean with her mother's cousins and their friends had been the highlight of her teenage years. It was there, under the azure skies of the Italian and French Rivieras and the tutelage of one young man in particular, that she had nurtured her passion for boats – and for her tutor Romeo. For more than a decade she had kept the memories of those magical days and even more magical nights locked securely away. She did not want to release them now.

The plane had aborted its initial approach and turned out to sea to circle round again. Below, a large motor yacht clove through the waves on a westerly heading. Could that be *Titania*? If so, was that where she would find Emily or a clue to her whereabouts?

So far, there were only two indications that Emily had actually joined the yacht: the postcard Amy had received in August, and one that had, according to Amy, just reached Emily's mother. It was dated September 16th and postmarked Puerto Banús. Through the vagaries of the

31

mail, it had taken nearly three weeks to arrive, but seemed genuine. The picture, as Emily's mother had described it to Amy, was an artsy composition showing a narrow passage between two blue-washed houses, labelled Typical houses of the Rif, Morocco. The message, in Emily's handwriting, was scrawled across the card. "Back to reality soon. Miss you more than I can say!" The strangest note was the signature: "Love Emy". Emily apparently hated that diminutive and never used it herself. Whether it had any significance remained to be seen.

CHAPTER THREE

The arrivals hall at Nice Airport was busier than Petra would have expected for a Monday lunchtime in October. There was a long queue for Passport Control. Most of the travellers were middle-aged, early retirees perhaps, following the sun south to the Riviera now that the summer crowds of backpacking students and families with school-age children had gone.

After a frustrating fifteen minutes in the queue, Petra stepped up to the desk and presented her Canadian passport. She stood waiting for the officer to acknowledge her presence, ready to answer any questions he might have in fluent French. When it became clear that he was more intent on his keyboard than on welcoming visitors to his country, she let her hand stray to the jewelled crucifix nestling between her breasts. She caressed it lightly. The tactic worked like a charm. He took a long look at her cleavage and stamped her passport with a flourish. After a wistful second glance, he handed her the document. 'Voilà, Mademoiselle. Bon séjour.' Thanking him with a wry smile, she followed the flow of people down the corridor.

With only carry-on baggage, Petra was one of the first to emerge after a handful of business-class travellers. The plane had been over an hour late and the hold-up at Passport Control had delayed her even further. She hoped the promised representative would still be there to meet her.

Scanning the expectant crowd of limousine drivers, tour company greeters and waiting relatives, she spotted a tall blonde wearing a sour look and sporting a sign that read MY *Titania* flanked by a crested logo. Petra took a minute to observe her. The fingernails on the hand holding up the sign were painted a shocking pink, visible at fifty paces. The sign wavered as the blonde shifted her weight from foot to foot, clearly uncomfortable in white ankle boots with stiletto heels and elongated toes. The square-cut platinum hair, bold black eyeliner, rouged cheeks and carmine lips left Petra in little doubt that this was the girl who had greeted Amy and Emily at the London hotel. Amy had an eye for detail that had enabled her to pass on a great deal of useful information.

The blonde adjusted her wide gold belt to sit lower on her hips and hugged the greeting board close to her chest. A ripple of interest ran through the men around her, though whether it was caused by the name on the board or her dark blue bustier and white micro skirt, Petra didn't bother to speculate. It was amusing to see how she haughtily dismissed a string of tanned, would-be suitors in need of a light. Petra felt sure that at another time, in another place, she would have given them a jolly good run for their money. Now she was doubtless anxious to get going.

'You must be waiting for me. I'm Petra Minx,' she said.

'You're late. Is that all your luggage?' The blonde made no attempt to disguise her hostility. She ignored Petra's outstretched hand and the reply to her question. 'Follow me, we need to get moving.' Her accent was hard to place, somewhat guttural, Eastern European perhaps, yet her English was colloquial and fluent.

'Where are we going?' Petra asked.

'Just stay close to me and keep quiet.'

The blonde led the way at an aggressively fast pace out of the building and across to the car park. She seemed to be heading for a white minivan parked next to a bright orange Lamborghini. As they neared the back of the Lamborghini, she let out a howl of horror.

'Holy shit! Look at that! What the fuck am I going to do?' Her micro skirt revealed a minimalist thong as she bent over the shiny surface and traced her index finger along a hairline crack in the paintwork. 'Don León will have my hide!'

'Who's Don León? And who are you?'

'Don Leonardo,' she said with emphasis, 'is *Titania*'s owner, your new boss. "Don" is a courtesy title. Everyone calls him Don León, or El Toro – the bull.' She gave Petra a hard look from under her long lashes. 'I'm Monica, his personal assistant. He'll kill me if he sees this scratch.'

'Why? It's not your fault. Someone must have keyed it.' Petra could understand the frustration, but not the fear in the other girl's voice.

'You haven't met Don León! He doesn't know I borrowed the Bat to pick you up.'

'Why do you call it the Bat?'

'Because this is a Murciélago, which means "bat", the kind with wings. Murciélago was the name of a famous Spanish fighting bull.'

And Don León's nickname is El Toro, the bull, Petra thought. How appropriate!

Monica pressed a button on the key fob in her hand and the Lamborghini's scissor doors tilted skywards. 'Put that bag behind the seat and get in, we have to get back before he does.' She folded her long legs into the car and pulled on a pair of supple white leather driving gloves before touching the wheel.

'How far do we have to go and when will he be back?' Petra asked.

'Over thirty kilometres, to Monte Carlo. He's been playing the tables all night so he'll be back soon. Now shut up and don't keep asking questions.' Monica glanced at the diamond-studded Cartier on her right wrist. 'The A8 would be faster unless there's a traffic problem, then we'd be stuck.' She hesitated. 'What the hell, I'm in shit anyway. I'll take the scenic route and show you what the Bat can do.'

Petra's heart began to pound as Monica threaded the Lamborghini through the traffic round the airport, impervious to appreciative looks and disapproving stares. Her gloved hands gripped the wheel with ferocious determination, yet her manoeuvres were well timed and gear changes fluid.

They were heading for the Grande Corniche with its spectacular panoramas and tortuous bends. Petra grabbed the edge of her seat and sank down as low as possible. It was on just such a road in the hills above Monaco that her teenage love Romeo had lost his life on a weekend jaunt with his mates, Carlo and Ben. She would never forget that terrible phone call a decade ago. The three young men had taken time out from their studies at the University of Genoa to celebrate Carlo's birthday. Tired but jubilant, they were riding abreast down a steep incline when Romeo's front tyre blew. As Ben had haltingly told her, Romeo had been thrown off his motorbike and over the guardrail. There was nothing anyone could do. The tragedy had changed Petra forever and made her reluctant to commit to a serious relationship.

Before Romeo's death, she had derived as great a thrill from speed over ground as speed over water. Now, fast cars and winding roads made her nervous, though she tried hard to control what she considered a weakness. Petra relaxed her hold on the front of her seat a fraction, took a deep breath and forced herself to focus on the views of the coast and the horizon as the kilometres sped by.

Monica seemed intent on keeping as close to the edge as possible while maintaining maximum velocity. She nudged the accelerator and gave Petra a sideways glance. Petra heard the revs go up a notch and knew that her nerve was being tested. She wondered if she could gain Monica's confidence without disturbing her concentration. 'You must drive this car a lot. You handle her like a pro,' she said.

'Listen to the expert! You college girls are all the same, think you know everything. Well, you don't know how to dress – jeans and running shoes and a denim jacket! That's no way to attract a man.'

'That wasn't my intention. These are my travelling clothes,' Petra said mildly. She tried another tack. 'I'm sorry I was late. You must have been waiting quite a while. Actually, it was lucky the plane didn't leave on time; there was such a long queue at Security, I was afraid I might miss it. Have you ever been to London?'

'No,' came the brusque reply.

'I'm surprised. London's very popular. It's not far by plane and the tickets are quite cheap.'

'I told you, I haven't been there. Stop prattling.' The look on Monica's face told Petra far more than she could have gleaned from further questioning.

As they swept round another vicious bend, the Principality of Monaco came into view. After dark, Petra remembered, the vista was stunning. At this hour of the afternoon, the sun bounced off the gleaming surfaces far below. The light that had attracted generations of painters to the Côte d'Azur shimmered, clear and white.

Directly below them lay the Port of Monaco and, to its right, the rocky outcrop on which stood the Palace of the Prince. Although Monica had seemed to relax a little during the drive, the tension became palpable as they descended towards the port. The brakes squealed as she nearly missed a red light. 'Look out for the flics – they don't like fast cars,' she muttered. But when they drew up at the barrier restricting access to the quay, the policeman on duty recognized the Lamborghini and waved it through.

From higher up, Petra had been unable to pick out *Titania* from the array of yachts and superyachts docked stern-to or moored further out in the harbour. Many of the world's leading yacht makers were represented: Benetti, Trinity, Horizon, Ferretti, Azimut. Some of the vessels resembled intergalactic battleships with their swooping windows and lofty radar arches bristling with domes and antennae.

Among the glittering white hulls, a single navy blue one stood proud in cool distinction. Monica steered the Lamborghini along the quay towards it and reversed into a spot in the shade close to the foot of the rock, no doubt to hide the damage to the back of the Bat. 'OK, here we are, let's get moving. It's three o'clock. There's a chance Don León isn't back from the Casino yet.'

Petra barely had time to climb out of the car and grab her bag before Monica activated the automatic locking and security mechanism. 'That's *Titania*?' she breathed, staring up at the majestic four-level vessel. She had expected something grand, but nothing as spectacular as this. Emily's word "awesome" was totally appropriate. The megayacht must be at least seventy metres long and nine metres in the beam. The deep blue of the hull served only to intensify the brilliant whiteness of her superstructure. Across the centre of the eurostern the vessel's name was emblazoned in gold. A midsummer night's dream indeed, Petra thought, even if it was October.

As Monica ran across the quay towards the yacht, the passerelle slid open to its full extent. At the top, watching them board, stood a crewmember in navy shorts and a white golf shirt embroidered with a stylized blue and gold T logo. Short and heavy set, he ignored Monica but scrutinized Petra as if to memorize her every feature. He nodded but did not speak.

'Take your shoes off here and be careful with that bag,' Monica instructed. 'Except for the ship's crew, only socks or bare feet are allowed on the teak decks on the main and bridge levels. Don León's very fastidious.'

Petra picked up her bag and followed Monica across the aft section of the main deck, past an alfresco dining area and along the port side of the vessel. The port side-door slid open.

'What took you so long?' asked a voice on the left. With another sense of déjà vu, Petra stopped short in front of a dumpy, unattractive woman whose age she could only guess at – probably somewhere between sixty and seventy. The face was square and heavy-featured, the upper lip shadowed by dark growth. The grin when it came revealed the stained teeth Petra had anticipated from Amy's description and reminded her of the gargoyles that grimaced from the College downspouts.

'The plane was late,' Monica growled.

'Well, you'd better give her a quick tour then take her down to her quarters. Don León and his guests will be back from the Casino any minute, so keep away from the master suite and the guest staterooms. Welcome aboard,

39

Miss Minx – Petra. I'm Olga, head of the ship's household. Monica will show you what to do.'

Petra watched the blonde's body language as Olga issued her instructions in accented English. Monica was clearly relieved to discover that her boss was still ashore, but disinclined to submit to the older woman's authority. Her stance was assertive, hands on hips. She had pulled on a pair of gold ballet slippers.

Motioning Petra to follow, she led the way past Olga, who was standing in the doorway to the galley, and gestured down a passageway towards the bow of the yacht. 'That's Don León's private suite. No one's allowed in there uninvited. That door on the right is the powder room and there's the library.'

Petra peeked through the stained glass panel in the library door as Monica continued on through a hallway hung with what appeared to be genuine Gauguin masterpieces. The Tahitian scenes in elemental colours were unmistakable. A circular staircase rose majestically to higher levels and disappeared below to what Petra guessed would be the crew cabins. They passed through an archway – the first Petra had ever seen on a private yacht – into a room decorated with embedded columns and wall sconces in the shape of flaming torches. Pastoral scenes against clear blue skies adorned the walls between the columns and an elaborate teardrop chandelier hung from the centre of a huge oval ceiling fresco.

'This is the formal dining room where Don León likes to have dinner when he has company. You'll be doing silver service here – and more,' Monica said.

'I'm sure I'll soon learn the ropes,' Petra retorted. As she suspected, the play on words was lost on Monica. She stopped to admire the wall paintings. The opulence of the room was breathtaking, the style more in keeping with a

Venetian palazzo than a megayacht. He's a showman as well as a manipulator, she thought; his presence is pervasive, even when he's not around, and he inspires fear, not respect. I wonder what he looks like…

'Are you listening, Minx? I said this is the grand salon and here's the bar.' Monica gestured to a black granite counter behind which tiers of fully stocked shelves rose on either side of an etched glass panel separating the salon from the dining room. 'You'll meet the new steward who looks after the bar later. He's cute – and a pretty good piano player,' she added, indicating the Steinway baby grand.

Petra nodded. The Italianate elegance of the décor and furnishings, all designed to impress and impassion, brought back other memories of those sun-kissed days with the trio, Romeo, Carlo and Ben. They had all been opera lovers and musicians, always ready to strum a tune or burst into song, eyes flashing, like a band of wandering minstrels. Yet in character they had been very different: Romeo, the romantic of course, Carlo – whom everybody called Mercutio – reckless and mercurial, and Ben, solid as a rock. If anyone should have been killed, it should have been Mercutio, the risk-taker.

'So I'm not the only new kid on the block,' Petra said. 'Has the steward been here long?'

'A few weeks now.'

'How's he getting on?'

'Carlo does what he's told. Don León likes that. Come on.'

They left the salon via the aft doors. Monica took off her ballet slippers and pulled on a pair of socks. She gestured up the stairway on the starboard side. 'We'll go up to the boat deck then forward through the guest suites to the communications room and the bridge.'

41

'I thought Olga said…'

'I don't care what Olga says.'

Petra was unprepared for the size of the boats standing secure in their cradles on the boat deck. Some of her Italian cousins had friends with power cruisers and she had seen plenty of good-sized motor yachts in Montreal and on the Great Lakes, but their tenders were inflatable dinghies or small open runabouts. These were high performance vessels in their own right. Out of the water they looked massive. The twelve-metre Scarab in front of her was instantly recognizable. Cigarette boats were a marine cop's nightmare. Graffiti-style decoration in neon colours launched a bold challenge to the senses against a background of *Titania* blue. On the stern the name blazed forth: *El Toro*.

The boat gracing the port side was the other face of the coin. Ten metres of pure classical lines and perfectly kept wood took Petra's breath away. To maintain the varnished hull and brightwork of a Donzi like that in pristine condition required hours of dedication and very deep pockets. *Dreambaby*'s master was not lacking in funds nor, Petra thought, in appreciation for quieter finer things, despite the testosterone and machismo of the Scarab.

A shout from the dock sent Monica running back to the stern. She flung a horrified look over the aft rail. 'He's here! Let's go.'

From the cacophony below, Don León was having trouble getting his guests safely aboard the yacht. They had evidently left behind in the Casino any sea legs they might have had, along with significant donations to the tables. Monica dragged Petra along between the boats, up a few steps and across a small seating area, then through a door leading to the guest suites. She gestured forward through another door. 'That's Captain Juan's domain. We'll have to skip it for now. Anyway, the Captain keeps the bridge and the communications room, not to mention his cabin, locked whenever he isn't here, and he's ashore today.'

Petra had no time to assess her surroundings as they flew down the circular staircase to the lower deck, two levels below. She still did not understand the element of fear and panic in Monica's reaction to her boss's arrival.

'Is it a problem if he sees us?' she asked. 'I thought you were his personal assistant.'

'I am. Look, you'll find out what he's like if you cross him or if he takes a dislike to you.'

Petra wondered whether Emily had done something to incur Don León's wrath. So far, she had seen no sign of her or any other girls on board the yacht, yet Monica had made a snide reference to college girls during the drive to Monte Carlo. Who were they and where were they?

At the bottom of the stairs, Monica pointed aft. 'Back there is the engine room and workshop,' she said, 'and behind that, the garage for the toys. Both are off limits to the household staff. Forward, through that door, are the male crew cabins and lounge, also off limits. This is the female staff area and here's your stateroom.' She opened a door on the port side to a twin-bedded cabin with an en-suite bathroom.

Petra took in the light cherry-wood panelling, the two beds with their blue and gold covers, the seascapes on the walls. These quarters were palatial by comparison with the cramped bunk and the rudimentary toilet facilities on her cousin's sailboat.

'Does anybody share this cabin?' she asked.

'Not at this time of year. The summer is busier. Unpack your things and take a shower. You'll find day and evening uniforms clearly marked in the closet. Put the

43

evening one on and wait for me here. I'll be back at six. I've got to go, Don León will be asking for me.'

Petra walked across to the porthole as the door closed with a bang behind Monica. She had succeeded in the first part of her mission, to get aboard the good ship *Titania*, one of the most impressive yachts in the harbour. Now she was keen to meet *Titania*'s master, her new boss Don León, and to follow Emily's trail, wherever it led. And if that meant playing a part, she would play it with gusto.

CHAPTER FOUR

A shaft of sunlight glancing through the porthole of Petra's cabin cast a dancing patch that moved like a will-o'-the-wisp with the slight but incessant motion of the megayacht. Petra knew from long and sometimes painful experience that boats, especially small ones, moved constantly. Underway the movement was expected, but even in a sheltered harbour, waves and wakes from other vessels could throw a person off balance. The famous rolling gait of the sailor just home from the sea was a legacy of the myriad compensations made by the body to keep itself upright on a shifting platform. On a megayacht like *Titania* in port, the motion was imperceptible most of the time.

Petra paused in the middle of the well appointed cabin to look at her watch. Only a quarter to four. It felt much later. There was ample time to explore the crew area before she needed to shower and dress for the evening. She took off her denim jacket then, as an afterthought, her necklace, which she placed on the bed underneath the jacket. Careful not to make a noise, she opened the cabin door.

The hallway was empty. To the left, Monica had said, were the male crew quarters. She had omitted to mention that access was through a gleaming laundry area fitted with washing machines and dryers on one side of the passage and what appeared to be floor-to-ceiling storage lockers on the other. None of the machines was in use and the locker doors Petra tried were locked. The access door to the male crew quarters was also locked.

Petra retraced her steps past her own cabin door and its twin opposite. Beyond the circular staircase that led to the upper decks, a small lounge opened off to her right. To the left was a galley with a fridge, but no apparent cooking facilities. Five metres further on, the corridor dead-ended at what Petra judged to be the engine room bulkhead. In the centre was a narrow, locked door.

All off limits, she thought, as she tried the door handles of another two cabins located opposite one another in the section between the lounge and galley area and the engine room bulkhead. They too were locked. She straightened up and turned towards the galley.

'What do you think you're doing?' a dry voice asked. Olga was hurrying down the corridor towards her.

Petra searched rapidly for a plausible excuse, hoping Olga had not seen her trying the doors. 'I came to look for something to eat. They only served a snack on the plane. I hope you don't mind,' she said politely.

Olga studied Petra's face. For a moment everything hung in the balance. Then she nodded towards the fridge. 'You'll find drinks and snacks in there,' she said in a softer tone. 'Help yourself to whatever you like, then come back to your cabin with me. There are a few routine matters I need to take care of.'

Relieved, Petra selected a tomato juice and a packet of cheese and biscuits. 'This should keep me going until dinner. Do the crew take meals together?'

'Breakfast and lunch will be put out for you down here. Dinner arrangements vary, depending on Don León's schedule. Most evenings you will be required to wait at table – silver service of course – unless Don León is ashore or dining in his stateroom. From time to time, he may invite you to join him for a meal.' Olga displayed her discoloured teeth in what Petra would have classified as a leer rather than a smile. She opened the cabin door and motioned Petra inside. 'Give me your passport. I'll put it in the safe with the others. And if you have a phone, I'll take that too for safekeeping. It won't work on the boat.'

Petra knew this was probably untrue provided they stayed close to the coast, but decided not to arouse suspicions by arguing. Tom was not expecting to hear from her anyway for a few days, and she could use a telephone on shore if necessary. The loss of her passport was unexpected, though not an insurmountable problem. She could always send for her Italian one if she needed it.

Olga smirked as Petra handed over her passport and phone. 'That's a good girl. Now have your shower and get yourself dressed for dinner. Monica will fetch you later.'

To Petra's surprise, Olga's tone was benign, almost motherly, the edge of steel tempered by obedience. On the surface she was a bulldog, stocky and tough; underneath there was a hint of something else. It was all about control, Petra thought, as she lay down on the floor to do a few exercises before showering. Everything would be fine as long as she complied.

She did not yet understand the hierarchy of relationships aboard *Titania*, but was eager to meet the formidable Don León. In her imagination, he was a tall, commanding figure, good-looking in a rather hard way. His age was difficult to guess, but she suspected he must be middle-aged to have accumulated sufficient wealth to acquire such a fabulous yacht and collection of toys.

Maintenance and crew costs on a boat the size of *Titania* would be huge. Although she had seen only one sailor on deck, there had to be several more in addition to the Captain and the First Mate. A total complement of a dozen including household staff would not be unusual. One of them must know something about Emily, who might even still be aboard. The stretching and deep breathing combined to relax and energize her at the same time and she practised a few of the moves Tom had shown her in London.

Ten metres above *Titania*'s waterline, Carlo the steward was busy on the sundeck, restocking the bar. The yacht was a hive of activity after the relative quiet of the previous week, during which Don León had taken himself away for a few days and only a skeleton staff had remained on board. The chef had returned, the Filipino houseboys had scrubbed and polished, the pool had been uncovered and cleaned.

A sudden commotion somewhere below alerted Carlo seconds before the VHF phone on his belt beeped at him. It was Olga.

'Coffee and Fernet Branca for Suites B1, 2 and 3,' she ordered. 'The usual for Don León.'

'No problem,' he said. 'Coming right up!' The espresso machine was primed and ready to go. The past three weeks had taught Carlo a great deal about the habits of Don León and his associates. After eighteen hours at the Casino, Sheik Kamal and his entourage would need a remedy for overindulgence and a dose of restorative sleep. Don León's ability to imbibe copious quantities of red wine with only catnaps to offset any effect was legendary among the ship's Mallorcan crewmembers. Hard drinkers themselves, they swore Sangre de Toro coursed through his veins and revered him as they did Spain's most renowned bullfighters. Behind his back, they called him El Toro, the bull.

Carlo made his delivery and returned to the sundeck by way of the port-side stairs. As he crossed the deck towards the skylounge, the door slid open and Monica stepped out in front of him. She thrust her bare breasts out to greet him, dark nipples fully erect. Her platinum helmet was a sham and the silicone support evident in the rounded fullness of her chest, but the effect was nevertheless incredibly sexy and he knew she knew it. She gazed up at him from under long black lashes.

'Look after this for me, darling, while I take a swim,' she said, fingering the VHF phone that hung low on the hip strap of her G-string bikini.

Carlo nodded. 'Of course.'

With a suggestive movement across her crotch, Monica handed him the phone and sashayed past him to the pool. She executed a neat dive, rolled onto her back and cut through the water with strong, disciplined strokes, then slowed the pace to give him ample opportunity to view her handsome chest. He had to admit it was worth a look.

During the week of Don León's absence, her interest in him had become overt. Whether out of boredom or because she found him truly attractive he was not sure, but the signals were clear. Equally clear was his response to temptation: them there apples were forbidden fruit. Maybe training the new girl who had just come aboard would divert her attention.

Monica's phone lying on the bar emitted a low roar like pounding surf. Carlo picked it up and waved it in the air. 'The boss calls,' he said, walking quickly to the edge of the pool.

Monica reached up and grabbed the now-silent instrument. She looked at the message on the screen. 'Master suite. Thanks, lover boy,' she said, placing it at a safe distance from the edge of the pool. In a lithe movement she lifted herself out of the water and climbed out of the pool. The diamond in her navel flashed a rainbow of colours as she picked up the phone and re-crossed the deck to the skylounge.

Carlo watched her go, glad to be alone again.

The master suite occupied the whole forward section of *Titania*'s main deck, two decks below the sundeck. Lavish in its spaciousness, decadent in its cushioned opulence, wild in its use of African motifs, the suite was at once impressive and overwhelming. Its creator paced like a caged beast in the area between the enormous bed and the plasma screen that dominated the teak panelled bulkhead. Beside the bed stood a half-empty bottle of red wine. The gold mesh on the bottle glistened temptingly in the dim interior light. Don León paused to replenish his glass and take a sip from the heavy crystal before resuming his beat.

The scratch on the Lamborghini was ugly and mean. It pained him, not because of the damage, which was superficial and reparable, but because the gratuitous desecration of such a beautifully conceived machine stemmed from an emotion whose destructive power he had struggled to overcome. On the cut-throat streets of Bogotá, he had grown up tough, disadvantaged, dishonest and envious. Envious of the people who had food when he did not, envious of the rich in their finery and limousines, envious of the young men he saw escorting stunning young women. A bitter taste flooded his mouth and he fought to suppress the memory that threatened to destroy his hard-won equilibrium.

There was a knock at the door. Don León opened it wide and confronted Monica. 'Where the hell have you been?'

'Up on the sundeck helping Carlo restock the bar. I ran through the shower to freshen up before coming down,' Monica ventured, unsure of her reception.

Don León accepted the lie for what it was. He no longer trusted her implicitly as he used to. Something had come between them to alter the shape of their relationship. It irritated him to feel himself losing control.

The first part of the summer season had been a dream: extravagant parties with nubile summer staff to stimulate the senses and bolster business. He had laughed with them, teased them and delighted in their svelte bodies as a connoisseur might appreciate exquisite objets d'art. He had revelled in their conversation on subjects Monica could barely comprehend, yet had never let her feel unwanted. Then she had begun to display signs of jealousy, pouting and interrupting his discussions with the blonde from Oxford, the one who challenged and tantalized him. Olga had warned him to be careful. He felt his anger rise. They were all interfering bitches.

Monica was looking at him with veiled eyes. He could smell her fear.

'Come here!' Don León hooked one finger into the centre of her bustier and pulled her towards him. He nuzzled her ear. 'What perfume are you wearing?'

'Jean Paul Gaultier, why?'

'It's distinctive. Like you.' Keeping one arm round her shoulder, holding his glass with the other, he propelled her past the bed and up the steps in the centre of the cabin to his private sitting room. The blinds were down and the mood was inward-looking, not expansive as it was when the circular picture windows revealed the full panorama of the sea and the sky.

Don León sank into his favourite armchair and let his blue silk robe fall open. His penis was flaccid, still curled in its nest of coarse dark hair, but large, even in repose. Monica knew what she had to do. She pushed the footstool aside and knelt in front of him. Don León leaned forward to draw her closer, resting the glass briefly on her shoulder before setting it on the table beside his chair. She winced at the cold. He ran his nails down her back and unhooked the gold bustier. Her breasts swung free and he placed his palms underneath, hefting them in his hands like a peasant gauging the size of melons in the local market. They were heavy and warm.

The wicked tip of Monica's tongue flicked his mind back to the matter in hand. He closed his thumbs and index fingers on her nipples like a vice and pulled her savagely towards him. Monica squeezed her eyelids together to block out the pain. With a swift tug on the waistband of her short, wraparound skirt, he released the Velcro fastening and the white fabric fell away to reveal a blue lace thong. The sight of her taut buttocks with their delicious cleft pushing upwards in glorious unison as she ran her tongue up and down his swelling member made him throw back his head and groan in anticipation. She was a whore and a bitch, but a turn-on nevertheless.

His fingers clutched at the smooth golden cheeks that dipped and rose with the rhythm of her work. Cupped in her left hand his balls were on fire as her mouth and lips kneaded and massaged. The scent of arousal hung heavy around them in the shuttered suite.

Then, like a breath of air stirring on a fetid night, Don León felt a coolness as her right hand moved away from its post to fondle her own breasts. He let go of her buttocks, seized a handful of her hair and jerked her head brutally backwards. 'Stop! Not now!' he commanded.

The pressure on Monica's scalp was intense. 'What's the matter? Let me go! You're hurting me!'

'I'm not in the mood.' He relaxed his grip slightly. 'Let's take the Lamborghini out. Do you know where the keys are?'

'How should I know? Pablo takes care of the car.'

Monica felt a searing pain at the back of her neck as Don León tightened his hold on her hair and jerked her head backwards for the second time. The strain on her larynx made it impossible to move.

Don León leaned forward and spat in her face. 'Puta! Don't lie to me. You might not know *now*, but you took the car this morning. Your perfume is all over it.' Monica's whimper brought him back to his senses. For a few seconds, he had reverted to the underworld of the *barrio*. Disgust, with himself and the woman, overpowered him. 'Get out,' he yelled, 'and don't let me down tonight. This is an important evening.'

After a long hot shower, Petra was ready to dress for the evening. The clothing in her closet was clearly marked, as Monica had said it would be, but skimpy in the extreme. That would explain the photographic selection process, she murmured, holding a slip of blue lace up to the light. She extracted a blue and gold sequined bustier and raised her eyebrows in mock horror. Monica might look good in that type of gear and Emily Mortlake certainly had the build, but she wouldn't do it justice. For a moment, she considered adding some padding then dismissed the idea as puerile. She would have to stand on her own merits.

Half an hour later, Monica had not reappeared. The waiting was becoming a bore. Inaction was a crime – that had been drilled into them at the Police Academy.

'All dressed up, so where shall we go?' Petra said aloud as she examined her silhouette in the mirror. The bustier was a surprisingly good fit, and the gold Lurex mini-skirt trimmed with blue satin sat neatly on her hips. Whoever had gauged her size from the photograph she had sent had an experienced eye. Only the gold sandals she had found in the closet were uncomfortable, mainly because she wasn't used to wearing ten centimetre stilettos.

As she reached down to liberate her feet, she saw something glitter in the soft pile of the carpet. The heart-shaped pendant had lost its chain, but none of its sparkle. A tiny diamond set in the corner of the left upper ventricle twinkled above the clear blue of the topaz in its cage of gold. It was a pretty piece. She placed it in the top drawer of the chest of drawers for safekeeping and slipped out of the cabin to explore.

Petra ran barefoot up the circular staircase that linked the lower, main and boat decks. Hearing voices on the main deck and guessing that preparations for dinner would be in progress, she did not stop. On the boat deck where the guest suites were situated, all was quiet and she continued on up to the sundeck via the starboard stairs.

Petra walked quietly past the deserted pool and bar to the skylounge. The sliding doors were partially open and she risked a look inside. Two middle-aged men with beards and a clean-shaven youth were sitting around a low table on which stood a carafe of water, a whisky decanter, ashtrays and partially full glasses. The older men were smoking and the air was heavy with the scent of Gauloises. All three were swarthy in appearance and dressed in formal Western business attire: Savile Row down to the last shirt cuff and tailored lapel. Immediately Petra thought of the men who had "interviewed" Amy and Emily in London. She would have bet her Christmas bonus that they were one and the same.

At the urging of the man closest to her, the one with the pointed chin and a close-cropped beard, the youth leaned across the table and picked up a remote control. A silvered plasma screen rose, silent and ghostly, from the credenza facing the doors. A few clicks through the menu brought the screen to life.

The first long shot through ornate wrought-iron grillwork showed an expanse of marble terrace dotted with palms and flowering plants in yellow and blue glazed pots; in the background, beyond a tiled fountain, was a turquoise pool. The zoom, when it came, went straight to the point: a pair of bronzed buttocks and a long tanned back capped by a sheaf of golden hair. Seductively, the camera panned from one sinuous young body to another, topless, bottomless, nubile and all unquestionably blonde. It paused for a time to showcase a couple of girls massaging each other in turn with deep, lascivious strokes. The man with the neat beard gestured with obscene intent to a roar of laughter from his companion. The beardless youngster seemed uncomfortable with their crudeness.

With another click, the silent panorama of sun-kissed female flesh faded from view. The haunting sounds of Arabian music, cacophonous to the untrained ear, filled the smoky space. Petra held her breath. A girl with long flaxen hair as fine as silk gyrated across the same terrace, lit now by hundreds of white mini-lights wound around the ironwork and the trees. A veil hid the lower part of her face and diaphanous pantaloons covered her naked nether regions. Tasselled, jewel-encrusted cups defined the contours of her breasts. The nipples were bare.

Petra watched entranced as the belly dancer wove her way across the marble terrace towards a group of sofas. The camera closed in on one of the reclining white-robed figures and she gave a sharp intake of breath as she recognized the man with the pointed chin and close-cropped beard. On screen he crooked his finger at the dancer and waved her towards him. Her hips dipped and rose to the increasingly vigorous tempo, jiggling the coins of gold that bedecked the hip band of her pants.

As the music squealed to a crescendo, she flung herself to her knees in front of him. The camera zoomed in on her outstretched belly with its topaz centre then inched upwards past her breasts to her throat. Petra gasped. The heart-shaped blue pendant around the dancer's neck was unmistakable. A hand flashed in front of the camera and tore the veil away. The face underneath was Emily's.

As Petra struggled with the implications of what she had seen, she felt a hard body press into her back. Immersed in the video, she had let her guard down. Hands clamped around her breasts, pulling her up and backwards. She tensed to punch behind her with one foot, aiming for her aggressor's groin.

'It's OK, Pablo. I'll take it from here.' Monica's voice cut through the confusion. 'Don't worry, Minx. Pablo was being overzealous. He probably didn't recognize you as the new girl.'

His memory must be crap then, Petra thought, placing him at once as the crewmember who had watched her come aboard. He just wanted a feel to confirm his visual. She was annoyed with herself for momentarily forgetting her training and wondered whether Monica would ask her for an explanation. It would be difficult to justify her presence on the sundeck when she was supposed to be waiting in her cabin. In the background, the music continued to wail and other dancers appeared on screen to weave their magic.

Monica cast a scornful glance at Petra. 'Your job is to entertain these men,' she hissed. 'Be sure you do.'

Petra watched as Monica arched her back and doubled over the table to refill the visitors' glasses. The ringside view was not lost on the two older men and Petra found herself sharing an embarrassed moment with the youngest member of the group. She gave him a rueful smile. He seemed more approachable than his colleagues.

'Where are you from?' she asked.

'Casablanca. Do you know it?'

'No, but I'd love to visit the Hassan II Mosque. I hear it's an amazing feat of engineering and architecture.'

'You're American, aren't you?' he said.

'Actually no, Canadian. It's hard to tell the difference sometimes.'

'I was educated in England, at Harrow. It was a wonderful experience.' The dark, hungry eyes lit up with joy.

'Was there something or someone special there?' she asked.

'My housemaster said I should…'

Before he could put his thoughts into words, Monica's voice penetrated the heavy air. 'Gentlemen, dinner is served. Don León requests the pleasure of your company.'

At the mention of Don León's name, Petra's heart seemed to skip a beat. This was the moment she had been waiting for. Now she would have the opportunity to assess the real man and see how closely he resembled the image she had formed of him. She accepted with grace the arm proffered by the young man from Casablanca, but felt him flinch at the contact. Monica was squiring the two older men with a hand under each of their elbows and a swagger that defied all comers. Outside the megayacht, the wind was calm and the Mediterranean swell, a gentle rise and fall.

As she crossed the threshold of the dining room a step ahead of her escort, Petra paused. The table shone with crystal and silver that flickered in the light of two elaborate candelabras. In the centre stood a three-tiered epergne overflowing with sweetmeats, chocolates and fruit. She wondered if the sweet tooth belonged to Don León or whether he was simply catering to the tastes of his guests. Looking around, she was disappointed to see no one who might be her host. Then, out of nowhere, a strong finger tipped her under the chin.

'And who have we here?' asked a low rich voice.

'Petra,' she managed to gasp, 'Petra Minx.'

'Miss Minx. At last. Welcome aboard *Titania*. You're comfortable, I trust?'

'Yes, Sir, thank you.' Petra looked up into a pair of deep brown eyes flecked with gold. They smiled with a warmth she did not think was feigned and held her gaze, the raw power palpable. Don León's head was huge and noble like that of a revered Emperor on an old Roman coin, though a laurel wreath would not have sat well on his leonine mane of hair. From his right ear, a cascade of silver rings and tiny fish glittered in the candlelight.

He continued to stare into her eyes as if he were trying to penetrate her soul. Petra was the first to turn away. In the far corner of the dining room, she could see the back of a man with short curly hair – presumably the steward – intent on his wine.

Suddenly, the huge head was nuzzling her ear and the same strong but gentle finger exploring the inner contours of her chest. 'I think you'll be more comfortable without this,' Don León whispered, undoing the front clasp of her bustier. 'You don't need any support. Carlo, what do you think?'

Nothing in the Police Academy's curriculum had prepared Petra for such a situation. Humiliated, she stood her ground as Carlo turned round at his boss's behest.

'Mercutio!' Petra's horror was audible over the opening bars of the Overture to The Abduction From the Seraglio. Carlo shook his head in a swift yet unambiguous reply.

'I'm sorry, Sir,' Petra stammered. 'You startled me.'

Don León draped a protective arm round her shoulders and she felt the cold metal of his earring brush the side of her face as he ushered her into the dining room. 'No apology needed, my dear. Come, my friends, let's enjoy ourselves. The night is young.'

CHAPTER FIVE

Thunder woke Petra briefly at 4 a.m. on Tuesday morning. With a groan, she rolled over and fell back into a profound, almost drugged, slumber. When the sound of waves slapping on the hull brought her to her senses again, the room was bright. For a moment, she was disoriented. Then her eyes fell on the seascape on the opposite wall: white surf smashing onto barnacle-covered rocks, a pair of gulls soaring into an azure sky sprinkled with clouds. She was in Monte Carlo, aboard motor yacht *Titania*.

Memories of the night before came in waves, each one more insistent: her first, unnerving encounter with Don León that had been nothing like she'd expected; the acute embarrassment of being stripped half-naked in front of a group of unknown men; then the shock of seeing Mercutio. Could it really be him? Or had being on the Côte d'Azur resurrected images from the past and superimposed them on the present? No, it was a one-in-a-million chance, yet she was sure.

The name Mercutio had fallen from her lips as soon as the dark, curly-haired man had turned to face her at Don León's command. When he responded to his boss's question with an expansive 'Bellissima!', she had needed no further convincing. His voice was the same as it had been a decade ago. She had often thought of him and Ben during those years, but always found another excuse for not making contact.

Even before he had managed to whisper a few words in her ear later, as he was pouring her a glass of wine, she knew that she must not reveal their relationship. Whatever he was doing on board *Titania* required discretion, just as her mission did.

The rest of the evening had passed without further incident. She succeeded in recovering her bustier and Don León said nothing when she reappeared with it on. Like a circus ringmaster, he had opened the show with a flourish to excite the crowd, then taken a back seat. The feast had been sumptuous, washed down with vast quantities of wine and champagne, and she probably drank more than she should. The older Moroccans had been introduced as Sheik Kamal and his aide Mustafa; they became more voluble and raucous as the evening wore on. She managed to keep out of their reach, leaving Monica to field their attentions. The young Moroccan, whose name she did not know, excused himself shortly after dinner and did not rejoin the party. Don León remained jovial but a little aloof, then surprised her late in the proceedings by asking Mercutio to accompany him on the piano. His fine baritone voice sat well with his physique and he gave an impassioned performance of a selection from Don Giovanni before suddenly announcing that he was retiring to bed.

Petra looked at the clock on the bedside table. It was almost eight-thirty. She threw back the covers and grabbed a blue robe off the adjacent twin bed. As she was putting it on, she noticed a folded square of paper someone had pushed under the door. She picked it up and opened it. The note was brief and unsigned: "Piano practice in the grand salon at 9.30. Romeo and Juliet's favourite songs".

61

Mercutio was most definitely aboard! It was a coincidence Petra could never have anticipated. A sceptic like A.K. would simply refuse to believe it.

Carlo was already seated at the piano when Petra entered the salon in brief white shorts and a blue T-shirt emblazoned with the yacht's logo. He greeted her with a wicked wink and an emphatic 'Bellissima!' as his fingers flew across the keys of the Steinway.

'Come and turn the pages for me while I fill you in on what's going on,' he said. 'The lingua franca on board is English, but be prepared to switch to Italian and break into song if Olga shows up. She's the only one up and about, apart from the ship's crew.'

'Won't she find that strange?'

'I'll tell her we're preparing something special for Don León. He loves Italian opera.'

'Do you think she'll buy that? I'd say she's street-smart.'

'Yes, but not well educated. The most important thing is not to let on that we know each other, and you'll have to get used to calling me Carlo. I'd love to jump up and fold you in my arms, but we'll have to save that for another day.'

'I assume you're working undercover.'

Carlo nodded. 'Interpol have been watching this vessel for some time. They have very strong suspicions, but couldn't prove anything, so they asked me to come aboard. What about you?'

'RCMP. I'm looking for a politician's missing daughter.'

'You're not a topless waitress?'

'Mercutio!' Ten years had not changed him.

'Scusi, scusi! I knew there had to be another reason.'

'I had no idea you were in law enforcement. Is it drugs?' Petra asked.

'Of some kind, almost certainly, but so far there's no evidence of cocaine smuggling which is what you'd expect. Don León grew up in Colombia and Olga seems to be of South American Indian descent. The rest are a mixture – the Captain and crew are Mallorcan and the houseboys, Filipino. The chef's a Basque from Northern Spain.'

'A tough lot, by the sound of it. What about Monica?'

'She's difficult to place. Probably Romanian. Her Spanish and English are fluent, but she has a heavy accent.'

'A whole lot of attitude, too! She's been antagonistic towards me from the moment she set eyes on me.'

'Because you're different, not Don León's usual style. A dark horse, one might say. Monica complained to me that he okayed you as soon as he saw your photograph. She dislikes anyone he singles out for special attention.'

'You seem pretty clued in – for a bartender! When did you join the crew?'

Carlo lifted his right hand off the piano to tap his nose. 'Hovering and listening are my speciality. I came aboard just over three weeks ago in Puerto Banús.'

Petra made rapid calculations in her head. That would be about the time Emily was due to fly to Geneva to visit her uncle and meet Amy. There was a chance Carlo had seen her. 'You say Monica doesn't like me because I'm different, but wasn't there another Canadian girl on board this summer?' she asked.

Carlo raised his eyebrows. 'There might have been.'

'Was her name Emily? Do you know what happened to her or when she left?'

'No idea. By the time I arrived, the temporary staff had gone. During the summer season, Don León acts like a regular jetsetter, moving from port to port around the

63

Mediterranean, surrounding himself with blonde bathing beauties, hosting parties…'

'So you didn't see her?' Petra said, disappointment in her voice.

'No, but I heard the houseboys talking about one of the sailors who'd become involved with an American girl, a favourite of Don León's. That might be your Canadian.'

'Didn't you wonder what happened to her?'

Carlo shrugged. 'Why should I? There are plenty of crew changes and comings and goings on this boat. Don León does a lot of entertaining. He has a number of businesses …'

He broke off suddenly and, with a warning glance at Petra, picked up the tempo and began to sing 'O sole mio'. Petra joined in the refrain then started to harmonize.

As the final chords died away, she heard rhythmic applause from the dining room. Olga was standing under the arch, a tight smile on her face. 'Beautiful, my children, beautiful. Such talent,' she said.

Petra exchanged glances with Carlo. This was another side to Olga. Unless she was a consummate actress, the music seemed to have stirred some emotion in her.

She beckoned to Petra and moved towards the piano. 'Petra, come with me. Don León wants to see you in his suite.'

'Of course.' Petra saluted Carlo and followed Olga out of the salon. The command performance was not unexpected. She had known there would be a sequel to the previous evening and wondered what mood Don León would be in. In a perverse moment, she had deliberately not worn a bra under her T-shirt.

Olga was silent as they made their way to Don León's quarters. Petra struggled to find a topic of conversation that would draw her out. 'The food was superb last night, especially the nettle and shrimp risotto,' she said.

'I'll tell the chef you enjoyed it,' was the clipped reply. 'Here we are. Go on in.'

Petra gave a short knock on the lacquered teak door and waited. She was about to knock again when the door was flung open.

'Miss Minx! Welcome to my boudoir or whatever the male equivalent is. Olga tells me you have a beautiful mezzo-soprano voice and Carlo is the perfect accompanist.'

She must have been watching for longer than we realized, Petra thought, and she keeps Don León informed of everything that's going on. I'll have to watch my step.

Despite the warmth of Don León's welcome, Petra felt like an intruder as she entered his bedroom under the hollow-eyed stare of the African carved heads that adorned the teak walls. She grimaced back at a singularly horrible mask with its tongue hanging out and followed him deeper into the room. It was too oppressive and over-furnished for her taste, her preference being for clean lines and simple painted walls, though she did share his love of animal prints.

He padded barefoot across the thick pile carpet, the muscles in his calves flexing below his blue silk robe. Petra trailed along behind him in silence. It was like tracking a wild animal to its lair, she decided. This was his refuge and retreat, the place where he gathered his strength before striking out at the rest of the world.

Don León paused on the threshold of his sitting room with its panoramic windows. After the orange glow of the teak-panelled bedroom, the brightness was dazzling.

Looking out at the array of pristine yachts in the marina, Petra was mesmerized. 'The view is stunning,' she said. 'A window on a world too few people see.'

'Yes, and if they do see it, it's only with eyes of envy,' he said, with a hint of bitterness that made Petra want to jump to his defence.

'Instead of admiration for the dedication and skill it represents! *Titania* is a magnificent vessel. You can be very proud,' she insisted.

He spun round to face her. 'Can I? Of what? That I clawed my way up from nothing on the backs of others?'

The harshness of his outburst surprised her. She would have liked to probe further, but he recovered his poise quickly.

'Never mind,' he said. 'Tell me about yourself.' He patted the chair beside him and leaned back, stretching his legs out on the chaise longue. The blue robe was tied loosely around his waist and stopped just above the knee. Petra focussed on his feet. The skin was dry and flaky, the toenails ragged and dirty, like those of a street urchin, not a man as wealthy as Don León. Repulsed, she stared out at the vista before her.

'There's nothing to tell really. I'm studying for my PhD. It became awfully intense. I needed a break and I love to travel, so I requested a deferment.'

Petra knew he would ask about her thesis and wondered if she could be sufficiently convincing. Tom had advised her to choose a subject as far removed as possible from Emily's Philosophy, Politics and Economics, but to keep her story close to the truth. Not wanting to venture into scientific realms, she had opted for an aspect of maritime history that she had studied at college.

Fifteen minutes later, she had no doubt that she was dealing with a fine mind. Twice he almost caught her out and she had to dredge for an answer. Then he seemed to lose all interest in her academic background. Leaning towards her, he looked at her with a curious expression on his face.

'We had another Canadian student from Oxford this summer,' he said. 'Her name was Emily. Do you know her?'

Astonished at his directness, Petra pretended to search her memory then shook her head. 'I can't think of anyone called Emily. There are quite a few North Americans at the University, but we don't hang out together. Unless she was in my faculty, I wouldn't know her.'

'A lovely girl. We were all sorry when she left at the end of August to travel.'

Don León's reference to Emily threw Petra for a loop. She had not expected him to mention the missing girl. If there had been any foul play, he almost certainly would not have done. Should she conclude then that Emily had left *Titania* of her own volition? If so, she could be anywhere, especially if she had been gone six weeks.

'Travel?' Petra repeated, in an attempt to elicit more information.

'Yes,' he said. 'She should have stayed with us, but she chose not to. And now you're here!'

Don León looked appraisingly at Petra. If he noticed that she was bra-less, he did not mention it. 'You have a good body and it shows well,' he said. 'I want you to do some modelling when we get to Spain.'

'Spain? Is that where we're going?'

The VHF phone on the table beside Don León buzzed before he could respond. He picked it up and listened for a few seconds. 'Right. I say we leave as planned. Load the car. We'll get underway as soon as you've finished.'

67

He turned to Petra. 'There's your answer,' he said. 'We'll be in Mallorca tomorrow morning.'

Without further ado, he sprang up and disappeared into the bedroom. For a few minutes, Petra contemplated the view. Beyond the seawall she could see the first hint of whitecaps forming, telltale signs of an increase in wind speed and worsening weather to come. When the door to the suite closed with a cushioned thud, she judged it safe to leave.

Dockside, a crowd of onlookers had formed. They watched in amazement as the starboard side of the main aft deck slid silently towards the bow of the yacht. Most of the time, there was no action aboard the megayachts in the marina to capture the attention of tourists or locals out walking. It was enough to gape at the dazzling superstructures and dream about the lifestyles of the yachts' absentee owners. But this was stuff to capture on camera and text home about.

Slowly, two booms extended out over the dock then locked into place. Hanging from these titanium arms was a reinforced aluminium platform. The four corners of the platform were attached to the booms by synchronized telescopic cylinders designed to minimize sway.

Petra could hear Don León shouting instructions as she walked through the grand salon, past his three guests who were enjoying a cup of coffee, and out onto the aft deck. Careful to keep out of the way, but eager to watch the action, she moved to the starboard side-rail from where she had a good view of the dock below. Pablo was signalling to the crewman in charge of the booms to lower the platform little by little until it was sitting comfortably on the dock.

A van from the local gendarmerie screeched to a halt fifty metres from the yacht. With whistles and sober expressions, the four policemen cleared the area then leaned on the side of the van to puff on their cigarettes and observe the action.

After checking the position of the platform, Don León strode to the row of cars parked below the cliff. His Lamborghini Murciélago VT Roadster might be standing in the shade, but it still outshone every other car in the Principality. Once again Petra thought how appropriate it was that a car that could go like a bat out of hell should be named after the famous Spanish bull Murciélago, the Bat. Its scissor door rose to the sky like an incandescent angel's wing seconds before he lowered himself into the driver's seat. The V12 580 engine roared to life and he began to manoeuvre the car towards the platform.

In the marina and so close to the water, of course, he could proceed only at a crawl, using only a fraction of the Bat's awe-inspiring capability. With impressive ease, he lined the Bat up with the platform and drove it up the short ramp. The colour, glowing now in full sunlight, was breathtaking. No ordinary man's colour, but a blatant challenge to the senses like the iridescent orange of a Mexican fire opal. Petra and fifty others stopped breathing as the car on its platform, wheels clamped in place, was hoisted off the dock and onto the yacht. The whole mechanism was designed with elaborate safeguards and the booms retracted at a snail's pace under the watchful eye of Don León.

'Romeo would have loved a machine like that!' whispered Carlo, coming to stand next to Petra. He felt her tense under the touch of his hand on her shoulder. Half a life away yet the wound had never healed.

69

Petra shook her head. 'Don't, please!' Mercutio was still the same – lovable, quixotic, vivacious, witty, and sometimes utterly tactless. 'We're leaving now the car is on board.'

'I know,' he replied. 'I was talking to Captain Juan. There's weather coming in from the Atlantic and he wants to try and beat it. With luck, we'll be in Mallorca early tomorrow morning. How was your session with Don León?'

'Interesting. After what happened last night, I was prepared for him to make a pass at me, but there were no sexual overtones at all. He's a dichotomy. His hands are perfectly manicured, but have you seen his feet?' Petra asked.

'Yes. I have a theory – corny I know, if you'll pardon the pun – that he keeps them that way to remind himself of his origins. From what he told me, he grew up in extreme poverty after his father disappeared. His mother took all kinds of menial jobs to scrape together enough money for food. He begged, and stole when necessary.'

'Then how did he educate himself?'

'Sheer luck. The local priest agreed to take him under his wing to keep him out of jail…'

'What are you two love-birds up to?' Petra caught a whiff of Jean Paul Gaultier as Monica thrust the tray of clinking glasses she was carrying into Carlo's hands. 'Take this back to the galley, I've got better things to do. Minx, Olga's looking for you downstairs.'

Before leaving, Petra surveyed the aft deck. The platform with the car on it had been clamped into position and the four telescopic cylinders were rising smoothly to their final nesting place in the underside of the deck above. Don León was supervising the installation of the Dacron cover that protected the Lamborghini from the elements.

On the dock, people were beginning to move away now that the excitement was over. One or two of them looked up and pointed skywards.

On her way to find Olga, Petra paused in the hallway to listen. A helicopter was coming close, the sound similar to that of the six-seater Eurocopter Twin Star used by her Marine Unit for search and rescue.

'Excuse me! Miss Minx!'

Petra turned. The young Moroccan was running down the circular staircase.

'Our transport is here. I just wanted to say goodbye.' Somewhat awkwardly, he held out his hand. 'I am sorry you were embarrassed last night. My father does a lot of business with Don León. He can be very unpredictable. Here is my card. If ever you are in Casablanca or you need anything, please give me a call.'

'Thank you, Ahmed,' Petra said, reading his name off the card. 'I appreciate that. I never guessed Sheik Kamal was your father. Have a safe trip.'

'You, too. There is a major storm coming. I wish you well.' He gave her a shy smile and ran back up the stairs towards the helipad on the top deck.

CHAPTER SIX

By midnight, the weather had worsened to the point where Captain Juan was beginning to regret trying to outrun the storm. It had been his decision, although the underlying pressure from Don León had been immense. Had he elected to stay in port, El Toro would have shown him nothing but contempt.

He had rechecked the weather forecast before they left Monte Carlo just after noon. All the reports showed a major storm front moving in from the west, but it was not expected to hit the Mediterranean for at least twenty-four hours. The front, however, had turned rapidly into a Force 9 gale and the waves had been building for the last six hours.

Now, with four metre rollers hitting her starboard fore quarter every few seconds, *Titania* bucked and reared like a bronco bent on unseating a rodeo cowboy. Her stabilizers shuddered as they attempted to compensate for the sideways roll. Spray drenched the pilothouse windshield, making it impossible to see anything outside.

Despite the array of sophisticated navigational instruments in front of him, Captain Juan was worried. He never liked running at night and in violent storm conditions such as these it was impossible to know what was out there. Ángel, a reliable crewman, had his eyes glued to two radar displays, one set to a fifteen nautical mile range to give early warning of other vessels, the other adjusted to detect and track any boat coming within five nautical miles of the megayacht.

'How are we doing, Juan?' Don León, who had come onto the bridge, scanned the dimly lit screens and dials. The anemometer showed a fifty-five knot wind from the west-northwest.

'We're over halfway, but we'll have to reduce speed. The wind's showing no sign of abating – if anything, it's strengthening and there are reports of heavy squalls between here and Menorca.'

'Damn it! We have to be there by eight tomorrow morning. Do what you need to do. Where are Pablo and Miguel?'

'Pablo will be on watch at 0200 hours. Miguel is as sick as a dog.'

'Tell Pablo to check the boats now, then to come and help me with the car. I want to put the extra cover on. And get Miguel up too – I don't care how sick he is. We need all hands in this wind.' With a shake of his huge head, Don León strode off the bridge. Ángel stared mutely at his screens.

'You heard what Don León said!' Captain Juan shouted. 'Call Pablo and Miguel. On the double!'

Don León stood for a few moments in the lee of the salon doors to assess the situation. *Titania* was pitching and tossing on the wild sea. For the time being, the rain was holding off, but the aft deck was slippery and wet from the spray. The starboard side especially was exposed to the worst of the weather.

A quick inspection of the drier port side revealed no problems with the Lamborghini's cover and he moved on, bending to double-check one of the fastenings. On the starboard side, one corner of the cover had come loose and was flapping in the wind. He wrestled with it and cursed under his breath, turning to see if there was any sign of Pablo to help him install additional protection for the Murciélago.

A sudden massive surge threw him off balance as the boat climbed a wave then rolled hard to port. His head hit the side of the car with a bone-jarring thud. Before he could steady himself, *Titania* was battling the next wave and his feet slipped from under him. He felt himself sliding on his shoulder towards the starboard corner, unable to slow his momentum.

Below in her cabin, Petra lay on her back feeling the seesawing motion of the boat and wondering whether she should get up to take a look round. The waves were smashing against the hull and water cascaded past her porthole. Her marine training told her the situation was worsening and anything could happen. Yet a young history graduate was hardly likely to get up in the middle of the night to offer advice to a professional crew.

After arguing with herself for a while, Petra could stand it no longer. She pulled on her jeans, running shoes and a sweater and let herself quietly out of the cabin into the dark corridor.

In addition to excellent hearing, she was blessed with above average night vision and her eyes adjusted quickly. At the far end of the passage, a glimmer of light showed beneath the door of one of the other female crew cabins. Petra heard retching and a groan, followed by the toilet flushing. Either Olga or Monica must be seasick. Seasickness was the bane of many people, even experienced sailors, and Petra was thankful she never suffered from it.

She made her way through the dining room, also in darkness, and into the grand salon. The blinds were up and a glow from *Titania*'s exterior deck lights shone through the picture windows. Here above the engine room, the vibrations were stronger. From time to time, one of the engines seemed to miss a beat as the hull juddered and cracked under the onslaught of a particularly big wave.

To her surprise, Petra saw that the aft doors leading to the car deck were ajar. She slid them open and paused on the threshold. Outside, the noise was deafening: a cacophony of crashing sea and howling gale. The seating area was empty, the cushions safely stowed. The teak dining table, salty to the touch, stood like a sentinel on its pedestal. Except for the car, forlorn under its cover, there was nothing else to see. She was not dressed for battling the elements and it would be foolish to venture further.

Petra turned to leave, then froze. What was it she had heard above the wind? Scanning the deck, she could see nothing out of place. The first icy drops of rain splashed onto the car and blew in to where she was standing. She shivered and shook her head to clear her ears. Something was not right.

Then, during a split-second lull in the wind, she heard a grinding noise to her left. The side of the boat was sliding forward. With the movement of the boat, the locking mechanism holding the starboard coaming in place must have failed. Water was pouring through the widening gap. She knew that with the next wave the coaming would begin to slide back towards the stern.

As the coaming commenced its return journey, she was horrified to see a dark mass slithering across the deck. Seconds before tumbling overboard, it came to rest against the aft corner of the gap in the side of the yacht. Oblivious to the danger and the rain, Petra sprinted past the

Lamborghini and grabbed hold of the prostrate form. It was Don León. She had no idea of his condition and no time to waste: the coaming was only a metre or two away and sliding rapidly towards him.

In the last few desperate seconds before it clanged shut and crushed him, or pushed him into the ocean, Petra managed to grab the collar of his jacket and drag him away from the side. She sank to the deck next to him to catch her breath. He was a big man and it had taken all her strength to haul him into a position of relative safety. The good thing was that she could detect a faint pulse and feel the rise and fall of his chest.

The same low grinding noise alerted her to the fact that the coaming was beginning its next slide forward, reopening the gap. The situation was still critical. They could both be swept into the water. She had to act.

Petra got to her knees and ran her hands over Don León's torso and legs. No blood and no apparent broken bones. She shook his shoulders. 'Don León! Don León! Wake up! We have to move.' Her efforts elicited a feeble groan and she shook him again. 'Don León, come on!' This time his eyelids fluttered then opened.

'Petra?' His voice floated on the wind. 'What are you doing here? Where am I?'

She saw the confusion in his eyes as the floodlights above the car snapped on. Help must be on its way. She wondered if he would remember that he had been sliding inexorably across the deck to the open sea…

Within minutes the drama was over. Ángel and Carlo were the first to appear on deck, followed by Pablo.

'Ángel! Make that coaming fast!' Pablo shouted.

Carlo raised Petra gently to her feet and steadied her back to the salon. Pablo waited for Carlo to return, cradling Don León's head in his hands. Ignoring his protestations, they carried him inside and laid him on the sofa.

'I'm fine! I'm fine! Just get me a brandy.' He sat up and turned to Petra.

'My dear, I am in your debt. You're strong for your size and your quick reactions saved my life. I won't forget.'

Looking at the enormous head and into the cat-like eyes, Petra felt a visceral tug. She was soaked and weary, but some of the wetness came from deep within.

An hour later, after a couple of Spanish coffees brought in by a solicitous Olga, Petra was ready to retire and Don León obviously restored to his old self.

'Mamma mia! Don't fuss, Olga, I'm all right. You're acting like a mother hen,' he complained.

Captain Juan came in to report that the weather was clearing and they should be in Mallorca more or less on schedule.

'I want a full investigation into what happened, Juan. Those mechanisms are built to survive extreme conditions – a failure's unlikely. I suspect it was that damn idiot Miguel. Where is he?' Don León asked.

'Still below. It was a waste of time trying to get him on his feet.'

'I've never trusted that man. He's useless. He was the one who locked the coaming after we loaded the car.'

'Leave it to me, Don León. I'll have a talk with him and watch him like a hawk.'

'If it was his fault, he'll regret it. The consequence of evil is retribution. Isn't that how we were brought up?' Don León stared hard at the men and women clustered around him. 'Unless, of course, you confess, in which case anything can be forgiven.'

CHAPTER SEVEN

As so often happened, an immense calm followed the storm of the night. The whole world seemed cleansed and purified. Petra slept like the proverbial log and woke next morning only when the sound of an engine penetrated her stupor. She lay back with her arms over her head, listening. The chug-chug of the motor was very near and water splashed against *Titania*'s hull. Strange that Captain Juan would allow another boat to come so close. Then she realized *Titania*'s own engines were silent. A glance through her porthole confirmed that the motor yacht had indeed stopped. She pulled on a T-shirt and shorts and went to investigate.

Titania was riding at anchor in a bay ringed with limestone cliffs. Pitted and hollowed from millennia of erosion, they formed an almost perfect semi-circle around the limpid waters of the bay. Petra rested her elbows on the side of the boat. The water was crystal clear and the sandy bottom seemed much closer than it was in reality. She could scarcely believe that only a few hours ago there had been a major dislocation and a near-disaster; now there was scarcely a ripple. Nature never ceased to amaze her. She noticed a small white fishing boat chugging its way north, making surprisingly good time. She watched it until it disappeared round the headland.

'So how's our little heroine this morning?' Monica appeared, looking trim in a white mini-skirt and somewhat more voluptuous in the upper regions where her blue Lycra shirt was stretched close to breaking point. She came to lean on the rail beside Petra. 'I hear you rescued Don León from a fate resembling death,' she whispered. 'Don't think you can ensnare him that way. Others have tried and come to grief.'

Petra's initial reaction was to dismiss Monica's comments as melodramatic; then she wondered if she could be referring to Emily. 'It all happened so quickly. I wasn't really conscious of doing anything. I'm just glad it turned out all right,' she said, cringing at her own words.

Thank God her boss A.K. – or Tom – wasn't around to hear such platitudes. But why should she worry what Tom thought of her? She had hardly spared him a thought in the last thirty-six hours. Tom was just a mild-mannered nerd. The Super was a different kettle of fish, known for his scathing comments. 'If you can't say something worthwhile, don't say anything at all,' he would bark at recruits.

A shout from above made Petra and Monica look up. Sidetracked by her thoughts of A.K. and Tom, Petra hadn't noticed the telltale sounds of activity on the boat deck. Remote control in hand, Ángel was signalling them to move out of the path of the Scarab, which was coming into view. 'Stay clear, we're bringing her down!' he warned.

The double davit swung slowly out over the water, the long-nosed cigarette boat secure in its grasp. The neon colours of the hull sizzled in the sun. On the stern, next to the name *El Toro*, Petra noticed the stylized picture of a bull with its head down ready to gore. It was almost identical to the logo on the Lamborghini, the perfect symbol of Don León's alter ego: powerful, irritable, cunning and stubborn.

'That's my baby,' Monica crooned as the boat touched the surface of the water and Ángel climbed in. He unhooked the davit cables, fired up the engines, manoeuvred her away from the hull and drove her round to *Titania*'s stern.

'Monica, let's go!' The cry came a few minutes later as Don León marched through the doors of the grand salon and across the aft deck.

She jumped to attention and threw Petra a supercilious smile. 'Enjoy your day, Minx; Don León and I have business to attend to.'

Petra followed Monica to the stern and watched her climb into the Scarab. Don León stood at the helm, a blue bandana round his head. The four exhausts gave their characteristic hollow bark as the engines idled, then a full-throated roar as he opened the throttle. Within seconds, the Scarab was well away from the yacht, heading in the same direction as the white fishing boat, which it would soon overtake. Behind her, Petra heard the chink of glassware and turned to see Carlo placing a tray on the table.

'Come and grab a bite to eat, Petra, then we'll go exploring,' he said. 'Ángel and Miguel are preparing one of the WaveRunners for us. Don León was totally at ease this morning. He said we should just relax and enjoy the day.'

'Do you know where he and Monica have gone?' Petra asked.

'He mentioned a meeting with some German associates. Mallorca is full of Germans and their imposing villas, though they're mostly on the other side of the island, on the west coast. As I started to tell you yesterday morning, Don León has a number of legitimate businesses, one of which is the manufacture and wholesaling of what he likes to call leisurewear. You were wearing some of it for a while the night before last.'

'I guess you'll never forget that!'

'It will be enshrined in my memory forever and hopefully I'll get a second look someday,' Carlo said.

'In your wildest dreams!' Petra shot back.

'In my wildest dreams, I might be looking for someone built more like Monica.'

Carlo danced out of reach as Petra lifted her hand to swat his shoulder. 'Mercutio, you're incorrigible.' It was just like the old days. She had always enjoyed the verbal thrust and parry with him, though his insouciance seemed somewhat forced at times.

'Is that why Don León employs young girls?' she asked. 'To model his "leisurewear", I mean. He told me he wanted me to do some modelling when we arrived in Spain and Emily, the politician's daughter who was here in the summer, was keen to be a model.'

'I'm sure that's one of the reasons. He also has a thriving film production company based in Marbella. It produces documentaries and serials for TV as well as promotional videos for a variety of clients, including the tourist board. Last year, at the request of Interpol, the Spaniards conducted an enquiry and found nothing untoward, even from a tax point of view – which undoubtedly means it's a front for something else.'

'You're a cynic, Mercutio, but probably right!'

'Don León employs a lot of people in those two businesses,' Carlo continued. 'They're his main ones and provide most of his declared income. The girl you're looking for could be working in Marbella for one of them.'

Petra nodded agreement. 'It's possible.'

'How come you've been sent to look for her anyway?'

Before she could reply, Pablo walked round the corner from the port side of the megayacht, his ear to his VHF phone. He cast them a glance full of suspicion.

'Ángel's ready at the stern,' he said, eyeing Petra.

She glared back at him, resenting the way his gaze lingered on her breasts and remembering how hard he had squeezed them with his calloused hands.

'If the sea's cold, there are wet suits in the aft locker,' he muttered.

Ángel was waiting on the swim platform next to a two-seater Yamaha FX Cruiser HO, painted in *Titania* colours. Petra noted once again the bull logo on the stern plate, El Toro's mark of ownership. The water, when she bent down to test it, was warm to the touch, the sun strong.

With Carlo at the controls and Petra seated behind him, hugging his waist, they shot away from the yacht. The speed was exhilarating and the sense of freedom unexpected. Petra had not realized how oppressive the atmosphere aboard the yacht had been.

Titania was anchored three hundred metres offshore, in eight metres of water. A seventy-metre yacht with a three-metre draft would need plenty of room to swing in the currents and wind, Petra thought. Now, in the absolute calm, she sat in the heart of the bay sparkling like a jewel on a velvet cushion.

For an hour or more, Petra and Carlo played on the WaveRunner like children, racing up and down, circling the yacht, wishing she were underway so that they could jump the wake. Then they beached the watercraft on the sandy shore and cooled off in the turquoise sea. The cliffs buttressing the beach were ancient and worn yet still formed an impenetrable barrier.

'Let's go and see what's beyond the headland, Carlo. There's nothing else here,' Petra suggested.

'It's further than it looks.'

'So? We've got all day.'

Carlo shrugged. 'Fine by me. Who am I to resist a beautiful woman? You take control, girl!'

The Yamaha responded well, not unlike the Bombardier Petra used in the summertime at her uncle's cottage on Lake Huron. Fifteen minutes later, they rounded the headland and entered a different world. There, the heavily indented cliffs rose up steeply from the water's edge. Jagged outcroppings of rock, some of them like small islands, lay offshore. The water was still clear but darker, reflecting the rocky bottom. Even the sun seemed to have lost its strength and a slight chop disturbed the surface of the sea.

Petra shivered. 'Much cooler this side. I need to pee.' She nosed the Yamaha between two high piles of rock some fifteen metres from shore into a long V-shaped crevice. She cut the engine and jumped off onto a convenient ledge. 'Close your eyes, Carlo, I won't be long!'

'The first chance I get to take a peek and you tell me to close my eyes!'

'Sure do!' Petra paused and put one finger to her lips. 'Shhh! Listen.'

The faint throb of an engine carried across the water. Petra scrambled to the top of the outermost pile of rock on which stood a cross-shaped cairn reminiscent of the Inukshuk stone markers built to guide travellers across the featureless wastes of the Canadian North. It served now to shield her from view. What appeared to be the white fishing boat she had seen earlier was heading towards her at a fast clip. At that speed, they're definitely not fishing, she thought.

She motioned to Carlo to stay where he was. As the boat drew nearer, she could see two, maybe three, people on board and a stack of boxes in the open aft section. The *Sant'Ana* came so close before turning to avoid the rocky islet that Petra wondered what the skipper was thinking about. With a feeling of relief, she watched him alter course to starboard and follow the cliffs away to her left. A change of tone in the engine and a sudden decrease in the wake confirmed that the boat had slowed to negotiate another crop of offshore rocks. But why cut everything so fine? Petra found her answer as the noise receded and Carlo climbed up to join her.

'Where's the boat?' he asked, surveying the empty coastline.

Petra pointed to the solid mass of cliffs. 'In there. There must be a hidden inlet, which would explain why the captain was hugging the rocks. You know how difficult it is to see entrances and openings from the water until you're right on top of them.'

'Sure do! Let's go and take a look.'

Rolling her eyes at Carlo, Petra climbed down and seated herself at the controls of the watercraft. Carlo pushed it backwards out of the crevice until there was sufficient room to manoeuvre. The 4-stroke Yamaha engine was quieter than the old 2-stroke her uncle had had on his first Bombardier Sea-Doo, yet even at close to stall speed, it sounded too loud. Petra was glad 2-strokes were being phased out – they rattled your brain as well as leaving a huge carbon footprint. Ahead of them loomed the cliff face, pitted and crazed but with no visible point of entry.

'Focus on the discontinuities,' Carlo murmured into Petra's ear.

'I am.'

She scanned the rocks in front of them. Still nothing. It was a solid wall. She was about to turn the WaveRunner away to make a pass further to the south when a wave breaking against the base of the cliff caught her attention. Carlo tightened his grip on her waist.

'There!' Petra said, and nudged the jet ski closer.

The cliff face was almost upon them before the gap opened up to view. A narrow channel led off at a tangent between high canyon walls. There was no sign of the fishing boat. The jet ski idled forward. At the point where the channel appeared to end in a massive rock face, it made a dogleg turn to port. Negotiating the blind turn, Petra held her breath. In tight situations such as these, the rules of navigation required a Sécurité call to warn other vessels of their approach. In the absence of a radio, she could have sounded the horn, yet some instinct warned her against it.

They rounded the corner and skirted a group of rocks, bare and damp in the shade. A few seconds later, Petra brought the WaveRunner to a stop and stared in astonishment. Storybook-like, the channel opened out into a lagoon surrounded by caves. In ancient times, the action of the water must have scoured out this unexpected refuge, no doubt refined and improved by generations of smugglers and buccaneers to meet their own needs.

Half a kilometre away on the other side of the lagoon, the fishing boat was moored port-alongside a rocky ledge. With the help of a davit, her crew were unloading the boxes Petra had seen on the aft deck. The electric arm rose and lowered and swung back and forth in a fluid, effortless motion.

Releasing Petra's waist, Carlo tore at the dive watch on his left wrist. 'Take us in behind those rocks. I smell something fishy, but I bet you there's no fish in those boxes!' he said.

85

'OK, let's try.' Petra wormed the Yamaha between two inhospitable clumps of rock with only a few fingers of water to spare on either side. Once through the narrow neck, they were hidden from view.

Carlo slid from his seat and began to clamber over the rocks. 'Stay here,' he instructed Petra. 'I want to take a few pictures.'

Petra nodded. Carlo slithered his way to a point where the rocks met the cliff face in a slurry of boulders. He propped himself against the cliff and angled his watch until the cross hairs on the miniature screen set into the back were centred on the fishing boat. At maximum zoom, he fancied he could pick out a scar on the captain's cheek. Focussing on the boxes, he tried to read the inscription beneath the stamped outline of a bottle. He zeroed in on each of the crewmen in turn, pushed a tiny button to set the video in motion and panned slowly round the lagoon. The tide was a metre below the high water mark etched along the base of the cliffs. Some of the caverns were unsuitable for storage, plunging dark below the surface to unplumbed depths.

Petra waited at the controls of the Yamaha, pondering on the significance of the fishing boat. The *Sant'Ana*'s engines were more powerful and her loading gear more sophisticated than those of the average fishing vessel, and fishing vessels invariably had seagulls circling overhead, watching and waiting for a discharge of fishy remains. There had been no gulls around the *Sant'Ana*. This was the second time she had appeared in the vicinity of *Titania*, yet there was no real reason to suspect any link between them. Most probably she was a local bootlegger, one of countless small-time smugglers that traded back and forth across the Med. With its concealed entrance and convenient caves for storage, the lagoon was a perfect hideaway.

A distant whine attracted Petra's attention. It sounded like another jet ski. She looked round. Carlo was out of sight. She hoped he would hear it and keep a low profile. The noise echoed between the canyon walls, building to a crescendo as the watercraft shot out into the lagoon. Astride it sat Pablo, his sturdy figure erect and full of pride, his face suffused into a lop-sided grin. As he passed close to her, Petra saw his elation and could almost smell the level of his arousal. Fast cars and boats were a real turn-on for some men. Perhaps in Pablo's case, the power of the machine between his legs excited him in a way that normal sexual relations never could.

He skimmed across the glassy surface of the lagoon towards the fishing boat. The skipper of the *Sant'Ana* signalled him to pull in alongside. Petra watched the interplay between the two men from afar. They seemed to be on good terms and intent on their business. From their gestures, she guessed they were discussing the boxes, perhaps a shipment or a delivery. After a few minutes, they clasped hands, slapped each other on the back and Pablo revved his engine in preparation for leaving.

From his rocky cover, Carlo observed the exchange between the two men through the camera lens. 'I took some great pictures,' he whispered, dropping onto the seat behind Petra. 'Pablo and his mate seem to know each other well. I suspect they were making some arrangements of their own.'

'That was my impression too. Could you see what was in the boxes?' Petra asked.

'I'm afraid it looks like champagne. That's what's stamped on the side, although the contents could be anything.' Carlo pointed across the lagoon. 'I think Pablo has finished his business and is getting underway.'

'Fine, let's go!'

'What are you going to do?'

'Just hold tight and wave when Pablo sees us.'

Petra edged the Yamaha forward through the narrow gap, opened the throttle wide and turned hard to the left. Like a heat-seeking missile, they hurtled across the lagoon towards the fishing vessel. The burly skipper was gesticulating and shouting in rapid dialect to the departing Pablo, who cast a startled look over his shoulder. Petra chuckled at his discomfiture. 'Wave! Wave and smile!' she urged.

Carlo followed Petra's lead so enthusiastically that he nearly lost his seat as she forced the watercraft into a tight U-turn.

'I told you to hold tight,' she shouted.

The canyon walls flashed past. Petra and Carlo streaked through the entrance fifty metres ahead of Pablo. Like a thoroughbred on the home straight, the Yamaha surged forward, bouncing across the waves as they raced for the headland followed hotly by the second jet ski.

CHAPTER EIGHT

Monica followed Don León and his business associate Theo through the great hall of Theo's villa, across the sun-dappled courtyard and up the steep spiral staircase to the tower room where their meetings always took place. The two men were deep in conversation and she had ample time to savour the atmosphere of the old house with its wooden beams, terracotta floors and sandstone details. Once a hunting lodge for a minor prince, it exuded warmth and contentment in a way that modern villas did not. She loved its redundancies, its nooks and crannies that resonated with the history of past lives.

Sometimes she fantasized about settling down with Don León in a house like Theo's, putting their nomadic existence behind them and becoming a family. She craved affection and stability, not a stream of guests and visitors and attractive young summer staff to divert Don León's attention. Olga had warned her not to get sentimental. Don León valued his independence and wanted no ties, 'least of all to someone like you', she had sneered. Monica wished she had trusted her own instincts and not listened to the old witch. With regret, she buttoned her dream into the back pocket of her mind. It would never become reality now.

The back-slapping prelude to the meeting came to a halt as the men entered the tower room. Theo ran his hand through his Teutonic brush cut and gestured to two of the three vacant chairs at the round oak table. The fourth chair was already occupied. On it sat a short, dark-haired man with thin lips and a sharp nose. Monica distrusted him instantly. Theo introduced him as his new estate manager Axel, and Monica found herself sitting next to him. She noticed that he inched his chair closer to hers as soon as she sat down.

'Axel has a number of ideas for streamlining production and increasing output. He has good connections in Hamburg and Berlin. Through them, we could build a much wider network,' Theo said.

Monica watched him run his hand through his short blonde hair again. He seemed more nervous than at their last meeting earlier in the summer.

'Our business is solid, Theo,' Don León replied. 'Demand is growing in the Middle East and North Africa. The Arabs want quality, not quantity. I've told you before that I don't want to get involved in the rest of Europe.'

Monica nodded. Don León had always been careful to stay out of the way of the big guys. Maybe they were beginning to put pressure on Theo.

Axel made a fist with his hand and brought it down hard on the table. 'You don't know what you're missing. All we need is a guaranteed supply, a little grease on the right palms and we could all be millionaires.'

Not the way to talk to Don León, Monica thought. He's not interested in making creeps like you into millionaires.

'I think your estate manager needs more time to understand our business, Theo,' Don León said. 'You should give him some training. What do you think, Monica?'

'I think he's a loose cannon.' Probably goes off at the slightest provocation, she added under her breath.

'Now, now, there's no need for insults. Axel has only recently joined us and is anxious to prove himself. We must work together.' Theo's hands fluttered. 'I know your feelings, Don León – some might call them prejudices – but I believe some of Axel's ideas have merit.'

'There are far more important issues we need to discuss today, Theo. For example, the recent restrictions on goods entering the European Union from certain South American countries,' Don León said. He began to expound on the diabolical nature of the directives emanating from Brussels.

After a few minutes, Monica lost the thread of the conversation and her mind drifted. Through the tall church-style windows of the tower room, she had a clear view of the mellow stone buildings surrounding the inner courtyard of the *finca* as well as a corner of the roof terrace.

Under a pergola draped in purple bougainvillea, a young woman with blonde hair hanging down her back was pulling a chaise longue into position. Monica did a double take. From the rear, she looked like the Canadian girl who had been on board during the summer, the one who had captivated Don León. She cast him a glance to see whether he had noticed, but he was arguing with Theo over shipments and in any case, his chair was facing the sea. It couldn't be the Canadian. There must be some mistake.

To her left, Theo's estate manager Axel seemed to be fidgeting in his seat. Monica bit back a laugh as she noted the direction of his gaze. He was watching the blonde on the terrace. With a quick movement, the girl gathered up her hair and twisted it into a knot that she fixed in place with a large clip. Then she unhooked her bikini top, stripped off her thong and dropped them both on the ground. Judging by the lascivious expression on Axel's face, he was imagining what he would do to her, given half a chance.

Monica turned her attention back to Theo and Don León. They had settled their differences and moved on to general topics. A few minutes later, Theo stood up, indicating that the meeting was at an end.

'We've made some good decisions, Don León,' he said. 'Join me tonight in Palma. We'll celebrate aboard *Nemesis*. And bring your steward and that new member of staff you mentioned – you said they could sing.'

At the thought of Petra muscling in on her territory, Monica felt a prick of jealousy. It turned rapidly to outrage as she realized that Axel's hand was under her skirt reaching for her crotch. In a flash, she caught hold of his wrist and dug her nail extensions into the soft underside. 'Leave me alone, punk,' she whispered through gritted teeth, 'or you'll wish you'd never met me.' She dropped his hand and was pleased to see him wince. As he stomped out of the room, she lifted a finger at his receding back. Had she been on the street, she would have spat in his direction.

Theo bade them a cordial goodbye and instructed one of his boys to take them back to the jetty where they had left the Scarab. The drive downhill from where the villa sat perched on the edge of the Sierras de Levante, the eastern mountains, was electrifying. Monica could feel the tension in Don León as they rounded every bend in the narrow, unprotected road. He had told her once in an unguarded moment that heights troubled him. Vistas and panoramas, fast boats and cars posed no problem, only heights – ever since the day he had witnessed a boy of about his own age drop from the top of a tenement in Bogotá. The body had fallen opposite the spot where he and his mother were begging for a few coins to buy food. He still avoided tall buildings and disliked mountain roads. Monica moved closer to Don León and tentatively placed a hand on his thigh.

An hour and a half later, she went looking for him. During the ride back to *Titania* on the Scarab, he had seemed preoccupied and had disappeared as soon as they re-boarded the yacht. She found him on the upper deck next to the pool, lying on his stomach on a teak sunbed topped with a blue and gold striped cushion. For a moment she gazed at his long tanned back and legs through cloudy eyes. Then she pulled the blue Lycra top over her head and let it drop to the ground. She undid the side zip on her white mini-skirt and stepped out of it, leaving it in a heap where it lay. Softly, she knelt down beside him and began to work his flesh, stroking and kneading with her strong fingers.

As she zeroed in on the knots in his muscles, she felt him stiffen then relax under her touch. She bent to her task and let her bare nipples caress his back. At times like this, when she and Don León were alone, naked together and joined not in sexual union but a profound intimacy of flesh and feeling, she could forget the petty arguments and slow-burning jealousy that sapped her confidence. However many Emilys and Petras there might be, he still needed her.

Monica worked deftly down from Don León's muscled shoulders to the base of his spine, smoothing the uninterrupted tan. She lingered for a moment on the tiny bull tattoo etched in black just above the crease of his buttocks, on the right-hand side. Concealed power seen only by a privileged few. And she was one of those.

93

The VHF phone on the table by Don León's side gave a peremptory buzz, shattering their peace. 'That's Olga. Give me my robe,' he barked.

The fine blue silk was a perfect foil for his golden skin and lion's mane of hair. Monica felt a surge of desire as Don León strode past the pool to the bow of the boat.

The wind had strengthened and changed direction so that *Titania* now rode with her stern towards the shore. 'The jet skis are coming in, Monica,' he called. 'Go and get Petra ready for tonight. We'll be underway in half an hour.'

As Petra and Carlo rounded the headland, the sun bounced off *Titania*'s superstructure in a shimmer of stars. Petra threw a quick glance backwards. Crouched low over the handlebars of his jet ski, Pablo was gradually gaining on them. She gunned the engine and spun the Yamaha in a hard turn to port. Carlo grabbed at Petra's waist to steady himself against her wild gyrations. She drove the machine in a tight circle behind Pablo then round again, waving crazily and venting cries of joy. By the second pass, she could see Pablo glowering at her.

'You've run circles round him, literally, and he doesn't like it,' Carlo whispered as they disembarked. 'Watch out for him – he's bad news.'

'Children, children! Have you had a good time?' A beaming Olga greeted Petra and Carlo as they emerged onto the main deck. 'Where did you go?'

'Pablo showed us the way to an amazing lagoon, didn't he, Carlo?' Petra matched Olga's insincere beam with an ingenuous smile.

Olga's face tightened. 'Did he now?'

Carlo took his cue from Petra and gave a brief nod of his head in acquiescence. Out of the corner of his eye, he saw Monica making her way across the deck to join the

94

group. The only things smaller than her white thong bikini were the blue and gold appliqués that covered her nipples and an infinitesimal portion of her overripe breasts. She bridled under his gaze.

'Now that you kids are back, we're leaving for Palma,' she said.

In confirmation of her words, *Titania*'s engines rumbled to life. Two of the sailors headed to the foredeck to monitor the anchors as Captain Juan used the remote control to retrieve and stow them from the bridge.

'Minx, you're to come with me to prepare for this evening.' Monica paused before continuing in a tone that conveyed a certain reluctance to deliver the rest of the message: 'And Don León wants you and Carlo to sing some opera tonight for his German friends.'

'Did he mention any specific pieces? Do you know what they like?' Petra asked.

'That's not my business. You'll have to ask him or talk to your mate.'

After the trauma of the storm the previous night, the four-hour run to Palma that afternoon was uneventful. *Titania* sliced through the tranquil waters with nothing to impede her passage; even the turn to the west at Cap de ses Salines brought no unpleasant surprises.

Don León never tired of the entry into Palma Bay. The vista from his sitting room was magnificent. On the east side of the wide bay ran endless expanses of fine sand beaches, more exposed than the indented west coast but still protected from the worst of the north and west winds by the Puig Major mountain range.

The old town was dominated by the Gothic cathedral. Its tall, pinnacled buttresses rose above the seafront in silent testimony to the city's medieval glory and maritime heritage. At this hour of the day, the walls of Santanyi limestone reflected pink in the rays of the setting sun. Like the Taj Mahal, to appreciate the cathedral fully, it needed to be seen at different times of day. For Petra, this was the first time yet she knew it would not be the last.

Standing on the foredeck, she took in the looming monument and, to the left, pointed out by Carlo, the ancient Moorish fortress converted centuries before into a royal palace. They had spent part of the voyage rehearsing their opera medley in the grand salon under Olga's eagle eye. Then Monica had appeared in a mini blue robe and whisked Petra away to instruct her in the art of modelling for the evening's reception. This, Petra had learned, was to be held aboard the megayacht belonging to Don León's business associate Theo, at whose villa the morning's meeting had taken place.

Palma's harbours were busy with commercial and passenger traffic. Cruise liners mingled with ferries, merchantmen with fishermen, sailing boats with speedboats, twenty-metre motor yachts with eighty-metre superyachts and everything in between.

Titania docked with an effortless ease that belied her size. Captain Juan's skill was unquestionable. Petra still preferred side-to docking along a wall, or reversing into a slip with side piers, to the Mediterranean-style stern-to docking. Inserting a large yacht between two others, even with plenty of fenders in position, then picking up a mooring line to secure the bow was something she preferred to avoid.

In this particular instance, she would have been petrified, for in the adjacent berth lay a sleek, shiny leviathan. The futuristic design was unlike anything she had ever seen. With its elongated profile, the sharp pointed nose of the bow, the slash of the mouth forward where the bridge would be, and the oval eye set halfway back in the hull, the vessel had the look of a gleaming predator. A shark, Petra thought, or a daring new version of a submarine poised to hunt and destroy its prey. Its conning tower – the radar mast with its array of antennas and satellite communication equipment – reached for the sky and caught the final glow of the sun.

'Are you impressed, Minx?' Monica enquired, coming up behind Petra and prodding her in the back. 'You should be, though you probably don't know what you're looking at.'

Petra ignored both the gibe and the jab. It wouldn't hurt to let Monica feel superior. 'She's amazing,' she said. 'Have you seen her before? Is this her homeport?'

'That's Theo's yacht *Nemesis* – the one we're visiting tonight. She's registered in the Cayman Islands, but spends a lot of time here. Come on, you need to get changed.'

Petra followed Monica down to the female crew quarters where, earlier that afternoon, Monica had attempted to teach her the model's arrogant sway and pouting pose. Professionals on the catwalk made it look easy. Posture was no problem, but Petra had found the walk and turns unnatural and could not help laughing at herself. In the beginning, Monica had remained true to type, maintaining her bossy, sneering attitude until Petra's hamming it up had reduced her to laughter too.

'Minx, this is serious stuff. Pull yourself together. These guys are tough. You've got to give them what they want,' she had said.

Not everything they want, Petra had murmured to herself. Remembering what Amy had told her about Emily wanting to model, she had decided to take advantage of Monica's more relaxed mood.

'I'm not sure I'll ever master this, although you're a pretty good teacher,' she had said. 'You must have taught other girls.'

'When I have to!'

'Don León said you had another Canadian student aboard, last July and August I think. Was she also involved in this modelling stuff?'

A shadow had crossed Monica's eyes. 'Yeah, for a while. She thought she was good, but she wasn't. She didn't want to do what she was told, so El Toro paid her off at the end of August.'

Monica's response had been interesting. A slightly different version, but still no one was denying that Emily had been aboard the yacht. The challenge was to find out where she was now. So far, the only trace of Emily's stay on the yacht was the topaz pendant she had found – if indeed it was Emily's. Certainly, the girl who looked like Emily had been wearing it in the movie Don León's guests had been watching in the skylounge.

Petra's thoughts switched back to the present. The theme for the evening was predictable – high stiletto boots, black leather micro skirt, tightly laced top. She had been involved in undercover operations before, but this one took the biscuit. Still, she was proud of her figure and would strut her stuff along with the best of them.

Theo's yacht *Nemesis* was slightly smaller overall than *Titania*. As the party of four boarded the steel and aluminium vessel, the sky darkened and the first stars began to appear. Trim and, Petra had to admit, sexy in black T-shirt and sculpted leather trousers, Carlo led the way across the passerelle. He nodded to the crewman standing guard. In gallant Italian fashion, he offered his arm to Monica and kissed his fingers to his lips as she stepped off the passerelle after him.

Petra was next in line. He gave her a slight bow and a steadying hand as she walked onto the deck. 'Madame, allow me.'

His tone was bantering and Petra felt an irrational stirring of anger. 'You look like a gigolo,' she hissed.

He gave her a deprecating look. 'And you?'

Petra was conscious of Don León following close behind her. The back of her neck prickled under his scrutiny and she wondered if he would reach out and touch her. She quickened her pace to stay one step ahead of him. It was too late. Her nerves tingled as he ran a manicured finger down her spine.

'You keep yourself in very good shape, my dear,' he said, admiring the neat flare of her waist, the firm butt and slim legs. His hand travelled back up her spine to the nape of her neck. He left it there, under the glossy black hair, for a few moments, squeezing gently. The underlying strength of the caress reminded Petra that she was dealing, by his own admission, with a powerful and ruthless man. She was glad she had decided to wear her cross for protection.

'Welcome, willkommen, friends! Welcome aboard *Nemesis*.' Their host came bustling forward, his brush cut gleaming yellow in the concealed deck lights. 'Don León! Monica!' Theo paused to shake hands with El Toro and embraced Monica closely but coolly. 'And who have we here Don León? You must introduce us!'

'Of course. Theo, this is Petra, Petra Minx, who has just joined our staff for a few months, and Carlo, our new steward. They're both talented singers and will be delighted to entertain us later.'

Theo kissed the air in the vicinity of Petra's cheeks then turned his attention to Carlo, who batted his eyelashes in a deliberate attempt to size up the opposition. Petra already had Theo's measure. She followed them across the deck.

The swooping glass doors that separated *Nemesis'* aft deck from her salon slid silently open and closed immediately behind them. The enormous side windows gave Petra the impression of being in a plastic bubble surrounded by the sea. After the rather florid decoration favoured by Don León aboard *Titania*, the stark juxtaposition of unadorned glass, leather, wood and stone was refreshing.

Theo whispered something into Carlo's ear and escorted him to an L-shaped white leather sofa where three men were already sitting. Judging by the number of wine bottles on the glass and bronze coffee table, the evening was well underway. Don León propelled the girls forward.

Theo clapped his hands in the air. 'Champagne cocktails for the ladies! Don León and Carlo, you'll have wine, I'm sure. The best Sangre de Toro!'

At Theo's command, a redhead stepped out from behind a mirrored screen, balancing a round silver tray on one emaciated arm. She couldn't have been much older than Emily Mortlake, but she showed no emotion as she handed Petra a crystal flute brimming with bubbly.

'Thank you, that looks great.' Petra's warm smile elicited only a blank stare. Curious. She glanced around. Monica was chatting in German with two of the three men on the sofa, Don León and Carlo were talking intently, and Theo had vanished. Petra took a sip of her champagne cocktail. The redhead was filling her tray with empty bottles.

'Let me help you with those. They're awkward.' Petra picked up two of the bottles.

'There's no need.'

'Please.' She followed the girl behind the screen and placed the bottles on the bar. 'My name's Petra. What's yours?'

There was a pause before the girl answered. 'Rosemary.'

'I've just joined the crew of *Titania*. She's a fantastic boat but *Nemesis* is incredible. Have you been aboard long?'

'Six months or so.' The flame-red hair curved around her pale, lightly freckled face.

'Do you like it?'

'It's a job.'

Extracting information from the redhead was like uncorking a bottle of wine with a pin. Rosemary moved across to a dinner table laid for eight with Danish silver on a black marble top. At each place she set a facetted crystal goblet overlaid in crimson, the colour of the far wall on which hung a selection of what looked like Escher drawings. Petra went to take a closer look. They had lost none of their appeal.

'My father loved these. He said you could never tire of something that worked in so many different planes at once. What do you think?'

Rosemary stared at Petra as if seeing her for the first time. 'Nobody asks me what I think.'

'Well I'm asking you. What do you think?' Petra repeated.

A flicker of interest passed across the redhead's eyes.

'You're different – not the usual type we get from *Titania*.'

'What do you mean?'

'Most of them are blonde, like my friend. That's what Theo prefers.'

'I got the impression that Theo prefers young men to women.'

'That too. He can swing either way. As long as they're properly trained, and your Don León does that well.'

'He's not my Don León.'

Rosemary showed no reaction. 'Whatever.'

'You said blonde. You're not blonde either,' Petra reminded her.

'No, so they leave me alone most of the time. I was an experiment that didn't work out. The clientele is pretty demanding.'

'What clientele? What are you talking about?'

'All I know is Don León supplies a lot of girls to *Nemesis* and other yachts.'

'Are any others on board now?'

'They come and go. Right now the crew is mostly male. There's just one other girl here, my friend Emy.'

Petra's mouth dropped open. She stared unseeingly at Rosemary, questions racing through her mind. Then she realized the redhead was still speaking.

'Her real name's Emily, but she prefers to be called Emy. She's due to leave at the end of the week.'

Petra felt her pulse rate spike. 'What did you say? A girl called Emy … and she's leaving at the end of the week?'

Rosemary shot Petra a worried look. 'Right! What's wrong with that? She's going to work for Sheik Kamal, the owner of *Lady Fatima*.'

'I'm sorry; you caught me off balance. Of course there's nothing wrong with that. Is she here now?'

'This is her afternoon off. She'll be back later.'

The news left Petra in shock. She remembered the postcard signed "Emy" that Emily Mortlake had sent her mother from Puerto Banús. Although, according to her mother, Emily hated the diminutive and never used it, she might have changed her mind once she reached Oxford. In which case, it looked to Petra as though her mission was coming to an end much sooner than expected.

If she could persuade Emily to return to England, it shouldn't be too difficult to slip away from *Nemesis* and contact Tom to sort things out with the local authorities. A.K. would be delighted to get Donald Mortlake off his back. And yet... the unqualified elation Petra knew she should be feeling was tinged with regret. With a jolt, she realized she would have liked to have more time to get to know Don León.

CHAPTER NINE

Rosemary's revelation preoccupied Petra throughout the modelling before dinner. As she strutted round Theo's salon in a leather combi slit to the navel, her mind was alight with questions. Why had Emily transferred from *Titania* to *Nemesis* instead of going to see her uncle in Geneva? Why hadn't Emily returned to Oxford? If she had decided not to go back for the beginning of term, why hadn't she contacted her family or friends or the University to let them know? Those were just a few of the questions Petra would ask her, assuming that Emy was indeed the girl she was looking for.

And what about Don León? What was he doing training and supplying female crew? If he had arranged for Emily to join *Nemesis* and now to transfer to *Lady Fatima*, why had he said that she had left to go travelling? He seemed to have his fingers in lots of pies. Sticky fingers in suspect pies.

Then there was Rosemary, another enigma. Why was she so painfully thin? Why were her eyes so glazed and her attitude so disinterested? Was she anorexic? Was she on drugs? Petra didn't have enough answers yet to make sense of it all.

She paused in front of Don León, who was sitting on the sofa next to Carlo. Although he was drinking along with the rest of them, he seemed detached now that the show had started and hardly glanced in her direction. Monica had implied that the modelling was a gimmick, not strictly necessary from a business point of view. Don León liked to titillate his audience. It was another way of exercising control.

A few minutes later, Petra reentered the salon in a mini dirndl with a wire uplift cut-away blouse. She saw Carlo lean towards Don León and whisper something. Her face flushed with anger and shame, as if Carlo had made a scathing comment on her attire. What was she doing here flaunting her body, allowing herself to be manipulated by Don León and Monica? Then she reminded herself that she was engaged in a delicate balancing act to discover Emily Mortlake's whereabouts without arousing suspicion. In fact, by pretending to be someone she was not, she was manipulating them.

With renewed determination, she pirouetted in her high-heeled patent leather pumps and surveyed the scene. Theo and his comrades were exchanging noisy comments in German accompanied by outbursts of laughter. A quartet of bronzed young men standing behind the sofa in crisp whites completed the audience. Rosemary was nowhere to be seen.

An hour and a couple of champagne cocktails later, Petra found herself seated for dinner between Erik, a burly bear of a man, and Axel, a wiry thirty-something with a narrow mouth. Across the wide table, Monica was sandwiched between Carlo and another man, whose name Petra thought was Johann. Theo and Don León faced off at opposite ends of the table. The four young men kept an impressive range of exquisitely prepared dishes coming to the table and ensured that nobody's glass remained empty for more than a few seconds.

Sighing with pleasure after the most delectable crayfish she thought she had ever tasted, Petra found her eyes drawn to the tanned neck and chest of one of the waiters as he bent close to Don León to refill his wineglass. Feeling her scrutiny, he lifted his hazel eyes to her blue-green ones and smiled lazily. Carlo watched the interaction with amusement.

'Pssst! Minx! You're up to no good, I can tell. Anyway, he's too young for you.'

'What do you mean?' Petra demanded.

'He's a nice boy, but not your type.'

'You don't know what you're talking about!'

Petra turned away to her left. She had neglected her neighbour on that side. He had a pinched look about him and seemed very drunk and morose. Theo had been talking to him quietly without eliciting much response.

'Hello, I'm Petra, Petra Minx. You're Theo's new estate manager, aren't you? Where were you working before you came here?'

Axel made a visible effort to pull himself together. He focussed his eyes on her pale, heart-shaped face, which contrasted starkly with her black hair. Her complexion was flawless, like that of a fine porcelain doll – a real doll. 'Hamburg,' he answered, without elaboration.

'You're so lucky!' she exclaimed. 'You have a wonderful opera house in Hamburg.'

'I wouldn't know,' Axel replied. In the shadows of the Reeperbahn, Hamburg's red-light district, opera didn't exist. He searched for something to say to pique her interest.

Across the table, Petra could hear Theo and Carlo arguing about the merits of various productions of

106

Wagner's Ring. She looked past Axel with his lack of culture and his weasel face. The animated discussion beyond him to her left was much more inspiring.

'Come on, Carlo!' she erupted. 'I agree with Theo, the Copenhagen Ring's brilliant!'

Axel clenched his teeth. The room was buzzing with conversation. Johann and Don León were talking in serious tones about the insurgency in Iraq, Monica was cackling at one of Erik's obscene jokes. As Petra leaned forward to interject into the Wagner debate, the cross at her neck caught the light. She stroked it lightly like a talisman, not seeing how Axel's eyes bored into her chest. His hand inched over to touch her thigh under the table. Without a second thought, Petra swatted it away like a fly.

The main course of estate venison was followed by a lavish selection of cheeses and desserts from a stainless steel trolley. Petra wasn't sure she could eat or drink much more. She had tried to limit the amount of alcohol she had consumed, but Theo was determined to give his guests a good time.

'Ladies! You must try the new Cuvée Ana León.' Don León clapped his hands and the waiter with the hazel eyes appeared at Petra's side with a V-shaped glass.

'No, thank you. I really can't manage it.' Petra waved the glass away.

The waiter made a moue and pressed the flute into her hand. 'Please! For me! You'll love it.'

With a small show of reluctance, Petra took the proffered glass. Tiny bubbles gushed to the surface of the delicate pink liquid like unstoppable geysers. At the first sip, she felt them tickle her nose and laughed, trying to put the glass down.

'You're right. It's delicious!' She couldn't seem to balance the glass properly. Then she realized it had no foot. 'What is this? A joke?'

Don León leaned towards her and smiled. 'Think of it as a rite of passage for new members of staff. It's all or nothing.' He raised his wineglass. 'Welcome, Petra, to our inner circle!'

Monica raised her footed glass in salute. Theo and his cohorts chorused their welcome. Axel sniggered. Feeling somewhat foolish, Petra drained her glass and handed it back to the waiter who exchanged it for a normal flute full to the brim.

'Thank you, Sir. Thank you all for accepting me.' Petra looked round the table then back to Don León. His gaze was compelling. She managed to hold it for several seconds before dropping her eyes.

When she looked up again, he had turned towards Monica. Their closeness sent a surge of jealousy through her. An urge that she fought to control made her want to run her hands over the aquiline nose, the high forehead and through his shaggy hair. She began to wonder what he would look like naked, how his skin would feel and smell…

He was leaning closer to Monica, across the empty chair where the man called Johann had been, pulling her towards him with her shoulder strap. It fell off her shoulder, revealing part of her left breast and a tiny black tattoo, the outline of a bull with its head down. Petra's eyes were riveted. The swell of Monica's breast fascinated her. She watched it rise and fall. With each breath, the bull's head seemed to flex and lift. Petra's own breath came in gasps. She wanted to reach out and touch.

Petra rubbed her temples in an attempt to clear her head. What was happening to her? Never in her life had she felt such confused stirrings as these. Despite her efforts, she must have had way too much to drink. At the Police Academy, all the cadets had been warned about situations in which disreputable characters forced people to drink in order to take advantage of them. Was this one of those situations? She wouldn't have thought so, yet there was something strange about the evening. The background music, unobtrusive during dinner, suddenly seemed to double in volume. Her head began to pound. She had to get out.

Over to her left, beyond Theo and Carlo, the salon stood in near darkness. The coffee table was still strewn with evidence of the early evening's intake. Petra watched as Rosemary entered with a tray and began to clear the debris. Where was Emily? Surely she should be back from town by now. The redhead came closer, but remained in the shadows. She appeared to be trying to tell Petra something. After a few minutes, Petra realized she was signalling her to leave the room. Petra excused herself and asked the young Adonis standing nearby to point her in the direction of the bathroom.

Forward of the salon and dining room in a rather odd arrangement of space, Petra discovered a bar and balcony area overlooking a plunge pool and Jacuzzi. The balcony floor was tiled in what appeared to be blue glass. In one corner stood discotheque equipment and a bank of speakers. On the lower level, strange circular beds flanked the pool. Petra floated between them as if on a cloud. Above her and to each side, the glass enclosure gleamed with reflected light from the outside deck lights, casting a subdued glow over the interior. She felt a sudden desire to sit down and was about to sink onto one of the beds when Rosemary ran into the room.

'Please come with me, Emy's back but she's in a terrible state. From what I can make out, Axel tried to rape her.'

'What? Is she hurt?'

'Battered and bruised, I can't tell how badly.'

Petra abhorred violence against women though she had seen plenty of it during her career. She had served for several years in the female protection division before transferring to the Marine Unit.

'I knew that bastard was rubbish!' The spurt of adrenalin helped to clear her fuzzy head and drive out any remaining lascivious thoughts. She flew with Rosemary past the pool, along a passage and down a companionway to the crew quarters. Rosemary opened one of the doors.

'She's in here,' she said.

The cabin was compact compared to Petra's aboard *Titania*. Rosemary's friend Emy lay on the lower bunk facing the wall, curled up in the foetal position. Petra hurried over to her and knelt by the bed. Carefully she placed her arms around her in the eternal gesture of comfort. Her voice was gentle but authoritative. 'You'll be fine. No one's going to hurt you now. We'll look after you.'

Petra held the girl close until she felt a shudder run through her thin body. With the lightest of touches, she stroked her head and neck and felt the girl's tears begin to ooze. 'Let it out, let it come. You'll feel better after a good cry.' The platitude sounded like a crock, but Petra knew it was true.

A spasm shook the girl. The release of tension had begun. Rosemary hovered behind Petra. 'I had no idea what to do. You're so clever,' she said.

'She might go into delayed shock. She needs to be kept warm. Pass me that blanket, then go and fetch some hot sweet tea.'

Rosemary reached up to the upper bunk and handed Petra the soft fleece. Petra cradled the girl in her arms, soothing her with quiet words. Ten minutes passed before Emily's sobs ebbed away. Of her own accord, the girl uncurled her legs and turned over.

'My jaw hurts.' She touched the left side of her chin. 'My head too. I need to sit up.'

'Let me help you.' Petra slipped one arm behind her and raised her up. As the light fell on the girl's damaged face, Petra bit back a string of expletives. Multiple abrasions and ugly black bruises disfigured the delicate structure. An egg-sized lump stood out above her right eye. There was dried blood round her nose, which could have been broken. It shocked Petra to see it. She had never grown inured to the consequences of violence. But the greater shock was the dawning realization that this Emily was not the Emily she had seen in the photograph Amy had shown her in Oxford. Of course, the world was full of Emilys. Why had she been so certain that this girl would be the one she was looking for? It was bad practice to jump to conclusions.

'Petra, are you all right?' Rosemary had returned with the tea. Concern tinged her voice. 'Don't worry, Emy's injuries probably aren't as bad as they look.' With the resilience of youth, Rosemary was bouncing back now that her friend appeared to be out of danger.

'I'm fine. It's just that I got my job aboard *Titania* on the recommendation of a friend named Emily. She worked for Don León during the summer then stayed in the area. When you said Emily was here, aboard *Nemesis*, I thought you were referring to her. And naturally when you said she had been battered, I was devastated. But now I know this isn't the same Emily.'

Rosemary looked a trifle confused, and Petra didn't blame her. Her explanation was rather garbled.

'Emy, are you sure it was Axel who did this to you?' Petra asked.

'Absolutely certain.' The tea seemed to have revived her and the words came tumbling out. 'At the end of this morning's meeting, Theo told him to drive me to Palma in the Mercedes. It was my afternoon off and I was looking forward to going shopping. Theo and Erik went off in the Porsche, and Rosemary was already on her way back here with Johann. I was stuck with that bastard Axel. He's been after me ever since he arrived at the villa a couple of weeks ago. Rosemary will tell you what a pain he's been. He's a horrible little man.'

Rosemary nodded in agreement. 'From the moment Axel set foot on the property, the atmosphere changed,' she said. 'Because he was estate manager, he acted as though everything was his to use as he wished, including the female staff. He was particularly taken with Emy, used to follow her around and spy on her when she was sunbathing. One night, to avoid his advances, she was forced to sleep with me. When she went back to her own room next morning, there was a nasty white stain on the bedcover.'

Petra knew exactly the kind of person Axel was. 'So you, Emy, had to leave in the Mercedes with Axel. What happened then?' she asked.

'I tried to keep as far away from him as possible. When he adjusted his seat forward, I pushed mine back. At first, we were behind Theo's gold Porsche. Theo had told Axel to stay close as it's easy to get lost on the estate. There's only one real road down the mountain through the pinewoods, but plenty of side-tracks. Axel seemed to be concentrating on driving, getting the feel of the big saloon. He didn't say anything and I could see the flashes of gold round the curves ahead of us, so I began to relax. It was hot in the car and I must have dozed off.'

'You always go to sleep in moving vehicles!' Rosemary interjected.

'I won't from now on,' Emy said. 'When I woke up, we were lurching along a track through an abandoned olive grove. There was no sign of the Porsche. We were completely alone. I was mad as hell at finding myself stranded with that creep. Before I had time to decide what to do, Axel stopped the car and pressed the recline button. Both our seats tilted backwards until they were virtually horizontal. Then he shoved me flat and straddled me with his left leg. He kept breathing in my face and pushing me down every time I tried to sit up, kept telling me I liked it.'

Emy broke off and shook her head, remembering how he had grabbed her low-cut top and ripped it off to expose her breasts, naked underneath. He had fallen on top of her groaning, rubbing his chest on hers, crushing it beneath him. With his right hand, he had felt under her skirt searching for the entrance, homing in on the moist heat. 'You're just like all the rest,' she had scoffed. None of them had touched her soul, not even El Toro whose mark she still bore.

Axel was heaving against her, humping and wriggling, taking a long time about it. It occurred to her that he might be incapable of maintaining an erection. She had laughed, a loud, raucous, relieved laugh. 'I was wrong! You're not like the others, are you? You can't get it up!' Pushing with both palms against his skinny shoulders, she had spat in his face. 'You're a fraud! You need Viagra! Why don't you ask Theo for some? You're useless without it…'

113

Her words had faded away in a hail of blows…

Gradually Petra elicited the whole story. During the telling, Emy was by turns belligerent, defensive, tearful and contrite. From the start, she had tried to discourage Axel's attentions. She knew he used to spy on her and admitted that her taunts might have fuelled his anger that afternoon. The bastard had hit her repeatedly in the face. She had turned aside to avoid the worst of the first blow, which smashed into her temple. The next blow connected with her nose. The last one she remembered socked into her jaw with such force that her neck snapped backwards and she lost consciousness.

When she came round, she was lying face down in a dry riverbed. The sun had moved round to the west and a chill was settling over the valley. Using the sun's position as her guide, she trudged back in the direction of the road. Eventually, she came to the olive grove and a shack, which proved to be a disused pressing room. In the corner stood a rusty pump. She succeeded in coaxing a trickle of water from the ancient machinery, drank some of it and cleaned up her face as best she could.

After a long wait at the roadside, she was able to cadge a lift from a lorry carrying fish from Cala Rajada. The driver had looked at her curiously, but apparently accepted her explanation in broken Spanish that she had had a fight with her boyfriend. In reality, he considered her fair game and just outside Palma, she had to fend him off. By the time she reached the marina, Emy was physically and emotionally exhausted and ready to give up the male sex for good.

Emy's narrative did nothing to change Petra's impression of Axel. While he might have had some provocation, that was no excuse for assault and attempted

114

rape. The old adage sprang into her mind: "Sticks and stones will break your bones, names will never hurt you". Obviously, Axel had never understood this.

'Rosemary, you stay here with Emy. I'm going back to the salon to find Theo. He has to know about this.' Over Emy's protestations, Petra left the cabin and retraced her steps to the pool.

Immersed in thoughts of Emy and her ordeal, Petra skirted the outermost sunbed, for that was what she surmised it must be. Her heels clicked on the glass floor. In the glow from outside, she fancied she saw a pale figure on the balcony and heard another faint click. This was followed by a low purring sound she couldn't identify. A breath of fresh air gave her the first clue. The domed glass roof was inching open to reveal the night sky. Star after star appeared in the gap above. She threw back her head to drink in the constellations. Orion the Hunter twinkled his ever-watchful presence. His constancy reassured her, wherever she was.

A split second later, Petra was knocked flat on her back by a human cannonball. She fell winded onto the sunbed. Her attacker pressed himself against her, pinning her down, groping with moist hands under her skirt. His wine-laden breath came in short erratic bursts. She could feel him hardening. He fumbled for his belt.

'Here, lover, let me help,' Petra murmured. She softened her voice to caress his twisted soul. He was the runt of the litter, the by-product no doubt of a fleeting passion, unwanted and unloved. Lead him on, let him believe he was getting what he so desperately wanted, then… turn the tables!

Her assailant gasped and pulled away as a sharp object tore at his cheek and blood poured from the gash. Petra knew she would have only a second or two before he turned on her in fury. With unerring accuracy, she drove the sole of her shoe and its vicious stiletto into his crotch. As he doubled up in agony, she jumped to her feet and slammed her knee into his face. Then she grabbed his thin shoulders, spun him round and threw him into the pool.

CHAPTER TEN

Captain Juan Vallidolid had been on the bridge of the megayacht for over an hour. *Titania* was close now to the African coast, about thirty kilometres north-northeast of the Spanish enclave of Melilla. The night sky was overcast, but the rain that had dampened everyone's spirits in the aftermath of Theo's party had stopped. Captain Juan gave the order to douse the running lights and stared with heavy concentration at the radar screens. With no rain to clutter the displays, targets were easier to identify. And the continuing threat of inclement weather made it unlikely that patrol boats would venture far offshore. The rendezvous was scheduled for 0200 hours. Captain Juan was anxious to offload the cargo and make tracks for Puerto Banús. A man of the sea, rough and ready, he understood the risks Don León paid him to take, but didn't like them. His greatest joy was to be alone at the helm on the open water.

A small blip entered the five nautical mile alarm zone. Captain Juan watched it traverse the screen then turn towards *Titania*. Its size and speed suggested it was their contact. Pablo had seen it too and began to slow down even before Captain Juan issued the command.

Taking its cue from *Titania*, the vessel advanced at a reduced pace until it was just over a nautical mile away. The pre-arranged signal was a short flash followed by two longer ones, repeated three times. Pablo used the remote-controlled searchlight to confirm and answer. There was to be no radio communication. Captain Juan brought *Titania* to a complete stop. She rode quietly in the gentle swell, nose to the wind. He checked the radar again then spoke to Pablo.

'Get Ángel and Miguel down to the main deck. Tell them to prepare our port-side fenders and be ready to take her lines.'

'Aye, aye, Cap'n.'

The Lazzara's skipper examined the megayacht through the night sight. Popularized by the military, it was indispensable for this sort of job. Half a nautical mile away to his port, *Titania* showed up in an eerie greenish light, riding easily over the lazy waves. He could see activity on deck. They were getting ready for him to raft alongside. Leery of a trap, he stayed well off with *Lady Fatima* until he was satisfied that everything was as planned. Slowly, he brought his vessel round. At the last moment, he gave a short burst on the bow and stern thrusters to bring her in tight. Five minutes later, they were safely tied on.

In her cabin below, Petra opened one eye to test it and quickly closed it again. It was no good, she still felt lousy. Champagne hangovers were the worst, and this one worse and of longer duration than any she had experienced before. Her second attempt was more successful. The luminous dial on her wristwatch read 2.15 a.m. Something had jarred her awake. She stumbled out of bed to the bathroom then back to her cabin porthole. A faint light shone through from above. Instead of the water she expected to see, the white hull of another boat obstructed her view. It was rafted alongside *Titania*. Petra was confused. Her head ached. They weren't in port. What was going on? There was only one way to find out.

Two nights ago, during the run from Monte Carlo to Mallorca, she had ventured onto the main deck at the height of the storm to find the starboard coaming open and Don León in danger of falling overboard. This time, Petra took the circular staircase up two levels to the guest suite area on the boat deck. She met no one on the way, and she knew there were no guests aboard. Careful to stay away from Captain Juan's domain, she exited via the deserted boat deck and tiptoed to *Titania*'s port side to take a look at the adjacent tri-level boat. The enclosed flybridge was empty. The captain must be manning the controls from the pilothouse on the main deck. Below the radar arch, the boat's name was etched in gold letters on black: *Lady Fatima*. Why was it familiar? The throb of her head prevented her from thinking clearly. Then she remembered. That was the name of Sheik Kamal's boat, the one Rosemary's friend Emy was to join at the end of the week.

She peered over the rail. The stylish motor yacht sat like an offshoot on *Titania*'s side. Petra recognized the make immediately. A Lazzara. It was, as she had told Tom, the boat of her dreams, well known in North America, but seldom seen in Europe. This was the new One Sixteen, the larger cousin to the Lazzara Eighty Four. Sheik Kamal certainly had good taste, but what was she doing rendezvousing with *Titania* in the dead of night?

From above, Petra watched as Pablo supervised the installation of a gangplank to bridge the gap between the two boats. As soon as it was secure, Ángel and Miguel began to ferry boxes from *Titania*'s aft deck to the Lazzara. Compact and not too heavy, they bore no markings. A short stout figure in a hooded anorak marked each one off on a clipboard as it passed. Fifteen minutes later, the work was complete and Petra heard the gangplank being removed. *Lady Fatima* drew away and disappeared into the blackness.

Petra glanced again at her watch. Thank God for Tom! She lifted her left wrist, pressed a button below the lower right-hand corner of the dial, held it for three seconds and waited for the reading to flash up. To determine where the rendezvous had taken place, all she had to do was look at a nautical chart to check the coordinates. Suddenly, in the fresh night air, she felt better than she had for the last twenty-four hours.

Titania's motors rumbled. Captain Juan turned her hard to starboard and set course for Puerto Banús. The clouds were beginning to disperse and one or two stars peeped through.

Petra leaned on the rail and tried to marshal her thoughts. As far as finding Emily Mortlake was concerned, she was back to square one. Although Rosemary's friend Emy bore a certain resemblance to the girl in the photo Amy had shown her in Oxford, there was no doubt she was a different person. Apart from her English accent, the roots of her hair gave her away as an artificial blonde and her nose was much less aquiline. What was intriguing was the appearance of *Lady Fatima*, which Petra now knew belonged to Sheik Kamal. On board *Titania*, Don León had treated Sheik Kamal as an honoured guest. Their relationship, however, appeared to have a darker side.

Petra cast her mind back to her first evening aboard *Titania*. Sheik Kamal had been sitting in the skylounge watching a movie – one in which he also featured. Not only that, the belly dancer in the movie had Emily Mortlake's face and had been wearing a topaz pendant that looked identical to the one Petra had found on the floor of her cabin. If Tom could confirm that the pendant did belong to Emily Mortlake, it would corroborate what Don León had said about her being on board. The next question was who had made the movie, and where. The why was obvious. It might be worth trying to contact Sheik Kamal's son Ahmed to see if he could provide some answers.

As *Titania* swung to the right and her running lights came on, Petra heard the deep tones of Don León.

'Having trouble, Miguel?' His booming voice carried up to where she stood.

She looked down. Miguel was struggling with the lock on the port-side coaming. She could see Don León bending to help him. He too appeared to be having trouble. Without warning, the coaming slid back a metre. Petra stifled a cry as Don León gave the unsuspecting sailor a crippling blow to the back of the neck followed by a push that sent him flying into the water. Unwilling to believe what she had seen, she backed away from the rail and stood shaking in the shadow of the deckhouse.

'You shouldn't be on deck at this time of night, young lady!' Petra jumped like a startled rabbit as Captain Juan placed a gnarled hand on her shoulder.

'I came up to get some air. I don't feel too well,' she stammered.

'Ah! You girls should be more careful when you drink. It can be dangerous to have too much.'

His words had an ominous ring. Petra wondered whether he knew what Don León had done and whether he had seen her leaning on the rail. She made a supreme effort to act normally. 'I know, but this whole experience is so intoxicating – Monte Carlo, Mallorca, the Med…' She waved her hands to complete her thought process.

'*Titania* is amazing. You must be so proud to captain her and you handled her so well during that storm.'

'Thank you, I am.'

'I love boats, though I've never been on one like this before,' Petra continued. 'Could you show me the bridge and the communications room?'

Captain Juan paused. This was the young woman who had saved Don León's life. Her enthusiasm and the pleading look in her eye made him want to accede to her request. Then he pulled himself together. 'I'm sorry. Nobody is allowed on the bridge except myself and the crew, and Don León of course. It's a question of safety and security.'

Petra shrugged her shoulders in mock disappointment. She would have been surprised at any other response. 'I understand. I shouldn't have asked.'

'No, no. Look, maybe I can arrange it one day.' The offer came out before he could stop it.

'That would be fantastic! You're so nice!' On impulse, Petra reached up and gave him a peck on the cheek. The stubble on his chin was abrasive. She had taken a liking to the Captain and was genuinely interested in seeing the bridge and the communications room. Apart from anything else, there would be a computer there, and she had not seen one in Don León's suite. With her feelings towards Don León in turmoil after witnessing his execution of Miguel, Captain Juan seemed unshakable and could make a good ally.

Captain Juan rubbed his cheek where Petra had planted her kiss. 'I don't think many people would consider me nice,' he said. 'Tough, capable, determined, perhaps, but not nice. Still, it makes a "nice" change.' He sighed and turned to look back at the boat's wake. *Titania* was up to cruising speed, gliding along with the grace and strength of a swan.

From the rail, Petra contemplated the rushing water below. A vision of Axel face down in *Nemesis'* pool superimposed itself on the empty surface. His unexpected attack had fuelled the anger she felt towards him over his attempted rape of Emy. She had no qualms about what she had done and no idea how she had managed it. It had been pure self-defence. Scum like that deserved all they got.

Petra threw a glance at Captain Juan who was standing a few metres down the deck, drawing on a strong-smelling hand-rolled cigarette. It would be useful if she could cement her relationship with him. 'Does *Titania* have a fixed itinerary?' she asked.

'Not really. We usually cruise the Western Mediterranean – Italy, Sardinia, Corsica, France, and of course Spain.'

'What about Morocco?'

'Occasionally.'

'You have so much experience docking in different ports,' she said. 'I wish I could dock a boat as well as you. You make it look so easy.'

Her flattery worked its magic and Captain Juan's face softened. 'There's no reason why you couldn't learn. Some women do. Of course, most captains are men,' he added quickly.

'I think one of the girls I know at Oxford has her licence,' Petra said. 'During vacations she sometimes helps her father with his charter business. This summer she worked here for a while. You might remember her: long flaxen hair, good figure. Her name's Emily.'

'I don't know. Perhaps. You say she's a friend of yours?'

'Not a friend, just a fellow student. She's so knowledgeable about boats, I'm sure she was a real asset on board.'

Captain Juan took a long drag on his cigarette and inhaled deeply. 'Actually no. She caused a lot of trouble. One of my crewmen fell in love with her, stupid boy.'

'How did that happen?' Petra asked, trying to make the question sound casual.

'She tried to inveigle her way onto my bridge by flirting with him. The idiot thought she really cared about him. He started to follow her about and neglect his duties. I had to reprimand him.'

'Was Don León aware of their relationship?' Petra asked. If he had been, she suspected he might have seen it as a threat to his authority, which would help to explain why he had meted out such summary justice to Miguel. She had no doubt that the sailor Captain Juan was talking about was Miguel.

'I think not,' he replied.

Petra waited for him to elaborate. When he didn't, she pressed him for more information. 'What happened after that?'

'Nothing much. When we left Puerto Banús in late September, she wasn't aboard. I heard that she wanted to travel.'

'And what about your crewman?'

'He stayed around, but his mind wasn't on the job.'

'Is he still here? I'd like to meet him.'

'I'm afraid he left us in Palma.' Captain Juan extinguished the butt of his cigarette in one of *Titania*'s sand-filled ashtrays. 'You should go to bed, young lady. I must get back to the helm. Make sure you're up in the morning for our arrival at Puerto Banús.'

At 9 a.m. on Friday the air was crisp and the sky cloudless. A light breeze ruffled Petra's hair. From offshore, she could see whitewashed buildings hugging the port on three sides, their terracotta tiled roofs rising tier upon tier above the breakwater. Beyond the port, the lower slopes of La Concha were dotted with villas. The mountain's shell-shaped summit shimmered in the clear morning light, casting its spell over the Coast.

Captain Juan reduced speed at the harbour entrance, crawled past the fuel station and turned into the first fairway. The berth immediately behind the fuel station was reserved for Don León. With consummate skill, Captain Juan brought *Titania* slowly in, starboard side parallel to the dock, reversing until her transom was a metre from the wall. A handful of early birds gasped and applauded. Pablo and Ángel worked seamlessly with the harbourmaster's staff to secure the side and stern lines. Petra moved out of the way as they struggled to attach the bow mooring line, and gave a double thumbs-up sign to Captain Juan on the bridge. The port appeared to have changed little since her last visit ten years ago: the boats in the row closest to the Moorish watchtower guarding the entrance were still the largest; the fast cars parked along the water's edge, the products of the world's best makers. Only the urban concentration beyond the marina reflected the passage of time.

Carlo sauntered onto the foredeck in white trousers, blue shirt and gold tie. He frowned in mock irritation when he saw Petra's grey sweat suit.

'Didn't you get the message, Minx? It's full regalia today. I'm on guard duty this morning to stop the plebs coming aboard.'

'Mercutio, we need to talk.' The tone of Petra's voice signalled urgency.

125

'Put on your dress uniform then, and come and stand with me at the stern.'

Ten minutes later Petra was on station at his side, similarly clad in white trousers, blue blouse and gold belt.

'Very smart! What's up?' Carlo stepped forward to ward off a pair of stray sightseers. 'Sorry, ladies, this is a private boat.'

'I woke up in the middle of the night...' Petra began.

'Hardly surprising since you were prostrate all day yesterday.'

'Mercutio, this is no time for jest. I saw Don León kill a man!' She recounted the events of the night while Carlo protected *Titania* from invasion. It was incredible how people considered boarding a yacht quite acceptable when they wouldn't dream of walking up the drive to someone's country cottage.

'That GPS reading you took will be very useful,' he said. 'A pity you weren't wearing your watch when we went jet skiing.'

'I can give you the coordinates of the bay we anchored in.'

'Why didn't you say so before?' Carlo shook his head in disgust.

'I haven't had a chance to speak to you alone.'

'Not my fault. When I came to see you yesterday, you were snoring up a storm.'

'OK, OK, mea culpa! But we need to decide how to play this. If you pull Don León and his cohorts in, my chances of finding Emily Mortlake are almost nil.'

'Before I can do anything, I need more evidence. The only thing I've seen so far is a few cases of champagne being unloaded.'

Petra nodded. 'I can attest to what happened last night.'

'Yes, but it would be your word against that of some very clever and merciless people,' Carlo reminded her. 'I'd prefer not to alert them to our interest in their activities yet, just send the coordinates to our database for use later.'

'How are you going to do that?' Petra asked. 'Do you have access to the communications room?'

'No. Nobody does except Captain Juan, Don León and perhaps Olga. I have a phone.'

'A phone? Olga took mine away for "safekeeping".'

'I'm part of the regular staff. My references are impeccable. You girls are just floozies. We men don't need coddling.'

'Mercutio! Cut the crap! Can I borrow your phone? I have to contact London.' Briefly, Petra told him about Tom and the topaz as they continued the battle to prevent uninvited visitors from coming aboard.

Carlo left her on guard while he went to fetch his phone. He had joked about his position on board *Titania*, but Petra knew he was right. The girls were controlled and subjugated in a variety of ways. Deep in thought, she failed to detect an elderly intruder until he was halfway across the passerelle and then only when he rapped his cane sharply against the metal handrail.

'My compliments, young lady. Permission to come aboard.'

'I'm sorry, Sir. We don't allow visitors.' Petra rushed forward to halt his progress.

'Nonsense! Just let them know I'm here: Henry Lawton, Commander, Royal Naval Reserve – the Wavy Navy. I know this coast like the back of my hand and I've seen and heard more than you could ever dream of.' He jabbed his finger at Petra to emphasize his point.

'Sir, I can't let you board without authorization,' Petra said.

127

'Then get the authorization, damn it! I'll wait here.'

He spoke with the impatience and irascibility of advancing years. Petra scrutinized his face. Above the gaunt cheeks and pale but piercing eyes, a fringe of white hair encircled his bald, sun-blotched head. Despite his walking aid, his bearing was dignified and he manifested the level of determination common among those who have survived great traumas.

'All right, I'll see what I can do. Stay where you are.' Implicitly, Petra felt she could trust him, yet experience made her wary. He's probably lonely and just wants to look around, she thought, as she began to move away from the passerelle.

His voice cut through her vacillation. 'You shouldn't desert your post, you know. A rating could get flogged for that in the Navy. If you're on guard, you're on guard.'

He was right on the money.

'Now you're in a dilemma. You need officer training,' he called after her.

Petra bit back a curt response.

'Anyway, what's a nice Canadian girl like you doing on a yacht like this?'

She turned in surprise. Few Europeans could tell the difference between American and Canadian accents.

'Aha! Got you there!' He pointed a finger in Petra's direction. 'Your accent's the same as the other girl's. She had beautiful hair, like Rapunzel's. You do know who Rapunzel is, don't you?'

Petra had a vague idea that Rapunzel featured in some fairytale involving golden tresses as long and as strong as rope ladders. Could this crazy coot know something about Emily? 'Sir, did you…?'

Before she could complete her sentence, Monica waltzed across the aft deck from behind the car and placed

128

a patronizing hand on Petra's shoulder. 'Let me handle this, Minx. Don't let yourself be taken in by this guy. He's got more movements than a Swiss watch used to have. Get lost, old timer. Go walk your dog.' She waved him off the gangway.

'Monica, he's…'

'Don't worry, young lady.' Henry Lawton drew himself up as close to upright as he could. 'She's rubbish!' he whispered to Petra from behind his hand. Then loudly he added: 'It's a treat to see someone decently dressed. Look for me tomorrow. I'll be around. Cheerio!'

Petra watched him stump across the road to where a small brown and white dog was tied to a bollard. At his approach, the dog began to pull at its tether and whine. Bending down with obvious difficulty, he scratched the side of the dog's neck and unhooked the red leash. 'Come on, old girl, they don't want to know what we've got to tell 'em,' he murmured.

CHAPTER ELEVEN

From the moment Petra left his sphere of influence, Tom Gilmore had been on edge, barely civil to his colleagues, moody towards his friends, and left to his own devices. Friday lunch was usually long and convivial, a fitting prelude to the weekend; an opportunity, too, to exchange information and iron out any problems affecting the department. Robert Mullings paused at Tom's office door on his way to their favourite watering hole.

'Coming, Tom? It's gone twelve-thirty. Those papers can wait.'

'I think I'll give it a miss. You go.'

'What's up? You've been like a bear without honey all week.'

'Nothing, I'm fine,' Tom lied.

Robert shrugged. 'Have it your own way! I'm off for a beer.'

For the umpteenth time, Tom glanced at the screen on one of the two mobile phones that lay on his desk. No messages. For the first day or two, he hadn't expected any communication. As time passed, however, he had grown progressively more anxious. This was out of character. It was well known among his colleagues that when he ran agents, he taught them to fly then set them free, let the chips fall where they may. With Petra, it hadn't worked that way. Somehow she had penetrated his shell. The more he worried about her, the angrier he became. He berated himself for allowing someone he considered an amateur to go into the teeth of danger, though he knew Petra would lambaste him if she heard him cast doubts on her professionalism.

A sudden squawk from Petra's red Nokia made Tom wish he had joined Robert and the others for lunch at the pub. He had been fielding increasingly irritated calls from Petra's irritating boss ever since he had exchanged her Canadian phone for a European Siemens.

Cursing, he reached out for the noisemaker. His hand was barely a palm's width away when the other phone – his own blue Ericsson – emitted a tiny beep. He paused. It couldn't be. The red noisemaker was still clamouring for attention. His hand hovered between the two. The blue one won. He snatched it up and stared at the words on the screen. "All OK. Beaut Lazzara in PBanús." Tom sent a prayer of thanks to the Gods in whom he didn't believe. The message continued. "Did poldaught own topaz pendant? My phone gone. Use this no. Suspect…"

He scrolled rapidly down the screen. There was nothing else there, nothing to end the sentence and no sign-off. He returned to the beginning of the message and scrolled through it again to make sure. No, that was all. Petra must have been interrupted while she was texting. He continued to ignore the insistent squawking from the red Nokia then abruptly changed his mind.

'Yeah! Who is it?' It was no surprise to hear the harsh tones of Petra's boss.

'Gilmore? Donald Mortlake's furious at the way things are going. The media are asking awkward questions. He's filing a missing person's report. It'll be circulated to Interpol so contact Minx and tell her to get out of there.'

'But Sir, I just had a text from her. Everything's going fine and she has some suspicions. She wants to know if Emily owned a topaz pendant, so she must be onto something.'

'No buts, Gilmore. I don't want jurisdictional squabbles. Just get her out.'

Before Tom could enquire or protest further, the phone went dead.

'Dammit! First he wants to go it alone, now he wants to play by the book.' Tom kicked the desk in frustration. He picked up the Ericsson and began to text back to Petra. He wondered what had happened to disturb her or corrupt her message. Was it the transmission or did something prevent her from finishing it? And where was her phone? Whose was she using? He thought for a moment then let his fingers fly over the keypad. He had better be discreet. "Prefer Azimuts myself. Bad news from A.K. Call ASAP. Larry xxx." He reread the message, sent it winging through cyberspace and decided to join Rob and the others at the pub. At least it would take his mind off the problem.

The Lamborghini swayed slightly as it swung out over the quay where Pablo and Ángel were waiting to receive it. Reverently, they monitored the progress of the exquisite machine as it was lowered towards the dock.

Petra, standing to attention at the passerelle, was still smarting over the highhanded manner in which Monica had banished Henry Lawton from *Titania*. She had sneered at Petra's handling of the situation and hung about on the aft deck waiting for Carlo to return. She needed him, she had said, to move some boxes of supplies. Her antipathy towards Petra had been manifest. Carlo made things worse by coming up to Petra from behind and putting his hands round her waist. He pulled her towards him murmuring

'Ciao, bella!' and managed to pass her the phone he had gone to fetch. Monica had been spitting with jealousy. Petra had slipped Carlo's phone into her pocket and acknowledged with an ironic salute Monica's final admonition to 'concentrate on what you're supposed to be doing'.

The car was now the focus of all eyes. From her station on the aft deck, Petra had a good view of the proceedings. It was fascinating to watch people's reactions to megayachts and their "toys". She smiled to herself as a well dressed couple, feigning indifference, skirted the growing crowd. The man shrugged in response to a comment from his wife, but could not resist turning his head to admire the Murciélago as it inched towards terra firma. A battery of cameras rose like periscopes from the sea of holidaymakers who turned them this way and that to capture the scene. An exuberant teenage girl clawed through the mob and hurtled towards the car. Pablo and Ángel raced forward to catch her before she could do any damage to the Bat or herself. In the distance, a siren howled as it approached the port. The cavalry was on its way to prevent the hordes from storming the castle.

Petra patted her pocket to reassure herself that Carlo's phone was still there. It was good to have communication with the outside world again. She had sent Tom a text about half an hour ago. It was too soon for an answer to her question, but an acknowledgement would have been nice. Petra pulled the phone from her pocket and looked at the screen. Nothing. She heard the aft doors to the salon slide open behind her, then heavy footsteps as Don León strode across the deck calling her name. Quickly, she bent over the stern seat in front of her and stuffed the phone into the locker beneath the cushion.

'Petra! What are you doing?'

'Just straightening up.' She patted the striped cushion and willed her heart to slow down. She should have guessed Don León would put in an appearance now the Bat had been unloaded.

'Leave that and come with me. There's something I want to show you.'

Was she imagining it or did his words hold a veiled threat? Petra wondered if he had found something incriminating that might have aroused his suspicions or link her to Carlo. Or had he seen her on deck at 2 a.m.? She didn't think so, but couldn't be sure. If he had, he would assume she'd witnessed Miguel's death. And who knew what effect that would have on him?

Don León shouted back to the salon: 'Monica, take over from Petra. We're going out.' Taking Petra's arm, he escorted her off the boat and through the crowd to where the Lamborghini stood ready to take off like a ball of apricot fire. In unspoken accord, the onlookers parted to give him room to reverse in the shadow of the tower.

Sitting low in the passenger seat, Petra felt a surge of pride then reminded herself that was not only foolish but dangerous. Someone for whom revenge for a simple mistake meant pushing a man overboard to his death surely had an ulterior motive for asking her to accompany him on a mystery drive. She must stay alert.

Like Monica, Don León drew on a pair of white leather driving gloves from the glove box before putting his hands to the wheel. He eased the Murciélago along the quay past the sterns of an impressive row of yachts. Petra scanned them as they passed. None could match *Titania* for size or sheer dazzling beauty.

Although it was not yet time for the locals to head home for siesta, the traffic in Puerto Banús and westbound on the N-340 was heavy. Don León focussed all his attention on the road. Petra sat quietly beside him, enjoying the envious looks of other motorists. Not until they reached the Ronda road did he break the silence. He turned right and accelerated hard. 'That's better. Now we can go.'

At the pay station for the toll road, the young man on duty leaned out of his window to take a long look at the interior of the Murciélago – and Petra. Admiration flashed across his face as he took in the blue blouse with its deep V-neck clinging nicely to her chest and her slim legs encased in white stretch trousers. 'Fantastic!' he breathed and waved them through with a grin. 'No charge today for Lamborghinis, Sir.' As the sports car drew away, the sunlight danced across the disfiguring scratch. The young man shook his head. 'There's no respect for beautiful things anymore,' he muttered and raised his hand again.

Don León threw back his head and roared with delight. Just like a little boy, Petra thought. He thrives on attention and loves to show off. In profile, his nose had a slight hook that was indiscernible from the front. The tiered cluster of earrings that adorned only his right ear fell away from his neck to reveal a scar that had healed badly. The skin was puckered and raised. He had been lucky to escape death on the streets of Bogotá or wherever in Colombia he had spent his youth.

He threw Petra a quizzical glance. 'I can feel your gaze.'

'You're incredible,' she said, and she meant it.

Don León was larger than life; he could never walk into a room unnoticed or slip quietly away. According to Carlo, his legitimate businesses alone were sufficient to provide for a jet-set lifestyle. He had panache and charisma, both useful qualities in the media and fashion industries he had chosen, yet she knew there were many more layers to the man. The challenge would be to peel them back one by one to reveal what lay underneath.

'Monica told me something about your business interests, particularly the lingerie,' she said. 'Who designs it for you? Do you have it made here or is it imported?'

Don León pulled into the left-hand lane to give a Mercedes clear entry to the toll road and racheted up his speed before answering. 'She did, did she? Why is it you girls have so many questions? My leisurewear collection is made mostly in the Far East, to the specifications of our own design team. Some of the specialty items come from Europe and elsewhere.' He paused to appraise Petra from the side. 'There'll be more modelling for you to do tomorrow night. I'm hosting a gala evening for my special clients. You'll look stunning in what I have in mind for you.'

Remembering how she had felt decked out like a Christmas tree in front of Don León and Theo aboard *Nemesis*, Petra forced herself to sound enthusiastic. 'That'll be…,' she searched for a suitable adjective, '…awesome. Who'll be there? Will it be aboard *Titania*?'

'Enough! You'll soon find out. Look at those mountains.' He pointed to the lower hillsides covered with gorse, cacti, yucca and aloes. Further up the slopes, the scrub gave way to barren rock. High above, the jagged peaks were stark against the sky.

The Lamborghini swept along the toll road, the needle inching up as they sped westward, the sea on their left, past tracts of fertile land given over to cultivation of the sweet white grapes of Málaga. To their right sat the white village of Casares, its castle high on a promontory, the houses piled one on top of the other like glittering cubes of sugar in the bowl below.

The scenery was so impressive that Petra forgot her phobia and began to relax. The car responded to Don León's firm yet tender touch like a racehorse rewarding its jockey with an extra spurt of speed – or a woman warming to the caress of a lover, she thought. Speedily she banished the second idea before it could lead her into areas best left unexplored. She had, after all, seen him kill a man in a despotic act of revenge.

As they emerged from a tunnel, the Mediterranean opened up before them. In the clear October air, the Rock of Gibraltar faced off with Jebel Musa across the Strait. The rugged coastline was visible far beyond.

'You're a lucky one,' Don León commented. 'Most of the time, from a distance, Gibraltar is completely veiled in cloud or mist. Now there she is, like a beautiful young girl from the harem who reveals herself to the man she calls master.'

An image of Emily Mortlake as the belly dancer prostrating herself in front of Sheik Kamal flashed into Petra's head. Was she just an entertainer, a girl who loved to belly dance, or was there a deeper connection between her and the Sheik? Did Don León supply the Sheik with girls for sexual purposes as well as to work aboard his yachts? Their relationship was an intricate one.

'That reminds me of Sheik Kamal,' she said carefully. 'You enjoy his company, don't you?'

'There are many people I enjoy. I entertain them, give them what they want, and sometimes what they aren't expecting. It amuses me to see how people react to different stimuli.'

'What kind of stimuli?'

Don León lifted one neatly gloved hand off the wheel. 'I don't know… Something offbeat or incongruous: an

137

educated girl acting like a whore, a studious blonde belly dancing.' He turned sideways to gauge her response.

For a moment, Petra wondered whether he had read her mind or if his choice of examples was mere coincidence. 'You can learn that at the YWCA in Toronto!' she shot back.

'What? To be a studious blonde?'

'No, of course not. Belly dancing. It's supposed to be very good for the abdomen.'

He reached over and placed a hand on her stomach. 'I'm sure you've tried it.'

'Actually I have.'

'What haven't you tried?' he asked, a light smile hovering on his lips.

Suddenly, she felt like the mouse in a crazy game where he was the big cat. Each deliberate swipe of his paw knocked her off her feet. She had to pick herself up, dust herself off, play along and try to draw him out on the subject of Emily.

'Let's see... cocaine, heroin... blowfish... Seriously, there are lots of things I haven't tried, and tons of stuff I still want to experience. I hadn't ever been on a megayacht, but when I heard on the Oxford grapevine that you could get jobs like this, I had to try it.'

'I thought you didn't know your compatriot Emily,' he said.

'I don't,' Petra replied. That at least was true. 'But a friend of a friend had a postcard from someone working on a megayacht. She said she was having a blast. It might have been Emily who sent the card.'

Don León stamped his foot on the accelerator. 'What in hell are my girls doing wasting their time with postcards? I've got better things for them to do. Obviously they need more training.'

To Petra, the ferocity of his outburst seemed utterly out of proportion to the apparent crime. She eyed Don León sideways. 'The description of you was pretty accurate.'

'What do you mean?'

Petra knew from his tone that he was rattled. It was her turn to strike back. 'It said you had a flowing mane of hair and a big head. Which you do, literally and figuratively,' she added.

Don León rammed his foot on the brake. With a squeal of tyres, the Lamborghini careened across the fast lane and scorched along the edge of the road, dangerously close to the barrier. Petra was flung hard forward. The seat belt pulled her up in an agonizing jolt.

'I'm sorry, I didn't mean it,' she said, to soothe his ruffled ego. 'You've every right to be proud of your accomplishments, but you are a dichotomy.'

'Don't try to psychoanalyze me,' he grunted. 'I had enough problems with that girl Emily. She caused a lot of trouble among the staff and crew. In the end, I had to ask Olga to get rid of her.'

'You told me she wanted to leave to go travelling.'

'She did. She was invited to Morocco.'

'And did she go?'

'Yes!' he roared. 'Now shut up. You educated girls are always questioning everything. It gets on my nerves!'

Then why hire us? Petra thought, but didn't say anything.

At the next exit, Don León left the highway and pointed the Bat's nose to the hills. Beyond a sleepy village, the road climbed steeply. The terrain became more rugged and human habitation sparse. Petra winced as the Bat took a sharp bend to the left. She caught a glimpse of curious limestone formations rising like fractured skyscrapers from

139

the bottom of a ravine. Don León extracted a clear plastic container, the size of a cigarette lighter, from his shirt pocket and passed it to her.

'Try these. They're a mixture of aloe and arnica with a touch of peppermint. A herbalist friend of mine makes them. They'll ease the pain. I'll have one too. I'm still sore from my slide towards eternity.'

Petra tapped two greenish pills out of the container and handed one to Don León. He nodded his thanks and lapsed into a heavy silence. On a far ridge, the heads of some of the province's gigantic wind turbines turned hypnotically. Spain derived a significant percentage of its energy requirements from wind power, but Petra dared not ask how much. The drone of the Murciélago's engine was a reassuring white noise. She sank down in the soft leather seat and let her eyelids close.

In her dream, Petra was stretched out on a sunbed under a towering palm tree. She could feel the sun on her skin and hear water tumbling over rocks. There was a heady smell of jasmine in the warm air. The long fronds of the palm were tickling her chest. Something cold made her wriggle.

'Stay still. It's my turn to minister to you. This is an arnica cream – good for bruises.' Don León was on his knees beside her, his thick curly hair tickling her chest. Her blouse, unbuttoned, had fallen open to display the pale perfection within. 'A lot of girls your age have tattoos. You don't,' he said. 'Not yet,' he added in a whisper. The mark would go there. He touched the spot lightly.

The contact sent a ripple of electricity through Petra's body. Don León bent to brush his lips over hers and she arched her body to meet him. In the instant before desire swamped common sense, she rolled to the left off the sunbed, flipped herself over on the terrace and jumped to her feet. The manoeuvre reminded her of rolling a canoe at summer camp when she was a child, except that the marble was hard. She ignored the pain in her ribs and ran across the terrace, past the dancing fountains towards the pool.

'Come on! Race you to the pool!' Her blue blouse was flapping so she tore it off and tossed it behind her. She risked a look over her shoulder. Don León was sprinting between the yellow and blue glazed pots that decorated the terrace. To distract him further, Petra unclipped her front-fastening bra and slung it towards him.

As soon as she reached the pool, she launched herself into a shallow dive and struck out for the opposite side. The white trousers clung uncomfortably to her hips and legs. There was no ladder to help her out, and Don León was propelling himself through the water with strong strokes. Petra placed her hands on the edge of the pool and lifted her body in an attempt to get out before he reached her. Too late! He grasped her legs and pulled her back into the water. She surfaced spluttering. Where was he now? An arm encircled her waist, fingers fumbled with the zip of her trousers and he stripped her of her last remnant of material protection.

In the gathering dusk, the Murciélago purred downhill, devouring the curves with ineffable ease. Below, the lights of the port began to twinkle. It had been a long day and Petra was exhausted. Since the early hours of the morning, she had been on a roller coaster ride of emotions, from incredulity and fear through excitement and hope to exhilaration and, finally, satisfaction.

The climax had come in the pool. Naked, she had thrust herself against him, entrapped him with her legs and peeled off his clothes. Instead of resisting, he submitted to her touch. The huge head bent backwards and he bellowed and roared like the lion he was. Then they had frolicked in the water like children freed from the restraint of parental supervision, raided the larder and eaten and drunk on the terrace until it was past time to go.

Don León took a hand off the wheel and laid it over Petra's. His yellow eyes lit up. 'By God, you're tough, and you swim like a fish!'

Petra responded with a high rippling laugh. Out of the valley of the shadow of self-reproach had come immense satisfaction – at the way the day had turned out and at her success in building a bond that transcended desire and would enable her, she felt sure, to accomplish her mission. Magnanimously she said: 'You know Monica was appalled to find that scratch on the car. Don't be too hard on her.'

'She should never have taken it,' was the curt reply.

The Bat rolled to a halt. Pablo, Captain Juan, Olga, Monica and Carlo watched mesmerized from *Titania*'s stern as Don León jumped out and ran round to the passenger side to assist Petra. Both of them were clad in short royal blue robes. With uncharacteristic gentleness, he helped her aboard the yacht.

'Pablo, park the car.' Don León tossed him the keys. 'Olga, collect our gear and get it laundered. We're going to bed.'

CHAPTER TWELVE

A thin coating of grease brought to the surface by early morning showers had made the streets of Puerto Banús slick and dangerous. The few residents going about their business at 10 a.m. that Saturday morning trod carefully. Wet marble did not provide the most secure footing.

Captain Juan came out of the communications room and locked the door. Using the port-side stairs, he climbed up to the sundeck and walked forward to survey the scene. Marbella's magical mountain La Concha was swathed in low-level cloud. Only the very top of the shell-shaped summit peeked out above the misty white wreath. He lit his first cigarette of the day and took a long draw. He checked *Titania*'s fenders on the starboard side. They were perfectly placed to prevent her from rubbing against the dock. The berth on her port side was, for the moment, empty, but the fenders were in position.

Making his way to the stern, he looked down on the boat deck and examined the Scarab and the Donzi from above. The blue covers on *El Toro* and *Dreambaby* were clean and secure. Below them, the aft deck was tidy and the passerelle properly stowed. Everything was shipshape. He gave a nod of satisfaction. Only the pick of the crop of megayachts was entitled to the outermost berth.

He raised his head to look down the quay as a horse came clip-clopping along, pulling a black-hooded carriage.

143

Due to the inclement weather, the hood of the carriage was up, screening the occupants from view.

The driver slowed as they neared the end of the quay and stopped when he reached *Titania*'s stern. He looked over his shoulder at his passenger. 'Is this right, Señor? There's nobody about.'

'We'll give it a few minutes. Be patient, man,' the hidden occupant instructed.

With a look of resignation, the driver climbed down from the front of the carriage and hooked the food bag for his long-suffering horse back into position. His insistent passenger had interrupted their usual morning routine. Smelling fresh food, the horse took the opportunity to create more space in his stomach.

Captain Juan shook his fist at the driver and cried at the top of his voice: 'What are you doing, man? Get that animal out of here!' He shouted down to Pablo whose timing to appear on the aft deck could have been better. 'Tell the driver to move on and clean up that mess!'

Pablo scowled. He opened his mouth to object, then thought better of it. With ill grace, he lowered the passerelle. As it fell into place, the driver of the carriage leapt back into his seat, slapped his horse with the reins to get him going, turned him in a tight circle and high-tailed it back along the quay.

Petra had slept through the night like a contented baby. When she woke, she had no idea of the time. Whatever it was, it didn't matter. A slow feeling of euphoria crept over her as she remembered her triumphant return to the yacht with Don León the previous evening. The five key members of staff had been lined up like a welcoming committee. Their demeanour, however, had been anything but. Pablo, surly as usual, hadn't spoken, Captain Juan had eyed them both with interest, Olga had stood grim-faced and Monica had been ablaze with jealousy. Petra chuckled at the memory of Mercutio with a face like the irate father of an adolescent daughter. The whole afternoon with Don León had been a dream, out of this world, parts of it bad, most of it amazing.

Then her true sober self came to the fore. She could not deny that she found Don León attractive, but that was no reason to forget everything that had been drilled into her at the Police Academy and act like an immature schoolgirl. Still reproaching herself, she pulled on a robe and went to fetch some fruit and a yoghurt from the fridge in the crew's galley. She was surprised to see Carlo sitting poker-faced in one of the easy chairs.

'What are you doing here?' she asked.

'Why shouldn't I be here?'

'No reason, although these are the female crew quarters. You usually have lots to do around the boat, helping Monica for example.'

'Like you were helping Don León yesterday?'

'Oh, so that's your problem!' Petra exclaimed.

'I don't have a problem,' he retorted.

'Yes you do. You're jealous!'

'You're making a real fool of yourself, Petra. That guy will make mincemeat out of you if he realizes why you're here. What are you now, another of his conquests to be palmed off onto someone else as soon as he's tired of you?'

'Mercutio, you're being an idiot. I confess I was seduced for a while by the luxury and pizzazz, and there is something about Don León that appeals to me, but that's as far as it went. I came to my senses just in time.'

'How lucky is that!' Carlo said.

145

'Don't be sarcastic. Actually, it was very strange. We had a bit of a tiff in the car, then I fell asleep. The next thing I remember is lying on a sunbed with Don León bending over me.'

'Were you sick?' Carlo asked.

'No, but he gave me some sort of herbal candy which might have contained something to make me sleep. Otherwise I'm sure I would have woken up when he carried me from the car. What do you think?'

'It's possible. We know he likes to experiment. That champagne you had aboard Theo's boat in Mallorca could have been "enhanced".'

'That would explain why I felt so heady and became so aggressive.'

'Mellow might be a better description. Although I must say that when you came back from the bathroom or wherever you disappeared to, you looked pretty upset.'

'I was shaken. I wasn't able to tell you before, Mercutio, but I was introduced to a girl called Emily – not Emily Mortlake, unfortunately – but another one. She'd been badly beaten up by that creep Axel, Theo's new estate manager. He must have followed me out of the room, then he jumped me when I was on my way back to join you all. I managed to throw him off and into the pool.'

'He won't thank you for that!'

'Last I saw he was floating face down, so with any luck he'll not be around to thank or hurt anyone again.'

'Jesus, Minx, remind me to keep out of the way when your dander's up!'

'If you'd seen the girl, you'd understand why I reacted so strongly. And the champagne certainly helped.'

Carlo thought for a minute. 'The boxes you saw being transferred to the Lazzara early yesterday morning, could they have contained this champagne?'

'I don't think so. They weren't marked like the ones you photographed being unloaded in Mallorca, and they seemed smaller and lighter. The delivery didn't take long.'

'I'd love to know what was in them,' he said. 'In the meantime, I'll send those coordinates you recorded on your watch to Rome. I'll need my phone – you went off with it yesterday.'

'I hid it in the locker under the aft deck seat when Don León came looking for me. I haven't had a chance to fetch it.'

'I'll do that,' Carlo said, standing up. 'Can you give me the coordinates?'

'Sure, I'll go and write them down.'

When Petra returned to the lounge, Carlo was talking on his VHF phone. She had twisted her hair into a topknot and pulled on some blue Lycra leggings, a V-necked white T-shirt and running shoes.

'The boss wants to take you to his TV studios. He said to meet him at the stern in five. It's ten-thirty now.'

'I need to shower.'

'The message was "Come as you are". There's some filming going on and he wants you to be there.'

'Monica will kill me!'

'She would have done last night if there'd been an opportunity. So would Olga. She was fuming too.'

'I don't understand that,' Petra said. 'I wouldn't have thought she'd care what my relationship with Don León was. From what I understand, there've been plenty of other girls in his "harem".'

'I'm just telling you to be careful. You're making a lot of enemies. On the other hand, you need to take advantage of his interest in you to get to the bottom of what happened to Emily.' He cocked his head at Petra. 'Anyway, Minx, you don't look bad, with or without a bra!'

If Don León noticed her rough and ready appearance, Petra was relieved that he made no comment on it as they headed out of Puerto Banús in the Lamborghini. Nor did he comment on the events of the previous afternoon and, if he had, she would not have known what to say. Instead, he maintained a studied silence until they reached a gated complex about fifteen kilometres west of Marbella and half a kilometre north of the main coast road. This, as he then told her, was his main studio from which various Spanish soap operas and spaghetti Westerns were directed. He was unapologetic about his business. His intent was to generate a consistent revenue stream churning out staple fare for the masses, not rich cream for the connoisseur.

Despite it being a Saturday morning, a dozen cars were parked in front of the E-shaped complex of sandstone-coloured buildings. Don León swung the Bat in next to a red Ferrari directly in front of the pillared entrance. A flurry of activity greeted his arrival. A young Spanish woman with highlighted dark hair snapped off her phone and came forward to meet him. She gave Petra a haughty stare before stepping aside to make way for a portly Spaniard a head shorter than Don León. Petra judged him to be in his mid-forties with a taste for good food and wine. He wiped a few droplets of sweat from his forehead before shaking hands with Don León, who introduced him to Petra as his Studio Director.

'How's the filming going?' Don León asked him.

'Good, good.'

'And the budget?'

'Fine, fine. I've got the latest figures in my office, if you'd like to go over them.'

148

The Studio Director led them out of Reception, through a waiting area and down a corridor past the Men's and Ladies' bathrooms, to what was in effect a T-junction. Signs in Spanish pointed left to Make-up, Wardrobe and Dressing Rooms, and right to Design and Production. They turned right.

Petra followed the two men down a short passage that opened out into a work area where a handful of designers and technicians were poring over computer screens. They acknowledged Don León and went back to their work. Beyond the work area was another corridor lined with named offices, all with closed doors. At the end of the corridor was a spacious corner office with an open door. Another sign pointed to the right, to the Sound and Recording Studios. As it was the weekend, the Studio Director explained, the studios were not in use.

'This won't take long, Petra. Have a seat,' Don León said. 'You might find it interesting.'

'I'm afraid I need the bathroom. I can find my way, I saw it when we came in.' Playing on a weak bladder was one of the oldest tricks in the book. Petra hoped Don León was too immersed in his figures to notice.

She made her way back to the T-junction, pausing only to ask for confirmation of the bathroom's location from a spike-haired girl with an armful of tattoos who was talking aloud to her computer. At the T-junction, instead of turning left, she kept straight on and began opening doors. Her ever-ready excuse was that she was looking for the bathroom.

There was no need to use it. Make-up was empty, the Wardrobe room was locked and there followed a series of empty dressing-rooms. All the notices, schedules, lists and signage that Petra saw were in Spanish. Her own knowledge of the language was fair, largely because of her

149

background in French and Italian and more than a few Mexican vacations. She could carry on a conversation, although she found the Andalucían accent difficult to follow.

She walked past the Ladies' bathroom without stopping and stood in front of the Reception desk where the girl with the highlighted hair was talking on her phone in voluble Spanish. Her consonants were well defined and Petra guessed that she might be Argentinian. The girl carried on talking for another two minutes while Petra worked out how to handle her. She didn't have a lot of time, but a little team-building exercise might work wonders.

'At least I can understand your Spanish,' she said. 'It's so much better than what a lot of people speak down here.'

The girl sniffed. 'You can say that again!'

'Are there any opportunities for foreign actors and actresses?' Petra asked.

'Why? Do you want a part?'

'It could be fun.'

The girl looked doubtful. 'We might be able to use you as an extra, but there wouldn't be a speaking part.'

Petra floated another balloon. 'What about modelling? I've been doing some for Don León, and I know he employs foreign models.'

'These are TV studios. We have enough to do to keep up with each season's demand for soaps and the occasional full-length feature, let alone fashions.'

Petra judged that her time was running out. She had one more question for the girl. 'Is all the filming done here?'

'No. A lot of it is done on location in the villages and mountains of Andalucía, the desert regions of Almería, and sometimes Morocco.

'Using locals?'

The girl nodded. 'With the occasional "name" to boost the popularity of a series.' Her phone began to ring and she raised her eyebrows. Petra slipped away with a half wave of her hand.

She retraced her steps in double-quick time and arrived back at the Studio Director's office just as Don León was approving an additional hundred-thousand euro retainer to one of Spain's best-known actors. The Studio Director suggested they take a short drive to the School of Equestrian Art where a new scene for the series in which the actor had a cameo part was being filmed.

The arrival ringside of the Studio Director's scarlet Ferrari followed by Don León's incandescent orange Lamborghini caused a stir among the watchers. To the credit of the actress on horseback and her mount, they missed not a beat, despite the scrunching of super-high-performance tyres on the gravel. The riding instructor whacked his polished riding boots with his crop to let the newcomers know how unimpressed he was and raised his voice a notch to maintain his position of authority. At his command, the girl used a light touch of her spurs to change the horse's pace, leading him fluidly from one step to the next.

Petra's riding experience was limited to the occasional trail ride on a plodding mare, far removed from this tall, proud Carthusian horse. The camera captured the girl as she executed a half-pass. She sat erect in the saddle, dark curly hair falling thickly down her back, the splay of her buttocks counterbalanced by the jutting of her generous breasts. Indeed, Petra was afraid she might topple forwards if her centre of gravity shifted even a fraction. Don León heard Petra's giggle and raised an enquiring eyebrow.

'The Andalucían horses make me nervous,' she confessed. 'They're all dense muscle and restrained power. I imagine that if you gave that one his head, he'd boil up like a pan of water when you take the lid off.'

'An interesting analogy. I might try it some time,' he said.

The Studio Director returned to their side after a brief conversation with his production manager. 'I'd like to schedule some filming at your villa this Tuesday evening, Don León, if that would be convenient. Three or four hours should suffice.'

'No problem. Just check with my man Raoul. He and Bettina will be on site. I'll probably be there. I have some work to do at the villa.'

In the ensuing silence, a crack rang out from beyond the ring, somewhere on the other side of the property's boundary fence. The girl slumped forward. Petra gave a cry before she realized that the cameras were still rolling. A posse of extras swarmed down the hill shooting into the air. The bandit in the lead looked familiar.

On the return journey to Puerto Banús, Petra tried again to find out more about Don León's film productions. Perhaps the man himself would be more forthcoming than the receptionist.

'Do any of the crew from *Titania* ever act in your productions?' she asked. 'And what about the fashion shows you produce? I'm sure you must film those. I wouldn't mind being in a movie.'

'Amateurs have no place in my productions. All my actors are professional,' he replied in a tone which brooked no argument.

Petra lapsed into a silence as deep as Don León's had been on the way to the TV studios. She wondered why he had taken her there. What had he wanted her to see? Did he want to impress her or prove to her that Emily Mortlake wasn't there? Like a United Nations inspector, Petra suspected that she had not been shown all there was to see. And if Don León did not employ amateur actors, where did that leave Sheik Kamal, the belly dancer Emily Mortlake or her look-alike, and the other girls in the blue-tinged movie the Sheik had been watching? If that movie had not been made in Don León's Marbella area studios, where had it been shot? Morocco perhaps?

Petra opened her eyes and drew herself upright in her seat. With sudden clarity, she realized the film had been shot on the terrace of the villa where Don León had taken her the previous day. In her mind's eye, she saw the yellow and blue pots, the golden bodies lounging under the palms, the fountains, the swimming pool in the background …

'A euro for your thoughts!' Don León said, picking up a coin from the centre console that separated them.

'They're not worth half that much.' Petra pretended to stifle a yawn as the Bat rolled to a halt at the security barrier protecting the port. 'I'm still recovering from yesterday.'

The rain clouds had blown away to the west, lightening both the sky and the hearts of the merchants around the port. It was still not busy, but business was starting to pick up. Petra saw that the touts were out, urging tourists to empty their wallets inside the boutiques and eating establishments.

The Murciélago cruised along the quay and discharged its occupants at the far end of the dock. Neither Petra nor Don León paid attention to the horse-drawn carriage bowling along behind them. Don León scanned Titania's aft deck. It was empty and the passerelle was up. Where was everyone? One less crewman should not make that much of a difference. Carlo, in the salon, heard Don León's holler and pressed the remote control to lower the gangway. Now that Petra was back, he would have to ask her again about his phone.

Don León steered Petra onto the passerelle. His touch was surprisingly light for such large hands. Halfway up the gangway, something wiry shot like a bullet between his legs. It streaked past Petra emitting high-pitched yelps, skittered across the aft deck and disappeared from view. Petra thought she recognized Henry Lawton's dog. She had looked for the old fellow that morning, not really expecting to see him because of the uncertain weather. Perhaps he was in the vicinity now.

Don León gave her a push. 'Go, go! It's that damn dog of Henry Lawton's.'

The brown and white dog reappeared as if bidden. It leapt up and down in front of Don León, springing a metre or more into the air. Petra gasped as Don León rewarded the display of acrobatics with a vicious kick that connected with the poor animal's ribs. With a heart-rending screech, it fell to the floor then stumbled to its feet and ran off whining down the port side of the main deck. Petra was aghast.

'You didn't have to do that. The dog didn't mean any harm! I'm going to find it – and a vet if necessary.'

'Do what you like, only get that cur off my boat!' Don León's eyes were on fire.

The rapport that had been established between them snapped like a twig underfoot. Petra sensed that Don León's fury concealed a deep-rooted fear. The obvious explanation was that he had had a bad experience with a dog at some time in the past. Yet that did not quite account for the savageness of his attack. In Petra's opinion, the punishment once again did not fit the crime. Having no idea of the dog's name, she whistled.

'That's not a whistle.' Carlo stepped out onto the aft deck through the doors Don León had left open. 'This is how you do it.' He put two fingers into his mouth and gave a resounding wolf whistle ending in a showy trill.

'I'm trying to find a dog, Mercutio, not some bimbo like Monica.' Exasperation rose in Petra's voice.

'Ah, but I'm trying to find Monica. Don León wants her.'

'What does he want *her* for?'

'How do I know? Sex?'

'Mercutio, stop it! Did you find the phone?'

'No. I was going to ask you where you put it.'

'I told you, it's under that seat over there.'

'It might have been, but it's not now. You shouldn't have left it in such a stupid place.'

'I had no choice; I didn't want Don León to catch me with it.'

'Then you shouldn't have gone off with him for the rest of the day.' Carlo scowled. 'Check for yourself, it's gone.'

Petra whistled again and the little dog limped round the corner. She scooped it up, tucked it under her arm, walked aft, and lifted first the seat cushion then the lid of the locker below. Carlo was right. There was no sign of the phone.

'Someone must have taken it.'

155

'Hey, Minx, why didn't I think of that? No wonder they recruited you for such an important job.'

'You underestimate me all the time. If you're such a whiz yourself, you figure out what's going on here. I'm going to return this dog to its owner.'

Exhausted and near to tears, Petra fought hard to contain her anger and frustration – with Mercutio, with Don León, with Monica and above all, with herself. In the close environment of the megayacht, emotions were running high.

CHAPTER THIRTEEN

London was cold. An unseasonably chill wind from the Russian steppes had swept across the country and made the capital a less than pleasant place to be. Tom went out at 9 a.m. for a run. He gave up after less than two kilometres and came back with an armful of the Saturday papers. Fortified by a pot of coffee, he slouched on the sofa to see what was going on in the wider world. Political upheaval, bribery, corruption – the usual stuff. There was nothing of great interest and he found it difficult to concentrate.

Halfway through a limp article on climate change, which never once mentioned the explosion in human population as the root cause of the increase in CO_2 emissions, he heard a beep from his phone. After rummaging through a pile of papers, he located it under a rather scruffy cushion. The message was from his service provider.

Deflated, Tom crossed to his desk in the corner of the room from where he could see the back of New Scotland Yard. The sheer bulk of the building was reassuring. He opened a file on his computer called Lazzara and began to make notes. He had heard nothing yet from Petra in response to the text he had sent the previous afternoon. The uncertainty as to what he should be doing was shredding his nerves. Should he jump on the next plane and go fetch her or wait for her call?

His phone beeped again, this time from the coffee table. The beep was only the precursor to a tune heard by millions, but recognized by few.

'Tom, have you seen the latest Interpol alert?' There was no mistaking the urgency in Robert Mullings' voice.

'No. I'm just vegging out with the papers. What are you doing in the office on a Saturday?'

'I came in to finish off a file the big boss wants first thing Monday. Tomorrow's my day in the country – sacrosanct as far as my wife is concerned. You should check out the new Interpol notice from Morocco. It might have something to do with your girl.'

Tom's worst fears surfaced in a rush of stomach acid.

'What colour is it?'

'Yellow.'

Tom relaxed a fraction. Yellow notices weren't as serious as the black ones used for unidentified bodies, but it was still worrying.

'Thanks Rob. I'll get right onto it.'

Within a few seconds, he had logged on to the restricted network. What the hell could Petra be doing in Morocco? Twenty-four hours ago, her message had indicated she was in Puerto Banús.

Below the heading "British Embassy, Rabat, Morocco" was a rather grainy photograph of a fair-haired girl in a pink kaftan.

Tom read the description, at first with relief then with growing interest. The girl, one hundred and seventy centimetres tall with long blonde hair, weighing a mere fifty kilogrammes, had turned up at the Embassy with no passport or papers. She had contusions to her head and arms and was suffering from anxiety, shock and trauma-induced amnesia. She could be British or perhaps Canadian. Any information as to her identity should be forwarded without delay to the Embassy.

Tom cursed. He would have to go into the office. After a full working week of Petra's squawking red Nokia, he had made a deliberate decision to leave it locked up in his filing cabinet. Now he needed to talk to her boss.

On Saturdays, the London Underground was slower than usual, though less crowded. Within minutes of boarding the train, Tom regretted his decision to ride instead of walking through St. James' Park and cutting through Mayfair to Grosvenor Square. Two teenagers were talking non-stop in shrill nasal voices about their Friday night encounters. In his haste to get to the office, he had forgotten to equip himself with the travel or puzzle section of the newspaper. Luckily he had remembered his keys. He closed his eyes and tried to decide how to handle Petra's boss. It was impossible to block out those insistent female voices. He wouldn't have been able to concentrate on the crossword or a Su Doku anyway.

The guard at the entrance to Canada House gave Tom's credentials a cursory glance. Tom did not stop to exchange pleasantries, but took the lobby steps two at a time and raced for the elevator. The doors were almost closed when he stuck his forearm between them. For a split second, it seemed as though they would destroy his arm. Then they opened.

'A bit risky, old boy,' said Robert Mullings. 'I didn't expect you in. What's up?'

'I have to call Toronto. Where have you been? I thought you were nailed to your desk.'

'For sustenance,' Robert said, holding up a brown paper bag.

Over a share of Robert's lunchtime sandwich, Tom outlined his plan to pick up Petra from Puerto Banús and take her with him to Morocco to interview the girl featured in the Interpol notice. Robert was sceptical.

'Why assume that the girl who has shown up at the British Embassy is Emily Mortlake? If she were Canadian, surely she'd go to the Canadian Embassy. And if she's lost her memory, interviewing her won't do much good. Does she have any distinguishing marks? There are thousands of blondes out there: Brits, Germans, Scandinavians, Americans, Canadians, and the rest.'

'OK, OK. I'm not handling this very well,' Tom admitted. 'At first when you phoned, I thought the Interpol notice might be about Petra. It worried me to death. That girl has a knack for worming her way into your psyche.'

'Do you even have a photo of the missing Emily Mortlake?' Robert asked.

'I don't. Petra did, on her computer, but it's locked and I don't have access. You have to remember this was no official operation. I was just asked to facilitate.'

'You could have a look for Emily on the social networking sites. All the kids are on them nowadays. And I'm sure you can wangle access without too much trouble. Tom, I've got to finalize this file. I'll let you know when I'm leaving.'

As the door closed behind Robert, Tom's phone beeped. He snatched it up. At last Petra had responded! It was a message though, not a phone call. Quickly, he ran through the new text. "Don't worry about topaz. All OK. Suspect I won't want to leave. Petra." The words rang true enough, but there were two problems: she had used her name not her password, and she made no reference to the urgent message he had sent her the previous afternoon,

160

shortly after he had received her first message. It looked as though this message had been written by somebody other than Petra. After a moment's thought, Tom decided to text back in case it was authentic. "You may 1 day! Call me ASAP. Any Azimuts in port? Larry xxx," he wrote. If Petra did receive the text, he hoped she would respond to his signal and call without delay.

Robert tapped on Tom's door midway through the afternoon. From within, he could hear Tom arguing in strident tones, although his actual words were unclear. He extracted a yellow sticky note from his briefcase and scribbled on it. "Good luck! Watch your back." He stuck it to Tom's door and whistled his way to the elevator.

Tom slammed the red Nokia down on his desk. Only his innate respect for property prevented him from hurling it across the room. A.K. had denied each and every one of his requests. No access to Petra's computer. No access to Emily's parents for information that might help identify her or track her down. No trip to Morocco, with or without Petra. The only thing A.K. had said that made sense, Tom realized as his phone slid across the desk, was that Petra must be extracted before the Interpol notice regarding Emily Mortlake's disappearance was circulated.

It was too late to catch the Saturday afternoon flight to Málaga, so Tom made a reservation for first thing Sunday morning. He was reluctant to give up the idea of going to Morocco, despite A.K.'s prohibition and Robert Mullings' scepticism. If there was even a slim chance that the unknown girl who had turned up at the British Embassy in Rabat was Emily Mortlake, the trip was worth the effort.

When Tom left the office a little after four o'clock, the scudding clouds had slowed to a snail's pace and the sun was putting in a late appearance. He decided to amble home to give himself time to think. Having drawn a blank with A.K., his only option was to do as Robert Mullings had suggested and try the social networking sites. It was a long shot because Petra had told him that, according to Amy, Emily Mortlake's parents had forbidden her to join any of the sites. Her father in particular had threatened to cut her off without a cent if she did anything to compromise his political career. Which she had of course done once already, Tom thought. But a girl like Emily would not easily be dissuaded.

As soon as he arrived back at his antiquated flat that was as comfortable as an old cardigan, Tom fired up his computer and began to trawl the Web. An hour of intensive effort turned up nothing on Emily Mortlake. There was plenty of interesting stuff on her father Donald, but it was as if his daughter didn't exist. Frustrated, he poured himself a glass of Rioja and sat at his desk with his hands behind his head, pondering.

The problem was that the Internet was chock-a-block with fake identities and artificial personas. After thinking up a storm and trying all sorts of avenues using complex keywords and even a special computer programme to try and find Emily, Tom pulled himself up short. If you didn't know where to start, the rule was to start with the basics.

He poured himself a second glass of Rioja and studied her name. After trying various combinations, he found the answer: Mylie Letromka. Emily Mortlake's pseudonym was a simple anagram. Tom cursed himself roundly for wasting time and demoted himself from computer whiz to computer nerd.

There were just two photographs on Emily's Facebook site. Tom was disappointed to see that the last photo had been uploaded on June 20th, shortly before Emily had left England to fly to Nice. There were no more recent photos and none of motor yacht *Titania* at all. Curiously, one of the two pictures showed a flaxen-haired girl in a red and gold belly dancing costume, her face half covered with a veil.

In the other photo, Emily was reclining in a punt on the river, wearing a long flowered dress and a wide-brimmed hat. She was laughing up at the young man standing at the other end of the boat holding the pole. Her face was in half-profile and semi-shadow. Her Facebook status said: Mylie is… on summer retreat. See ya'll in fall!

'I sure hope she's right,' Tom muttered as he reheated some leftover pizza and poured himself a final glass of Rioja.

CHAPTER FOURTEEN

Podencos were very lively, loyal and even-tempered dogs, and Henry Lawton loved his with a passion many men reserved for their mistresses. He used to tell the tale, over and over again, of how he had been up in the Andalucían countryside, far from the madding crowds on the Coast, when a gypsy approached his car. This, in the days when he was still driving, cap firmly on his head, ramrod straight, hands planted on the wheel.

He and his wife, a flighty little French woman, whom he also adored, had gone to lunch at one of their favourite weekend haunts in the hills. On the way back, they stopped to admire the view of the Mediterranean spread out before them – and to give Henry a break from the concentration required to negotiate the winding, broken-surfaced country road after a five-hour eating and drinking marathon.

The gypsy appeared out of nowhere and, faster than any Vegas magician, produced a rabbit out of a bag. Several rabbits, in fact. This contraband the gypsy was keen to sell. Jocelyne waved him away, but Henry had his eye on something else. The gypsy's hunting dog jumped up to the window, not once or twice but three times, as if to impress the occupants of the car with its prowess. Henry was enchanted.

'How much for the dog?' he asked in his English-accented Spanish.

The gypsy waggled the rabbits in his hand. 'The dog's a very good hunter.'

'I know that,' Henry said. 'How much?'

'What would I do without it?' the gypsy asked.

'Get another one, of course,' Henry retorted. 'Come on, how about twenty?'

The gypsy upped the ante. 'I don't want to sell the dog, but I might if you buy the rabbits as well.'

The negotiations continued in the same vein until Jocelyne became bored.

'Here, I'll give you forty.' She extracted two twenty-euro notes from her purse and thrust them towards the gypsy. 'And you can keep the rabbits!'

Henry guffawed at the memory. 'She had a way with her, my Jocelyne did. It was hard to refuse her anything, right up to the day she died. Now you see, my dear, why I'm so attached to Lila here.' Hearing her name, the dog turned her head to look at her master, on whose lap she lay in the carriage. 'I can't thank you enough for bringing her back to me,' the old man continued. 'Podencos will follow a scent that intrigues them for miles, and Lila loves boats. I just sold mine.'

Petra scratched the dog's head. After her first encounter with Henry Lawton on the morning *Titania* had arrived in Puerto Banús, she had been keen to see the old man again. He had intimated that he knew a lot about what went on along the Coast and had spoken of a Canadian with long, blonde tresses – Emily Mortlake perhaps? She wasn't going to jump to any conclusions this time, but it was worth investigating further. She wondered how she could bring the conversation round to Emily. Elderly people tended to ramble and she would be missed if she didn't get back to *Titania* soon.

'Mr. Lawton…' she began.

'No, no, call me Henry, Sir Henry actually. Knighted for services to His Majesty during the war. Dangerous missions they were, with the coastal forces. The worst was in May 1943. I'm sure you remember it.'

At the risk of being rude, Petra had to put a stop to what was sure to be an avalanche of reminiscences. 'That's way before I was born! Can't we talk about what you do now? You must live nearby. Did you keep your boat here? Was it a big one?'

'This place is too expensive. The people who own yachts like these…' he waved a hand towards *Titania*, docked fifty metres away, '…don't care what it costs. Mine was nothing like these gin palaces. You should see the parties.' He sucked in his breath. 'And the girls! I see them in the morning when I'm walking the dog, cleaning up in their short shorts. Sometimes they swan around in their bikinis – real show-offs some of them, like that blonde there with the square-cut hair. Mostly silicone, I'd say.' He gestured towards *Titania*'s aft deck where Monica was standing at the stern poring over something in her hand.

Sir Henry leaned forward and exchanged a few words with the driver. To Petra he said, 'We'll go and get some lunch.'

Before she could object, the driver had whipped his horse into action. Petra shrank back beneath the hood of the carriage.

'Afraid they'll see you, are you?' Sir Henry fixed her with his sharp eyes. 'My little friend was scared too!'

'I'm not scared,' Petra countered. 'I have jobs to do this afternoon.'

166

'Stuff and nonsense! That lot will never miss you, and if they do, just tell 'em you were with me. Now where was I?' Sir Henry knit his brows. 'Ah, yes! In the beginning, she wasn't afraid. She loved the high life and the parties. Some of the goings on she told me about made my scalp prickle so hard I thought my hair would start to grow again.' His eyes twinkled at his own joke.

Petra choked back laughter. She didn't want to interrupt Sir Henry's train of thought, but needed to find out who he was talking about. If the friend he kept mentioning was Emily Mortlake, as seemed likely, she had to learn as much as possible about her movements during the summer. If not, she didn't want to waste her time, however delightful Sir Henry's company might be.

'What was your friend's name?' she asked. The question vanished into the air like smoke.

'A pretty girl she was, in a rather brassy way. Blow me if I haven't forgotten her name. My memory's terrible. I've got Alzheimer's, you know. I've forgotten yours too, young lady.'

With a wince at his vocabulary, Petra realized she hadn't told him who she was.

'It's Minx, Petra Minx.'

'Well, Petra Minx, how come you're not blonde? They always are.' He paused to study her. 'You definitely don't fit their mould, and you're no spring chicken either. How did you get this job?'

'I heard about it through a friend at Oxford. A girl she knows was working on board *Titania* this summer and I wanted some time out from my studies.'

'You a student? Don't give me that bull!' Sir Henry banged his hand against the side of the carriage. 'I'm not stupid!'

Far from it, Petra thought. Her reaction at their first meeting had been to dismiss him as a semi-senile old man. Yet behind the eccentricity lay a shrewd mind. Would he believe her story as she hoped Don León had done?

'I'm doing an MA in Maritime History. It's a special two-year programme of in-depth research plus a thesis. I ran into a real mental block with my thesis so I came away to clear my head.' Petra shrugged. 'And I'm not blonde because I'm not!'

'Well, whatever you are, you're a cracker!' Sir Henry patted Petra's knee then tapped the driver on the shoulder. 'Take us right up to the main door. Don't pay attention to those signs.'

The hotel grounds were a symphony of colour and texture. Orange, purple, red and yellow bougainvillea vied for control of the garden walls; camellias, hibiscus, oleander, frangipani and cacti grew effortlessly and in abundance. Over them all towered huge rubber trees with shiny dark green leaves, fig trees with small pearlized leaves and, of course, the palms.

Petra was distressed to see two soaring palms topped with a mat of dead leaves and brown fibrous material. She pointed them out to Sir Henry. 'What's wrong with those palms? Something must have attacked them.'

'It's the damned palm weevil. Nasty thing, hard as nails, looks a bit like a cockroach with a long red spike for a nose. It's destroyed hundreds of palms along the coast, and thousands more will die as it spreads.'

'Can't anything be done?'

'They inject poison into the core to kill the blighters, but in most cases it's too late. No good shutting the gate after the horse has bolted.'

No good, indeed, Petra thought. I'll have to be proactive.

168

As soon as the carriage drew up in front of the hotel, the doorman hurried out to assist them. 'Sir Henry!' he exclaimed. 'Welcome. Are you lunching with us?'

'Same as always, Manuel. Why change a good thing, eh? Take the dog and give her some water, would you?' Sir Henry handed the woven red leather leash to the young man. Lila reared up on her hind legs like a miniature stallion and waved her front paws as if to say goodbye, all the while emitting a series of tonal yelps.

Petra raised her hand in admiration and farewell as the little dog trotted away. Animals were fascinating. It was a pity humans regularly underestimated their capabilities and intelligence. 'She's so human, it's as though she's speaking to us,' she enthused.

'Don't you start! Just like my friend! She fell in love with Lila, wanted to take her home with her at the end of the summer, she said.'

'But she wasn't going home,' Petra interjected, thinking of Emily Mortlake, 'only back to College.'

'Well, wherever she was going, I wasn't about to let her take my baby. She was selfish that way, thought she could do anything she wanted. Of course, she found out fast enough on that yacht that she couldn't. I'll tell you about it as soon as we've ordered lunch.'

The Maître d' greeted Sir Henry as effusively as the doorman had. He led them to a corner table overlooking the pool which appeared to be the old man's regular spot. Petra found it hard to concentrate as Sir Henry explained the intricacies of the local dishes on offer through the month of October. She wondered if he were deliberately testing her, he was certainly wily enough.

Forty minutes later, she had begun to despair of ever being able to extract any useful information from him. He was halfway through another convoluted story about the war when he stopped in mid-sentence and drew himself bolt upright.

'E. Her name begins with an E.'

'Are you sure, Sir Henry?'

'Of course I'm sure, girl. Perhaps I don't have Alzheimer's after all – they say you don't if you can remember the initial letter of a word.' He scratched the top of his bald head. 'That's it, her name was Emily! She accosted me one morning as I was walking along the quay with Lila, started petting her and saying how much she missed her own dog.'

'When was that, Sir Henry? Do you remember what month that was?'

'Don't ask me about time, girl! When you get to my age, it's a blessing if you can remember what day of the week it is. All I know is that I used to see her whenever the yacht was in port. My apartment overlooks the water not far from here. Occasionally she would come and visit, but mostly we walked and talked around the marina.'

'You said you'd tell me what happened on board *Titania*. I'd really like to know,' Petra urged.

'If you ask me, she got too involved with her boss. She loved spending time with him, answering his questions about Oxford and discussing philosophy. And he was training her to model lingerie. I wish I'd seen that,' he said with a wink.

Petra said nothing, willing him to continue. Now that Sir Henry was on the right track, she didn't want to do anything that might distract him.

'She was a natural exhibitionist, you know, one of those that likes to shock and tease. But there were limits. Everything was fine as long as she made the rules, and at first El Toro let her.'

'You know Don León's nickname?' Petra asked in surprise.

'It's no secret. He's like the Osborne bull you see on top of the hills, something of an icon on the Coast. You must have seen his car and his boats. All his toys bear the bull logo. I warned Emily to be careful. She thought she could take the bull by the horns, but she misjudged him. Bulls can be erratic.' Sir Henry leaned across the table to add in an undertone: 'If you want my opinion, I'd say she led him on, then teased and goaded him until he turned on her.'

'What makes you think that?'

'She often complained of his mood swings, that she couldn't "figure him out" as she put it. Then she and that blonde bimbo, the one who was on deck when I picked you up, had a real run-in.'

'You mean Monica?'

'Whoever! Don León's permanent girlfriend, as jealous as all hell. She and the grey-haired woman were on Emily's case from morning till night, giving her extra jobs to do. Then the yacht left and I didn't see Emily for a while. Even when the yacht came back, she wasn't aboard. I didn't know what had happened.'

As Petra listened to the old man, she couldn't help but wonder why she should risk her neck to search for someone who was so patently a troublemaker. Even Emily's best friend Amy had intimated that the girl created problems for herself. Then Petra recalled some of her own behaviour over the previous few days.

'Did you see her after that?' she asked, to hide her confusion. Given Sir Henry's sense of time, she expected a snort of incredulity. He surprised her, in the way of many dementia patients, by answering without hesitation.

171

'Turned up like a bad penny in mid-September. She was in quite a state, said she'd had enough and wanted to leave. The problem was they had her passport and phone. I didn't like the look of her at all. She'd lost a lot of her verve and arrogance.' He tapped the side of his nose. 'My guess is she'd been experimenting with drugs. Plenty of those on this coast.'

'Did you find out where she'd been?' Petra asked excitedly.

'I tried, but she seemed ashamed to talk about it. All she would say is that she had had an invitation to visit Morocco.' Sir Henry put down his coffee cup and gave a loud yawn. 'There, I've tired myself out with talking. I'll take you back to the marina. The bill if you please, Waiter.'

Petra stared at her host in disbelief. The torrent of words that was providing her with such valuable information could not be allowed to dry up. She had sacrificed half her lunch on the altar of necessity, preferring to let the waiter think she had finished rather than interrupt Sir Henry's steady flow. 'Go on, go on!' she urged. 'Don't stop now! Did Emily tell you anything else?'

'Nothing that made much sense to me! Don León was a bastard, the new girl was a moron, Morocco was a waste of time.'

'So she did go there! Who invited her? Which part of the country did she visit? What did she do there? And who was the new girl?'

Once again, Sir Henry leaned across the table, bringing his face close to Petra's. 'You ask a lot of questions. Are you sure you aren't a private investigator?'

For a moment, as she looked into Sir Henry's eyes, Petra toyed with the idea of telling him the truth. Then she shook her head. The danger to them all was too great.

'What a crazy idea! It's my natural curiosity. I heard on the Oxford grapevine that Emily was still aboard *Titania*, but she's not. You said you didn't like the look of her when she came back to see you in mid-September.'

'That I did. She looked bloody awful.'

In the hope of eliciting a more meaningful description, Petra spread her hands in the quintessential French gesture of enquiry. 'What do you mean?'

Sir Henry made no response, but rummaged instead in the inside pocket of his sports jacket. He pulled out a crumpled photograph. 'There she is, with Lila, on my terrace at Playas del Sol. That's not far from here. Jocelyne and I used to have a marvellous villa in the hills above Marbella. Stupendous coastal views from there. She designed it, you know, in the French style. At the back, we had an orchard – grew our own oranges and lemons as well as avocados and walnuts. Her lemon tart was out of this world. Better than my mother's.' He chuckled. 'But you wouldn't expect the British to be any good at real lemon tart, would you? Eventually, the villa became too much for us and we sold it for a fortune…'

While Sir Henry wallowed in his memories of golden days with his beloved wife, Petra perused the photograph, which was printed on ordinary white paper. In the centre of the picture, a girl with long flaxen hair sat on a patio chair, facing the camera. The dog on her lap, back erect, ears pricked up, faced the camera too. Petra studied the girl's face. There could be no doubt that it was Emily Mortlake, though she was thinner than in the photograph supplied by Amy and her skin had a waxy pallor. She was smiling a tight-lipped smile, but did not look happy. In fact, her eyes were reddened as if she had been crying.

'I'm sorry, Sir Henry, but had Emily…?' Petra broke off the question as her attention fell on the pendant around the girl's neck, hanging just above the dog's head. It was the blue topaz. And on the fourth finger of her right hand, with which she was cradling the faithful Lila, Petra spotted a matching topaz ring.

'A good one, eh?' Sir Henry gave her a friendly jab in the ribs. 'She took one of me too.' He delved again in his pocket.

'Can I get a copy of this one of Emily and Lila?'

'May, girl, may, not can. Don't you young people learn any grammar these days? Of course you may. Take them both; they're on my computer. I should have used proper photographic paper though. When you're out shopping, perhaps you could bring me some and while you're at it, there's a new camera I'd like to get.' For the third time, Sir Henry reached into his jacket pocket. 'This is it, the Pentax Optio A40, 12 megapixels with Divx recording capability…' He waved a newspaper advertisement in front of her.

I won't underestimate you any more, old boy, thought Petra. If you have the smarts to keep up with electronics at your age, you still have more tight screws than loose ones. Sir Henry's words had given her an idea. As soon as she could get away, she would buy a phone and text Tom. There was no longer any need for him to bother Emily's family to confirm ownership of the necklace.

'Thank you, Waiter,' Sir Henry said as the young man brought the bill. 'Lend me your pen for a minute.' He took the photo of himself from Petra and smoothed it out on the table. After a moment's thought, he wrote in bold letters: "To my bosom friend Petra, a minx if ever I saw one and up to no good!" He signed it with a flourish and returned the pen to the amused waiter.

Anxious to get going, Petra proffered Sir Henry his cane and they made their way ponderously to the lobby.

While Sir Henry went for an essential pit stop before the bumpy carriage ride home, Petra amused herself by looking at the tourist brochures in the stand near the door. Most of them related to sports: tennis, golf, horse riding on the beach, quad-biking up in the hills, scuba diving and even ultra-light rentals. She pulled a few out of the stand and placed the two photographs inside one of them for protection.

By the time Sir Henry returned, relieved and complete with doorman and dog, Petra had learned a lot about what was on offer to denizens of the Costa del Sol. She rose from her chair and hurried forward to meet them. Lila jumped high in the air in sheer delight, causing Petra to drop some of her handful of papers. Quickly, she gathered them up and followed Sir Henry out to the carriage.

Inside the lobby, a swarthy, thickset man stepped out from behind a potted palm, from where he had observed the entire scene. He crossed to the chair recently vacated by Petra and bent to retrieve a piece of paper she had unwittingly left on the floor. Immediately, he recognized the girl in the picture. In the bottom left-hand corner was a digital date: 16:09:2007. How had she managed to visit the old codger then and what might she have told him? Petra chumming up with Sir Henry was an unwelcome development. He would have to talk to Olga.

Pablo pushed his way out of the hotel through a gaggle of Japanese tourists arriving with multiple suitcases and determined to capture every second of the adventure on their phone cameras. In front of their bus, a single taxi waited.

'Follow that carriage but don't get too close. Horses can be skittish,' he ordered the driver.

'I can pass if you like, there's plenty of room.'

175

'No, don't bother. My wife's taking a short ride with a friend and his dog. I don't like horses myself – or dogs.' Pablo lapsed into silence.

The carriage made good time through the quiet residential streets of the Rio Verde neighbourhood. Most Spaniards were at lunch or taking their siesta and traffic was light. As they approached the roundabout at the head of the avenue leading down to the sea, the driver pulled over to the right to allow the taxi that had been crawling along behind them to overtake.

Tired of travelling well below the speed limit, the taxi driver ignored his passenger's instructions, accelerated past the carriage and round the circle, thus restoring the natural order of things along with his ego. 'Where to now, Señor?' he asked.

Pablo craned his head to see where the carriage was heading. 'Pull in over there, you idiot,' he growled, indicating a Smart-sized spot at the kerb. With the luck of the devil, he had chosen well. The black-hooded carriage negotiated the roundabout at walking pace to a chorus of car horns and stopped behind the taxi.

Petra planted a kiss on top of the dog's head, then a longer one on Sir Henry's stubbly cheek. 'Thank you for lunch and for the photos – and for lending me the money. I'll be in touch.'

'Look after yourself, my girl! Don't do anything I wouldn't do or haven't done,' he said, blinking back tears as she leapt to the ground.

The taxi driver watched her through his rearview mirror. 'Some wife, buddy!' he muttered.

'Shut your mouth,' Pablo snarled. He threw a ten-euro note on the back seat of the taxi and hurried off to catch up with Petra who was sprinting across to the shopping centre.

176

CHAPTER FIFTEEN

From a safe distance, Pablo watched Petra purchase a phone from a dealer in the shopping centre. For some reason, she insisted on taking one of the demonstration models. The dealer had to search for some time until he found the box containing the battery charger and other accessories. Once the purchase was complete, Petra extracted the charger and the instruction booklet and dumped the box, along with the rest of its contents, into the nearest refuse bin. It was easy to tail her back to the yacht. She never once looked round and paused only to stuff the phone, charger and booklet into the pocket of her leggings underneath her long T-shirt.

Petra was surprised to see Captain Juan standing watch at the passerelle. Fifty metres behind her, Pablo saw him too. He slowed his pace to let a rowdy group of tourists catch up and engulf him. Amid the confusion, he succeeded in slipping unnoticed into an alley running between two restaurants. To avoid awkward questions about his absence that afternoon when he was supposed to be on duty, he would wait until Ángel or one of the other crewmen replaced the Captain.

'Petra! You've been a long time,' Captain Juan said. 'You're in trouble with Olga.'

177

'That's nothing new. I took Sir Henry's dog back then went for a walk. I got lost up by the bullring trying to avoid the Saturday market.'

Captain Juan made no comment.

'Why are you standing here?' she asked.

'Pablo didn't show up to take his watch. You haven't seen him, have you?'

'Negative, Captain. Shall I take over?'

'Olga wants you up at the party venue. Carlo and Monica are there with the catering staff setting up for tonight.'

Petra had first glimpsed the extraordinary building the morning before as *Titania* entered the marina at Puerto Banús. The imposing block of apartments had a distinctive oriental flavour. On each of the seven storeys, a peppering of purple-gilt domes shimmered above semi-circular floor-to-ceiling windows that reminded Petra of the picture window in Don León's suite aboard *Titania*. Copper accent tiles ran across the top of the pearl-grey marble cladding the walls and below the immense curved balconies, giving definition to the building's fluid lines. Regal palms rimming the beach in front of the complex soared as high as the fourth floor, and lush vegetation, cascading in green rivers over the balconies, flowed down to meet them. Stately and opulent, like something out of the Arabian Nights, it fired Petra's imagination: a desert potentate's pleasure palace set in an oasis of palms.

By nine-thirty that evening everything was ready in the rented premises. The outside staff and caterers had worked tirelessly since noon to prepare the enormous apartment that spread over three floors for the evening's celebrations.

Resplendent in a burgundy velvet smoking jacket, Don León was in his element. He called to Carlo to accompany him on a final tour of the buffet tables and sitting areas. The sumptuous Moroccan *diffa* or feast had been set on a long, beaten-brass table surrounded by low, plump-cushioned sofas for comfortable lounging. Through an archway, in a separate area, the Mediterranean seafood and dishes of roast lamb, beef and venison sat in tempting array on carved wooden tables. With unusual sensitivity to the tastes of some of his guests, and to encourage mingling, Don León had forbidden any pork to be served.

In the dining rooms, the music was soft and neutral. The loud noise and beat would be reserved for the discotheque on the top floor. Arabian music would be played in the smoking room where hookah pipes were provided for those who wished to indulge. The selection of cigars in the cigar room was worthy of Sir Winston Churchill himself.

'Carlo, did you stock the bar upstairs with the Cuvée Ana León?' Don León asked.

'Yes, Sir,' Carlo replied. 'Just as you asked.'

'Then let's begin!' El Toro declared.

They made their way to the entrance hall where white-coated staff were relieving the first female guests of their fur wraps and embroidered shawls. After half an hour in the receiving line, Petra's cheeks were on fire and her hand was aching. The cosmopolitan crowd kissed, shook, bowed or grovelled, depending on their ancestry and personal preference. Petra noticed that many of the "gentlemen" bowed long and low over Monica's cleavage as well as her own, while Olga in mannish tuxedo kept her eagle eye fixed on them all. Carlo, to Petra's right, whispered irreverent comments in her ear at the approach of each guest.

179

'Talk about mutton dressed as lamb! Next stop the abattoir!'

Petra poked him in the ribs.

'Pink's last year's colour, mate. Forget to tell you, did they?'

'Mercutio, he'll hear you!'

'Ah, the gold brigade! Nice, nice, old son!' Chameleon-like, Carlo could adopt any accent and vernacular he fancied. And probably have any woman he fancied too, Petra thought, noticing the warmth with which many of them greeted him.

Don León ushered the last arrival into the vast panelled drawing room where generous servings of drinks and canapés were teasing his guests' palates prior to dinner. He spotted Monica across the room, engaged in heavy conversation with a rival studio owner. Her snakeskin-patterned sheath, cut to her navel in front and to the crease of her buttocks in the back, writhed with every word.

'Monica darling, check with Carlo for me to see if the models are here.' Don León's commanding touch on her shoulder left her no choice. With a scowl at being interrupted before she had had time to hedge her bets, she sidled away.

In the far corner, Petra stood tall and slender in her silver lamé. The erectness of her bearing drew El Toro's eye away from her deep décolleté to the fine-boned structure of her face. Her elfin features danced with animation as she responded to the young Spaniard standing close beside her. The pang in Don León's chest was a terrible reminder of the older sister he had idolized.

The recollection came unbidden and unwelcome. In the midst of the revelry, he saw again the lamplight fall on Ana's pale, heart-shaped face seconds before it exploded in

180

a shower of crimson. True to their word, the drug lords of Bogotá had taken their pound of flesh.

Petra was impressed by the range of languages being spoken in the convivial atmosphere created by Don León. He had, it seemed, invited representatives of all the pillars of Marbella society: genuine European aristocracy and old money with good manners and good taste, flashy "nouveau riche" types, prominent local and foreign citizens and politicians, business people from around the world, social climbers and self-styled socialites along with borderline criminals and assorted hangers-on. A true melting pot or witches' brew, depending on one's degree of cynicism.

Carlo paused next to Petra and her beau. 'I'm sorry, Sir. I have to steal this magnificent lady. Boss's orders.' Deftly, he balanced the inlaid tray with its cargo of heavy silver tea and sugar pots and multi-coloured glasses on his left arm, and placed his right hand under Petra's elbow, little by little drawing her away.

'What are you doing, Mercutio? You're not part of the waiting staff tonight.'

'Special request for mint tea from Sheik Kamal's entourage. Anyway, I like carrying a tray. It gives me an excuse to listen in on lots of interesting conversations.'

'Well, you spoilt mine. That guy owns a paragliding outfit.'

'One of the most dangerous things you can do,' Carlo commented. 'I don't think Don León would let you try, the way he was staring at you just now.'

'What do you mean?' Petra asked.

'First he was admiring your tits, then he looked as though he'd seen a ghost, next he ordered me to fetch you. I deduce: 1) he can't get enough of your body, 2) you remind him of somebody significant, 3) he's jealous. Ergo,

181

he's falling in love with you,' Carlo expounded. 'Gotta go – tea's getting cold.' Indicating the opposite end of the lounge, he said: 'El Toro's over there, talking with Monica'. He darted off before Petra could turn the full beam of her wrath on him.

To avoid confronting Don León until she had sorted out her emotions, Petra pushed through the chattering crowds and sought refuge in the Spanish dining room. Absent-mindedly, she picked up a peeled shrimp from the buffet. Mercutio was such a clown. As in the past, he frustrated her with his desire to be so smart. In his own way, he was as much of a manipulator as Don León. He could make people believe anything.

Through the open archway, Petra heard the guttural tones of one of the Scandinavian languages. Her sanctuary would shortly be invaded. With her mind still in turmoil, she opened the glass door leading from the dining room to the balcony. Outside, the air was cool enough to make her shiver.

The balconies on the rear of the building faced extensive, well kept gardens across which could be seen a row of more traditionally styled white-painted buildings with blue and white awnings. In the pale light cast by the lamps dotting the gardens, Petra fancied she saw a piebald dog chase a black cat. Hundreds of feral cats eked out an existence along the Coast. Perhaps the aggressor was Lila, Sir Henry's precious pet. Perhaps he was watching. Perhaps…

The introspection of the moment came to a brusque end. Guests filled the room with laughter and noise. A clutch of under-dressed Brits in boots, jeans and glitzy T-shirts spilled over into Petra's territory She decided the time had come to sample the delights of Morocco.

Of all the dishes she tried, Petra preferred the *tajine* of chicken, olives and preserved lemon, with its smooth texture and flavourful sauce. The *mechoui*, an entire lamb stuffed with couscous, almonds, prunes and other dried fruit, basted with butter, garlic and spices, and slow-roasted to the point of disintegration, was a sensation as a centrepiece and for the taste buds, but too rich to receive top marks. The Moroccan food proved popular with many of El Toro's international and Spanish guests who quickly adapted to the recline-and-slouch mentality that Petra suspected was not good for the digestion.

Mindful that the silver lamé would not tolerate second helpings, she wandered out onto the balcony facing the harbour entrance. She needed to order her thoughts and was still keen to avoid Don León for as long as possible. The moon had risen. A slight distortion of the perfect circle suggested that it was not quite full. Full enough, though, to make people crazy.

Blotting out the sounds of revelry emanating from the apartment, Petra began to analyze what she had learned about Emily Mortlake over the last few days. Since her mistake in jumping to the conclusion that the Emy aboard *Nemesis* was the politician's missing daughter, she was loath to make any more hasty judgements. Yet everything pointed to the fact that Emily had gone to Morocco.

As if the power of her thinking had brought a monster to life, a long, low, metallic snout followed by sixty metres of polished steel and aluminium slid past the end of the seawall and turned to enter the port. *Nemesis*. The vessel's unexpected appearance destroyed the remnants of Petra's composure and the whine of its gas turbines perturbed her inner ear. In that instant, she failed to hear the steps behind her. Her stomach leapt to her throat as strong hands massaged her shoulders.

'I've been looking everywhere for you!' Don León rumbled.

Petra tried a light-hearted response. 'I'm often to be found looking at the water.'

'As long as you're not found in it,' was his unsettling reply. He gestured to the disappearing tail fin of the boat. 'Theo's on time as usual. They should be here before the show begins. Come with me up to the roof terrace.' Don León pulled Petra closer. Her initial impulse was to throw him off, then she forced herself to relax.

The roof terrace was a shadowy fairyland of stately palms studded with white mini-lights, branched cacti, and flowering shrubs in ornate pots. Petra found it somewhat ironic that this vast garden in the sky bore many more times the weight of earth and flora than the marble terrace at Don León's villa in the hills.

The marquee that had been erected for the fashion show was ablaze with lights. Guests in various stages of intoxication were already taking their places in anticipation of another Don León spectacular. The buzz was that he had had to negotiate special visas for the models he had hired to display his wares in this show. Speculation was rife.

Don León led Petra past the rows of chairs and tables to the front of the marquee where Olga pecked at her like a mother hen with an unruly chick.

'If we're late starting, you're to blame,' she grouched. 'Thank God you're with the second group. Go and see Natasha, quickly!' She pointed out a dark-haired girl with heavy eye make-up that emphasized the pallor of her skin.

An expectant hush fell over the audience as the marquee lights went out. For an instant, there was darkness and a hint of unease. Then a single spotlight fell on Don León, standing centre-stage. He spread his hands.

'Ladies and Gentlemen, I have brought you here today to enjoy yourselves and each other, to indulge your senses, to experience and experiment, in short to celebrate the essence of life. What you are about to see may surprise, shock or disgust you, move, touch or arouse you in ways too complex to understand. My purpose is to entertain you. To you falls the task of processing what you see and of living by what you distill.'

Waiting in the wings, Petra felt a tremor run up her spine. A goose on her grave, her mother would have said. Then the screen behind the catwalk exploded in a maelstrom of psychedelic colours, strobe lights and throbbing sound. Monica, in black stilettos and a loosely crocheted white nano-bikini in which there was absolutely no room to hide, appeared at the head of a dozen statuesque Brazilian mulattos loosely chained together at the ankle and wearing white leather anklets studded with emeralds and diamonds. Similarly studded collars encircled their necks and waists.

As the tall, proud, honey-coloured women advanced in time with the beat, it became apparent that the waist collars were chastity belts. Their full breasts were bare, only the area surrounding the nipple camouflaged by intricate green and white painted tattoos. Monica bent to unlock the first anklet with a silver key. The girl shook herself free and, to raucous cries from the crowd, exposed the cruel teeth of the belt. As the model held her pose, Monica turned her attention to the next member of the chain gang, then the next. When all were freed, she shooed them off stage and held up the ring of silver keys.

On the giant screen, Christ the Redeemer spread his arms in blessing over Rio de Janeiro. His lost sheep reappeared in Don León's swimwear collection of sombre zippered and buckled black, mesmerizing green and white

185

dots, sixties' swirls of pink, green and purple. They paraded along the beaches of Ipanema and Copacabana to the strains of the South American harp, then retreated into the Amazonian rainforest. As they disappeared into the dense undergrowth, a volley of gunfire shook the audience out of their seats. The picture on the screen dissolved in a splatter of blood and all the lights on the terrace went out. Someone screamed.

After a moment's silence, a dirge struck up and a single white strobe light started to flash. One after the other, Monica, followed by the twelve mulattos chained together again at the ankle, passed through it. The flickering ceased. They formed a semi-circle around her in a swath of yellow light that emphasized the lustre of their skin. Monica extracted the key ring from the V front of her bikini, undid it and lobbed the keys into the audience. Cameras flashed around the marquee. It took some minutes for the clamour and scuffles to subside.

The implications of the staging were too much for the feminist contingent to accept and a posse of women in tailored evening suits ostentatiously vacated the front row of seats. On the opposite side, Sheik Kamal's aides grinned knowingly as their master pressed one of the silver keys to his lips.

A change in the tone and tempo of the music alerted the crowd that more was to come. Silence fell. Black and white images of emaciated beings as far from human as it was possible to imagine expanded and condensed against a background of concentration camp fences.

At a push from Natasha, Petra emerged onto the runway dressed in black fishnet stockings, a crimson demi-chemise and French knickers. In her wake, like the children of Hamelin following the Pied Piper, danced a dozen urchins with big eyes and dishevelled hair. Their pubescent bodies in sheer white slips shone pale in the eerie half-light. To a haunting melody, they mimed with infinite sadness the depths of their distress.

The contrast with the first group could not have been more extreme. Whereas the Amazonians had dwarfed Monica, Petra felt like a giant among the "petite gamine" models with their pixie faces and anorexic bodies. A cloud of dry ice began to envelop the stage. Petra had been warned, but found it difficult not to cough.

As the smoke cleared, the urchins reappeared against a changing backdrop of iconic images of Paris – the Eiffel Tower, Sacré Coeur, Montmartre, the Arc de Triomphe – and Berlin – Kurfürstendamm and Kaiser Wilhelm Memorial Church, a section of the infamous Wall, and the Brandenburg Gate.

To a street rap beat, accompanied by catcalls and enthusiastic applause, the troupe presented Don León's latest lingerie collection of sheer tulle thongs, see-through slips, ruffled and laced corsetry, sultry zip-ups and seductive robes designed only to be taken off. One after another, the models completed their routines and strutted off stage through the Brandenburg Gate. As the last one disappeared from view, the Gate morphed into footage taken at the end of the Second World War when the Allies arrived to liberate Auschwitz. The urchins returned to complete their terrible ballet of hunger, cruelty and exploitation.

Caught up in the drama of the final tableau, Petra was near the end of the runway before she paid any attention to the audience. Directly in front of her, a few metres away, Theo stood with Axel. So the bastard was back! Petra threw him a look that she wished could kill, since she hadn't succeeded so far by other means. Axel grabbed Theo's sleeve and whispered urgently to him, tapping the

187

dressing on his cheek as he did so. At least she had hurt him.

The last waif vanished from the stage along with the last of the dry ice. Carlo ran forward into the spotlight, every inch the gentleman in his top hat and tails. He doffed his hat and bowed.

'Ladies and Gentlemen, on behalf of Don León and the whole team, I would like to thank you for your participation in tonight's celebration. Let's give another round of applause to our fabulous performers.' He waited for the noise to die down before continuing. 'Now, for your dancing pleasure, the discotheque and champagne bar are open downstairs. For those of you who don't like to show off, cards and roulette are available in the library, also one floor below. However, before you go to try your luck on the floor or the tables, I must tell you that this hedonism comes with a price. Our waifs will be out and about with collection boxes, begging for contributions to The León Foundation whose aims are set out in the information leaflets they can provide. Those of you who would like to spend more time with them tonight are invited to buy the privilege. And those of you who have keys to release the passions of our Brazilian dancers should know that each one carries a price tag of twenty thousand euros.' A gasp went up from the crowd. 'Our cameras know who you are. Don León will make special arrangements with you if you don't have the funds available tonight. Finally, Ladies and Gentlemen, breakfast and brandy will be served in the dining rooms and on the lower terrace at sunrise, after the fireworks. Off you go! Get those feet tapping!'

Carlo returned his hat to his head, tucked his cane under his arm and broke into a Fred Astaire routine that drew cheers and whistles from the departing guests.

188

'Beautiful, Carlo, beautiful! And both my girls were brilliant!' Don León kissed his fingers to his lips. 'Let's join the fun.'

The discotheque had been set up in a cavernous room with a vaulted ceiling inlaid with thousands of silver particles. These twinkled like stars in the reflected light of dozens of candles that stood in sconces around the walls. Down one side of the room, a short distance away from the dance floor, canopied beds with ample space for at least two people offered exhausted dancers and amorous couples a chance to relax. In other areas, more conventional armchairs and sofas were arranged around marble tables. Already these and the dance floor were filling up. The beds would fill up later.

Don León acknowledged with a slight inclination of his head the compliments showered upon him as he escorted Monica and Petra across the floor.

'Monica, go and circulate and don't get cold!' He patted her behind and sent her off in the direction of an impeccably dressed couple who were looking rather at a loss.

'Dora, I'll come back to you in a moment. Don't go away,' he said to a shapely redhead who was waving a cheque in his face. He steered Petra towards a group of men in white *jellabas*, seated around a tall blue and silver hookah pipe.

'Petra, you've already met Sheik Kamal. Sheik, I hope you remember our newest recruit, Petra. I'll leave her with you for a while. Then I'll be back to collect the money for your key to heaven.' He winked and strode away.

'Of course.' Sheik Kamal turned to Petra and patted the seat beside him. 'Sit, my dear.'

Petra did as she was bidden.

'Your performance was spellbinding. I shall enjoy this opportunity to get to know you better,' he said formally. 'You are a refreshing change, my dear. My son Ahmed, who accompanied us aboard the exquisite *Titania*, always tells me brunettes have more depth than blondes. I must say I am ready for a new challenge.' Sheik Kamal scrutinized her for several seconds before continuing. 'I understand you are American.'

'I can't think where you got that idea. I'm Canadian.' Petra found him irritating.

'Ah, a feisty one! I thought so. Forgive me, Canadians are so sensitive about their nationality. Don León seems to have a penchant for them this year.'

Petra knew at once that he must be referring to Emily Mortlake, even though he didn't mention her name. And that was the strange thing. From the beginning, nobody seemed to want to hide the fact that she had been on board *Titania*. Everything was above board, so to speak. She cocked her head to one side and gave him a quizzical look. 'So it appears,' she said. 'But two Canadians in a season don't make a horde. Anyone would think we'd overrun the whole Mediterranean.'

Sheik Kamal ignored her sour tone and leaned forward. Petra caught a trace of aniseed. 'The two of you would have made a lovely pair. Both educated, beautiful, good bodies, contrasting colours.' He ran a practiced eye over Petra and smiled at the annoyed expression on her face.

Under his urbane exterior, he was as bad as Don León: needling, baiting, watching her reactions. Was this how they manipulated girls into doing what they wanted – by using pseudo-intellectual banter, instead of coercion and force, to stimulate, coax, and gently push towards the objective? Petra was not going to let herself be subjugated by those or any other means.

Sheik Kamal stroked his beard. 'You Canadians are all fighters, it seems. As you know, in my culture, women are not encouraged to be aggressive, so a little thrust and parry with someone like yourself is appealing. Would you care to try the hookah?'

Accepting the challenge, Petra took the proffered nozzle and put it to her lips. The smoke made her cough.

Sheik Kamal laughed. 'The water pipe is an acquired taste. It is worse than dry ice. Let me get you something more palatable.' He signalled to a passing waiter. 'Have you been to Morocco, Petra?'

'Never, but I'd love to visit. I've heard there's a lot of development across the water from here: new apartment complexes, resort hotels and marinas. I expect Don León takes *Titania* there from time to time.'

'He used to join us in Marina Smir. It is our equivalent of Puerto Banús – the place to see and be seen on the Moroccan side. Then the Customs people started to make it difficult.' Sheik Kamal sighed. 'There are always problems when men become hungry for power.'

'Do you keep a…?' Before Petra could ask him about *Lady Fatima*, Carlo came hurrying over with his tray.

'Champagne for the lady? There we are.' Carefully, Carlo placed a brimming glass on the table in front of Petra. 'It's the Cuvée Ana León. Very potent.' He looked round expectantly. 'Here's Natasha, our leading waif. Perhaps you'd like to make a contribution to her upkeep, Sheik?' Taking advantage of the distraction, he whispered to Petra: 'Can you get away?'

'I'll try. When?' she breathed.

'Meet me at 2.30 a.m. in the entrance hall.' Carlo straightened up and addressed himself to Sheik Kamal.

191

'The gogo dancers come on in half an hour. Things will really start to hot up then. Can I get you anything else, Sir?'

'No, thank you. I have this lovely lady to keep me company, at least until Don León disturbs me.' With narrowed eyes, he waved Natasha away and waited for Carlo to leave. 'Tell me, Petra, have you been to Cádiz? I am right that you are studying Maritime History, am I not? I am sure I could not be wrong about a girl twice in one evening!'

With consummate skill, Sheik Kamal turned the conversation to the great sea battles between England and Spain and blocked all attempts by Petra to change the subject. For appearances' sake, she took a few careful sips of her drink. After what seemed an interminably long time, the gogo dancers bounced their way onto the dance floor. The DJ cranked the music up even louder and Sheik Kamal craned his head to watch the antics of the dancers.

'Do you enjoy this type of gogo dancing, Sheik?' Petra asked. 'Or do you prefer belly dancing?'

'I am a man of the world, Miss Minx. I will take whatever is on offer,' he said. 'What about you?'

'I'm just a poor student, I'll take whatever's on offer too. But they are good!'

Petra shuffled her chair as if to get a better view of the dancers. In doing so, she contrived to knock over her glass of champagne, which shattered on the table. She jumped up. 'I'm so sorry! What a mess! I'm soaked,' she said, indicating the wet patch spreading across her crotch. 'And I'm covered in shards of glass,' she added, picking one off the front of her crimson knickers. 'Let me go and change, and find someone to clear up. I'll be right back.'

Before Sheik Kamal or any of his entourage had time to react, she melted into the seething mass of people.

CHAPTER SIXTEEN

Petra elbowed her way through the revellers on the dance floor, hoping that no one from Sheik Kamal's entourage would try to follow her. She headed in the direction of the ladies' room before exiting onto the rear terrace. Running down the two external flights of stairs to the main floor of the apartment she saw nobody, just the indistinct outline of an embracing couple on the middle balcony. She was thankful to find the dining rooms empty. The buffets had been cleared away and large baskets of fresh fruit had been placed on the tables in preparation for breakfast.

In the panelled drawing room, all was tidy. The only heart-stopping moment occurred when a white-coated waiter emerged whistling from an unobtrusive door cut in one of the panels. Petra concealed herself behind a carved screen. Intent on his own business, the waiter made his way towards the entrance hall.

Petra followed at a discreet distance, ready to flop down into one of the chairs and tell a convoluted story about the spilled champagne. The stain on her French knickers was uncomfortably wet and she would have liked to have had time to change. Spying a white mink wrap on the arm of a chair, she scooped it up and draped it over her arm as if she were looking for the owner. She reached the entrance hall in time to see the waiter disappear into the gentlemen's cloakroom. Ten seconds later, Carlo came out of the same door and they stepped into the waiting elevator.

'Good girl, you made it!' he said.

'My ruse worked.' Petra showed him the spreading stain then pulled the wrap tight round her shoulders as the elevator door opened. The night air was cool.

The golf cart Carlo had used to ferry supplies of the Cuvée Ana León to the party venue was standing in the lobby. 'I'm surprised it's still here,' he commented. 'Hop in!' He put the cart into gear.

'Why did you want me to get away?' Petra asked, as they purred along the drive to the guardhouse.

'This is the perfect opportunity to take a look at some of *Titania*'s locked areas while everyone is living it up at the fiesta.' Carlo waved to the security guard who barely looked up before raising the barrier for them.

'How do you intend to do that? Don León is certain to have left somebody on watch and you're surely not going to suggest that we break doors down?'

'Captain Juan told me all the crew except Pablo have been given the night off. Apparently Pablo didn't get back until six when he should have taken over the watch at four. As punishment, Juan ordered him to take the midnight to eight shift as well, instead of Ángel.'

'Then only Pablo should be on board?'

'Right. And I have Olga's keys!' Carlo patted his trouser pocket.

'How did you manage that?'

'I was talking to Captain Juan while the poker game was being set up in the library after the fashion show. Olga came in with Theo and that jerk Axel. She called for some tequila shots – I think she'd already had a few; it's her favourite tipple. Axel joined the poker players, Theo and Olga sat at the roulette table. I've never seen Olga so

194

animated! She took off her tuxedo jacket and put it behind her on the chair. When I returned with the tequila, it had fallen to the floor. I picked it up and whispered to her that I was going to put it on the coat rack in the corner. The wheel was spinning, so she just nodded and waved me away. I felt the keys in the jacket and took them.'

'A stroke of genius!' Petra muttered.

Carlo suspected she was being sarcastic. 'Do you have a better idea?'

Petra shook her head. 'I was planning to leave this morning anyway.' She told him briefly about her lunch with Sir Henry and what he had said about Emily accepting an invitation to Morocco.

'I'll show you the photo Sir Henry gave me. According to the date on it, Emily was here on September 16th. The general consensus seems to be that she left to go travelling, a.k.a. lost her job, at the end of August. My guess is that she went to Morocco for a couple of weeks and then came back to Spain, although it's possible she didn't go there until later. The date on the camera could be wrong too. Either way, I need to check out Sheik Kamal's boat *Lady Fatima*. There's a definite connection between him and Emily Mortlake.'

Carlo put a warning hand on Petra's arm as the golf cart approached the end of the alley near *Titania*'s berth. 'We'll get out and walk past the yacht to the parkette by the tower. We'll have to be very quiet. Snuggle up to me as if we're lovers.' He buttoned up his black tailcoat with one hand. 'It's unlikely Pablo will be on deck, but keep your eyes peeled as we go past.'

Petra did as she was told. This was not the time to question Carlo's motives. Besides, she felt comfortable with her arms around him and her head against his chest. She heard shouts and music carried on the breeze from the other side of the port. At this end of the marina, the restaurants were closed and the street was quiet. In the berth next to *Titania*, *Nemesis* lay in darkness like a sleeping whale, her silver-grey metallic hull gleaming in the pale streetlamp light. Petra shivered despite the fur wrap and Carlo's closeness.

Pablo was sitting on *Titania*'s bridge with his feet up on the console. He was livid with Captain Juan for forcing him to miss the party. He had been hoping to "persuade" one of the models to spend a few hours with him after the show. Even better, he could have kept company with Petra. And thanks to Captain Juan, he had not yet been able to tell Olga about Petra's outing with Sir Henry. He would have to find a way of presenting the information without revealing his own secret. Then, if Olga gave him the go-ahead, he would enjoy putting pressure on Petra to find out what she knew.

Earlier that evening he had searched Petra's cabin. He had lingered over her clothing, but found nothing incriminating. He shuffled in his seat. The memory of her breasts in his hands on her first evening aboard *Titania* in Monte Carlo still aroused him. He half-closed his eyes to indulge in a few moments of fantasy.

In front of him, the bank of monitors flickered. The black and white screens showed the main deck forward of Don León's suite, the mid-ship section of both side decks, the stern of the vessel and a portion of the street. Earlier the quay had been crowded with locals and tourists having a good time on a Saturday night. Now it was deserted. Most of the rowdies had repaired to the late night bars and discotheques, a few of them to bed to sleep off the evening's excesses.

Don León's fiesta would continue until dawn. The hard cases would carry on partying as long as he allowed. There was no need for Pablo to stay on the bridge. He could keep an eye on things from the skylounge and would be able to see the fireworks from there.

Pablo threw a last glance at the monitors. Nothing of interest. Just a couple sauntering by, arms around each other, the girl leaning heavily on the man. A working girl judging by her outfit. Nice long legs. Probably going to make out on a bench at the end of the quay. Or maybe she'd just service him in the shadow of the tower. He might be able to watch them from upstairs.

Petra hugged Carlo tightly as they passed the yacht. *Titania*'s security lights were on, but the salon drapes were drawn and no light showed through. Carlo steered her towards a bench in the corner of the parkette next to the marina's fuel station. It was partially screened from view by a large rubber tree.

'I want you to take a good look at *Titania* while I'm kissing you,' Carlo said. He twisted Petra into a position from which she should be able to see the yacht and pressed his lips to hers, softly at first then more urgently.

After a few seconds, Petra pushed him away. 'Multi-tasking's one thing, Mercutio, but you don't have to make it so realistic.'

'Sorry, I got carried away.'

'OK. A light just went on in the skylounge. Someone's up there, probably Pablo.'

'He's supposed to be on the bridge watching the security monitors.'

'Come on, Carlo, you know what he's like, always playing his cards to suit himself. He's probably gone up there to watch a movie. Kiss me again,' she added, ' in case he can see us.'

'I knew I could win you over, Minx,' Carlo said. 'Seriously though, we can't risk being caught on camera. I think I know how we can get aboard *Titania* unseen.'

Petra and Carlo got up from the bench, arms firmly around each other. They lurched across to the wall of the fuel station, leaned against it for a few moments, then ducked behind the building on the water side. The moon slipped behind a cloud. Petra prayed for it to stay there.

Two metres below the level of the fuel dock, the harbourmaster's inflatable Zodiac dinghy bobbed on the water. Carlo pulled it in close to the dock and held the line taut while Petra sat on the cold edge of the wall and took off her stilettos. She threw them into the water before jumping down. The small craft danced under the impact. Carlo untied the line, threaded it through a metal ring set in the wall and handed the end back to Petra.

'Haul it in as tight as you can. She's going to bounce,' he said. He dropped to his knees, put both hands on the edge of the dock and swung his body over the wall, feeling for the side of the inflatable with his feet. As anticipated, the boat tipped and rocked.

Carlo found his balance, and the paddles. In less than five minutes, they had paddled quietly round the end of the fuel dock, under *Titania*'s bow and close along her port side. There was just enough room to squeeze between the enormous fenders separating *Titania* and *Nemesis*.

Carlo reached up and tied the dinghy next to the fender closest to *Titania*'s stern. With great care, he balanced on the bow of the dinghy, reached up with his hands to grasp *Titania*'s upper rubrail and placed first one foot then the other on her lower rubrail. In this precarious position, he inched along towards the corner of the swim platform. Reaching the safety of the platform, he held out his hand to assist Petra.

'Stay low,' he whispered as she joined him on the swim platform. 'Keep out of the field of vision of the cameras.'

Petra nodded.

'We'll go in through the "toy room". I know how to open it from down here,' Carlo said. 'There's a release catch in case of malfunction.' He felt around in a recess next to the eurostern steps on the port side and pressed a button. After a few seconds, he released it, having raised the hatch just enough for them to crawl underneath. 'I'll leave it open as an escape route.'

Again Petra nodded. The "toy room" was as impeccably clean and tidy as the rest of the yacht. The two jet skis were stacked one above the other on hydraulic cradles. On the starboard side, two ocean kayaks hung above a rigid-bottomed inflatable. Water skis, tubes, fishing rods and nets stood in labelled racks. Petra also noticed scuba diving equipment along with spearguns and knives in a special rack.

The "toy room" led into a well organized workshop fitted with cupboards and wall-racks. From one of the racks, which housed enough tools to stock a small hardware store, Carlo took a rubber mallet and a roll of duct tape, then opened the heavy engine room door. The latent power of the twin diesels hung over the area like a pall.

Petra followed Carlo through the gap between the engines. They were incredible machines, complex yet simple, tough and reliable. 'Don León doesn't scrimp on maintenance!' she said, looking around in admiration.

'Or gadgets!' Carlo said, surveying the sophisticated machinery. 'Come on, let's get out of here. I'll find Pablo and disable him for a few hours.'

'What if he sees you first?'

Carlo shrugged. 'I'll tell him I've come for more champagne.'

'OK. I'll help you search as soon as I've changed into more practical travelling gear,' Petra said.

'After we've finished, I'll go back to the party. I should be able to cover for you for a while.' Carlo slipped his feet out of his shoes and left them in a corner of the engine room. 'What I'd like to do is stop you from going. I still think you're making too many assumptions.'

'Call it a hunch, Mercutio. Whatever you think, I'm going to Morocco.'

'Right. Quiet now.' With extreme care, Carlo opened the door at the far end of the engine room that led to the crew cabin area, alert to any sound or hint that somebody might be there. He put his head round the door and held his breath. 'All clear! See you in the laundry in a few minutes.'

Carlo took the circular staircase from the crew level to the main deck. The galley, library, dining room and grand salon were all in darkness. He hurried on up the stairs to the boatdeck and made his way forward to the communications room and the bridge. He tiptoed past the guest suites, Captain Juan's cabin and the communications room. He was sure they would all be locked.

The communications room was dark. A dim light shone through the glass pane of the closed door to the bridge. He approached cautiously. The room was empty. Pablo must be up in the skylounge, as they had surmised. Carlo was pleased to see that the cameras trained on

Titania's aft deck did not pick up the partially open hatch to the garage.

He decided to take the port-side stairs to the sundeck. The pool area and bar were deserted. He crossed to the skylounge and peeped through the gap in the doors. Pablo was sprawled on the sofa with his back to the doors, a tumblerful of whisky in his hand and an open bottle on the coffee table to his right.

On the plasma screen in front of him, a platinum blonde with overripe breasts was kneeling on a daybed, fingering herself with one hand and massaging the engorged penis of the man lying on the bed with the other. A second man, endowed with a very square but very erect penis, entered the room and pressed himself against the girl from behind. Another girl entered, this time a skinny redhead. She began to fondle the blonde's breasts. Pablo's eyes were riveted on the screen. He took another gulp of whisky and unzipped his trousers with a sigh.

Carlo stepped sideways through the doors. The gasps and moans from the two couples on the screen were more than enough to camouflage his entry. Pablo was gradually bringing himself to seventh heaven as he immersed himself in the action. Carlo waited for the right moment. In the instant before climax, Pablo groaned as if he were mortally wounded and dropped his head. With a calculated swing of the rubber mallet, Carlo knocked him out. The blow was enough to immobilize him for a few hours, but not sufficient to kill him. Pablo slumped sideways, his erection taking a moment to subside.

In the movie, the action had moved to a more exotic locale featuring not two couples but four. After checking that Pablo was indeed out for the count, Carlo picked up the remote control, put a stop to the actors' acrobatics and ejected the disc. He slid it into the pocket of his tailcoat.

Taking out the duct tape, he bent over Pablo's prostrate body and bound his ankles together. He lifted Pablo's feet and dragged him off the sofa onto the floor. He turned him over, twisted his arms behind him and taped his wrists. Then he rolled him over and stuck several pieces of tape over Pablo's mouth, pressing them firmly into place. Finally, he turned him over again so that he was lying face down on the floor. Satisfied with his workmanship, he switched off the light and ran to join Petra.

Petra opened her cabin door and stepped over the threshold. She knew immediately that her blue deck shoes had been moved. Her training had taught her to be aware of detail and to recognize when something was out of place or not quite right. They had been moved from where she had left them in front of the dressing table – not by much but enough to put her on the alert. Her gut told her it wasn't the houseboys.

A glance through the two banks of drawers confirmed her suspicions. Someone had been rifling through her belongings. Her clothes hanging in the closet had also been moved. The search had been discreet but thorough. She hoped it had not been thorough enough to find the place where she had hidden the topaz, her new phone, her watch and some papers, including the brochure containing the photos from Sir Henry.

Quickly Petra stripped off her still-damp French knickers and the fishnet stockings. There was a large hole in the back of the left leg where she must have caught it on the parkette bench. She pulled on her jeans, replaced the demi-chemise with a T-shirt and her denim jacket and slipped her feet into the blue deck shoes. Then she knelt in front of the lower drawer on the left-hand side of the dressing table and lifted it out.

Because of the curve of the hull, there was a void that ran behind the drawers and the kneehole opening. Searching earlier for a truly secure hiding-place, Petra had felt in all directions to the full extent of her reach until she had discovered a ledge high up under the centre section of the dressing table. She had placed the pendant, phone, watch and papers in a plastic bag on the ledge. The bag was still there! She pulled it out and extracted the contents.

The safest place now for the topaz, if she could find a suitable chain for it, would be round her neck with the cross she always wore. She placed the papers and the phone into a money belt that she strapped round her waist under her shirt, then stuffed a change of clothing along with a few other necessities into the small backpack she had brought on board less than a week ago. At the last minute, she remembered to pick up her discarded party clothes, which she placed in the plastic bag. She would dispose of them later. Tempus fugit... Time flies... there was none to waste. She had to go and meet Carlo.

As Petra approached the laundry area, she saw a light go on. Carlo was just ahead of her. 'How did it go?' she enquired.

'No problem, he was exactly where we thought he'd be – in the skylounge, drinking himself into a stupor and watching a porno flick.' He tapped the side of his jacket. 'I whacked him on the head and pocketed the disc. It's probably one of Don León's creations.'

'Or Sheik Kamal's. There's no evidence Don León is involved in the blue movie business. I didn't see anything shady at his studios, and you said yourself that they had been investigated and were clean,' Petra protested.

'That's the reason we're here: to look for anything incriminating, whether it's movies or drugs or anything else. Why are you being so protective?' Carlo pointed to a set of lockers. 'The bar stock and the champagne are kept in there. I want to send a couple of bottles of the Cuvée Ana León away for analysis.'

'You search here,' Petra said. 'I'll take a look at Olga and Monica's cabins. Do you have the keys for those? I need to find my passport.'

'You'll be lucky! Olga keeps all valuables in her massive safe. It's rumoured to be built into the hull and so heavy that *Titania* has a permanent list to starboard. You can have the key ring after I've unlocked these cupboards.'

The third key Petra tried opened the door to Olga's cabin. It was the mirror image of her own. She crossed immediately to the dressing table. The surface was bare. She opened each of the drawers in turn, but did not disturb their orderly contents. Kneeling down, she lifted out the bottom right-hand drawer to check for anything hidden in the space behind. It was empty, as she had guessed it would be. A few pairs of trousers, two suits, and a couple of skirts hung in the closet.

The safe was easy to find. It was in a cupboard adjacent to the closet, built into the hull as Carlo had indicated, solid steel and festooned with dials. Carlo was right. She would have to sneak into Morocco without a passport.

As she felt for the switch to turn out the cabin light, Petra noticed a large portrait photograph of Don León next to Olga's bed. It was the only personal note in the whole room. In front of it stood a row of small white votive candles like the ones you paid 20 cents for in Italian churches. The strong-burning flames of such candles had helped Petra through several dark spots in her life. She wondered what they meant to Olga.

Petra crossed the corridor to Monica's cabin. Unlocking the door, she felt a trifle guilty. This was more about curiosity than necessity. A trail of clothes littered the furniture and the floor. Perfumes and cosmetics cluttered the top of the dressing table. The only similarity with Olga's spartan retreat was the photo of Don León on Monica's bedside table. It was the same photo, but a different kind of shrine. Gold and silver trinkets fought for space with a miscellany of bottles and jars. Wax from a fat, pink, cherub-shaped candle had spilled like pale blood across the surface of the table.

To justify her incursion into Monica's den, Petra repeated the process she had carried out on the other side of the corridor. The first drawer she opened was full of colourful thongs and uplifting bras. The second was jammed with bikinis that spilled onto the floor as she lifted out the drawer. Picking one up, she noticed a small black velvet bag lying on the carpet. With nervous fingers, she felt the hard shape inside, loosened the red drawstring top that held the bag closed, and tipped out the contents. Emily's topaz ring and the chain for the pendant sparkled up from the palm of her hand. Petra was elated with the find. She wondered how and when Monica had obtained the jewellery. Had she stolen it, or taken it forcibly from Emily, or come by it honestly? There was also the possibility that the topaz set belonged, not to Emily, but to Monica and that she had just lent it to Emily. That scenario was unlikely, though, given Monica's resentment of Emily.

Petra searched the remaining drawers and, purely for completion, made a cursory exploration of the void behind the dressing table. Her fingers brushed against something cold that had been pushed in a long way. Intrigued, she struggled to retrieve the object. A feeling of triumph gripped her as she brought it out. It was Carlo's phone. Monica must have found it in the aft-deck locker. Quickly, Petra replaced the drawer, looked around to make sure she had disturbed nothing else, relocked the cabin door and went to find Carlo.

She could tell by the frown on his face that he had not found as much as he had expected.

'There's nothing here except a stash of DVDs.'

'Yes, but look what I've got for you!' Petra waved the phone at him.

'Fantastic! I feel much better now. Where was it?'

She explained as briefly as possible where she had found the phone and the jewellery.

Carlo added the phone to the pocket of his tailcoat. He still seemed unhappy. 'I'm frustrated because I know there's other stuff on this boat. What I have so far isn't enough for me to call in the authorities. They'll laugh at me. If these were child pornography, it would be a different matter.'

'How do you know they're not?' Petra asked.

Carlo took three DVDs from the top of the stack in the locker. 'I don't for sure, but look at the covers and the titles. These look like soft porn to me, not hardcore. The girls are young, but probably not underage. This one's called "Susana's Sailors" and here's "Rosemary At Sea". And what about "Emily Swings"? You should take that with you, see if it's your girl; and I'd like you to take the two bottles of champagne for analysis too. Drop them at your Embassy.'

'Forget it, Mercutio! I'm not a packhorse and it'll look bad if I'm caught with dubious goods and no passport!' Petra extracted her new phone from her money belt and

206

punched in a text for Tom: "Pls send Ital pport to Can Emb Rabat. Looking for a Lazzara. Petra xx".

'Here's that photo of Emily with Sir Henry's dog I told you about.' Petra pulled out the brochure on paragliding from her money belt and opened it up. The photo of Sir Henry alone stared up at her. She riffled through the pages. 'Damn! I must have lost the other one.'

'Petra, this isn't getting us anywhere. I don't know exactly how long Pablo will be out.'

'What about other areas of the boat?' she asked.

'Since I came aboard I've been taking every opportunity to investigate the living and general areas. Of course, I've only been in Don León's suite in his presence. Captain Juan showed me the bridge and the communications room, and I've scoured the sundeck, the guest suites and boatdeck, and the rest of the main deck, including the rope and tackle lockers.'

'I don't think Don León would risk hiding contraband in his own suite. It would compromise his defence if the boat were searched by police with dogs, for example,' Petra said. 'The same goes for the bridge – he's too much of a seaman.'

'I'm inclined to agree with you. There's not much else down here, just the workshop and the garage. I've already checked the male crew quarters.'

'It might be worth taking another look at the communications room. You said Olga might have a key. I'd really like to see if there's any information on Emily and the summer staff on the computer up there. Don León has to keep some sort of accounting and personnel records, in addition to emails and photographs.'

'Not necessarily here on board. That sort of stuff's handled by the offshore company that owns *Titania*. My salary's paid regularly into my Italian bank account, for example. And there's a danger Pablo will wake up and somehow raise the alarm.'

'If we both go up, I can try the communications room while you check on Pablo. I've been helping you, Mercutio, now you need to help me.'

Reluctantly, Carlo agreed, but when Petra tried the keys on Olga's key ring, none of them worked. Frustrated, she paused to think. Perhaps Pablo had the key or had left it somewhere on the bridge. She looked through the glass panel in the door to the bridge and was about to try the door when the radio crackled to life. Someone was calling *Titania*.

She jumped as Carlo tapped her on the shoulder.

'Pablo's still unconscious,' he said, 'but there's no time to do any lock-picking. We need to get going. Whoever's calling *Titania* will expect Pablo to answer.'

They ran down the circular staircase to the crew level and Petra picked up the backpack she had left at the bottom of the stairs. Carlo collected the plastic bag in which he had placed the two bottles of champagne. They retraced their steps through the engine room where Carlo slipped on his shoes.

'What about the workshop?' Petra asked him.

'The cupboards are unlocked and full of tools, spare parts and cleaning materials,' Carlo said. 'I was down there the other day helping Ángel repair one of the jet skis. We can have a look on our way out.'

It took them only a few minutes to verify what Carlo had already determined. The cupboards were neat, but brimming with boat paraphernalia. On the front of most of them was a list detailing the contents.

'Oh well!' Carlo sighed. 'That's basically it unless we get someone to tear the boat apart. Let's go.'

Suddenly, Petra stopped and pulled at the tail of Carlo's coat.

'What is it?' he asked.

'I want to go back into the engine room. The mid-ship bulkhead is really deep. I noticed it as we came through the door. I know you need it for sound insulation, but it seems unusual. Can we look?'

'I suppose so.'

'See what I mean, Mercutio?'

Carlo stared at the area just inside the engine room door. He went back out into the workshop and reentered, scrutinizing the panels on either side of him. They were nearly a metre wide.

'You're right! It's unusual. Space is always at a premium in a boat, even one as large as this.' He looked again at the flush panels. They were not full height. There was a break halfway down. 'Get me an epoxy trowel, Petra. I'll try and pry off this panel.'

Petra found what she thought was the right implement hanging on a pegboard with other tools and handed it to Carlo. The top panel moved slightly at Carlo's first attempt to dislodge it.

Excitedly he said: 'This must have been done recently. It's too easy!' With a firm upward motion, he levered the panel off. Petra caught it and leaned it against the wall. In front of them was a tower of small, unmarked boxes.

'Eureka!' she breathed. 'This is exactly what we've been looking for!'

CHAPTER SEVENTEEN

The boxes were stacked tightly in two columns. With difficulty, Carlo prized one out and handed it to Petra. There were no markings on the outside of the box, except for a couple of letters and a serial number in the bottom right-hand corner of one end. Petra grasped the box firmly as Carlo cut the tape that held the top together with a utility knife he had taken from the workshop. Carefully, he pulled the flaps open.

'They look like packs of soluble aspirin!' Petra exclaimed.

She took a pack out of the box. The foil pack contained eight tablets, each enclosed in a separate bubble. Carlo used his fingernail to break one of the bubbles and extracted the tablet. Holding it between his finger and thumb, he sniffed it.

'There's no smell.' He held it up for Petra to inspect. It was round, white and devoid of markings.

'I doubt if it's a commercial drug or medicine. They usually bear the imprint of the maker or an abbreviated name,' she said.

Carlo took out another pack and gave it to Petra. 'Take two with you. Ask the Embassy to contact Interpol and have them tested. I'll take two as well.' He took his phone out of his pocket. 'Hold the box open while I photograph it.' He took a picture of the contents of the box and another of the stacks of boxes hidden in the engine room bulkhead. Petra found some tape and they re-taped the box they had opened. Carlo replaced it in the stack then reinstalled the panel.

'That was a stroke of luck!' he chortled.

'What do you mean, luck? It was sheer genius, my genius, don't you forget!' Petra countered.

'Of course, of course! Now you need to get started for Morocco, and I have to get back to the party. If anyone asks where you are, I'll say I saw you with that young Spaniard you were talking to at the beginning of the evening. That'll make El Toro jealous!'

The party was in full swing. The discotheque reverberated with the beat of the music. The gogo dancers, as lithe and savage as tigers, led the frenzy. From the side of the dance floor, Axel watched the dancers shaking and stomping and waving their arms. Some of them looked ridiculous. The professionals, though, were alluring. If it hadn't been for his foot, which still hurt as it had since Petra sent him flying into Theo's pool, he would have joined them, seduced them with his pelvic thrusts, and bedded at least one of them.

Axel surveyed the room. All the daybeds were occupied, the petting getting heavier as the night progressed. Some couples had already disappeared to find an isolated corner out on the terrace or in a less frenetic area of the apartment. If only he had caught one of the silver keys Monica had tossed into the crowd, he could have used one of the bedroom suites that Don León made available to his most important guests. He had seen the discreet entrance to those suites on the other side of the bar. But of course the bitch had deliberately thrown the keys in the opposite direction.

One of the mulattos was making her way across the room. She was probably the tallest, with a fine head, defined cheekbones, full lips and a posture worthy of an African queen. With her was one of Sheik Kamal's men. Axel followed them. He leaned his back on a pillar and withdrew a foil pack from his pocket. Ripping it open with his teeth, he placed the tablet it contained in his mouth, grabbed a beer from a passing waitress's tray and took a long swig. Sheik Kamal was motioning the mulatto to sit down beside him. Axel moved as close as he could. He wanted to hear what they were saying.

Sheik Kamal turned to the Brazilian girl. 'You are a fine woman. What is your name?'

'Paula, Sir, from Rio.'

'Well, Paula from Rio, I am paying a hefty price for the pleasure of inserting this key into your lock. But I can see that you are worth every penny. Mustafa, go and arrange payment with Don León, then I can get down to business. Sit with me, Paula, and have a glass of champagne. Tell me about your country.'

Axel found a wing chair that had been dragged away from its table grouping. He pulled it further into the shadows and sat, brooding and listening to the mulatto's alto voice. Ten minutes later, the Sheik's man returned. 'Deal done, Sire. She's all yours.'

Sheik Kamal smiled as he placed the silver key on the table in front of him. He loved symmetry so he moved it a little to the left until it lay directly in the middle of Paula's ripe breasts. 'Paula, you are a delight: talented and witty as well as sexy. I wish I could use this key to sample what I have bought, but my wife would kill me. She is a Berber princess. Her wrath hath no equal.' He pushed the key towards Paula. 'Take it and set yourself free.'

She looked him directly in the eye and nodded.

Shock registered on the faces of Sheik Kamal's aides. Mustafa began to say something then fell silent. As Sheik Kamal inclined his head to end the interview, a hand shot in front of him. The fingernails were bitten almost to the quicks. Axel curled his fingers round the tiny, slippery key. Before he could pick it up, Mustafa was out of his chair. His left hand closed over the top of Axel's. With his other arm, he grabbed the thief around the waist and hauled him backwards.

'What shall I do with this cur, Sire?' he asked, keeping the pressure on Axel's abdomen. For effect he added: 'Cut off his hand?'

Axel wriggled and kicked. Mustafa tightened his grip and refused to let go.

Sheik Kamal gave a slight shake of his head. 'That malformed dwarf is not fit to look after my camels. Throw him out and make sure he learns his lesson.'

Don León was pleased at the way things were going. The show had been an immense success. The actresses and models would raise a quarter of a million euros for his charitable foundation, the primary aim of which was to help street children by providing shelter and education. One of the leading real estate lawyers on the Costa del Sol had just given him another fifteen thousand euros after discussing his strategy in minute detail.

He scanned the room. Monica was pushing her way towards him through clusters of guests standing, drinks in hand, around the dance floor. He had seen her again with the rival studio owner, dancing with him first in wild abandon then in a close embrace. Olga and Juan were still in the library, intent on their games. Carlo had been running backwards and forwards with drinks, and Petra should be keeping Sheik Kamal well entertained.

'Monica! Where have you been? I missed you!' He pulled her to him and ran his manicured finger down her spine.

She thrust her buttocks backwards to meet his hand. 'Mm, that's sexy. I missed you too,' she said. 'Why don't we take a little break?' She pressed herself harder against him.

'Why not? I need some stimulation after my marathon with our lawyer friend.'

'I'll be happy to oblige, Señor.'

With Monica clinging to him like ivy on an old English manor house, Don León threaded through the crowds, pausing only to exchange a polite greeting or respond to a compliment. 'I must just thank Sheik Kamal in person. He sent Mustafa to tell me that he's donating twenty-five thousand euros to the cause. He's over there,' Don León said.

Monica stifled her objections as Don León steered her to the Sheik's corner. The sound of raised voices reached them as they drew near. Some sort of dispute was in progress. Sheik Kamal was on his feet, speaking in a harsh tone to a furious little man whose arms were being twisted firmly behind his back.

'What's the matter, Sheik? Is somebody bothering you?' Don León asked. 'I'll have him removed.'

'It's Theo's estate manager Axel,' Monica whispered. 'Serves the prick right!' she added under her breath.

'Please do not worry, Don León. A minor incident. Nothing can spoil your wonderful party. My men will take care of him. I can assure you he will not come back in a hurry.' Sheik Kamal gestured to Mustafa to take the kicking thief away.

214

Axel found himself lying face down in the gutter outside the apartment building. He had no idea how long he had been there. His head was throbbing and he tasted blood on his lips. In an attempt to get to his knees, he pushed up on his hands. Pain shot through his ribs, warm blood ran down his cheek and neck. He subsided back into the gutter and waited until he felt able to roll onto his side. Bit by bit, he dragged himself into a sitting position. After another pause, he managed to stand up. Sheik Kamal's men had punched and kicked him, splitting his lips and his already damaged cheek wide open. They had worked him over well, but it was nothing he couldn't take after years in the red-light districts of various ports.

Axel checked his pockets. His key card and multi-tooled penknife were still there. If he had had a chance, he would have cut the grins off the bastards' swarthy faces. He began to limp slowly towards the marina, keeping to the alleys to avoid having to answer any questions from the police or curious late night revellers.

He reached the dock painfully but without incident. *Nemesis* brooded in the dark. In a benevolent moment, Theo had given his Captain and the whole crew the night off.

The vessel was equipped with a state-of-the-art alarm system comprising motion-activated spotlights and thermal surveillance cameras. As soon as Axel crossed the remote-controlled passerelle using his electronic access card, he deactivated the system, switched on the interior lights and made his way to his cabin to clean up.

The thugs had torn the stitches in his cheek so that the wound inflicted by Don León's bitch Petra had opened up. He would have to get it attended to in the morning. In the meantime, he needed to talk to Pablo about their business deal. He took out a handheld VHF radio he had purchased in Palma and struggled back up to the salon. His body ached. He poured himself a stiff brandy to wash down a couple more tablets and switched on the radio. Slowly, he began to regain his strength.

'*Titania*, *Titania*. This is *Nemesis*, I repeat, *Nemesis*. Over.' There was no response. Axel repeated the call to no avail. The signal might be better from the aft deck. He tried from there twice more. Still no response.

He wondered where Pablo was. All was quiet and there were no lights on the yacht next door. Pablo was probably feeling victimized at having to stand watch all night. He might be in his cabin watching a movie. Axel knew the sort of movies Pablo enjoyed. In fact, he suspected Pablo's tastes were very like his own when it came to women. The more the better, the rougher the better. He scratched his groin as he gave full rein to his imagination.

Leaving *Nemesis*, Axel walked past *Titania*'s stern then made a turn to the left along her starboard side, which was parallel to the dock. The pain in his leg had lessened, but his cheek was raw. Still he could see no sign of lights on the main or upper deck levels.

Pablo's cabin was close to the bow on the starboard side. The porthole was completely dark. Frustrated, Axel retraced his steps. For a moment, he thought he saw a glimmer of light through the engine room vents then decided it was a reflection from one of the streetlamps on the dock.

Suddenly, *Titania*'s underwater lights flashed on. In the blue glow Axel saw hundreds of small fish. A second or two later, the lights went off. Glancing down at *Titania*'s swim platform, he realized that the hatch to the garage where the jet skis and other toys were kept was not completely closed. He hadn't noticed it before. Strange, he thought, Pablo must be in there – or if not Pablo, someone else. Careful to make as little noise as possible, he swung down onto the swim platform, cursing as his foot made contact with the unforgiving fibreglass.

'Shit!' Carlo said. 'I was looking for the garage sidelights and I put the underwater lights on instead.' He flipped the sidelights on so that they could get their bearings, then quickly switched them off. Petra followed Carlo towards the stern, blinking to adjust her eyes to the darkness.

The plan, as outlined by Carlo, was for them to return to the fuel dock the same way they had come, replace the dinghy and find the golf cart. Carlo would rejoin the festivities after dropping Petra at the nearby taxi stand. Petra would take a taxi to the bus station in Marbella and wait there for the first bus to Algeciras. She wasn't sure how she would get from there to Tangier without a passport, but would have plenty of time on the bus to come up with an idea.

Ahead of her, Carlo came to a sudden stop. Going down on one knee, he stooped to take a look under the hatch. Abruptly he pulled back, motioning Petra to go the other way, and pushed the inside button to close the hatch. The mechanism whirred.

'What's the matter?' Petra asked. 'I thought we were going out that way.'

'Change of plan. Someone's standing on the swim platform. We'll have to get off from the main deck. You take the Zodiac and I'll distract whoever it is until you're away,' he said.

'It can't be Pablo, can it?'

'I don't think so. He's securely tied up and this guy is wearing black dress shoes. You'd better get going.'

'I'll need to start the motor without a key,' Petra reminded him.

'Take this,' Carlo said, handing her a light-duty jumpstart lead from the small craft repair bench.

Petra helped herself to a speargun from the rack as they passed. It never hurt to have some sort of weapon to rely on as well as her wits. They hurried back through the workshop, engine room and crew area, and climbed the circular staircase to the main deck. There was no sign of Pablo or anyone else.

Carlo took his leave of Petra. 'Good luck. Text me if you can. I'd like to know what you find out.'

'Don't worry, Mercutio, I'll be in touch. Take care,' Petra said as she exited through the port-side sliding door next to the galley.

Carlo paused for a moment to listen. As far as he could tell, no one was in the dining room or the grand salon. Assuming the intruder was still on the swim platform, the best thing would be to leave via the starboard-side door next to the library.

Carlo placed his bag of champagne on the deck and vaulted over the starboard rail. As soon as his feet hit the dock, he grabbed the champagne, veered left and disappeared behind the harbourmaster's office that formed part of the fuel station. He worked his way quickly back to the parkette where he armed himself with several decent-sized stones. Cautiously, he approached the dock wall and looked down at *Titania*'s swim platform. Whoever had been standing there had gone. Then he heard a man call Pablo's name and saw movement on the aft deck. The intruder was walking towards the salon doors. Quickly, Carlo took aim. The first stone hit him right between the shoulder blades and forced him to look round.

Carlo lobbed another stone at the figure on the deck. 'What are you doing aboard *Titania*?' he shouted. With a rush of adrenalin, he recognized Theo's estate manager Axel. He had to draw him away from the port side of the boat to give Petra time to escape. 'I know you! You'll never amount to anything; no girl wants you. You're a complete failure!' he taunted. He made as if to turn away, hoping that Axel would take the bait and follow him into the alley where the golf cart stood waiting.

What happened next took both of them completely by surprise. A barrage of sound shook the marina. Golden rain plummeted from on high, lighting up the port and the surrounding area. They looked up, transfixed.

Petra was poised on *Titania*'s port side about to jump into the Zodiac when the pyrotechnics began. She steadied herself on the rail, dropped her backpack and the speargun into the dinghy, then jumped down after them. It took her a few precious minutes to worry the cowl off the motor. As soon as it was off, she attached one end of the jump lead to the battery and touched the other end to the ignition. A volley of rockets roared skywards.

In the lull that followed, Carlo heard the outboard motor start. Petra would soon be away. Axel must have heard it too, for he turned to his left towards the source of the noise. When another stone hit his shoulder, he hurled it back at Carlo, but continued to move to the port side of the yacht.

Petra looked up as more spectacular fireworks lit the heavens. In the same instant, Axel identified his quarry: it was the whore who had caused all his pain, who had disfigured him so that he was no longer attractive to women, the one who was the root of all his troubles.

As Petra nosed the Zodiac between the two megayachts and their massive fenders, Axel launched himself from *Titania*'s rail. There was nothing she could do to move the small craft out of his way. It bounced under the impact of his weight. He landed badly, but recovered his footing and felt in his pocket for his army knife.

Clear now of the two yachts, Petra turned the dinghy past the fuel station towards the harbour entrance. She steeled herself for the attack she knew would come. Unfortunately, the speargun had slid backwards on the floor of the dinghy and was just out of reach. Now she had only her wits and some of Tom's down-and-dirty tactics to fall back on.

Axel leapt onto her back, grabbed at her throat with his left hand and slashed at her right arm with his blade. Bent double and choking under the force of his assault, she tried to pick up the speargun. Axel continued to slash at her arm. She knew that sooner or later one of his furious lunges would cut through the tough denim of her jacket.

Overhead the man-made stars burst and crackled. Carlo stood speechless under the tree in the parkette. He could do nothing to help Petra, but it might be useful to record Axel's assault. He took out his phone and began to take pictures.

The Zodiac shot forward as Petra accelerated rapidly, then seemed to stop in its tracks as she pulled the throttle back. She accelerated again and twisted the wheel from side to side, weaving like a competitor in a downhill slalom race. At the same time, she thrust backwards with all the body strength she could muster.

Axel clawed wildly in the air and fell to the floor. This was the break Petra had been trying for. She shook herself free and seized the speargun, plunging it deep into the soft side of the Zodiac. She pushed the throttle all the way forward, turned the wheel hard to port, grabbed her backpack and dived over the side of the dinghy into the water.

Watching in awe from the shore, Carlo saw Axel struggle to regain his feet. It was too late. The Zodiac hurtled on at full speed for another ten seconds before tearing itself to pieces on the rocks at the outermost end of the breakwater.

CHAPTER EIGHTEEN

The smoke from Don León's firework display hung thick in the air, obscuring the beach and the water beyond. Sonic booms from something that could have been mistaken for an interplanetary invasion force rattled windows and woke residents. Old Puerto Banús hands gave a mental shrug and simply turned in their beds; those less accustomed to the excesses of the Coast cowered or cursed depending on their personality. Carlo was torn. The desire to go to Petra's aid was overwhelming, yet he knew she could fend for herself and swim better than many fish. He could tell from the state of the Zodiac that any assistance he might have contemplated would have been futile. It was more important for him to return to the party and establish his alibi. Sooner or later the authorities would spot the debris and begin their investigation. Axel had drunk his last drink.

The golf cart was still parked in the alley. With relief, Carlo put the bag of champagne down by his feet, started the vehicle and whirred along the deserted quay at maximum speed. As he approached the security barrier at the apartment complex, Carlo could see no sign of the guard. He left the cart against the wall of a nearby antique shop and walked round the end of the barrier. The guardhouse was empty. High above him, Carlo could see multiple starbursts, the intensity beginning now to build towards the grand finale. He had to find a secure hiding place for the champagne.

A few minutes later, he found what he was looking for: a large, square cedar bush in an unlit corner of the garden. The dense foliage was difficult to penetrate and would withstand any scrutiny except a determined search. He planted the bag with care and backed out of the bush on his hands and knees. He felt a transient pain as a twig scraped the back of his hand, then a series of sharp tugs at his right trouser leg. Something was gripping it hard and not letting go. Carlo twisted round to investigate.

Seeing the movement, the Yorkshire terrier released the cloth and bared its teeth, growling. Carlo stood up and dusted the dirt off his trousers. He bent to talk to the dog. 'Come here, you demon! Mrs. Wunderkind will be looking for you.' The bundle of fur growled more threateningly. A late-blooming rocket burst overhead and plummeted to the ground, falling a few centimetres away from the two of them. Yipping and yelping, the tiny dog took off across the garden. Carlo stamped on the rocket to put it out then ran after the dog. He caught up with it in the hallway to the west wing. There stood Mrs. Wunderkind, wheezing and wringing her hands.

'Oh what a wonderful man you are, Carlo, you've found my Timmy! He's so scared of these horrible fireworks, aren't you baby?' Her chins wobbled as Carlo handed her the dog.

'Timmy's fine, Mrs. Wunderkind. Are you leaving?'

'No. I had to bring Timmy down to… you know.' She threw an embarrassed glance at Carlo. 'He ran away and I didn't know what to do.'

'Don't worry, I'll take you back upstairs. Let me handle it.'

Carlo escorted the nervously grateful lady and her pet back to the scene of the festivities. Monica was in the entrance hall when they arrived. She gave Carlo a sharp look.

'Where have you been? Olga's looking for her jacket. She's cold. She says you hung it up for her.' The words sprayed out like machine gun bullets.

'I went to help Mrs. Wunderkind take care of Timmy's needs.' He squeezed the elbow of the stout lady at his side. 'Olga's jacket isn't down here. I'll fetch it for her. Where is she?'

'Where we all are, on the balcony watching the firework finale.'

'Right. Why don't you look after Mrs. Wunderkind?'

Monica began to protest, but changed her mind. 'I'm cold too.'

'I'll come and warm you up in a minute.' Carlo gave Monica a lascivious wink. He hoped that his luck would hold and that he would be able to drop the keys back into Olga's pocket and deliver the jacket with no one the wiser. As he started up the stairs, he heard Mrs. Wunderkind singing his praises.

'If it hadn't been for Carlo, Timmy would have run away forever. I'm going to increase my donation...'

The discotheque was quiet. Most of the partygoers had had their fill of wine and song. Now was the time to delight the senses with coffee, brandy, cigars or a pipe, to engage in a little desultory conversation and anticipate the hearty breakfast soon to follow.

Monica steered Carlo around an upturned table and chairs, past several daybeds occupied by sleeping couples to one which, after peeping through the curtains, she declared to be available. With the determination of a playful tigress, she knocked him backwards onto the bed. She climbed on top of him, closed the curtains behind her and straddled him with her knees.

'How do you like these then?' Monica undid the white bikini top and allowed her breasts to fall free. She cupped her hands underneath them.

Carlo exhaled. They were splendid. Tentatively, he ran his right hand across the top of her left breast, then did the same with the opposite hand and breast. He fancied that the silicone gave them a rather robust, bouncy feel, different but not unpleasant. Less tentatively, he began to caress them. In the background, Julio Iglesias crooned a heart-rending tale of abandonment and despair. Monica arched her back to bring her breasts closer, offering them to him to suckle like an infant. Carlo could feel his own arousal, slow at first then insistent. Monica's hands were busy undoing his waistband and flies.

'Take off my thong,' she whispered, 'just rip it off.' She thrust her pelvis forward in encouragement.

Trying not to lose the breast on which he was working, Carlo followed Monica's instruction. The slip of material peeled away to reveal a mound as bare as a napalmed hill. He emitted a primordial groan. 'Let me go inside you.'

Monica laughed. 'Not yet baby!' She rubbed herself against him, moving up and down. The torture was exquisite. Just when Carlo thought he would lose control, Monica pivoted on her hands to face his feet. Silicone-free, her buttocks were rounded and firm to the touch. His hands played over the smooth surface and he drew her to him. She pushed herself into his face then dropped her head.

The music climbed to a crescendo. Lost in each other, Monica and Carlo did not hear the approaching footsteps. Only the swish of the rings as the curtains were swept

225

apart caused Monica to look up. A bolt of pure fear shot through her before she felt the mighty slap across her face.

'Bitch! Can't you keep your hands off anyone, even the waiters?' The disgust and hatred on Don León's face made her cringe. He stormed away before she could offer any excuse.

Petra felt the pressure on her lungs as she swam underwater back to the marina, towing the backpack. When she could hold her breath no longer, she surfaced. She was close to the dock that ran along the inside of the breakwater. A steel-hulled tour boat painted red and black was tied up, port-alongside. Petra trod water as she checked for lights and movement. If any crew or guards were on board, the firework spectacular should have roused them. Confident that no one was about, she pulled herself up onto the swim platform, climbed the ladder to the deck and moved into the lee of the aft doors.

In the aftermath of her struggle with Axel, she trembled, partly because she was cold and partly because of the release of tension. She knew she had been a whisker away from being overpowered and killed or, at the very least, maimed by the nasty little man.

The most important thing now was to strip off her wet clothing and shoes. Her backpack had a plastic lining and she had packed a small towel along with the change of clothes. The black leggings, long top and sweatshirt were cold and damp, but still an improvement on her soaked jacket and jeans. Petra replaced her blue deck shoes with a pair of black ballerinas, wrung out the wet gear as best she could and repacked it in the backpack. She would have to dry it out later. A quick comb of her towel-dried hair and she was ready to look for breakfast. Her money belt was a little soggy but had stood up well to the dousing. After taking a final look round, Petra left the tour boat by way of the side access gate, ran up the steps to the top of the breakwater and walked briskly towards the port.

Behind her, the sound and light show continued unabated. Rounding the corner of the boatyard, she jumped in alarm as a black cat shot across her path – a streak of luck, she thought. She could certainly do with it. At this end of the port, far from the fancy boutiques and restaurants, the streets were dark and deserted. Petra felt a huge weight of tiredness settle over her as she searched for a refuge.

In a narrow alley, a hole-in-the-wall establishment catering to locals and fishermen caught her eye. Two old men sitting in the rear looked up as she entered. They exchanged a few words that she could not catch and returned to the serious business of drinking in silence. At the counter, Petra paid for a coffee and a Spanish brandy then chose a table not far from the door. The warmth and the alcohol made her drowsy and her head fell onto her chest.

When she woke with a start, Petra did not know how long she had been dozing. Her coffee was cold, so she bought another, and a dry-looking bun. The sky was beginning to lighten and there was a faint hint of activity to come.

Petra reviewed the dramatic events of the night. She had no regrets about what she had done to speed Axel on his way. She had heard the Zodiac smash onto the rocks and waited for the fire. He had been spared that, but she prayed he was dead.

Mercutio was a dear; she loved him as you would a frustrating, mischievous child, the kind her father used to call an imp. She wondered if he would stay aboard the yacht now that they had found what he was looking for.

She certainly could not return to *Titania*. Her priority was to find a means of getting to Morocco to search for Emily Mortlake. All her instincts were driving her in that direction, though Mercutio obviously thought it was a wild goose chase.

The issue was where to start. A few hours ago at the party, Sheik Kamal had mentioned Marina Smir, well known as a mecca for boaters. If *Lady Fatima* were the yacht Sheik Kamal kept in Marina Smir, she had been a long way from home when she had made her rendezvous with *Titania* in the early hours of Friday morning. Petra hoped *Lady Fatima* would be in Marina Smir when she got there. It might be a long shot, but she had no other starting point for her enquiries and she was sure there was some connection between Sheik Kamal and Emily's disappearance.

Petra was annoyed with herself for losing the photo of Emily posing with Sir Henry's dog. It would have been useful to show people at the marina, to see if they recognized Emily. And if Rosemary's friend Emy had already joined the crew of *Lady Fatima*, she might be able to provide more information. There had been no sign of either Emy or Rosemary since *Nemesis* had arrived in Puerto Banús.

The noise of a motorcycle engine outside the door disrupted Petra's thoughts. Seconds later, a rush of cool air heralded the arrival of a young man who staggered up to the counter. He purchased the usual coffee and brandy and sat down heavily at the table behind Petra. The old men mumbled; then for a few minutes there was silence. Petra could feel the fellow's eyes on her back.

'Hey, baby! Wanna come for a ride?' the biker asked, taking his keys from his pocket and jangling them.

Petra turned slowly to look at him. His eyes were glazed and his face puffy with overindulgence.

'Thanks but no thanks, I don't like bikes.'

With careful deliberation, he unwound the scarf from round his neck and placed his keys on the table. 'Suit yourself.'

Silence fell again over the establishment, broken only by the occasional slurp from the biker. After a resounding belch, he pushed his chair back and lurched up to the bar. Petra heard the bartender direct him to the facilities out back.

On an impulse, Petra stood up and shouldered her backpack. She took a few steps towards the bar and the old men at the rear, saluted them and made for the door. On her way past the biker's table, she lifted the keys and clasped them firmly in her palm.

Outside, the sun was rising. The biker's black and silver helmet was strapped to the pillion of the motorcycle. Petra released the bike from its stand and pushed it along the alley, away from the café. She grabbed the helmet. It was a little big, but would have to do. She strapped her backpack to the pillion, inserted the key into the ignition, started the machine and drove down the street. It was true that she didn't like bikes, particularly since Romeo's death, but she had learned from him how to ride one. To borrow one from a hung-over biker when she needed transport was, she rationalized, doing him a favour.

Petra emerged from the port near the statue of El Marbellero greeting the new day with outstretched arms. As she sped west along the avenue, a plan formed in her mind. She would drop in on Sir Henry to get another printout of the photograph of Emily with Lila. He would have to take the dog out for her morning constitutional, so the earliness of the hour should not be a problem.

At the bottom of the road near the apartment where the party had just ended, there was a huge amount of activity. Private limousines and taxis were lined up two deep waiting to ferry Don León's guests to their homes or their next port of call. To evade the crush and avoid being recognized, Petra took the path along the beach. She would wait at the back of Sir Henry's building until the crowds had dispersed.

In the absence of Don León and the other members of staff, Olga was thanking the partygoers for their generous contributions and supervising their departure. Don León had disappeared in a huff; Captain Juan had gone back to *Titania* to relieve Pablo and ensure that the rest of the crew returned from their night on the town. Of Monica, Carlo and Petra there was no sign. She would take the matter up with them later.

Sheik Kamal's helicopter was late. He had taken his leave of Olga and stood waiting on the roof terrace with his entourage. Shading his eyes to protect them from the red ball of the sun, he looked across the placid waters of the Mediterranean towards the majestic Rif Mountains. This morning there were indistinct shapes above the horizon that could be the ridge of mountains or simply banks of cloud. From the south, he heard the characteristic beat of rotors.

Riding the motorbike up the winding ramp at the end of the path, Petra also recognized the noise. She stopped halfway to watch. The red, white and green Eurocopter swept in over the lighthouse at the harbour entrance, heading straight for the rooftop helipad. Suddenly, it turned to the left and circled round again. Petra guessed that the pilot had seen the wreckage of the Zodiac. Her suspicions were confirmed when the helicopter dropped ten metres as it neared the lighthouse and hovered above the inside end of the breakwater. No doubt the pilot was radioing the authorities. From where she was positioned, it was impossible to see anything other than a tangled mess on the rocks. After a couple of minutes, the helicopter moved off and she saw it land on the rooftop.

Petra parked the motorbike. She sat on a bench contemplating the horizon for a while to plan her strategy. Once Don León's guests had departed, she would go to the front of Sir Henry's building, to Reception, and ask the concierge on duty to call him. She was certain he would be at home. Then, as soon as she had a copy of the photograph, she would ride to Sotogrande and find a boat to take her to Morocco. Her biggest problem was not having a passport.

Sheik Kamal's helicopter passed overhead, flying south towards Morocco. Though she had found his manner irritating, why hadn't she thought to hitch a ride with him? It could have saved her a lot of hassle. From the direction of Marbella, Petra thought she heard another helicopter, probably the search and rescue services. Time was running out.

She stood up and glanced over the hedge into the garden of the property behind where she had been sitting. She was surprised to see a number of policemen cordoning off a large area with yellow incident tape. Her eyes widened as she zeroed in on the source of the activity.

The little dog had been strung up in a tree, garrotted with her red plaited leash. The brown and white body hung lifeless, paws up in a macabre dance. Lila had gone down fighting. Petra blinked back tears. Her gaze fell on the form that lay beneath the tortured animal's feet. The old man was face down in the dirt, his arms extended in a fruitless attempt to reach his pet. The shock alone would have killed him.

Involuntarily, Petra made the sign of the cross. In a corner of the wall, she sank to the ground and buried her face in her knees. Slowly, she began to rock backwards and forwards, sobbing at the waste, the cruelty and the enormity of it all.

CHAPTER NINETEEN

Captain Juan was in a poisonous mood. His luck had run out after the third game of poker. He had carried on playing and drinking with the best and the worst of them, including a jumped-up cheat from *Nemesis* who had won more than his fair share of the pot. Despite a copious breakfast and a large quantity of coffee, his temper had not improved.

His anger deepened as he returned to *Titania*. Lately, he had begun to feel too many undercurrents aboard the yacht. Don León could be generous to a fault; in fact, he paid his Captain well to ignore certain things, but his behaviour was becoming more and more erratic. Juan wondered if Don León were ill. There were diseases, he knew, that sapped the mind as well as the body. He had recently come to the conclusion that he would do well to retire before matters got out of control.

At this hour of the morning, Captain Juan expected Pablo to be on deck, swabbing off the dew or at least keeping an eye on early risers out for a walk or a jog. Instead he was nowhere to be seen. With every area of the yacht that he searched, Captain Juan's frustration increased. Up on the bridge, the surveillance cameras were on. The duty log was blank except for Pablo's scrawled signature at 1800 hours the previous evening. When Captain Juan rang down to Pablo's cabin and the crew lounge, there was no answer. He had already checked the main deck living areas. If Pablo had gone ashore, there would be hell to pay.

As a last resort, Captain Juan climbed the port-side stairs to the sundeck. He opened the skylounge doors to the stench of urine and fear. 'Madre de Dios!' His eyes swept the room. The whisky on the table, the flat screen and the remote control, the bound figure on the floor told a sorry story.

Pablo was lying half on his side facing the sofa with his back against the coffee table. His face was pale under the sailor's tan, his eyes livid. He could make up as many Spanish excuses as he liked, but this could not be explained away.

Captain Juan decided to take his time. For a while now, he had sensed that Pablo was irked by Don León's blatant success. El Toro had a magic touch that turned every endeavour to gold. Pablo wanted some of the gold to go his way. Captain Juan suspected that the envious sailor was setting up alternate networks to siphon off some of the profits.

He sat on the sofa and jabbed Pablo with his foot. 'I guess you came up here just to tidy up, right? Then somebody must have jumped you from behind.'

Pablo made a noise in his throat. Captain Juan kicked him again, hard, this time in the solar plexus. Pablo convulsed and Captain Juan was afraid he was about to vomit.

'Breathe through your nose, you scumbag,' he said. He bent over Pablo's face and used his fingernail to scratch and lift up a corner of one of the tapes covering the sailor's mouth. He peeled it off. The adhesive did not let go easily. Pablo yelped. Captain Juan ripped off the remaining tapes. Pablo squealed and covered his mouth with his hand.

'So what were you doing up here?' Captain Juan asked.

'Nothing.' Pablo inhaled and exhaled heavily through his mouth. The area around it was raw.

'Don't lie to me, man, just look at yourself!'

Pablo hurriedly zipped himself up and gave the Captain a rancorous look. 'I heard a noise. It was the fireworks.' He wiped his nose on his sleeve. 'The whisky was here. Somebody had been watching TV. That's all I remember.'

'You're vermin,' Captain Juan said. He didn't believe Pablo's story for one second, but he was a countryman nevertheless.

It was five minutes before closing time when Tom Gilmore checked in at the ClubWorld desk to catch the early BA flight from Gatwick to Málaga. The unexpected detour to fetch Petra's passport had made him late. Fortunately traffic was light on Sunday mornings.

The arrival of Petra's texted request for her Italian passport had thrown him for a loop. Sent at 4 a.m. Spanish time, it was in his inbox when he switched on his phone. The inference was that she was on her way to Morocco. Since it was impossible to change his flight at the last minute, he decided to go to Puerto Banús anyway, despite the fact that she might leave before he arrived. He would pay a visit to *Titania* then continue on to Rabat, with or without Petra.

By the time Tom's flight touched down in Málaga, he was feeling more relaxed. The breakfast had been decent and the vacant seat next to him had relieved him of any necessity either to be rude or to endure a forced conversation with a stranger. Since he had only hand luggage, he was able to go directly to the car rental agency ahead of the pack. The Category D vehicle he was offered held no appeal. He sweet-talked the rental agent with his high-school Spanish and ended up with a quadruple upgrade for the price of a double.

The metallic blue BMW responded well to his touch. Most of the traffic heading west stayed on the old coast road, leaving the toll road to the serious drivers and wealthier foreigners. In his rearview mirror, Tom saw a black Ferrari join the road and accelerate across two lanes. The low-slung vehicle swept past like a Derby hopeful racing for the post. Tom kept his foot hard on the pedal, slowing only when he reached the tollbooth. After paying the toll, he maintained a more sedate pace until he rounded a curve and glimpsed the sleek black roadster gearing away from a service station just ahead on his right. He was still in with a chance. With his foot to the floor, he chased the Ferrari until reason reasserted itself.

Tom parked the BMW in an underground car park in the centre of Puerto Banús and extracted his somewhat old-fashioned camera from his bag. He had travelled in his best pair of check trousers. To the casual onlooker, he would easily pass for an American on vacation.

The port was already humming. The slight nip in the air was a far cry from the icy winds that had been sweeping the UK, and the sun was strong. Tom strolled along the row of megayachts, marvelling at their diversity. A Maltese-flagged sailing vessel with computer-controlled sails and rigging lay alongside a Chinese junk that doubled as a real estate office.

Further along the quay, he passed a sleek, futuristic mono-hull lying silently next to the megayacht he was looking for. *Titania*'s decks were empty. The challenge was to attract someone's attention and make some discreet enquiries to find out whether Petra was still aboard.

Tom wandered along the dock until he reached a concrete bench at the far end. Perching himself on the bench, he scanned the marina through the viewfinder of his camera then fiddled with the focus. Delving into his bag, he brought out a paparazzi–length lens which he screwed onto the camera. Panning to the left, he trained the lens on *Titania*'s foredeck then focussed on the panoramic window of Don León's suite. It might not have the strength of some of the most modern zooms, but it could still penetrate deep into a room.

Carlo charged out of *Titania*'s starboard-side door like an irate bull. He strode towards the bow and placed himself between the window and the camera's field of vision.

'Hey, you there!' Carlo waved his arms to distract the cameraman. 'This is a private boat.'

Tom lowered the camera. 'I'm just taking a few pictures.'

'Well you can't invade people's privacy like that. If you don't back off, I'll call the police,' Carlo said sourly. *Titania* attracted a massive amount of interest every day from all kinds of people. This man looked harmless enough, but he was being intrusive.

'Sorry!' Tom said, approaching the rail where Carlo was standing. 'I wanted to get some good shots for Petra.'

Carlo stiffened. 'Petra? Whose Petra?'

'My niece. She's working on board. You must know her.'

'Who are you?'

'Her Uncle Tom.'

'Does she know you're in Spain?'

'No. I flew down to surprise her. Is she here?'

Carlo considered his options. The man fitted the description Petra had given him of Tom Gilmore, but he had to find out if the fellow was genuine.

'How did you know she was in Puerto Banús?'

'She sent me a text. Who are you?' Tom asked. The young man on the deck of the yacht did not look like a sailor, yet he was obviously a member of the crew. Tom needed to know how he fitted in with Petra.

'I'm Carlo, the steward. Your niece joined us about a week ago. She's doing fine. She told me a little about you.'

'She did?'

'She told me you were knowledgeable about 18th century Italian antiques.'

'True enough. Petra wears a beautiful black and silver cross, a family heirloom. What else did she say?'

'That you were good at martial arts, but lousy at Pilates.'

Tom ignored the dig. 'Can't be good at everything, but I love horses and the Mounties' Musical Ride. Is she here? Can I see her?'

Carlo decided they had tiptoed round each other long enough. He had to trust Tom. Sooner or later another member of the crew would come on deck and their conversation would have to end. 'I'm afraid she's gone to look for a Lazzara.'

Tom leaned closer. 'Where? When?'

'Morocco, this morning,' Carlo replied.

'Morocco's a big place!'

'That's all I know. Look, Tom, we haven't got long. I'm Interpol. Can you do me a favour?' Carlo spoke urgently to Tom for a few minutes. Then he bent over the rail and handed him a small packet wrapped in a paper handkerchief.

Tom slipped it into his pocket, stepped back and pointed the camera at Carlo. 'Thanks for the info. She's a fantastic boat! Wish I could take a cruise on a yacht like this some day.' He swung the camera round to the left and got a good shot of a buxom platinum blonde making her way towards him.

With her pride hurt and her face smarting from Don León's slap, Monica had hooked up with one of the mulattos whose ministrations had gone some way to alleviating her distress. Feeling refreshed after a few hours' sleep, she was now ready to tough it out aboard *Titania*. She had managed to find a discarded pair of red hot pants to replace the white nano-bikini.

As she sauntered along the quay, she saw an American tourist using a chunky camera to take pictures first of Carlo, then of herself. On Don León's behalf, she marched up to the offender and jabbed a long-nailed finger into his chest.

'What do you think you're doing?' she mouthed.

'I was just talking to your husband, Ma'am. You have this magnificent vessel and lead such a wonderful life! You are very lucky and, if I may say so, very sexy,' Tom said in his most grovelling voice.

'What a creep!' Monica muttered under her breath. The blarney washed over her like the tide at the Giant's Causeway. She looked hard at his thinning salt and pepper hair. 'Haven't I seen you somewhere before?'

'I don't think so. I'd know you anywhere!'

'Just keep out of my way,' she growled.

'Anything you say, lady.' Tom hurried down the dock and joined a group of gesticulating locals heading west.

Monica stepped into her cabin. It was stuffy and, she had to admit, a tad untidy. Time for a clean-up. She picked up a couple of pieces of underwear from the floor and shook them. A small black stone bounced off the top of her foot onto the carpet. She bent down to pick it up. It was square and shiny. Looking closely, she saw that it was a semi-precious stone of some sort. She put it on the table next to her bed. Various rings lay among the clutter. As far as she could recall, none of them had black stones. A half-formed idea niggled at the back of her mind as she continued to pick up stray items of clothing. She had seen somebody wearing a black sapphire or onyx necklace at the fashion show.

Thinking of jewellery, she remembered the topaz ring and pendant she had stolen from the no-good Canadian, Emily Mortlake, a few weeks before. She cursed herself for losing the pendant. She made a half-hearted search through her dressing table drawers for the bag in which she had put the ring and the chain. Where was it? Everything was such a mess. Strangely enough, there had been a message about a topaz on the phone she had found. Whose phone was it and who would have sent such a message? In the run-up to the party, she had had no time to investigate further and had hidden the phone in a safe place.

She knelt down, lifted out the bottom left-hand drawer of her dressing table and felt in behind. The phone had gone. To make sure, she put her shoulder as far as it would go into the void and searched around carefully. She moved back out with care and sat on her heels. The niggle in the back of her mind condensed into a certainty. The black stone had come from Petra's cross.

Carlo whistled his way downstairs. He heard raised voices coming from Olga's cabin. Olga was laying down the law to Pablo.

'If you had suspicions, you should have come to me at once. The trouble with you is you're always lusting after what you can't have. I suppose you thought you could get close to Miss Minx yourself.'

Pablo growled an answer Carlo could not quite hear. He tiptoed closer to the door.

'I tell you, she was up to no good, talking to that old fellow,' Pablo shouted. 'She dropped this photo of the girl that caused all the problems.'

'So? She can't know anything.'

'Olga, I'm warning you, she's a snoop. She'll get in the way and she's much too chummy with the new steward,' Pablo insisted. 'Let me handle her.'

'The steward's all right,' Monica piped up, 'but I agree Minx is dangerous. She's entrapped Don León, just like the other one did.'

Olga glared at her. 'You don't know what you're talking about.'

'Trust me, I do. You want to be careful! He thinks more of her than he does of you. What's more, she searched my room. She left this stone behind.'

Carlo decided that the moment had come for him to interrupt. He retreated to the bottom of the stairs and whistled loudly as he walked towards Olga's cabin. He rapped sharply on the door.

Olga pulled it open, a set look on her face. Her eyes revealed anger with a tinge of sadness. Behind her stood Monica and Pablo, staring grimly at him.

'What is it?' Olga snapped.

'The police are here. They want to speak to everyone,' Carlo said.

'Don León's not to be disturbed. Where's Miss Minx?' Olga asked.

'As far as I know, she's with Don León,' he answered. 'Last time I saw them, they were together.'

CHAPTER TWENTY

Petra could not shake off the terrible feeling that somehow she might be responsible for the deaths of Sir Henry and Lila. The tragedy had occurred so quickly after the lunch they had shared. She had no clue who could have done it or why. It took a particularly vile type of person to inflict such pain and terror on a harmless animal and traumatize its owner. Pablo might have the right temperament, but he was the only one alive Petra knew for certain could not have been involved.

The police had cordoned off the section of garden around the tree and would no doubt have sealed Sir Henry's apartment. She would have to do without the photo of Emily wearing the topaz. She had also been planning to quiz Sir Henry further about Emily's return to Puerto Banús in mid-September and ask him what she had done afterwards. His death changed all that.

The steady beat of rotors drew Petra's thoughts away from the ugly scene in the garden behind her. A search and rescue helicopter was hovering low over the port's outer breakwater. A cameraman was leaning out of the cockpit to photograph what must be the wreckage of the Zodiac. She could see several police vehicles and an ambulance making their way along the top of the breakwater towards the lighthouse. Their activities were beginning to attract attention from passers-by. It was time to go.

Petra picked up the helmet that lay on the ground beside her and stood up. She put it on, adjusting the strap as tightly as possible. There was a lot of play in it. She checked the pillion of the motorcycle. Her backpack was still there. She looked again at the breakwater where three policemen were clambering down to the water's edge.

With a jolt, she realized she was deliberately procrastinating. She was reluctant to mount the motorcycle. It was a powerful machine, silver and black, not unlike Romeo's. Memories of that terrible moment when she had learned of his death engulfed her, compounding her anguish over Lila and Sir Henry. The world was not fair. If there were a God, why did he take away the people one loved?

Frustrated and angry with herself, she forced her mind back to the task in hand. She had to get on the road; the owner of the bike could have reported it stolen by now. In an unconscious gesture, she touched the crucifix at her neck. In the centre where the two pieces of silver crossed, one of the black stones was missing. Loosened by the action of the water, it was no doubt lying at the bottom of the harbour.

A few high clouds were starting to blow in from the west. Petra hoped they did not herald a change in the weather. Her sole protection was the medium-weight sweatshirt she was wearing. It would be cold enough on the bike without wind and rain. And if it did rain, her clothes and the black ballerinas – not the most suitable footwear for riding a bike – would soon be soaked.

She made up her mind to take the old coast road, the N-340, to Sotogrande and look for a sailboat to rent, or perhaps borrow. With under a hundred euros left out of the money Sir Henry had lent her and no proper documentation, she had to find a less than orthodox way to enter Morocco. Hundreds of boats sat in marinas all over the world, unused by their owners for long periods of time. A small seaworthy but neglected sailboat would be ideal.

In her youth, she had done some night sailing on the Med though never as far as the north coast of Africa. She would need a decent nautical chart to determine where to land. Then she could input the latitude and longitude of the chosen spot into her GPS watch and use it to navigate by. It was a stroke of luck that whoever had searched her cabin on Saturday had not found the watch and the other items she had stashed behind the dressing table.

The coast road was quiet. The silver and black motorbike cornered well and Petra began to feel a certain exhilaration. With the sun still sparkling on the waves, the luminous quality of the light and the rich foliage and flowers, the area's natural beauty easily eclipsed the coarseness of the new urbanizations mushrooming along both sides of the road.

The ride to Sotogrande took less time than she had anticipated. She parked in a far corner of the marina, away from the main pedestrian areas. A short walk around soon confirmed her initial impression. Shops, restaurants and modern apartments with picture windows and large balconies overlooked the mooring basin. The port was too built up, the majority of vessels too well kept and the piers too well protected by security gates for it to be an easy place from which to take a boat. Disconsolately, she returned to the motorbike. She would have to find another means of getting to Morocco.

As she drove along the road back to the N-340, Petra noticed a service station. Although the bike's fuel gauge showed a quarter full, she decided it would be prudent as well as a guilt-assuaging thank-you gesture to fill up the tank. If she ran out of fuel, there was a risk that a passing police patrol would stop and ask her for identification.

The service station shop offered a range of convenience foods and a selection of maps. Petra realized she was extremely hungry. She bought a loaf of bread, some cheese and a bottle of water. Had she been relaxing on the banks of the Seine in Paris and not trying to find a way to enter a country illegally, she would have purchased a bottle of red wine instead of the water. She added a map of Southern Spain and Morocco to her basket and paid for it all with her dwindling supply of cash.

Ten kilometres further on, Petra came to a turn-off to a place called Santa Margarita. She followed the narrow road down to the coast and turned west. At the end of a long strip of barren sand dunes, a few fishing boats were drawn up on a small half-moon beach. The hamlet's single restaurant was serving *chocolate con churros*, hot chocolate and fritters dipped in sugar and cinnamon, to a vociferous group of Spaniards.

Petra drove past the restaurant to where the seawall ended in a pile of rocks. She parked the bike in the shade of a large palm, unhooked the strap of her helmet and shook out her hair. Keeping the helmet with her, she collected her backpack and climbed over the seawall onto the beach. She sat with her back against the wall. When she opened the backpack, a mingled odour of cheese and damp clothing greeted her nostrils. It was hard to tell where one smell began and the other ended. First she devoured half the cheese and half the bread. Then, her initial hunger assuaged, she pulled out her deck shoes, jeans, T-shirt and jacket, and laid them over the nearby rocks to dry. She found the village of Santa Margarita on the map she had bought. The Moroccan coast was over forty kilometres away. Further west lay Algeciras, a bustling port with strict controls over commercial and passenger traffic. It would be foolish to try to cross into Morocco from there.

The clouds had stayed high and the sun was hot. Petra covered her face with one hand and began to think through her strategy. Why didn't she go to the Canadian Embassy in Madrid and explain everything to them? Why was she so intent on getting to Morocco? What was she going to do when she arrived?

The first question was easy to answer. She had no proof that anything untoward had happened to Emily, only suspicions and a strong sense of urgency. Furthermore, she was not acting in any official capacity and could not expect any assistance from the authorities. Her involvement in the drug question was coincidental. That was Carlo's baby. She had no right to interfere.

On the second point, Petra's mind was clear. Captain Juan, Don León and Sir Henry had all told her Emily had been invited to Morocco. Those references were not conclusive yet they offered a feasible explanation for her absence that had to be checked out – and checked out quickly. She feared for Emily's safety. Part of that fear stemmed from her encounters with El Toro. By his own admission, he was a manipulator and a ruthless survivor. He used women as playthings then cast them aside; he demanded obedience and total loyalty. She had no doubt he would destroy anyone who obstructed him.

For a moment, she stopped to wonder whether there was any truth in Mercutio's assessment of Don León's feelings towards her. The rational half of her being hoped not, the other half glowed with a guilty excitement.

The third and last point was more problematic. If and when she reached Morocco, she had no real idea of what she was going to do. Everything would depend on what awaited her in Marina Smir.

Petra felt the temperature change as something came between her and the sun. She stared at the map on her lap, keeping her face down. Below her hand, she could see brown feet, dusty with sand. They were men's feet, calloused but not unkempt. Slowly, she raised her head. His shins were lean, the knees bony. A pair of ragged shorts was anchored round his waist with a piece of rope. Emblazoned across his chest on a washed out T-shirt was the name Princeton University. Tousled dark hair framed a sun-beaten face that was full of sympathy and concern.

'You need help, Mademoiselle?' he asked, addressing her in French.

'No thank you, I'm fine,' Petra replied in the same language.

'I think not,' he said.

'No, really, everything's fine,' she insisted.

He shook his head and sat down in the sand, facing her. He hugged his knees.

'I will wait.'

'Please don't,' she said. 'It's not necessary.' She looked away to blink a tear out of her eye.

'A pretty lady like you should not be crying.'

'I'm not crying.'

They sat in silence for a while.

'My name is Karim.'

Petra nodded.

'And yours?'

'Petra.'

Karim nodded.

They sat in silence for a while.

Karim began to doodle in the sand. He drew a boat and some wiggly lines for waves. Then he drew a fish, and another fish. Then he looked at Petra. And drew a question mark in the sand.

'You're a fisherman?' she asked.

'Yes.'

'Where do you fish?'

'Out there.' He waved his hand. 'From here to Morocco.'

'What do you catch?'

'Fish of all kinds. Some big.' He extended his arms as far as they would go. 'Some small.'

'Do you throw them back into the sea?'

'Sometimes.'

'Can I come with you?'

'Perhaps. If that is what you want.'

'Yes.'

'Then you must come and see my mother.' Karim stood up and beckoned Petra to follow.

She folded the map into an untidy package, picked up her backpack and the helmet, and snatched her half-dry clothes off the rocks. She stuffed them into her bag as they walked.

Karim's mother lived in a low, whitewashed house with a brown tiled roof and a single window, a hundred metres from the beach. Karim ducked through the beaded curtain that protected the doorway, gesturing for Petra to wait. She heard the muted sounds of conversation in a language she did not understand, but guessed to be some form of Arabic.

Karim returned to the doorway and pulled the curtain aside. 'Please come in.'

After the brightness of the sun, it took Petra's eyes several seconds to adjust to the dim interior. A woman in a black robe and *niqab* sat opposite the door on a green plastic settee. Her hair and face were completely covered.

249

'Mother, this is Petra,' Karim said, speaking again in French.

The woman nodded.

Petra inclined her head in obeisance.

'Sit, my child.'

Petra sat.

The woman gazed at Petra through the layers of sheer material that fell in soft folds from the headband of her *niqab*. The headdress reminded Petra of a Catholic nun's wimple with a double veil.

'My son wishes to help you.'

'I would appreciate his help.'

'You have a motorcycle.'

'I borrowed it. I must return it.'

'Ah, that could be a problem.'

Petra thought rapidly. 'I will leave it here for five days. On the sixth day, if I have not returned, you must call this number.' She opened the side pocket of her backpack and pulled out a notepad and pen. The paper was damp, but useable. Petra scribbled a note and handed it to the woman, who turned to her son.

'Karim, fetch the motorcycle.' She threw back her head covering to reveal her face. The velvet cheeks were firm, the eyes shrewd. 'Your task is difficult.' She touched a corner of the black cloth. 'You will need one of these.'

'That could be useful,' Petra acknowledged.

'Tonight you will go with Karim. He will show you the way.'

'Thank you, ma mère, I won't forget your kindness.'

'I know you will not. Now you must rest. You have seen and suffered much this day.' The woman laid a comforting hand on Petra's arm and lowered the veil over her face.

Don León deliberately broke his own rule of drinking nothing but Sangre de Toro. The whisky was harsh and burnt the back of his throat. After the third glass, he felt it less. He drank steadily to dull the hurt. After half a bottle, he became morose, then maudlin.

The tears flowed first for his sister. He had never mourned Ana in the conventional way. Instead, he had avenged her violent death with more violence. Inflicting pain obliterated his pain. Success at each level drove him onwards and upwards. It eluded him in one area only: his relationships with women. Like Ana, they abandoned him. So he developed a new modus operandi. He encouraged them, ensnared them, played with them, marked them as his own and cast them off. And it worked. Why then was it changing? Was it the retribution for evil that Father Lucanto had spoken about?

The tears turned briefly to resignation. Then came fury. He loathed weakness. His head was sore. He let out a string of expletives and threw himself onto the bed. Finally, he slept.

His convoluted dreams woke him with their vividness. He heard a helicopter pass overhead and sirens blaring not far away. He got up and pulled his blue robe around him. Through the blinds on the starboard side of his stateroom, he saw a police car and an unmarked limousine draw up alongside *Titania*. He recognized the Chief of Police's vehicle. It must be something important for the top man to be here after partying all night.

Don León let his robe fall to the floor. The hair on his strong chest and lean, muscled legs was thick and black. He walked into the shower and took a deep breath. The jets of cold water stung his back. He let it sluice over his head and face, drowning the curly mane into submission.

When he emerged coughing and spluttering, he felt restored. He buzzed Carlo. 'Coffee in the salon in five.'

Five minutes later, Don León greeted the Chief of Police.

'Sorry to keep you waiting, Chief. The party last night took its toll. I'm not as young as I used to be.' He shook the Chief's hand firmly. 'How can we help you?'

El Toro looked round at the assembled members of his staff. His lips tightened when he saw Monica. 'Do sit down. Carlo, the coffee if you please.'

The Chief nodded his thanks and placed his cup on the glass table. 'Is this the whole crew?'

'These are my senior officers. Olga is in charge of the household staff and Captain Juan, the ship's crew. Monica is my personal assistant and Pablo, First Mate. I presume the rest of the staff are available if we need them,' Don León said, addressing Olga and Captain Juan who nodded their assent. 'So, Chief, what is all this about?' he enquired.

'The body of a white Caucasian male was found a few hours ago. We think he might have been a crewmember on one of the boats here in Puerto Banús.'

From where he was standing behind the sofa with the tray, Carlo had a good view of the others' reactions. Don León was quick to respond.

'We have lost no one. Our chef is from the North of Spain and our houseboys are Filipino. The Mallorcan crew are like my First Mate, not very white, eh Pablo?' Don León noticed the raised redness around Pablo's mouth and chin.

Pablo scowled but made no comment.

The Chief of Police studied the First Mate. 'You look sore around the gills. What have you been doing?'

'Nothing,' Pablo growled. 'Just a little argument last night in a bar.'

'Let's hope it didn't involve the victim.'

'How did this Caucasian die, Chief?' Don León interjected. 'And what makes you think he was a crewmember?'

'His body was found on the rocks inside the breakwater near the lighthouse, close to the wreckage of a dinghy.'

'So he could be anybody,' Don León pointed out.

'He had a handheld VHF radio in his pocket. The coastguard picked up a call to your boat early this morning. Probably not long before he was killed. We're visiting all the boats in port to determine if anybody of his description is missing.'

'Do you have a photograph?' Don León asked.

'Not one you would want to see. His face was completely destroyed. It looks as though he was thrown out of the boat at high speed. What I can tell you is that he was short and slight, with dark hair. He was carrying cash, but no ID.' The Chief looked from one to the other. 'We also found part of a speargun trapped between the rocks. Do you have any on board?'

Captain Juan indicated that he would answer the question. 'We have three we keep for scuba diving. I check our garage and equipment every day. I can assure you they are all there.'

'I'm glad you're so meticulous,' the Chief said with a hint of sarcasm. 'Why only three? Isn't that a strange number for a yacht this size?'

Catpain Juan shrugged. 'There's rarely a call for more than two. What more can I say?'

'Nothing, I would imagine.' The Chief allowed his eyes to rove around the room. 'At about the same time this morning, we discovered the body of another white Caucasian male. This one was elderly, probably in his eighties, medium height, balding with a fringe of white hair. He showed only one sign of trauma: his dog had been hung from a tree with what we presume was its own leash.'

Carlo blanched and sucked in his breath. The Chief turned to him immediately.

'What do you know about that?' he asked.

'Nothing, Sir. It's just too horrible to contemplate. I abhor violence towards animals.'

'And towards humans?'

'That too,' Carlo said.

The Chief shot him a warning look. 'Watch your step, boy! I don't like flippancy.'

'I'm not being flippant, Sir. I hate violence of any kind,' Carlo replied.

The Chief appeared satisfied. 'One last thing,' he said. 'I received an Interpol notice this morning regarding a missing Canadian student. Her last known whereabouts were a megayacht on the Mediterranean, a yacht like this one.'

Before he could continue, Olga asked: 'Do you have a name for this girl?'

'Emily Mortlake, if I'm not mistaken.'

'There's no one of that name here,' she said.

'I didn't think there would be,' the Chief said, studying each of them in turn. 'Just let me know if you hear or remember anything.' He got up to take his leave. 'Thank you for your hospitality last night, Don León. Superb as always.' He shook El Toro's hand. 'There were of course some denunciations regarding the fireworks from some disturbed neighbours, but don't worry, I'll deal with those.'

The senior members of *Titania*'s staff watched the police cars drive away. Don León was more relieved than he would ever show. He made every effort to stay on the right side of the police and knew they could impound the yacht on a whim if they so desired. He was confident of the Chief's support, but at the lower echelons there was a potent envy factor that his enemies could exploit. And he had no doubt that, sooner or later, his enemies would catch up with him.

'Olga, tell Petra to come up and join us. I could do with a little music.' El Toro smiled. 'Carlo, you and she can sing to us for a while.'

Olga looked bewildered. 'Of course, Don León.' She reappeared a few minutes later. 'She's not in her cabin or the crew lounge. I thought she was with you, Don León.'

He shook his head. 'I assumed you knew where she was. There aren't many places she can be. She must be up top, by the pool on the sundeck or in the skylounge. Carlo, go and find her and bring her to me.'

CHAPTER TWENTY-ONE

Word of the police activity in Puerto Banús spread like a highly contagious strain of Spanish flu. Tom spent half an hour taking photographs in the port and jostling for a decent view of the helicopter that was winching the remains of the Zodiac onto a breakdown truck parked on top of the breakwater. Some enterprising boaters had taken their own boats out to get a closer look, much to the annoyance of the rescue workers and the harbour patrol. Megaphones and flashing lights disturbed the peace of the day. All the restaurants and cafés within sight of the action were full of ambulance chasers and gossip.

Tom managed to find a tiny unoccupied table outside a bar facing west at the town end of the promenade. Standing, he could just see the top of the lighthouse. He cadged a spare chair from a noisy group at the next table. Sometimes being single was an advantage.

He ordered a beer and a sandwich and amused himself by listening to the conversations around him. One of the men at the next table was holding forth in a thick Irish brogue about a Rottweiler that had been found hanged in a nearby garden. Apparently, it had taken several hours to die and had woken the whole neighbourhood with its cries. Tom thought it a likely tale. To his right, he could see the unusual domed apartment building Carlo had described.

He calculated that now was a good time to retrieve one of the bottles of champagne Carlo had hidden.

A five-minute walk brought him to the guardhouse at the entrance to the complex. As he had hoped, the porter was watching the local news on TV. On the screen, the harbour patrol boat was attempting to intercept a squad of jet skis coming from the west. The jet skiers were trying to skirt around the patrol boat and enter the harbour. It looked as though some of them might succeed. Tom settled his camera bag more comfortably on his shoulder, gave the porter a cheery wave and walked briskly round the barrier into the complex. The porter barely glanced in his direction.

Tom walked up the drive, through the first archway and into an elevator lobby. He could see the garden through the arch on the other side. A golf cart was parked next to the elevator. A bag of golf clubs stood in the rack at the back of the cart and a lady's jacket lay on the front seat. The elevator light was on and he could hear the mechanism whirring. Madam Golfer must have forgotten something. He would have to wait until she had gone before beginning his search for the champagne.

The elevator door opened. A woman Tom guessed to be in her mid-thirties, richly dressed and holding a pair of designer sunglasses, stepped out into the light. She raised her eyebrows enquiringly at Tom.

'Nice clubs,' he said.

'Callaway,' she replied.

'I'm a Taylor man myself,' he lied.

'Is that your walking stick over there?' she asked. 'It's been here since last night.'

Tom paled. He might be the wrong side of forty, but surely he didn't look old enough to need a stick. It must be the worry of the last week. He glared at the stick leaning on the wall.

Instead of the gnarled, knotted thing he had envisioned, it was a sleek, ebony cane with a silver top. 'So that's where I left it!' he cried, seizing it with glee and great relief. 'It cost me a fortune at Harrod's. Thank you so much.'

'We're lucky to have such good security here, just like in America,' she announced. 'Adiós!'

Tom strode out into the garden swinging the cane. He made a tour of the flowerbeds, looking around carefully as he poked at the odd rose and hibiscus. No one was about. He tucked the silver cane under his arm. Through the viewfinder of his camera, he checked the balconies overlooking the garden. There was no sign of movement. The residents of the building had either moved closer to the police action or were not interested in it. Tom hoped they would show no interest in him and what he was about to do.

Following the instructions Carlo had given him, it didn't take Tom long to identify the cedar bush in the far corner of the garden under which the champagne was hidden. Quickly he went down on one knee. He felt underneath the bush with the cane and heard it strike something hard. The foliage was dense and rough. He plunged his right arm under the bush and brought out a plastic bag containing two bottles. He extracted one and placed it in his camera bag. Then he stuffed the plastic bag containing the other bottle back under the bush. He stood up and dusted himself off. His jacket sleeve was a mess. Still, the job was done. With some regret, he left the silver cane leaning on the wall of the elevator lobby where he had found it. This time when he walked past the guardhouse, it was empty. A sign in the window said the porter would be back in five minutes.

Out of habit, Tom looked at his pocket watch. It was nearly three o'clock. He had not realized how much time he had spent on the champagne recovery project. He would have to hurry if he were to catch the five o'clock ferry from Algeciras to Tangier where the Canadian Embassy was sending a car to meet him.

Up on the toll road, Tom put his foot down. Built in the foothills of the Sierra Bermeja and the Sierra Crestellina, the road was high enough above the coastal plain to provide some incredible views of the sea to his left and of the mountains to his right before it entered a series of tunnels. As he rounded a corner, the Rock of Gibraltar came into view, its rhombic silhouette unmistakable even in the haze that dulled its edges.

Tom pulled into the left lane to overtake a pair of trucks that were labouring up a hill. His next routine glance in the rearview mirror caused him a heart-stopping moment. A few seconds earlier, there had been nothing in sight. The car now being forced to slow down behind him must have been travelling over twice as fast as he was.

The driver of the Lamborghini flashed his lights. Tom felt like sitting in the fast lane and letting him sweat. Then he realized it was pointless. Why be bolshy when the car tailgating you is a 300-kilometre-per-hour orange Murciélago? Before he could move over to the right, the pinnacle of automotive art hurtled past him on the inside, blaring its horn. Tom floored the accelerator and gave chase. After a few minutes, he gave up. Better to arrive alive and without the assistance of the Spanish police.

Once he stopped chasing the Lamborghini, Tom was able to take in the scenery as he descended towards Algeciras. Over the tops of the higher mountain ridges, he

259

caught sight of the swirling blades of enormous wind turbines. As he drew closer to the Rock, it presented a very different aspect, rugged and imposing, a bastion of imperialist ambition.

Tom dropped off the rented BMW then, after picking up his ferry ticket, spent the enforced wait capturing his surroundings on camera. A refinery disfigured the north shore of Algeciras Bay, while squat rows of unadorned concrete apartment buildings gave the town a dated look. The port, though, was fascinating. He particularly admired the way it had been built out into the centre of the Bay, with controlled road access to the marine terminal. Ranks of blue and yellow ship-to-shore cranes towered above stacks of containers waiting to be loaded or unloaded, the great names of shipping stencilled on their sides. Cargo ships, coastguard boats, tugs and ferries of all shapes and sizes manoeuvred in and out of the port in a stream of perpetual motion.

Scanning the rows of vehicles waiting to board the ferry, Tom fancied he could see the orange Murciélago. He had examined a yellow model in the manufacturer's London showroom barely a year ago – not that he could afford to buy one, but he was something of a car buff. What a coincidence if the Lamborghini driver was also going to Morocco!

Throughout the afternoon and early evening, Petra slept the sleep of the dead and the dog-tired. When she awoke, she was ravenous. Someone had placed a white cotton robe on a chair next to the bed and some slippers beside it. Her clothes had gone. She sat up and reached for the robe. Her skin felt slightly salty from her dip in the waters of the marina. The back of her hand gave off a faint oily smell and her hair was rank. Embarrassed, she slid the robe over her head and padded out of the little room. Fragrant odours and the characteristic sounds of cooking came from the kitchen at the back of the house. Karim's mother was preparing a dish of lamb with prunes, one of her son's favourites, to sustain him through the long night at sea. Petra put her head round the door.

'Ma mère, that smells delicious. I'm sorry, I'm dirtying your lovely robe.' Almost reverently, Petra touched the fine fabric.

The black-clad woman shook her bare head. Her eyes smiled. 'Do not worry, my child. Any dirt will wash away. Supper will be ready as soon as you have had a chance to clean up.'

After a hot shower in a stall decorated with blue and brown Moroccan tiles, Petra ate a copious meal with Karim and his mother. Karim informed them that the sky was overcast, but the wind and waves light.

'It will be a good night for our venture. Take these, they are for you.' He handed Petra a heavy fisherman's jersey, an oilskin jacket and a cap. 'Put them on over your other clothes. If anyone asks, you are my young cousin from Cádiz, my mother's sister's son.'

Karim's instructions reminded Petra of her schooldays acting in Shakespeare plays in which the heroine invariably dressed up as a boy and performed amazing feats, undiscovered until she herself revealed the ruse. Now Petra prayed for the same incredible luck.

Karim's mother presented her with a black robe and headdress, and some plastic bags in which to wrap all her clothes before placing them in her backpack. She spent the last hour before their departure teaching Petra enough Berber and Moroccan Arabic phrases to deflect any unwanted attention.

261

'I'm sure I shall get them hopelessly muddled,' Petra said.

'No, my child, you are a natural.' Karim's mother clasped Petra to her ample bosom. 'If your cause is just, you will succeed.'

Karim's boat was the last one on the beach. Petra heard him talking and laughing with his mates in a mixture of Spanish and French as they readied their boats for the night's fishing.

'Always late, our Karim! Too much good food.'

'You need to divorce your mother and find a wife. Then you'll want to get away early!'

The wooden blue and white boat was barely five metres long. There was no protection from the elements and little room for anything besides Karim's nets and other fishing gear. Petra was reassured to see that the outboard motor was clean and well maintained, and the boat sturdy if small. She admired the men who spent hours at sea in such small craft without radios or instrumentation.

Karim placed his spotlight on the floor. He pointed to the bench seat in the middle of the vessel. 'Sit as low as you can. I am going to head south for an hour or so, then locate a friend who will take you the rest of the way.'

'What speed will that motor give you?' she asked.

'In these conditions, about nine knots.'

'Not bad. So we'll be about halfway across when you hand me over.'

'It is better that way. It cuts the risk for both of us and I can be back in time to make a decent catch.'

'How will you find your friend?' Petra asked. 'It's a big sea out there.'

'We have all the necessary equipment, Mademoiselle,' Karim said. He pulled a GPS from his pocket. 'Better than the old compass, but I have that too.'

Petra laughed. Technology was everywhere.

For the first hour, there were other boats around. Occasionally, Karim would call a greeting to someone he recognized. He had eyes as sharp as a cat's, and hearing to match. He explained how the big fishing boats used strong white lights at night to attract the squid.

After a while, out on the open water, Petra began to feel the cold. Karim made no complaint. He could have been relaxing on the beach on a hot summer's day. They talked about his childhood in Morocco, how he grew up in Oued Laou, south-west of Tetouan, and became a fisherman like his father.

'I've met your mother. What about your father?' Petra asked.

'He died when I was a young man.'

'You're still a young man. Do you want to tell me what happened?'

'He was drowned trying to save a woman who could not swim. She had paid to be taken to Spain by boat, but the boat was not very large and the sea was very rough. She panicked and jumped overboard.'

'Was it your father's boat?'

'No. This is my father's boat. It was the boat we are meeting.'

'How did you end up in Spain?'

'My mother did not want to stay in Oued Laou after my father died. She would have become the responsibility of his brother, whom she blamed for the tragedy. My aunt, her sister, lives in Cádiz. First we went there, then we moved to Santa Margarita. Despite the bad memories, I prefer Mediterranean fishing.'

Petra heard the profound sadness in Karim's voice and wished she could bring him some comfort. She was about to speak when Karim put his finger to his lips and cocked his head to listen. 'Shhh!'

Petra's ears picked up the faint sound of an engine carried on the night breeze. The beat was powerful. It was definitely not a fishing vessel.

Karim spoke quietly, with certainty. 'It is a patrol boat.' He threw one of his nets over the stern and slowed the motor to trawl speed. 'They will wonder what we are doing so far out,' he said, 'but they might not bother us. It depends on the mood of the captain and what kind of mission they are on.'

The noise of the approaching vessel became louder. Petra glimpsed its white running light and green starboard light. Karim turned the bow of his boat towards the Spanish coast and accelerated to widen the gap between the two vessels. If they were lucky, the patrol boat would pass far enough behind them to discourage a detour. Karim eased off on the throttle.

'I do not want to go too far in the wrong direction,' he whispered. 'It will make us late.' His boat's engine seemed to labour and they felt a heaviness in the stern.

'Fish!' Karim exclaimed. 'Just our luck!'

'I'll help you,' Petra said.

Loading the fish took valuable time. The patrol boat came close enough to shine a spotlight on them to see what they were doing, then dashed away in the direction of Gibraltar. By the time they had finished hauling in the fish, Petra's hands were raw. When they reached the rendezvous point, they were half an hour late. Karim was muttering under his breath and Petra's teeth were chattering.

After a few minutes' sitting in silence, Karim reached for the spotlight. He switched it on, holding it face down, and picked up a lid from one of the fish storage bins. Swiftly, he raised the light, covered it with the lid, exposed the light again, hid it with the lid, and so on, three times in total.

Several minutes passed. Karim repeated the signal, then sighed. 'I think we are too late.'

As he spoke, a single light flashed.

'Over there!' Petra pointed.

'Yes, that is them.'

Karim had an infallible sense of direction that astounded Petra. Driving a boat at night was challenging even with the best of modern radar and chart plotters to show you where you were in relation to other boats and obstacles. With only a handheld GPS, it was the work of a true seaman to find a tadpole in such a large pond in the dark. Karim brought his small boat port-alongside the larger fishing boat.

'They will throw us a couple of lines. You take the bow. I will take care of the stern,' he said.

Petra caught the bow line and made it fast to a metal hoop.

'Stand on the middle seat and give Jojo your hands. He will pull you up.'

'Aye, aye, skipper! Thanks for the ride. I'll see you in a few days.' Petra touched Karim lightly on the shoulder and reached up to grasp the wrists of the burly fisherman who was leaning over the side of the other vessel. Karim gave her a push up from behind.

'Do not worry about the clothing. Take it with you if you want, or leave it with Jojo. Go well!'

Petra walked her feet up the side of the hull and clambered aboard with relative ease. She muttered her

265

thanks to Jojo, who appeared to be in charge. His crew had already pulled in the lines, and Karim was turning his boat away. Jojo disappeared into the wheelhouse and motioned Petra to follow him. She wasn't sure how much Karim had told him.

'You're late. We nearly didn't wait.'

Petra began to explain, but Jojo cut her short.

'No matter. Sit back there.' He gestured to a wooden seat behind him. 'I'll let you know when I'm ready to drop you off.'

Petra sat without talking and watched him steer. Jojo's boat was equipped with rudimentary instrumentation. He seemed taciturn and disinclined to conversation. Every few minutes he would turn his head and take a look at her. Petra began to feel uncomfortable in his presence.

'Do you mind if I go outside for some air?' she asked.

Jojo grunted.

On deck, Petra felt more at ease. She took a few deep breaths. In the bow was a small lifting crane and a variety of fishing tackle. This was a bigger operation than Karim's. The compass in the wheelhouse had shown their heading to be about 230 degrees. Essentially, they were running southwest towards Mount Hacho on the peninsula housing the Spanish enclave of Ceuta. Karim had told her that she would be dropped on a beach south of Ceuta, a kilometre away from Marina Smir.

Petra walked towards the stern of the boat, sniffing the salt air. She heard a slight noise behind her and turned. Jojo grabbed her. He pulled her roughly to his chest and folded his huge arms around her. She could smell his breath on her face.

He rubbed his body hard against her. 'Yes, I knew it! You're a woman.'

266

Petra struggled against his embrace. He tightened his grip and angled his face towards her. His wet mouth brushed hers. She turned her head to one side and breathed in deeply. Tensing her abdominal muscles, she thrust her pelvis forward into his groin in a strong, swift movement that took him completely by surprise. At the same time, she pulled her face away. The force of her reaction deflated Jojo completely. Cowed, he dropped his arms.

'Leave me alone, or you'll regret it. I'll tell Karim everything,' she threatened. For a moment, he stood facing her and she thought he might try again. Then he spat on the deck and walked away. She had hurt his pride, but his livelihood could be destroyed if Karim took up arms against him.

Two hours later, a faint lightening of the sky and freshening of the wind heralded the onset of a new day. A crewman came to fetch Petra from where she had been resting in the stern of the boat, as far as possible from the wheelhouse. The headland of Cabo Negro loomed in the distance.

'I can't go much further in than this or we'll run aground,' Jojo complained.

'Karim said you would drop me on the beach,' Petra protested.

'Karim hasn't been here lately. Things have changed.'

Petra thought things might well change for the worse if she pushed her luck any further with this man. She wondered if he was Karim's uncle, the one his mother disliked.

'Fine. Take me in as close as you can.' She stood at his shoulder as he slowed the boat to idle and inched forward. At a guess, they were two hundred metres from shore when he put the engine into neutral.

'That's it.' Jojo scrutinized Petra. 'You're a beautiful woman. No hard feelings?'

'No.' Petra shook her head. 'I'm surprised you could tell under this gear.'

'I have an eye for the best,' he said modestly.

She took off the cap she was wearing and shook her hair out. Then she removed the oilskin. 'Give that back to Karim. Thank him for the cap and the jersey and tell him I'm fine.'

'Right. I'll take you to the stern. That'll be the easiest.' He stood by with a proprietorial air as she dived off the boat into the sea.

For the second time in twenty-four hours, Petra found herself in cold water. Despite her heavy clothing, she surfaced quickly. The long hours spent in rigorous training with her Marine Unit had given her the strength as well as the technique required for survival swimming. She retrieved the backpack Jojo threw after her and struck out for the shore.

CHAPTER TWENTY-TWO

For Don León, crossing the Strait of Gibraltar was always a moving experience. There was something about going from one continent to another that captured his imagination, especially when one of them was Africa. He tipped the man in charge of the car deck handsomely to look after the Bat and reminded him that he would be returning in a day or two. If there were no problems, the man could be assured of an even larger reward.

Having once again bought what he wanted, El Toro made his way to the Club section. His seat on the port side, though not next to the window, would give him a good view of the lesser-known face of the Rock. He had just made himself comfortable and settled down to think when a strident "Excuse me" in a transatlantic accent announced the arrival of the occupant for the window seat. With ill grace, Don León stood up to let him pass. The man looked like an American tourist with a large camera bag and lurid check trousers. Don León closed his eyes firmly to eliminate any possibility of conversation.

During the ferry crossing, Don León had ample time to reflect on his motives for his precipitous decision to visit Morocco. As soon as the Chief of Police had left *Titania*, a thorough search of the vessel had failed to reveal any sign of Petra. He had ranted and raved like a madman.

The force of his reaction had stunned his staff as well as himself.

'When was the last time you saw her?' Olga had asked him, as soon as he had quietened down.

He recalled with great clarity Petra's presence at the party: the shape of her face as she talked to the handsome young Spaniard; finding her out on the terrace watching *Nemesis* enter the port; her outstanding performance in the fashion show; and finally, leaving her to entertain Sheik Kamal for a while. Clearly, the Sheik had abused his hospitality and spirited Petra away against her will. His action left Don León no option but to go after her. It was a matter of pride. His girls were his to control. In his reasoning and rationalizing, he still did not admit to himself what Carlo had divined.

The other disturbing thing had been the Chief of Police's reference to the Canadian student who had preceded Petra. He would have to let Sheik Kamal know they were looking for her.

From his frequent visits to Tangier, Don León knew the fastest and safest way to cut through the city centre. He followed the road west to Cap Spartel through the ritzy suburb of La Montagne to the pine-covered headland where Sheik Kamal had built a fabulous villa. He had not alerted the Sheik to his visit, preferring to surprise him. If Sheik Kamal had taken Petra away with him in his helicopter after the party, which seemed the most likely explanation for her absence, she might still be at his villa.

The Lamborghini roared up the private road to the massive wooden gates that blocked the way to Sheik Kamal's domain. Don León opened the window of the Bat to speak to the uniformed guard who had stepped out of the guardhouse at the first sign of the car. As far as the guard knew, Sheik Kamal was expecting no visitors that evening. After a rapid conversation with Don León and a confirmatory telephone call to the main house, the guard logged him in and let him through the gate.

The driveway continued upwards through thick stands of trees before emerging onto a plateau overlooking the Strait of Gibraltar. There Sheik Kamal had erected a veritable palace surrounded by manicured gardens and tiered marble terraces. As soon as the car came to a halt, the brassbound oak door was pulled open. Sheik Kamal himself in a lounging robe appeared in the doorway.

'Don León! Welcome! Please come in. I never dreamed I would see you again so soon. To what do I owe this unexpected pleasure?' Sheik Kamal embraced him in the Arab manner.

'I'm sorry to arrive unannounced, Sheik. I hope I'm not disturbing you.'

'Not at all. I am happy to be able to return your hospitality.' Sheik Kamal studied his surprise guest, whose usual poise appeared to have deserted him.

'My apologies once again, but there are some developments I think you should know about.' Don León scanned the foyer with its circular staircase and elaborate carved panelling as if he might see Petra step out from behind a pillar.

'Developments? That sounds most ominous, my friend.' Sheik Kamal clasped El Toro's arm. 'Let us relax for a while. I am sure you are tired. We will enjoy a drink and a good meal, perhaps some entertainment. Then we can talk.'

Don León allowed himself to be escorted into the lounge, which was furnished with low purple and gold plush sofas. He stood at one of the full-height windows for a few minutes, losing himself in the splendour of the sunset sky and the dramatic ocean view.

271

Sheik Kamal indicated the sofa next to his facing outwards. 'Come, Don León. Take the weight off your feet.' He clapped his hands and ordered the best Moroccan red wine for his guest and champagne for himself from the white-coated waiter who instantly appeared. 'You put on a memorable show last night. One could lose oneself for days in those Brazilian girls. Tell me how you found such beauties.'

Though he was avid for information about Petra, Don León knew that the niceties had to be observed. Sheik Kamal would not permit him to express his concerns until they had "chewed the fat" awhile, as he supposed the Americans would say. The conversation ranged back and forth as they drank to the accompaniment of some low-key jazz, which Don León infinitely preferred to the wailing Arabian music. Another waiter brought a plate of *briouates*, triangles of pastry stuffed with herbed goat's cheese, pigeon, spicy fish and other savoury fillings. A little later, after a selection of traditional main dishes washed down with more wine, Don León attempted to raise one of the topics that had brought him there. Sheik Kamal brushed him off with a wave of his hand.

'Please, please, Don León. I beg your indulgence. The evening is still too young for us to engage in serious discussion. Alisha will serve us some of your favourite desserts along with the most fragrant mint tea.' He nudged Don León. 'She is a stunning young woman from one of the desert tribes, a true desert rose and a consummate belly dancer. I know you will enjoy her company.'

Not for the first time Don León felt manipulated by Sheik Kamal, a sensation he abhorred. The pressure was subtle but insistent. It was served up with impeccable politeness and the occasional touch of irony, making it all the more difficult to resist.

The girl Alisha was indeed a beauty. Her light cream skin, lustrous long dark hair and soulful dark eyes rimmed in kohl reminded him a little of Petra. His eyes wandered round the room. In the subtle light thrown by the coloured glass hanging lamps, he could almost feel Petra's presence.

Alisha returned in the diaphanous costume of the belly dancer, swaying like a snake to the hypnotic music, jiggling the coins on her hips. She turned the full force of her display on Don León, contorting her hips and belly, favouring him with intimate glances, inviting him to reach out and touch her. He had little doubt this was Sheik Kamal's doing.

Like a spider spinning its silk tighter and tighter to bind the fly, the dancer wove ever more intricate patterns designed to charm and entrap. The tempo and pitch of the music increased until the girl's body became lost in a whirl of motion. As the final note sounded, she prostrated herself in front of Don León.

For a moment the silence was absolute. Then he sighed. The sigh was a complex expression of admiration for the dancer, relief that the music had ceased and frustration that he had made no progress in locating Petra.

'Did I not tell you she was a marvel?' Sheik Kamal asked. 'She is your companion for tonight if you want her. I presume you will stay with us overnight, Don León?'

The excesses and emotions of the past twenty-four hours had left behind a deep well of fatigue that Don León knew could impair his judgement. 'Thank you, Sheik. I shall be pleased to accept your generous offer, but I would rather sleep alone.'

'As you wish.' Sheik Kamal shrugged. 'You may change your mind later. Now join me in a pipe.' He indicated a round brass table in the corner of the room on which sat a hookah of impressive proportions.

'I'll take another glass of wine instead, Sheik. You go ahead with the pipe.' Don León knew that his refusal to participate in the ritual would be considered ill-mannered, even threatening. It was a deliberate counterstroke to Sheik Kamal's machinations.

He could no longer contain his impatience. 'You must know why I'm here, Sheik,' he said.

'My dear friend, I have no idea. Tell me.'

'You have taken something that belongs to me and me alone.'

'I have?' Sheik Kamal looked puzzled. 'What might that be?'

It was as if Don León had never heard the question. 'Without my permission!' he ground out. 'I sent her only to entertain you for a while.'

The pained expression on Sheik Kamal's face turned to a sly smile. 'Ah! Now I understand. You have come looking for someone.'

Don León cleared his throat. 'Yes, but that is only half of it.' He drew himself erect and said formally: 'I insist on her immediate return.'

Sheik Kamal leaned forward and banged his fist on the table, making the pipe jump. 'I like neither your tone nor to be accused of things I have not done, least of all stealing. The girl you are looking for – I presume Miss Minx is the one – is not with me. I have no idea where she is. I have not seen her since early this morning.' Sheik Kamal explained the circumstances of Petra's sudden departure to change her clothes. Don León looked perplexed and unconvinced.

'I can see that you do not believe me,' Sheik Kamal continued. 'I can assure you Miss Minx is not here, nor at my workshop.'

'Which brings me to the second issue,' Don León interrupted. 'Emily Mortlake.'

'Another troublemaker!'

'Miss Minx is not a troublemaker. She and I have a special relationship.'

'Of course, Don León, forgive me.' Sheik Kamal was forming a good idea of what that relationship might be. 'Your two feisty Canadians hardly fit their country's peacekeeping image,' he said. 'Feistiness can be a curse if it cannot be channelled. But I am sure you will agree that Emily Mortlake was in a much more docile frame of mind when you took her back in mid-September, after Zahra had used her in the workshop.'

Don León nodded. 'Her attitude had improved, though she was still rebellious – and jealous. Some of them are tough nuts to crack.'

'The problems of the harem, my friend. When women feud, only ill can come of it.'

'How right you are, Sheik. And I have to tell you that Interpol has circulated a notice regarding Emily's disappearance. The police came looking for her this afternoon.'

'I thought she had already returned to her studies.'

Don León shook his head. 'I gave Olga instructions to send her back to Zahra. I didn't want to bother you with this matter, Sheik, knowing that your wife Fatima has insisted you distance yourself from the workshop. But now we must wine and dine Emily and arrange for her transport back to England. She'll only remember the good parts. If she has any recollection of the rest, it will seem like a bad dream.'

'You may be trying to lock the cage after the bird has flown, my friend. Mustafa advised me a few days ago that one of the girls has run away. My son Ahmed is picking up a replacement tomorrow. He manages the workshop now, although sometimes I think he is too soft. We can go and see for ourselves.'

'Damn it, Sheik, you'll bring trouble on all our heads!' Don León glared at his host. 'And I'm sick and tired of women!'

'Except for Miss Minx,' Sheik Kamal reminded him.

The touts in Tangier were not as aggressive as Tom had been expecting. He managed to exit the marine terminal with minimal annoyance until a small boy on the lookout at the main door grabbed his overnight bag. Tom was close to losing the tug-o'-war when he found a packet of chewing gum in his pocket. As soon as he handed over the loot, the boy dropped his end of the bag and fled. The driver from the Canadian Embassy was waiting with a placard and the car right outside the terminal building. Tom was thankful for diplomatic immunity as they pushed their way through the chaotic city traffic.

After the first hour in the Embassy car, during which he tried to put his thoughts in order, Tom fell asleep. It was past ten o'clock when the driver stopped at the wrought iron gates to the Canadian Ambassador's residence in Rabat and requested admittance.

'Good to see you, Gilmore, it's been a long time.' The Ambassador shook Tom's hand warmly.

'It has indeed, Sir. I was astonished to see your name on the staff list. I thought you were still in the Middle East.'

'I was, then they offered me this posting when my predecessor took early retirement for health reasons. I've always been fond of the Maghreb so I jumped at the chance. Good people, the Moroccans.' The Ambassador looked past Tom to the car standing at the bottom of the steps. 'I thought you were bringing a young lady with you.'

'Yes, Sir, Petra Minx. That was my intention. However, when I reached Puerto Banús, I found out she was already on her way here. Has she made contact?'

The Ambassador shook his head. 'Not to my knowledge. Of course, the Embassy is closed on Sundays. Once you've freshened up, you can bring me up to date.'

Over a late supper, Tom and the Ambassador talked first about their early days together in the diplomatic service, then their parting of ways and the intervening years.

'Why does the time go so quickly?' Tom asked.

'Because we're so deeply involved in everything we do,' his senior replied. 'It doesn't matter what it is, we give it our all. Like you, with this case.'

'It's not my case, I was only asked to render assistance, but I have a moral responsibility and commitment that I can't just shrug off.' Tom hoped he was making his point clear. The Embassy wine did not help.

'You always were one of the most conscientious ones, Tom.' The Ambassador leaned back in his chair. 'I've arranged with the British Embassy for you to visit the unidentified girl tomorrow morning. One of their people will meet you at the hospital at eleven. The doctor has requested that you keep the interview short. She's under sedation so I don't know if you'll get the information you want.'

'I'm not after information. She might be the girl Miss Minx is searching for, the one who disappeared a few weeks ago in Spain or Morocco.'

'Don't get your hopes up too much, Tom,' the Ambassador said. 'In this turbulent and over-populated

277

world of ours, dozens of children and young women go missing every day, and the tragedy is they're rarely found.'

The Ambassador's words rang in Tom's head as he accompanied the doctor and the British Embassy official through the labyrinthine corridors of the hospital next morning. He took the opportunity to ask the doctor what they had found out about the girl. The doctor had little to relate.

'She was brought in two days ago, clearly in pain and incoherent. I prescribed painkillers and a sedative, and placed her under observation while we carried out various tests. She had a very bad first night, with hallucinations and a fever. Last night was better.'

'I'm sure you tested for drugs,' Tom said.

'Of course. The panel test was negative, although she could have taken some local concoction that it would not detect.' The doctor paused as his pager beeped.

'Did she say anything of interest during the hallucinations?' Tom asked.

'The night nurse said she was moaning and crying out to be left alone, then calling for her bustier.'

'Her what?'

'Her bustier, probably the one she was wearing under her T-shirt when she was admitted. Quite a showy, sequined affair. She has an infected tattoo just above her left breast.' The pager rang a second time. 'I have to attend to a case in emergency. This is her room. The nurse will come in when your time is up. Any problems, just press the alarm button by the bed.' The doctor opened the door for Tom and his companion then hurried off.

The girl lay facing a curtained window. She was curled up in a semi-foetal position, one thin shoulder jutting out from under the sheet. A tangled mass of washed-out blonde hair covered the pillow. The Embassy official seated himself on a chair by the door. Tom tiptoed round the bed. He scrutinized the long, narrow face with its high cheekbones. Blank blue-grey eyes stared back at him. Tom put out a hand as if to touch the girl's shoulder. She flinched.

'I'm not going to hurt you. You're quite safe now. I'd like to help you remember who you are.' Tom squatted down by the bed. He smiled with as much compassion and gentleness as he could muster, while his mind raged at the severity of the trauma that had caused the girl to block out not just the bad memories but all recollection.

'Your friend Amy sent me to see you. She wants you to get better. Then you can take that holiday together in Switzerland that you'd planned.' Tom smiled again. The girl's expression did not change. 'Amy gave me a very nice picture of you.' He extracted a folder from the camera bag he had placed on the floor beside him. 'You look really pretty here on the river.'

Tom showed her the photo with a sinking feeling in his heart. She looked like a wounded gazelle, shy, frightened and vulnerable. And he knew she was not Emily Mortlake. The shape of the face was not right, the eyebrows were too dark and the hair too often dyed. He had hoped, by talking about a friend, to elicit some response.

For a moment, there was nothing, then a tentative hand reached out for the picture. Tom gave a short intake of breath. The girl's fingers and the back of her hand were covered with intricate patterns in reddish brown.

The Embassy official who had been watching in silence spoke with quiet authority. 'It's a temporary henna tattoo in Berber style. Very popular with foreigners as well as Moroccan women.'

Tom thought the doctor had said the tattoo was over her breast. He waited while the girl examined the picture. Finally, she looked up and handed it back to him with a slight shake of her head.

Taking care not to startle her, Tom pointed to the designs on her hands. 'How did you get those?' he asked.

There was no answer. He tried again. 'They're beautiful, so delicately executed, the work of a true craftsman!' he enthused.

With a sudden movement, she pulled the sheet aside and turned down the top of her nightgown. A patch of oozing black blisters disfigured her chest.

'God in heaven! What's that?' The angry sympathy in his voice swept away the last of the girl's defences and she closed her eyes. A tear trickled from under her right eyelid then the first sob racked her body.

Tom pressed the bell and the nurse came running. He was cradling the distraught girl in his arms. 'I'm afraid I've upset her terribly,' he said.

The nurse reassured him. 'It's what she needs. Doctor will be pleased. You're a clever man.'

Tom brightened at the compliment. 'All in the line of duty, Ma'am. May I stay with her for a while?'

'If you could, I'd appreciate it. I'll be back with the doctor as soon as possible.'

Little by little, the girl's sobs subsided and she began to talk. Her recollections were disjointed. She was certain her name was Melanie, but couldn't tell Tom her age or birthday. She thought she was British, but wasn't sure.

Tom probed gently. Was she a student? No. How come she was in Rabat? She had no idea. Had she been travelling or working? She hesitated. Working. What kind of work? In a factory. What type of factory? Her response was slow. Lingerie, she whispered. That could explain why

280

she was wearing such an exotic piece of underwear when she was admitted to the clinic, he thought.

The Embassy official, who had moved his chair to the side of the bed, confirmed that there were many garment workshops in Morocco. The country was becoming popular with young European fashion designers for the manufacture of their clothing, and approximately a third of working women were employed in the growing industry.

Tom pressed Melanie for more information. Could she remember where the factory was? How long had she worked there? She shook her head in despair. The patchiness of her memories was scary.

Tom greeted the doctor's arrival with relief. 'What's the prognosis for her now?' he asked.

'Recovery can be very slow in these cases. She may continue to block out details relating to the trauma even if she remembers other events, names and places. She needs to be taken home or into a caring environment where her self-esteem can be restored.'

After discussion with the Embassy official, Tom decided to return to London on the next available flight. The British Embassy would circulate a new Interpol notice now that the girl's first name was known. A call to the Canadian Ambassador confirmed that there was no news of Petra, but the Embassy would hold her passport.

Tom was still in possession of the Cuvée Ana León he had retrieved from the garden in Puerto Banús, as well as the foil pack of drugs Carlo had given him. Although they had not raised any eyebrows when he entered Morocco, he would feel much happier when he could hand them over to the appropriate authorities for analysis. He also needed to let Petra's boss A.K. know that the girl in Rabat was not Emily Mortlake and that Petra herself was missing. She had not responded to his urgent text message and if he

281

didn't hear from her soon, he would have to consider requesting an Interpol alert himself, to try and determine her whereabouts. He was not looking forward to A.K.'s reaction to the news.

CHAPTER TWENTY-THREE

By the time Petra emerged from the sea, the sun had risen. To her left, the small fishing port of M'diq nestled in the lee of Cabo Negro. Karim had explained that Marina Smir lay on her right, to the north. The Coast was much more built-up than she'd imagined. She had expected a vast expanse of pristine sand edged with palms and few signs of habitation. Instead, villas and apartment blocks lined most of the shore. At this hour, there was no one on the beach. Water dripped down her legs from Karim's sodden jersey. She pulled it over her head and wrung out the heavy wool. The fine sand clung to her wet feet as she searched for a place to rest and dry off.

A few minutes' walk brought her to a less developed area, then to a structure that appeared to be derelict. Whether or not it had ever been finished was difficult to determine. The surrounding wire fence had been breached many times. Petra found a half-built room facing the water where the sun would provide at least some warmth. In fresh clothes that were only slightly damp, she attacked the dried fruit and cake supplied by Karim's mother. Tiredness enveloped her after the tension of the voyage. Her head nodded and she dozed off.

After two hours' sleep, Petra woke feeling refreshed and ready to investigate. She sauntered along the beach past an imposing white building that could only be a hotel, garnering a few strange glances from a security guard and some early morning sunbathers. A short distance beyond the hotel, she came to the entrance to what she assumed was Marina Smir.

The channel into the marina was marked with a row of red buoys. Petra watched a seventeen metre Sunseeker execute a wide turn round the end of the outer breakwater then hug the inside of the wall, keeping the red buoys on its port side. Silting was clearly a problem on the beach side of the marina. She remembered that in Europe red buoys had to be kept on the left when returning to port, not "red right returning" as in North America. It would make life easier and safer if globalization also meant global standards, she thought.

The marina was crowded with boats, ranging from basic sailing dinghies to glamorous motor yachts. Petra scrutinized the larger ones. It was an easy matter to spot *Lady Fatima* riding in pride of place in the berth next to the harbourmaster's office. With her sleek, smooth lines and swooping side windows she was a quintessential Lazzara.

Petra took a seat on the terrace of a nearby café, from where she had an unobstructed view of the Lazzara and the port beyond. She ordered a coffee and settled down to wait. Most of the activity seemed to be on the other side of the marina, along the row of restaurants and shops that occupied the ground floor of the first line of apartments. The buildings were lower, flat-roofed, less dense and squarer than their counterparts in Puerto Banús, the walkways wider and the whole port much more open.

The Lazzara's decks, shining white in the clear North African light, were empty. It was impossible to tell if anyone was aboard. Petra paid for her coffee and stood up to leave. As she did so, a figure appeared on the aft deck. It was Rosemary, the redhead from Theo's boat *Nemesis*.

She looked relaxed and at home though it was only five days since they had all been aboard *Nemesis* in Palma, Mallorca. Petra had not realized Rosemary was joining Sheik Kamal's staff as well as Emy. She wondered if Theo had dropped them off in Morocco before attending Don León's extravaganza in Puerto Banús.

Petra gave a low whistle to attract her attention. 'Rosemary? Is that you?' she called. She had to find out if Sheik Kamal was on board. If so, she would make a fast exit.

'Petra! What on earth are you doing here?'

'Looking for someone. I'll explain later. Are you alone?'

'No, Emy's with me.'

'Is anyone else on the yacht?'

'Not at the moment. The Captain has gone into Tetouan for supplies. Come aboard.' Rosemary crossed the aft deck to lower the passerelle.

Petra hugged her tightly.

'Emy will be delighted to see you! You were such a comfort to her that night. It seems ages ago, yet it was only last Wednesday,' Rosemary exclaimed. 'We're much better off here. Our quarters are right below where we're standing,' she added, tapping the aft deck with her foot. 'They're tighter than they were aboard *Nemesis*, but far safer.' She led Petra down the port-side stairs to the swim platform. 'That door in the centre gives access to our area.'

Petra stopped in amazement as they reached the bottom of the stairs. 'Isn't that a Quadski?' she asked, pointing to the black and orange machine sitting in a cradle on the hydraulic swim platform. 'I've seen the prototype on the Internet.'

'If you say so,' Rosemary said doubtfully. 'It looks brand new. Emy might know more about it. She's been keeping out of the sun and doing a lot of reading. Her face is healing, though it's still very tender. She also wants to stay away from the Captain. She's very leery of men at the moment.'

Emy's face had turned from black and blue to purple and yellow. It was not a pretty sight, but Petra knew that with the rapid healing of youth, she would soon regain her physical health. The psychological scars from Axel's beating and attempted rape would take longer to fade.

'You don't need to worry any more about Axel,' Petra told them. 'He was killed on Sunday night in a boating accident in Puerto Banús. Too much partying and not enough self-control!' She deemed it better not to reveal her own part in his demise.

Emy was ecstatic. 'Serves the bastard right! No one will miss him.'

'Too much partying is right!' Rosemary chipped in. 'He was very sorry for himself last Thursday after Theo's party on Wednesday night. Somehow he tripped, fell into the pool and concussed himself. And he had a great big gash in his cheek. The fuss he made about it, you'd think someone had attacked him.' Rosemary directed her gaze at Petra. 'You didn't tell Theo about Axel beating Emy up, did you?'

'No, I didn't. I knew you'd prefer me not to,' she said. And I didn't want to draw attention to Axel's absence after I threw him into the pool, she thought.

'We made up a story about a jealous boyfriend that Theo seemed to buy,' Rosemary explained. 'When I told him I wanted to leave with Emy, he just said he would call Sheik Kamal and arrange it.'

'Have you seen the Sheik yet?' Petra asked.

'No,' Rosemary replied, 'but he's sending someone at lunchtime to pick Emy up. She's had enough of boating.' Rosemary looked across at her friend for confirmation.

'That's right. I'm going to do some modelling for Sheik Kamal,' Emy said.

'For Sheik Kamal? Modelling what?' Petra asked. 'And where?'

Emy spread her hands. 'I don't know. The person who's coming to fetch me will have all the details.'

Petra failed to understand the mania for modelling that drove young girls to compromise their safety and wellbeing. Their desire for self-abasement seemed infinite. From the beginning, Emily Mortlake had been seduced by the idea of modelling. It was a euphemism that hid a multitude of sins, as she herself had found out. Now Emy was jumping into the same bottomless pit. She appeared to have no idea where she was being taken, nor by whom. Would she disappear too?

'Do you think what you're doing is sensible?' Petra asked her.

'What options do I have? I have to earn my keep, and I'll get to see more of the world,' Emy said defensively.

Petra shook her head in disbelief. 'I'd like to wander round the port for a while to get my bearings,' she said.

'Go ahead,' Rosemary replied. 'It's a lovely morning and we have jobs to do.'

A hawker in a hooded pink and green *jellaba* accosted Petra as soon as she turned towards the working end of the marina. The woman's face was lined, her eyes greedy. Petra waved the tawdry beadwork away. She had no use for it. A few seconds later, she changed her mind. 'How much for all your necklaces?' she asked. The negotiations were concluded swiftly. The woman snatched at the ten-euro note and tucked it inside the front of her robe.

An hour later, Petra took up station on the dock within sight of *Lady Fatima*. She was covered from head to toe in the black robe and headdress Karim's mother had given her. In one hand, she clutched the recently purchased strings of seed beads. Patiently, she waited for Sheik Kamal's envoy to arrive.

A beige Land Rover rolled along the quay and came to a halt alongside *Lady Fatima*. A clean-shaven young man with short, dark hair got out of the driver's seat. Petra approached the yacht to take a closer look, crooning over the beads. The young man waved her impatiently away. Petra drew nearer. He shouted at her in Arabic, most of which she did not understand. She was convinced he was Sheik Kamal's son Ahmed. She uncovered her face and called out to him: 'Ahmed!'

Immediately he recognized the young woman who had suffered such humiliation at the hands of Don León in Monte Carlo. 'Miss Minx! I had no idea it was you! I am sorry if I was rude, but the hawkers are such a nuisance. Please come aboard.'

Petra lifted the hem of her voluminous robe and crossed the passerelle onto *Lady Fatima* for the second time that day. She had not expected to find Ahmed in Marina Smir. What was he doing acting as Sheik Kamal's envoy and where was he taking Emy? Not only that, how was she going to explain her disguise? Perhaps it was time to tell the truth. She had already promised to explain to Rosemary what she was doing, and Ahmed might be able to help. From the moment he had given her his business card in Monte Carlo, she felt she could trust him.

At Petra's suggestion, they sat inside the elegant motor yacht, both to avoid prying eyes and to keep out of the midday sun. Petra loved the tiger maple panelling and the art deco-styled furniture. The Lazzara Eighty Four might be the boat of her dreams, but she would never refuse a One Sixteen. Over a sandwich lunch that Rosemary prepared for the four of them, Petra recounted the purpose of her visit and the essentials of her quest for Emily Mortlake.

'I think I know the girl you are looking for,' Ahmed said. 'She was here for a time in early September. My father brought her back from Cannes in his private plane.'

'Was she his concubine?' Petra asked before she could stop herself.

Ahmed frowned. 'My father is an upright man. He is very loyal to my mother. And he has done business with Don León for many years. He would not take one of his girls for himself.'

'I'm sorry, Ahmed, I didn't mean to offend you. You said Emily was here for a time. Am I to assume then that she is no longer here? Do you know what she did during her stay?'

'Of course!' Ahmed looked surprised. 'She was put to work in the atelier, the workshop you would call it.'

'What workshop?' Emy asked.

'My father produces exotic lingerie and dance costumes to special order, mostly for Don León; occasionally, we supply direct to a colleague or a friend in the Middle East.'

'If that's what Emy is going to do, it doesn't sound like modelling to me,' Rosemary said.

'We need to have foreign girls as models,' Ahmed said, 'to ensure that the garments are a proper fit.'

'Foreign girls supplied by Don León?' Petra asked, knowing that Sheik Kamal and Ahmed had been "interviewing" girls like Emily Mortlake in London and wondering if he would say anything about it.

For a moment Ahmed looked uncomfortable. 'My father does not involve me in all aspects of the business, although I am now manager of the workshop where I am to take Emy. Apparently she has been through a bad time. She will find peace and quiet there.'

To Petra, it sounded as though Ahmed did not believe entirely what he was saying.

'If you come with us this afternoon, you can see for yourself,' he said. 'Mustafa tells me one of the girls is ill and cannot work. She has gone away until she recovers.'

'Who's Mustafa?' Petra asked.

'My father's senior aide. He was with us in Monte Carlo. You met him there.'

Petra recalled the hawkish advisor who was never far from Sheik Kamal's side. He had been at Don León's extravaganza in Puerto Banús too. 'Will he be at the workshop today?' she asked.

'I do not think so. My father has a meeting in Rabat and Mustafa will accompany him.' Ahmed paused. 'Zahra is the shop supervisor, a nosy woman. If she sees you, she might say something to my father and he to Don León. To avoid trouble, you should wear that disguise; it is most effective and you will blend in well with the older seamstresses. Zahra forces them to dress in black and to cover their ageing faces.'

The road climbed steeply up into the Rif Mountains. Ahmed was a careful driver. He avoided the larger potholes and slowed for the dangerous bends, ever mindful of his passengers' comfort and safety. Once they passed the town of Chefchaouen with its beautiful blue medina, traffic was sparse. On the plateau before the next rise, olive trees grew in abundance. An argan tree full of goats reaching high to assuage their appetite for the foliage entranced Emy and Petra. The road continued to climb. At a thousand metres above sea level, the air was thin, cool and clear. Petra ran a gentle finger along her eyebrows to relieve the tightness in her sinuses.

Half an hour later, Ahmed brought the vehicle to a halt outside a pair of brass-studded cedar doors set halfway along the towering red-hued wall of an ancient *kasbah*. The back of the old citadel was built into the mountain itself. A few rectangular windows with elaborate wrought iron bars looked down on visitors from the third floor level. Emy shuddered as she eyed the smooth, forbidding walls.

Ahmed jumped out of the Land Rover and rang the bell. After a short wait, the right-hand door scraped open over the hard-packed sand floor. A slim but hippy young woman, whom Petra guessed to be about thirty-five years' old, greeted Ahmed with bare civility and scrutinized his two companions. No doubt this was the nosy Zahra. Clad in the black robe and *niqab*, Petra hung back. She lowered her head and shuffled into the courtyard behind Ahmed and Emy, carrying Emy's small suitcase. In the centre of the courtyard where one might expect to see a fountain, a circle of plain concrete suggested a work in progress.

'I will escort the new girl to her quarters, Zahra,' Ahmed said as planned in English. 'Your services will not be required.' He gestured towards Petra. 'The woman is old and deaf, but she still knows how to prepare a girl, and sew.'

Zahra gave him a sardonic smile. She responded in flawless English. 'I see you have already taught the blonde one to submit to your will, just like your father used to do.' She tossed her long, black hair. 'I doubt she knows the many ways in which to please a man yet. But then, are you a real man or an English schoolboy?'

Ahmed raised his arm as if to strike her. 'Get back to the workshop, daughter of Satan!' The show of strength convinced Zahra to leave them alone. She flounced across the courtyard in her jeans and high heels and disappeared through an archway in the far left-hand corner.

Ahmed cast a rueful glance at Emy and Petra. 'I apologize,' he whispered. 'Zahra was my father's favourite before he met my mother. She was very young then and truly loved him. She hates me because I am the eldest son. She gave birth to a daughter when she was eighteen, but lost her to cholera. My father tried to compensate by sending Zahra the best teachers to complete her education. Now she is in charge of the women here.'

He led them into the tower on the right-hand side of the courtyard and they climbed the stairs to the second floor. Four rooms opened off the central landing. Each of the rooms was small and dark, though furnished comfortably enough with a low double bed covered in a striped blanket and strewn with embroidered cushions. On a carved wooden dresser stood a jug and bowl for washing.

'Downstairs there is a hammam, a bathhouse,' Ahmed said. 'I am afraid the facilities are not the most modern. Upstairs there are more rooms like these.'

Emy ran up to investigate. 'They're just the same,' she said. 'Which one is Zahra's?' Now that she was inside the *kasbah* she seemed fascinated by the place and not at all dismayed by Zahra's innuendoes.

'She lives in the other wing near the local women,' Ahmed told her. 'This tower is reserved for the foreign models.'

Petra was examining dozens of framed photographs that papered the walls of the landing. In them, various young women stood or sat in provocative poses. Most were blonde. Some wore ruffled corsets and garter belts, others French knickers and sequined bustiers. A few were dressed as belly dancers, their faces half hidden behind masks or veils. The turquoise and gold costume of one of the dancers caught Petra's eye. She studied the picture closely.

'I'm sure that's Emily Mortlake,' she exclaimed. There was no mistaking the blue topaz pendant and the way her flaxen hair curled round her shoulders. 'You said Emily was here for a while in September. Do you know when she left and where she went?'

'My recollection is that she went back to Spain around the middle of the month, although I am not certain. My studies at the University of Fez keep me very busy. I prefer not to come here unless I have to.'

'Zahra would know, wouldn't she?' Petra asked.

'Of course, but to get any information from Zahra I will have to be very careful. She is cleverer than a fox. I will ask her first what happened to the girl Mustafa says is sick. Come now to the workshop. Remember to walk a few paces behind me. We will leave Emy here to settle in.'

Petra embraced the girl. 'Take care of yourself. I'll come back to fetch you as soon as I can.' As she took her leave, she pressed the special button on her watch to record the latitude and longitude of the *kasbah* on its built-in GPS.

Ahmed led Petra under the archway through which Zahra had disappeared, into an inner courtyard. In the centre of the courtyard, a tiled fountain tinkled and played. She followed Ahmed through a second archway and they entered the workshop from the rear.

293

At the far end of the room, Zahra sat on a dais facing rows of hooded figures hunched over individual worktables. She could have been a teacher invigilating a roomful of students writing their final examinations. Instead of writing, however, the figures in the front rows were operating electric sewing machines that whirred softly as their slippered feet pressed the pedals. These were young local women in colourful *jellabas* whose slim fingers and agile minds manipulated the machines, fine fabrics, ribbons and lace with dexterity and care.

Closer to Petra, towards the back of the room, black-clad senior women were embroidering and sewing on sequins with the mastery of old hands. Long tables along the wall on the left-hand side of the room held pre-cut materials and partly finished work. Windows on the right-hand side allowed light from the courtyard to filter through the delicately carved tracery screens.

At the far end of the back row, there was an empty worktable. Ahmed gave Petra a gentle push towards it. She understood his ploy and sat down quickly – but not too quickly, as befitted a woman her age – on the wooden chair. The woman to her right cast her a fleeting glance before returning to her sewing.

Ahmed walked briskly to the front of the room and addressed Zahra in Arabic. She stood up, truculent at being disturbed, and followed him to the arched doorway at the front of the room. From there, she had no direct line of sight to Petra.

Petra appreciated Ahmed's ingenuity. It gave her the opportunity to study the women around her. They all seemed intent on their work. Her neighbour was stitching a gold floret with quiet concentration. She heard Ahmed raise his voice and Zahra utter a low, vicious response.

Ahmed retaliated in kind. Petra would have liked to know what they were saying.

Over the sound of their raised voices, Petra detected the beat of rotors. The noise became deafening as a helicopter flew low over the *kasbah* and landed in the outer courtyard. She reached to her left and grabbed a padded brassiere from the long table. The well in the worktable at which she sat contained separate compartments for needles, thread, pins, sequins and other essentials of the seamstress's trade. She selected a needle and thread and began to sew a line of sequins onto the brassiere.

Ahmed and Zahra turned to greet the arrivals. Petra heard the mellifluous voice of Sheik Kamal then, to her horror, the sonorous tones of Don León. What could have brought him there? Had Sheik Kamal told him of her desire to visit Morocco? Could she escape out of the rear doorway without being seen? Before she could formulate a plan, Sheik Kamal and Don León entered the room. Heart pounding, she bent over her work. Zahra was standing very close to Don León.

'These are local craftswomen,' she said. 'I trained them myself. You can see the quality of their work.'

'Zahra is right,' Sheik Kamal said. 'She also trains our models in the sensual art of belly dancing.'

Don León made no reply. He took in the whole room at a glance. Slowly he walked down the narrow aisle along the window side of the workshop, pausing to study each row before moving on to the next. When he reached the last row of younger women, he paused. With care not to disturb the tables, he made his way along the row and stopped in front of the girl in the middle. The girl turned the silk as she came to the end of a seam. Her hands were long and slim, like Petra's. They bore none of the henna designs that marked the other young women. Don León seized one of her hands and threw back the red and yellow striped hood and scarf that concealed her head and her face. Her gasp of consternation mirrored his sigh of disappointment. Pushing his way through the tables, he strode back to where Sheik Kamal stood with Zahra and Ahmed.

Zahra plucked at his sleeve. 'These are simple country people, Sire, not cultured like myself. If you are looking for a consort, I can help you.'

Sheik Kamal laughed. 'You are such a delicious flirt, Zahra! And a fine teacher. But I hear you have been having problems with some of our foreign guests.'

Zahra paled. 'Not I, Sheik! The girl your son brought in today had problems before she arrived. I will help her adjust.'

'No doubt,' he said drily. 'But what about the one who fell sick, the one Mustafa tells me is now in hospital in Rabat? You must be careful, Zahra. Sometimes your methods are too harsh. Ahmed, look after the workshop. Take us to the models' quarters, Zahra. My friend wants to see for himself who is there. We will discuss the remedies later.'

Don León scanned the rows of older women quickly as he walked with Zahra and Sheik Kamal towards the back of the room. Petra bent lower over her work. To her relief, he did not stop.

As they went out through the rear doorway, Zahra spoke to Sheik Kamal. 'Sire, I can assure you, we have only one girl here now, the one who arrived today.'

'What about my girl Emily? I instructed Olga to send her back here a few weeks ago, into your care,' Don León said. 'Where is she? What have you done with her? Did you mishandle her too?'

'What do you mean? I have not set eyes on the little white whore since you came to fetch her in mid-September!' Zahra's angry voice faded as they moved across the courtyard.

Petra forced herself to continue sewing with shaking fingers. Her sequins were out of line where her heart rate had doubled with the fear of being discovered and the shock of what she had overheard. After a minute or two, she ventured a look at Ahmed who had taken the place of Zahra on the dais. He inclined his head in the direction of the doorway. She nodded in reply. A few seconds later, she rose from her chair, passed behind the last row of women and slipped through the door out into the daylight.

CHAPTER TWENTY-FOUR

Ahmed revved the engine and put the Land Rover into reverse. The tyres squealed as he executed a tight turn and took off down the mountain road. 'My father is sure to come looking for me,' he said. 'I think we had better not travel tonight. I know a place where we can hide until the morning. If you still want to go to Rabat tomorrow, I can arrange it. For myself, I will return to Fez and continue my studies. One of these days, I will be free of the constraints that are placed upon me. Then you will be pleased to acknowledge me as your friend.'

Petra put a reassuring hand on his arm. He was little more than a boy. 'You are already my friend, a good friend. I understand the difficult position in which your father puts you. The important thing is to be true to yourself. Don't let him railroad you.'

Petra wondered whether she should continue on to Rabat. Her intention had been to look for Emily in Marina Smir and, if she found her, to take her to the Canadian Embassy. There, she could have picked up her Italian passport and arranged for Emily to be issued with a temporary travel document and flown home. Now she was unsure what to do. There had been no sign of Emily at the marina, nor at the *kasbah*. Only the photograph on the tower wall was a fading reminder of her stay.

'Did you find out from Zahra the name of the model who fell sick?' she asked Ahmed.

'She called her Melanie. A sweet girl, she said, but prone to hysterics, particularly if things did not go the way she wanted. When I pushed her for details, she refused to discuss the matter further. I did not dare enquire about Emily Mortlake.'

'Don't worry. I heard Don León and Zahra talking in the courtyard. He asked her himself what had happened to Emily. Apparently, Olga was instructed to send her back to Zahra a few weeks ago, but Zahra was adamant that she had left with Don León and not returned. Something must have happened after Emily came back to Spain, something that caused Don León to send her away again. There's no doubt he was expecting Emily to be here in Morocco.'

'Unless someone is not telling the truth,' Ahmed said.

He turned off the road onto a rutted track that brought them, after a short uncomfortable ride, into a dense forest of majestic pine and cork oak. Under the towering trees it was dark and cool. 'As long as you do not mind spending the night with me here, we should be safe. In the back of the car, I have an emergency pack containing food rations, water, and a blanket.'

'You would have made a good Boy Scout!'

'It is better to be prepared, given the state of the roads here in the Rif. You never know when you might have a breakdown or some other kind of trouble. The roads are often washed out by heavy rain or blocked by avalanches of rock.'

'This seems as good a hiding-place as any,' Petra said. 'The tree cover should prevent us from being seen from the air.'

'I hope my father will not spend too much time looking for me here. I told him I had lectures tomorrow morning, so he will think I have taken the road to Fez.'

'Will the seamstresses say anything about my leaving with you?'

'I doubt it. I promised them a large bonus if they carried on with their work. The mountain people understand the need for discretion.'

An hour later, they heard the helicopter fly over. Ahmed paused in his description of the research project he was working on at the University. Sheik Kamal made several passes over the area searching for his son. When quiet returned, Petra squeezed Ahmed's hand.

'Thank you for your support, Ahmed. I know there will be trouble for you after this.'

'It does not matter. You were right when you said I should not let him railroad me. The time has come for me to assert myself. My father's values are not always the same as mine. For too long, I have tried to maintain a balance between what my father wants and what I can achieve without incurring his wrath. I cannot tell you how many times I have been mortified by my own lack of confidence and chivalry. If my mother will allow it, I would like to return to England to study.'

Petra was moved by Ahmed's obvious distress. 'There's no need for self-recrimination. You have an inner strength that I know will enable you to stand up to your father. And when all this is over, I'll help you as much as I can,' she promised.

On the return ferry crossing from Tangier to Algeciras, Don León sat in the Club bar at a table in the bow of the ship and drank steadily. He had left behind a furious

Kamal trying to contact his delinquent son by phone, and a much subdued and disappointed Zahra.

During their visit to the foreign models' quarters, Sheik Kamal had berated her for using excessive force with the girls, a charge she denied vehemently. At one point, they had come close to blows as the argument reached a climax. Don León tried to defuse the situation by drawing Zahra aside and apologizing for what he had implied about her mishandling Emily Mortlake. She wrenched her arm from his grasp and threw back her long hair with a haughty toss of her head. In general he was not attracted to brunettes, yet Zahra's fire and spirit reminded him of Petra. She had stood facing him, hands on her hips.

'You send me your whores to soften up and teach new tricks so that you can make them do whatever you want. Then you complain, both of you, if they lose their heads and go off the rails. It's not my fault.' She glared at the two men, then focussed again on Don León, her tone changing from petulant to wheedling. 'Why do you waste your time with immature children? You need someone properly versed in the art of love, someone who knows how to make a man writhe and beg for more, someone with a stamina to equal yours, a woman who will never let you down – like me. Look,' she said, ripping open her blouse to reveal a small black tattoo above her left breast. 'I am yours. Take me with you.' The naked desire in her eyes had shone like a beacon.

Don León finished his glass of Sangre de Toro and called for another, reliving the scene.

Sheik Kamal had watched Zahra's performance with apparent cool detachment. 'I could never allow you to leave, Zahra, you know that,' he said. The menace in his voice left her in no doubt as to her position. The door of her gilded cage would remain firmly shut.

301

Zahra's outburst had perturbed Don León. She was a liability to them all, acting like a prima donna. Such behaviour might be refreshing or seductive at first, as he had found with Emily Mortlake, but it soon became tiresome, even dangerous.

In anger, he had shouted at Sheik Kamal: 'You're losing control of your organization, Sheik.'

'My friend, you have already lost control of yours. If indeed you ordered Olga to send Emily back here for more training, for which no doubt there was a reason, I can assure you that your orders have been ignored. Neither I, nor any of my staff have seen her since you yourself took her away in mid-September. The problem is yours not mine!'

Don León had to admit that Sheik Kamal could be right. The tour of the models' quarters had confirmed the presence of only one girl, who appeared delighted to see Zahra but nervous of the two men. The problem lay in the fact that he had made two assumptions: first, that Petra had left Puerto Banús with Sheik Kamal; second, that Olga had carried out his instructions regarding Emily. Both assumptions had been proven wrong, although he did not trust Sheik Kamal entirely, and Zahra could be keeping the girls elsewhere. His priority was to find out what had happened to Petra, then to confront Olga. If she had disobeyed him, he wanted to know why. And with the police asking awkward questions, he needed to find Emily quickly.

During the last half hour of the ferry crossing, the sea had become rough. Don León stood up to return to the car deck ahead of the rush and knocked his empty wineglass to the floor.

A hostess hurried to help him as he lurched against the back of the chair. 'Hold on tight, Sir. It'll be calmer once we turn in behind the breakwater. If you wait a few minutes, I can assist you.' She bent down to sweep up the glass, her buttocks pushing upwards under her tight red skirt. Copper hair cascaded down her back.

She stood up tall and firm under his scrutiny, returning his gaze from steady green eyes. She had seen him on the ferry before. His yellow-flecked eyes were extraordinary.

'Can you drive?' he asked her, clutching the chair back.

'Of course, Sir.'

'Then leave that and come with me.'

The car-deck steward waved the Lamborghini forward. Gingerly, the hostess let in the clutch. Don León patted her leg where her skirt had ridden up and left it exposed. 'You'll do all right. Don't be nervous.'

Cognizant that he had drunk too much and exhausted by the conflicting emotions that his search for Petra and Emily had aroused, he had taken the unprecedented step of asking someone to drive for him. The girl had looked at him in astonishment, but agreed at once.

The lights of Algeciras and Gibraltar twinkled behind them as they cruised onto the toll road. Don León slumped in his seat, speaking only to tell her which exit to take. She wasn't a bad driver once she overcame her nervousness and he knew she would never have a chance to drive such a car again. They turned onto a country road that wound upwards past a field of giant wind turbines.

Don León sat up. 'Pull over,' he ordered. 'Stop here.'

'What's wrong? What have I done?'

'Nothing. I want you to feel their power.'

He got out of the Bat and walked round to the driver's door to help the girl out. His gait was already steadier than it had been on the water. They stood at the base of the nearest monolith looking up at the blades cleaving the night sky. Their swoosh was a vibrating pulse that penetrated right to his core. This was what he had wanted to show Petra that Friday afternoon which now seemed so long ago.

'You can feel it, can't you, deep inside, in there?' he said.

She shivered as he pointed at her pubis. His intensity was scary. With relief, she heard him say: 'You're cold. Let's go.'

They continued on up the deserted country road. After two or three kilometres, they turned onto a narrow road that appeared to end at a pair of heavy steel gates set in a three-metre-high perimeter wall. The girl slowed and looked enquiringly at Don León. He motioned her to carry on. The gates slid open to let them through, then closed immediately behind them.

They were in a kind of no man's land: a waterless moat between the solid exterior wall that screened the property from view and a wrought-iron fence of elaborate scrollwork surmounted by halberd points, through which the extent of the estate could be seen. The driveway continued to a pair of electronically controlled crested gates then curved to the left, skirting the lamp-lit formal gardens. Along the classical front of the villa with its two tiers of arched windows ran a colonnaded porch that gave onto a white marble terrace set with fountains and benches, potted plants and shrubs. On the right-hand side of the terrace, a blue-tiled pool gleamed.

'Can we swim?' breathed the girl.

The aphrodisiac properties of his possessions were not lost on Don León. 'Later. Let's get comfortable first. Drive round to the back of the house.'

The courtyard behind the villa was enclosed on two sides by a garage block and extensive outbuildings with small shuttered windows. There was none of the grace and light of the front.

'Shall I put the car away?' the girl asked, confident now of her driving ability and reluctant to abandon such a fine vehicle.

'That won't be necessary. No one can get to it here.' His words froze her libido. She was alone with an unknown man in an unfamiliar place.

A flight of marble steps led up to a porticoed door in the centre of the villa. There was no sign of life. Don León escorted his companion to an unobtrusive door to the left of the steps at ground level. She was somewhat taller than Petra, more angular, but in his present state of mind, still acceptable. He unlocked the door and urged her down the stairs in front of him.

Below the villa, Don León had created a subterranean recording studio complete with mixing, dubbing, editing and screening rooms, wardrobe, sauna and whirlpool, bar and lounge. 'This is my indoor entertainment area,' he said with a sweeping gesture as they emerged into the dimly lit lounge.

The girl's eyes popped as she took in the mirrored walls and ceiling and the red, black and chrome décor. A plasma screen as big as a king-size bed filled an alcove. In front of it, loafing sofas invited decadent relaxation.

Don León strode over to the bar and poured a glass of the Cuvée Ana León for the girl and a Sangre de Toro for himself. He placed the glasses on an asymmetrical table comprised of two moveable glass discs that opened like water lily leaves off a polished chrome stem. Picking up a slimline remote control, he turned to the girl.

'That jacket doesn't look too comfortable. Why don't we take it off?' He seized both lapels and peeled it back off her shoulders. 'Sit down, relax, kick off your shoes, enjoy!'

Don León ran his hands through her lustrous copper hair, lifting it high then letting it tumble down. She laughed nervously. He pushed her down onto one of the sofas, scrolled through the movie selection and pressed the play button. A redhead appeared on the screen, white-skinned and thin to the point of anorexia, but with breasts that could only have been hers through augmentation or trick photography. They overflowed out of a high-leg, zip-fronted black leotard, the zip already halfway to her navel.

She walked towards them, the crispness of the image and the clarity of the colours bringing her right into the room. She lowered the zip until the leotard fell outwards over her slim hips, put her tongue out to wet a finger and began massaging her clitoris. All the time, she looked directly at them, drawing them into her game. The music pounded to an insistent, erotic beat. With infinite slowness and her other hand, she drew the zip all the way down. The leotard fell to the mirrored floor. The hand that had released it moved upwards to her full breasts, thumb and middle finger extending fully to encompass both ripe globes.

The girl on the sofa gave a lascivious sigh. She unbuttoned the top of her once crisp white blouse and released one pert breast, about the size of Petra's. Don León felt himself growing. Sitting beside her on the sofa, he pulled up her skirt and parted her legs. Still holding the first breast, she released its twin, squeezing them up and together like a medieval maid in a secret garden of delights. Her other hand reached downwards to her groin.

Don León pressed another button on the remote control. A man in a black cloak and a Zorro-like mask stepped forward, filling the centre of the screen. The cloak swung wide as he pivoted in shiny, black, spurred boots. Now his back was facing the camera. He took two paces towards a four-poster bed hung with heavy tapestries. He pushed the tapestries aside and the camera closed in on a girl with flaxen braids lying face down. She was spread-eagled on the bed and loosely tied to the four corner posts with silken ribbons. Her medieval dress was bunched up round her waist, the velvet skirt and ruffled petticoats the perfect foil for her bare raised buttocks.

'Come, my lovely,' Don León said, gathering the copper-haired girl in his arms, 'time to go upstairs.'

The night's conquest was, for Don León, a shallow victory. The drugs, as Sheik Kamal had said during the helicopter ride to the *kasbah*, were excellent. His potency did not abate until the time came for the dawn to lighten the sky and he abandoned the girl with a final shuddering climax. But his pleasure was in the chase, the challenge, the weaning and the wearing down of the ones who thought themselves above the pleasures of the flesh. He despised himself for resorting to the drug. Yet it was useful to test it and experience its effects for himself. He still felt as strong as a horse.

Taking a towel to cover his nakedness, he climbed the stairs to the pool terrace. The sun was just peeping over the horizon. He threw off the towel and dived into the pool. Twenty lengths cleared the last cobwebs of the night. He pictured Petra in white trousers, Petra without the white trousers, Petra in red, Petra in black tights and ballerina pumps.

That was it! He had been chasing a ghost in the back of his mind ever since he left Sheik Kamal's workshop. Of all the female workers there, only one in the back row had not been wearing the traditional slippers. Her hands sewing the sequins were slim and white, not hardened or henna'ed...

307

Accustomed to rising early, Sheik Kamal answered his phone. 'You are crazy, my friend, eaten up with lust for this chit of a girl.'

'Just check, Kamal, do me this one favour, that's all I ask,' he begged. 'I need her,' he added to himself.

CHAPTER TWENTY-FIVE

For Ahmed and Petra the night passed without incident. Ahmed made her comfortable in the back of the Land Rover and said he would wake her at sunrise. But when sunrise came, Petra was in a deep sleep and he did not want to disturb her. He deliberately kept his phone switched off so that his father could not contact him. When the sun was high, Petra stirred. Among the cork oaks and pines, it was still cool, but shafts of sunlight penetrated their branches and lit up the forest floor. She sat up and rubbed her eyes. During the night, her brain had continued to work and pieces of the puzzle had begun to fall into place. She knew now with certainty what to do.

'I must get back to Spain, Ahmed. Olga's the key! Don León will be livid with her for flouting his orders to return Emily to Zahra's care. He won't rest until he's found out why. And I can't rest until I find Emily!'

Ahmed reversed the Land Rover and performed a three-point turn between the trees. 'Will you go back to *Titania?*'

'Not immediately. I want to take a look at Don León's villa. I've been there with him and I have a few ideas.'

'How will you gain access?'

'Today is Tuesday. Don León's Studio Director has organized a film shoot at the villa this evening. I was with them when they established the schedule. Don León said

309

he would probably be there, and I'm guessing Olga and Monica will be with him. I should be able to get in early with the film crew. It will be perfect cover.'

During the rest of the drive back to Marina Smir, Ahmed was pensive and Petra respected his mood. She knew he was struggling with conflicting emotions and would be heavily censored for his behaviour at the workshop.

Rosemary welcomed them back aboard *Lady Fatima* with a brunch of scrambled eggs, mushrooms, tomatoes and fried bread. The Captain, she said, had picked up extensive provisions at the new supermarket on the outskirts of Tetouan. She was eager for news of Emy and information about her new circumstances. After the food and a quick shower, Petra was impatient to start her journey back to Spain.

'Why don't you take the Quadski?' Ahmed said. 'It can do seventy kilometres an hour on land and water, and the fuel tank is full. The conversion from quadbike to jet ski and vice versa takes just a few seconds. I have tried it myself. It is amazing.'

'How will I return it to you?' Petra asked.

'Perhaps you will ride it back in triumph. If not, it is of no consequence. My father can replace it in less time than it takes to pump a barrel of oil.'

Petra was taking her leave of Rosemary when she heard a faint noise and saw a speck on the horizon. She had discussed with Ahmed the possibility that his father might come to look for him at the marina. Those fears were now a reality. Cutting short her goodbyes, she climbed down onto the swim platform of the Lazzara, sat astride the Quadski, fastened her helmet and waited with bated breath while Ahmed undid the locks on the cradle and activated the controls to lower the hydraulic platform into the water.

The amphibian was already in sea mode. At the touch of a button, it surged forward. Petra bent low and careened round the bow of the yacht towards the harbour exit. Sheik Kamal's red, white and green helicopter buzzed *Lady Fatima* and banked to the right over the boatyard and the turquoise sea. Petra had to assume he'd seen her, though there was a chance he hadn't. If she stayed on the water, she would never lose him.

As the helicopter made its turn, Petra drove out of the water onto the beach in front of the colonial-style hotel, to the astonishment of a couple of beachcombers. She raced along the hard sand at the edge of the water, the waves obliterating the heavy-tread tyre tracks as fast as she made them. A minute or two later, she turned inland to the half-built structure where she had sheltered twenty-eight hours earlier. At the southern end of the site, the fence had been trampled down and partly pulled to one side. With extreme care, Petra negotiated her way through the broken wire into the protection of the derelict building. From the marina, there was silence. The helicopter had landed.

Sheik Kamal was angrier than he had ever been with his son. 'You made me look like a fool!' he shouted. 'I had to return to the workshop this morning and ask demeaning questions. Then I find out – it was not too difficult for Zahra to make one of the old women talk – that you brought someone into the workshop and left with her as soon as my back was turned!' The outrage to his dignity was worse than the actual offence.

Privately, Ahmed thought his father was indeed a fool. The garment factory was lucrative, as were his other businesses. He did not need to get involved with the

311

seedier side of things that Don León seemed to enjoy. Ahmed hoped Zahra's methods had not involved too much force.

His father seemed to have read his mind. 'See what your interference has done,' he said, pushing his phone under Ahmed's nose. The resolution of the picture was poor, but the woman's plight was clear. Ahmed turned his head away.

'Poor Mummy's boy!' his father taunted.

'If you respect my mother, you will respect my sensibilities,' Ahmed said. It was time to stand up to his father.

Despite his displeasure, Sheik Kamal felt a stirring of pride in his son. The Berber stock was tough. 'I do, but you must understand the importance of maintaining discipline, even when it involves harsh measures.'

Sheik Kamal's sharp eyes had noticed the absence of the Quadski as soon as his helicopter landed. He decided that if he were to achieve any reconciliation with his son, it would be better not to question him about it. Besides, he was intrigued by Don León's infatuation with Petra Minx. He would wager El Toro had met his match. For the time being, he would keep his suspicions to himself.

It was one o'clock when Sheik Kamal's helicopter took off. It flew south, low over the beach towards Cabo Negro, then lifted up over the black cliffs to head inland. Petra waited a while longer before she deemed it safe to emerge. A group of young Scandinavian sunbathers stared in amazement as she thundered down the beach on the Quadski and drove straight out into the water until the vehicle floated free. With the flick of a switch, the wheels retracted and a jet ski was born.

The sense of freedom left Petra breathless. The wind of the night before that had moaned through the pines had died down. The Mediterranean sparkled silver and blue as she opened the throttle and sped across the top of the waves. On her watch, she set the GPS waypoint she had created for Santa Margarita.

Half an hour out, she spied a twenty metre Azimut running effortlessly over the lazy swells, heading for the Strait of Gibraltar. It was time to put the Quadski through its paces! With the exhilaration she once felt in the company of Romeo on the back of his motorcycle, she accelerated hard and jumped the motor yacht's wake in a cloud of spume. Considering the compromises necessary in the creation of an amphibious vehicle, the machine handled amazingly well. She crisscrossed the turbulent wake several times before reason conquered excitement.

Karim was sitting in his boat, relaxed and content. From time to time, he tended his nets. He counted the vapour trails in the brilliant blue canopy above him. He watched a search and rescue helicopter head for the Rock, and called out to a friend in another boat. Life was good. His only concern was for Petra. If she had not returned by the end of the week, he would have to deal with the motorcycle. And that would mean that she had encountered a problem.

The sound of the watercraft reached his ears long before he could see its shape. It looked like a wide, curved plate skimming over the surface. The helmeted rider was coming in close, perhaps too close. What was he doing? Karim cursed the lack of consideration of certain types of water users and prepared to haul his nets out of harm's way. In a shower of spray, the craft came to a stop two boat-lengths away. Petra greeted him with a gleeful cry.

'I knew it would be you, Karim!' She laughed at his expression as he recognized her voice. With care, she manoeuvred alongside *La Gitana*, the horizontal tyres acting as fenders. It took her only a few minutes to bring him up to date.

'Crazy girl! I cannot keep up with you on that thing. Go and see my mother. She has been keeping vigil for you since Sunday. She will make arrangements to look after your new toy.'

With the Quadski safely stowed in a lock-up at the small fishing port not far from Karim's mother's house, Petra set off later that afternoon for Don León's villa. She was riding the borrowed motorbike. She felt guilty at not yet having returned the bike to its owner or at least to the café from where she had borrowed it.

Once again, she used the GPS function on her watch, this time to retrieve the location of the villa. Her recollection of the route Don León had taken from the toll road up through the village and on into the hills was good, at least to the point where she had been drugged or fallen asleep in the Lamborghini. From there, she would have to rely on a combination of the GPS, her map and her innate sense of direction.

After a few false starts and dead ends, Petra found herself on a narrow but well maintained road. The GPS indicated that she was on the right track. Ahead of her, the road appeared to end at some heavy metal gates set between three-metre-high solid walls. This must be the entrance to El Toro's estate.

When she had left the property with him in the Lamborghini the previous Friday evening, she had committed to memory the layout of the villa, its outbuildings, the gardens and the winding drive to the entrance gates. She had also noted the advanced electronic and infrared surveillance systems that would alert El Toro's staff to any unusual activity on the perimeter of the estate or within its confines. He maintained only a skeleton staff at the villa, preferring the anonymity of caterers and local hired help to assist with occasional functions. With luck, her timing would be right and she could enter the estate with the studio staff and equipment.

To avoid being picked up by the cameras at the gate, Petra turned off the private road onto a rutted track through what had once been an orchard. Lemon trees bore fruit four times as large as the commercial varieties found in supermarkets; oranges pecked to pieces by birds littered the ground; avocados dangled overhead like opaque Christmas tree baubles. A safe distance away from the gate, Petra found a place to wait unseen.

Her ears picked up the noise of the cavalcade before it came into view. In front was the Studio Director's red Ferrari. Behind him, a couple of outriders on Harley-Davidsons revved their engines with macho enthusiasm. Two mini-vans containing actors and actresses in flamenco dress followed, then the studio trailer carrying the technicians and their heavy equipment. Bringing up the rear was a caterer's van. Petra nosed the bike in behind it and passed through the gate.

The procession moved through the no-man's land of cacti and scrub to a pair of wrought-iron gates and onto the main property. As she followed the line of vehicles up the drive, Petra looked across to the terrace. Three people were sitting round a table near the pool. Don León's unruly mane of hair and Monica's platinum helmet stood out even from a distance. The third person was a stocky woman, no doubt Olga. The trio had, as she had hoped, come to the villa.

As the procession approached the courtyard, the pace slowed. The caterer tried to overtake the trailer and managed to block the courtyard entrance. In the ensuing chaos, Petra seized her chance to pull in behind the first outbuilding on the left. She parked the motorbike next to a stack of eucalyptus logs and settled down to wait.

Twenty-five minutes later, the din in the courtyard had subsided. From the entrance, Petra saw that the trailer was partially unpacked. Arc lights and other equipment stood on trolleys at the bottom of the flight of steps leading up to the open door of the villa. Nobody was in view, but she could hear the babble of voices inside and the Studio Director calling out instructions. The Bat was parked in the far corner of the courtyard next to a courtesy car from the marina in Puerto Banús. If the Studio Director or Don León, or one of the other members of the trio, came out of the villa and recognized her, she would be unable to carry out the plan she had devised during her enforced waiting times that day. And what about Pablo? Was he at the villa too?

The rear doors of the caterer's van were open. Petra noticed a short white chef's coat hanging on a peg just inside. She ran to the van, grabbed the coat and put it on. A bulge in the pocket of her denim jacket reminded her that she had kept the cap Karim had lent her. With an elastic band she also found in her pocket, she tied her hair back in a ponytail and planted the cap on her head. At the sound of a door opening and shutting halfway along the row of outbuildings, Petra picked up a tray of hors d'oeuvres. The cap and jacket looked strange over her jeans, but she hazarded a guess that the studio staff did not know the catering staff and vice versa. Unless she was unlucky enough to walk into someone who knew her well, she might pass muster.

Petra watched from the cover of the van as a woman whose build and facial features, mainly the cheekbones, reminded her of Olga picked her way through the gaps in the vehicles and climbed the steps to the villa. Petra fancied she had seen the woman in the background the previous Friday, during her visit with Don León.

A tight sensation hit Petra in the pit of her stomach. She had loved Don León that afternoon. Not in the physical sense, the way in which the others assumed she had, but in a quasi-mystical, life-altering sense that would forever define her. Through the sheer force of his personality, he had reached into her soul and taken her out of herself, beyond the bounds of rational behaviour, further than she knew she should go. And next time, if there were a next time, she feared she might not say no to the physical consummation of their relationship.

The hors d'oeuvres tray tipped to one side and she deposited most of its contents on the ground. Salacious thoughts had no place in her present enterprise. Ruefully, Petra put the tray back in the van, checked that nobody was in the courtyard and ran under the cover of the vehicles to the far side of the flight of steps.

Among the dizzy memories of that Friday afternoon with Don León were more pragmatic recollections. He had extolled the virtues of the villa like a real estate agent to a client with money to burn. He had been particularly proud of the media rooms on the lower level, as keen as a small boy to demonstrate the latest technology. When she tried the door through which they had exited into the courtyard, she gave a mental thumbs-up. It had been unlocked to give the technical staff access during the film shoot that evening.

Petra hurried down the stairs. The bar and lounge were empty. She hoped Don León, Olga and Monica were still sitting on the terrace. How long they had been there and what they were discussing she had no idea, but they had been sitting drinking and talking in apparent harmony. Don León might not yet have confronted Olga over the question of Emily.

Part of Petra's plan was to try and shock information out of them. There was no more time to lose. If something serious had happened to Emily, she could be dead. Don León had mentioned that the Studio Director kept some props and costumes on hand, along with make-up and various back-up supplies. These were stored in the wardrobe room, one of a number of small rooms located behind the screening room. On her second attempt, Petra found the right door and vanished inside.

Don León had forgotten all about the film shoot until his Colombian manservant Raoul had come to ask him about arrangements. That had been at lunchtime after he had slept for several hours.

'And what about the girl, Sir?' Raoul ventured. He had seen the state she was in and instructed his wife Bettina to minister to her.

'You know the routine. I'll get Pablo over here. He can deal with her. Give her five thousand euros and a memory pill. She had a good time!'

Don León had picked up his VHF phone and dialled Olga. When there was no reply, he had tried Monica, then Captain Juan, Pablo and finally Carlo.

'Carlo, where is everyone?'

'At the police station.'

'What?' He listened carefully as Carlo explained.

'The Chief of Police came round this morning to ask more questions. He insisted on coming aboard even though Captain Juan told him you weren't here. The victim of the boating accident has been identified as Theo's estate manager Axel. They're treating the death as suspicious since they found part of a speargun with a bull logo on it that could have been used to disable the Zodiac.' Carlo hesitated.

'And?'

'Olga told him Petra Minx had disappeared and might know something about it. Monica also claimed Petra had stolen some items from her cabin. Pablo went with them to make depositions.'

Don León refused to believe that Petra could have had anything to do with Axel's death. Sheik Kamal had not returned his phone call. He must find Petra before the police did. Then he could protect her. 'Tell Olga, Monica and Pablo to come up here to the villa as soon as they get back. This is serious.'

Carlo agreed. He had no news of Petra and was wondering at what stage he should go to the authorities and explain their undercover activities.

According to Olga, the police had been suspicious and unsympathetic. 'You should have been there, Don León. With you, they would not have taken such a high-handed attitude.'

'Why did you tell them Petra had disappeared? I told you I was dealing with it.' His voice was as cold and brittle as a thin sheet of ice. 'You've overstepped your authority one time too many. And you!' He rounded on Monica. 'You're as bad or worse. I'm certain Petra's not a thief.'

Olga and Monica exchanged looks. El Toro was close to the edge.

'You won't countermand my instructions again, any of you, I'll guarantee that!' he said.

Monica had spied the procession of vehicles making its way up the drive. El Toro's vicious tone sent a shiver up her spine. To defuse the situation, she drew attention to the newcomers. 'The film crew is here, Don León. Shall we go and meet them?'

'No. Stay where you are. Raoul will handle everything.'

He refilled the three wineglasses.

'Let's talk about what happened in September. As you know, the police are looking for Emily Mortlake…'

The wardrobe room was a treasure trove of unusual and exotic items. Some of them Petra recognized, others she could only fantasize about. The costumes ranged from thigh-high leather boots and accoutrements to heavy lace peignoirs, via an entire lingerie collection labelled "Dream". One closet housed dance gear of all types: slinky leotards, frou-frou cancan dresses, tango and flamenco dresses, belly dancing outfits… She selected the creation she had seen in the movie on her first night aboard *Titania*. The wig was more of a problem. The first one she tried made her look like Monica with long hair, the second like Rapunzel with enough curly footage to attract more than a few suitors. Finally, she found a decent blonde wig that should enable her to pass for Emily Mortlake. She was already wearing Emily's topaz pendant and ring.

In the front hall of the villa, the Studio Director was addressing a recalcitrant actress with more boobs than brains. His patience was fast evaporating as she tripped over her skirt again at the bottom of the stairs. The assembled cast of acolytes waiting to greet the lady of the manor did not notice a belly dancer slip through the hall and out onto the terrace.

The strains of Arabian music filled the garden. Don León's pride in his state-of-the-art systems had enabled Petra to find a suitable tune and select the right speakers. She undulated onto the terrace, the coins on her belt jingling with each sway of her hips and shake of her butt. The three of them were still in the same places, sitting, not far from the pool, around a marble table that held a wine bottle and glasses. Petra inched closer, staying in the shadows until she was near enough to hear their words.

'We did exactly as you instructed, Don León, and sent Melanie away after her fight with Emily. You can only play girls off against each other so far,' Olga said accusingly.

'Ah! So what happened here that night was my fault! Then what do I need you for, woman?' Don León pounded his fist on the table as he spoke to Olga. 'But Melanie's not the issue. We have to find Emily. Why didn't you carry out my orders to return her to the workshop? If you had, we wouldn't be in the position we're in now.'

The tempo and level of the music increased. Weaving snake-like patterns with her arms and balancing on the ball of her right foot, Petra moved her right knee up and down and her left hip in and out, faster and faster in time to the music. Melanie? She knew that name. Melanie was the girl who had fallen ill at Sheik Kamal's workshop, the one Emy had replaced. So Melanie had been at the villa. But where was Emily? Petra was as close as she dared to be.

Don León was stamping his foot, raging at Olga. 'Why did you defy me? Answer me, woman!'

'Emily's dead,' Olga said flatly. 'An overdose. She collapsed. There was nothing we could do.'

Appalled at Olga's words and her tone, Petra completely lost her timing and wobbled out of synch with the music.

Monica nodded. 'That's right, Olga's right,' she said.

'Why didn't you come to me, instead of keeping quiet about it?' Don León roared. 'Now we have a real problem. What have you done with her body?'

The music wailed to a crescendo. Monica covered her ears. 'I hate this music! I thought it was flamenco tonight.' She cast her eyes round the terrace as if to locate the source of the irritation and looked straight at Emily Mortlake. 'No!' she shrieked. 'It wasn't my fault. We didn't know…'

Olga grabbed Monica's arm. 'What are you saying? Get a hold of yourself! She's just a dancer!'

Monica began to babble. She was beyond reason, and Emily was beyond help. Petra melted into the back of the terrace, swaying on feet that felt less than secure. If what Olga had said was true, she had failed in her mission. She did not want to be the one to convey the bad news to A.K. or Donald Mortlake.

CHAPTER TWENTY-SIX

Pablo was pleased with his handiwork. The tattoo had come out crisp and clean. It was a precision task that he executed with the meticulousness of a plastic surgeon. Only once or twice had the results been less than perfect – through no fault of his.

At first, the copper-haired girl had struggled against her bonds and he was forced to knock her out. Then he had run his hands slowly over her body examining the texture of her skin, gloating over his prize. He took his time to appreciate the girl fully before selecting the perfect spot. Without Olga there to interfere, as she often did, Pablo could indulge his desires for as long as he wanted. Don León always lost interest in the girls once they were ready to be imprinted with his mark.

Pablo left the copper-haired girl tied to the four-poster bed. He would do as Don León had instructed and take the girl back to Algeciras later. Right now he was eager to know what was causing the noise outside on the terrace.

On the landing, Pablo paused. He had been so busy with the girl that he had put everything else out of his mind. Now the film shoot was in full swing. The entrance hall with its cathedral ceiling and massive porcelain and coloured glass chandelier was teeming with a mixture of technical staff and Spaniards in flamenco dress.

The Studio Director's frustration with his leading lady was apparent from his careful enunciation. 'Darling, could you lift the front of your dress just a teeny bit higher? Then we might actually finish this scene tonight.'

The actress with the hourglass figure flounced back up the stairs leading to the east wing of the villa. The other side of the double staircase was clear save for a cameraman at the bottom. Pablo watched from the landing as she began her descent once again. This time, she succeeded in reaching the hall without mishap.

Pablo followed her progress with greedy eyes as he made his way down the stairs opposite those she had just vacated. In the melee, he glimpsed someone with blonde hair clad in what could have been a belly dancer's outfit slipping through the crowd. As a sailor, he was alert to anything out of place. The incident struck him as peculiar, but he dismissed it as unimportant. He had delayed long enough inside the villa.

Petra ran back through the hall and down the stairs to the lower level of the villa. As soon as she reached the wardrobe room, she stripped off her costume, leaving it in a heap on the floor. She pulled on her jeans, T-shirt and denim jacket, replaced the topaz necklace with her cross, put the topaz necklace and ring into her money belt for safekeeping until they could be returned to Emily's parents, and strapped on her watch. The filming was coming to an end and soon the staff would be gone. With a little luck, she should be able to leave the estate with them, either on the motorbike or in the back of one of their vans. The important thing was to get away and contact the authorities.

It had been a shock to hear Olga state so unemotionally that Emily was dead. Throughout the last week, Petra had been clinging to the belief that Emily was alive and she found it difficult to abandon all hope. Monica's timing had been unfortunate. If she had not turned round and seen Petra at that very moment, Olga might have revealed the location of Emily's body. The most likely spot was somewhere near the villa, either in the grounds or in the surrounding countryside.

Petra wondered if Monica had recovered her sangfroid. Had she had time to find her and talk to her, she might have been able to obtain more information. Now it would be up to the police to take all those involved into custody and unearth the details. Petra gave a hollow laugh at her inadvertent pun. She glanced at her watch. Her thoughts were taking up precious time. She must focus on escaping unseen. There had been no sign of Pablo at the villa and she did not know where Carlo was.

As a precaution, she copied the GPS coordinates of the villa from her watch onto her phone and sent a short text to both Carlo and Tom. "Saw Lazzara in Morocco. Now at villa." She pasted in the coordinates then continued. "Pls advise police EM dead. Suspect foul play by Olga/Monica. Petra." After sending the message, she was careful to delete it. She opened the wardrobe room door and checked the corridor. It was safe to leave.

Out on the terrace, the Arabian music continued to wail. Pablo took in the surreal scene at a glance. Monica was close to hysteria. She clutched frantically at Olga, who thrust her aside and faced off against Don León. He bared his teeth and roared at Olga like a lion turning on its tamer.

His eyes sparked with rage as he raised his arm to hit her. 'Have you taken leave of your senses, woman? You and that slut!'

325

He changed his tack and swung round, swiping Monica on the side of the head with the flat of his hand. The intensity of the blow sent her reeling across the terrace.

Olga stood firm, undeterred by Don León's show of temper. She had anticipated a strong reaction to the news of Emily's death. The decision to tell him had been taken by the three of them on the way to the villa in the car. In retrospect, perhaps it had been the wrong one.

Pablo hurried to Olga's side. 'What's going on?'

She cautioned him with her eyes. 'Some dancer appeared, looking like Emily Mortlake. Monica flipped. She thought she'd seen a ghost.'

Pablo paled. 'I saw the dancer – in the hall. It couldn't be her, could it?'

'You're the one who took care of the body,' Olga said. 'You tell me!'

Before Pablo could respond, Don León intervened. A deep melancholy had overtaken his rage. Another of his girls was gone. Sheik Kamal was right, he was losing control. 'You're wasting time,' he cried. 'Find the dancer, but don't hurt her. I want to know who she is. And turn off that damn music!'

The premonition of danger hit Petra a split second before she was grabbed from behind. She was standing at the top of the basement stairs just inside the door that led out to the courtyard, waiting for the film crew to finish loading the trailer. The last piece of equipment was being placed in the back as Pablo's thick hands grasped her in the centre of her ribcage. He pulled her backwards, using enough force to wind but not seriously hurt her, and gave a satisfied grunt. Olga opened the door from the courtyard side and grinned widely.

'Miss Minx! I knew we hadn't seen the last of you. Don León wants to hear all about what you've been doing.'

Petra lashed out with both fists. Because of the pain in her ribs, she was a fraction slower with the punches than she might otherwise have been. Olga ducked and seized first one wrist then the other. She had come prepared with a piece of cord that she used to bind them together. Then she did the same with Petra's ankles.

'OK, let's take her up, Pablo.'

They hauled Petra up the stairs like a trussed turkey. No one in the courtyard paid any attention to her shouts, and she heard the vehicles' engines revving and the gravel crunching under their wheels as they left.

'Sing, songbird, sing!' Olga chortled. 'You'll soon be singing louder than the opera singers you love so much. No one's going to come and help you here!'

Petra hoped she was wrong. She wriggled and twisted as they carried her into one of the guest suites on the upper floor of the villa. Her struggles garnered her a knee in the back and a whiff of heavy breath from Pablo who was holding her arms, as well as a stern admonition from Olga who was gripping her feet. Petra recognized the suite from her tour of the villa with Don León. Olga and Pablo threw her unceremoniously onto the first of the half-poster twin beds. She rolled to one side and used her wrists and her ankles to push herself up towards the top of the bed.

Olga cuffed her on the head and addressed her sternly. 'Look, Minx. You can struggle and force us to hurt you, or you can wait for Don León. He wants to deal with you himself, but if you give us a hard time, we won't have any choice.'

Petra thought about her options. She would do better to keep her senses about her. And she wanted to confront Don León. Olga turned her onto her back and held her shoulders down while Pablo bent to take care of her feet.

'Don't untie her, you fool! You'll never hold her,' Olga shouted. 'Tie a second piece of cord to one of her ankles and attach it to the foot post before you remove the first cord. Then do the same with the other leg.'

With reluctance, Pablo did as he was told. As he worked, he muttered under his breath. Losing her patience, Olga told Pablo to hurry up, which flustered him even more. Remembering Tom's instructions, Petra tensed her leg muscles and tilted her pelvis back, to maintain some play in the cords. As Olga went to work to tie her wrists to the head posts of the bed, she used her Pilates technique to lower her shoulder blades several centimetres, to give herself as wide a range of movement as possible. The money belt containing her new phone and Emily's jewellery was still round her waist. She had no way of hanging on to it when Olga tugged at it and broke the clip.

'Monica said you were a thief,' she said, examining the contents of the banana-shaped bag. 'And Don León will be interested in this,' she added, brandishing Petra's phone. 'You're a traitor and you know what happens to traitors.'

'You're a murderess and you know what happens to them!' Petra retorted.

Pablo took a step back from the fighting women, a helpless look on his face. Olga scowled at her opponent, then at Pablo. 'You're no damn use!' she said to him. 'I'll watch her. Go and fetch El Toro, then take care of the other business.'

Pablo's face darkened. For a moment, Petra thought he might disobey Olga's orders. Then he took one long last look at Petra's chest and turned to the door. As he left the room, he slammed the door behind him.

Don León entered the room without a sound. Olga was standing with her back to the door studying Petra. She gave a low chuckle. Petra stared up at her, seeing the malevolence in her eyes.

'Not in such a good position now, are we Minx?' She reached down and drew a fingertip across the top of Petra's right breast, down into the cleft and up again, across the top of the other one. Then she stabbed at a point in the soft tissue. Petra had guessed what was coming and steeled herself not to react. She refused to give Olga the satisfaction of seeing her flinch.

Instead, Petra turned the full force of her blue-green eyes on Olga until she saw her resentment boil over. Olga poked Petra again, digging her nail deep into the soft flesh. It was a power play and Petra knew it. This time, despite the protection of the T-shirt, she winced, but continued to challenge the older woman with her gaze.

'Enough, Olga! Get away from her!' Don León crossed the room in two paces. 'It seems I can't trust anybody to do the right thing anymore. Leave us alone.' He escorted Olga to the door, closed it hard with his foot and walked over to where Petra lay. The anger subsided from his face as he looked down at her. 'I'm sorry about that.'

'I'll survive,' she said.

He sat down heavily on the edge of the adjacent bed and stared at the floor, lost in thought.

Petra lay without moving a muscle and studied him. Except in the low light of the terrace, she had not seen El Toro since the party in Puerto Banús three days before. The change in him was acute. The leonine head seemed to sag on his shoulders, the mane of hair hung limply, and there was a weariness in his voice that made him sound like an old man. Only the yellow-flecked eyes, when he raised them to meet Petra's, retained a flash of fire. Her heart lurched.

'Why did you come into my life?' It was an appeal, not really a question.

Petra cast about for an appropriate response. She wasn't yet ready to lay her cards on the table.

'I didn't. I came to work,' she whispered.

'Until you arrived, I had everything planned, everything under control.'

Except for Emily, Petra thought, and Monica, who had taken the Lamborghini without permission. Don León shook his head as if he had read her thoughts and wanted to eradicate those niggling exceptions.

'The problem was, you reminded me of my sister, the sweetest and purest girl in the world,' he said. 'Ana believed in me and I lived for her. With my mother, she was the focal point of my existence. The money I made was for them. When she was assassinated, I swore to avenge her death by never being at the mercy of anyone again.' He stood up and began to pace like a caged animal searching for a way out. 'I became as ruthless as the men who killed her. I silenced my conscience, the one Father Lucanto had so carefully nurtured, and I turned a blind eye to the horrors around me.'

In the next breath, he answered Petra's unspoken question. 'Yes, I made my money from running drugs into Mexico and from there to the USA. I had it all – the laboratories, the mercenaries, a fleet of boats. I amassed a fortune, more than I had ever dreamed of and could ever spend. Life was tough, rough and fun. The girls and the friends came like flies to honey. But it was the old story. It didn't bring me satisfaction or happiness.'

'Did you really think it would?' Petra murmured.

'I never stopped hoping. Then new drug lords contested my patch, took my women, set me up. In the end, to protect myself, I turned them in and left that arena forever. Being here was a revelation. Sophisticated women, educated girls, a jet-set life of luxury without the constant looking over my shoulder.'

'Won't they follow you here?'

'It's possible,' he said, 'but unlikely.' In truth, it was one of his deepest fears. That was the reason he was constantly on the move, preferring to be on the water rather than on land and to keep only a small entourage of trusted staff. 'I stay out of the big guys' space. All my businesses here are legit.'

'Some of them, maybe, but why are you involved with people like Theo and Sheik Kamal?' Petra said.

He shrugged. 'Habit, I suppose. It's small stuff and I need the rush.'

To Petra, it was a poor excuse. Criminals often rationalized their actions by playing down their involvement. She decided to confront him.

'Did killing Emily Mortlake by forcing her to take drugs give you a rush?' she asked.

'I don't know what happened. I had no idea she was dead.' His voice was full of despair. 'She was an interesting girl; I enjoyed her intellect…'

'And her body,' Petra interrupted.

He shot her a quizzical look. 'Who wouldn't? She was a beauty and talented in so many ways. Her downfall was that she made people jealous.'

'Is that why she was killed? Because you were jealous?'

'I like to shock and keep people off balance, not kill.'

331

Petra knew he was lying. She had witnessed his ruthlessness the night of the rendezvous with the Lazzara.

'What about Miguel?'

'Miguel?'

'Yes. One of your seamen.'

'Oh, that! An accident. Man overboard. It's impossible to find anyone at night at sea.'

The callousness of his attitude was beyond belief, yet she knew also that he was capable of intense emotion. 'You asked me a question,' she said. 'Now I'll give you the real answer. I came into your life because I had to – to investigate Emily Mortlake's disappearance. To do my duty I had no choice.'

'But you do have a choice! Emily's dead – an accident. We can be together.'

'Another accident?' She paused before continuing. 'And what about Monica?'

'Monica is nothing. A girl I picked out of the gutter. She won't bother us.'

Until that moment, he had not touched her. Deliberately, he knelt beside the bed, as he had done on the terrace just a few days before, and placed his lips on hers. The jolt of electricity made Petra's whole body tingle. For a nanosecond, she was tempted. When he released her, he sat back on his heels. The golden eyes were tinged with regret.

'I know,' he said quietly. 'Don't say anything. I wish circumstances could have been different.'

She acquiesced with her eyes then let them close. Despite the strength of her attraction to him, she could never condone what he had done.

His voice broke the tension between them. It had a harsher edge that had not been there before. 'I shall have to decide what to do with you.'

Petra had already realized that after her rejection he would have no option but to consider her a liability. Her situation was precarious at best.

In the silence that followed his bald statement, they heard the familiar sound of a helicopter. Petra's heart leapt to her throat. Could it be the authorities? Don León jumped up and went to the window.

'It's Sheik Kamal. What's he doing here so late at night?' Don León's astonishment was evident in his tone. Petra wondered whether Sheik Kamal had somehow found out about Emily or if he was simply coming to pay his respects. Whatever the cause, his arrival could not have been more opportune.

Don León left the guest suite in a hurry to switch on the landing lights for Sheik Kamal. As soon as he had gone, Petra turned onto her right side and wriggled towards her right wrist. The play in the cords she had managed to obtain by tensing or expanding her muscles and lowering her shoulder blades enabled her to reach the binding on her wrist with her mouth. She struggled for a minute or two, trying to undo it. It was no use. She did not have enough purchase to make any headway, and she did not know how long Don León would be gone. It was time to implement Plan B.

Carefully, she turned onto her back again. Then, by making small jumps with her pelvis and pushing with her feet, she managed to raise her chest higher than her neck. The first time she tried, she became too tired and collapsed back onto the bed before the job was done. After a short rest, she began again. She was afraid Don León or Pablo would return before she had freed herself. This time, she moved with less enthusiasm and more precision.

Gradually, she worried the black and silver cross that hung on the chain round her neck out of the loose neckline of her T-shirt. She worked it into a position where, by lying on her right side again, she could use her mouth to pick up the top. Now she knew how Houdini felt. With the metal in her mouth, she gagged and had to drop it. On the second attempt, she succeeded in clamping it between her teeth at the base of the crosspiece. She bit down on the release mechanism and the bottom of the cross fell away to reveal a five centimetre stiletto.

Like her Italian priest ancestors, Petra kept the blade razor sharp to be ready to serve in time of need. Three minutes later, her right wrist was free. It was bleeding from the cuts inflicted on it during the process, but she gladly picked up the blade with her right hand and attacked the bindings on her left wrist. When both wrists were free, she released her ankles and wiped the blade on the bedcover. She picked up the jewelled sheath and slid it over the knife. The mechanism clicked into place. Pressing a tissue over her cuts to stem the bleeding, she ran out of the room.

CHAPTER TWENTY-SEVEN

In the far corner of the garden, the red, white and green helicopter sank slowly down onto the concrete pad, its rotors beating a sonorous tattoo. Don León had switched on the lights and was there to greet Sheik Kamal on his arrival. He extended his hand and pretended a bonhomie he did not feel. 'My friend, you return the surprise! What brings you here?'

'I am on my way to Puerto Banús,' Sheik Kamal said. 'I came in person to tell you I have found no sign of Petra Minx. I can assure you she is not at the workshop, nor at my villa. And I wish to arrange for some extra shipments, as we discussed,' he added.

A flicker of uncertainty crossed Don León's face. He could not help thinking there was some other reason behind Sheik Kamal's late-night visit. Nevertheless, he put on his most genial expression. 'Let's go inside. We can continue our discussions over a drink.' He hurried his guest across the lawn towards the terrace and the double glass doors in the centre of the villa.

Petra was halfway down the stairs leading to the hall when she heard the Lamborghini fire up. The film crew had packed up and left, and the hall was empty. She wondered who was using the car. It couldn't be Don León, because he had gone to meet Sheik Kamal, and he would be

335

unlikely to allow Olga or Pablo to use his precious toy. Apart from the servants, the only other person on the premises was Monica, who had gone into hysterics at the sight of Petra in the belly dancing costume. It was possible she might be trying to flee from a situation that had got out of hand.

Petra crossed the hall to the front door and risked a peek into the courtyard. She was surprised to see Olga and Pablo sitting in the car. They appeared to be arguing. How long they would remain there blocking her escape route she didn't know. The only other way to reach the courtyard where she had left the motorbike was via the gardens. If she could make it out through the French doors onto the terrace before Don León returned, she might have enough time to run round the outside of the villa, retrieve the bike and follow Olga and Pablo down the drive. If they realized they were being followed, she could only hope they would think the motorcyclist belonged to the film crew. There was no other way she could think of to get off the property.

The dimly lit sitting room was empty and the French doors were open. Petra could see Sheik Kamal and Don León walking across the lawn. Provided she stayed close to the house, she should be able to slip away without being seen. As they reached the open terrace, she drew back into the angle of the wall where the colonnade turned in on itself. It was costing her valuable minutes, but the delay was preferable to being caught by Don León. She was relieved when she heard the French doors close and saw the helicopter landing pad lights go out.

To make up for lost time, Petra ran as fast as she could. She pushed a white wicker chair out of her way as she passed through another outdoor seating area. She still had not seen the Lamborghini go down the drive. To her right now was the bougainvillea-covered courtyard wall and ahead of her, directly in her path, a swing seat.

She was nearly upon it when she realized it was occupied. Monica sat slumped over in the seat. Thinking she was asleep, Petra slowed to tiptoe by. At that moment, the Lamborghini roared past and Monica uttered a tortured sound.

'Monica! What's wrong? Let me see.' Petra bent to her aid. 'Oh my God!'

Blood was seeping from underneath Monica's hands as she clenched them over her abdomen. She appeared to be pressing down on the sides of a jagged incision. The loss of blood had left her face a ghostly white. Petra had seen enough marine accidents involving severely wounded victims to know that Monica would likely die if she didn't receive immediate medical attention.

'I'll fetch Don León; we'll get you to hospital and you'll be fine,' she said, trying to imbue her voice with as much reassurance as possible.

Monica put a restraining hand on Petra's arm and blood welled up from the gash in her stomach. 'No, don't. It's too late. I'm tired, so tired … and this is retribution for what I did.'

'For taking the Lamborghini? I don't think so,' Petra said.

'No, not that, although I know that was wrong. I went to Olga…' Monica's voice was raspy.

'Did Olga do this to you?'

'No, not Olga.'

'Was it Pablo?' Petra asked, thinking of him sitting in the car arguing with Olga.

Monica shook her head. 'No. It's all my fault. I told Olga I was pregnant with Don León's child. She insisted I have an abortion. She arranged it, then he found out.' She paused to gasp for air.

'When was this? Recently?'

'Six months ago. He blamed me, not Olga. Things started to go wrong between us.' Monica doubled over as pain shot through her gut. 'I wanted that child. I should never have listened to her. I love Don León, and I would have loved our baby.'

In the presence of such raw emotion, Petra suddenly felt ashamed at the way she had responded to Monica. From the beginning there had been friction between them, but they had also shared some laughs. If she had made more of an effort to understand what lay beneath Monica's bravura, she might have been able to prevent the terrible trauma the girl was now enduring. Instead, her complex feelings for Don León had clouded her judgement.

'So it was Don León who did this to you?' she asked, to confirm what she had guessed.

Monica nodded. Her breathing was becoming laboured. Petra recognized the signs and knew that her life force was ebbing away. 'It's not too late to get you to hospital. Sheik Kamal can take you in his helicopter. I'll call the police to arrest Don León.'

'No!' Monica's voice was suddenly strong and determined. 'He saved me from a life of drugs and debauchery. This is my fault.'

'It isn't, Monica. This is a crime.' With immense sadness, Petra realized that Monica did not want to live. She put her arms around her and asked gently: 'Can you tell me what happened to Emily Mortlake? Did he kill her too, with drugs?'

'No,' Monica whispered. 'He fell for her tricks. He couldn't see she was manipulating him.' The hurt in her voice betrayed her jealousy. 'I was glad when Sheik Kamal took her to Morocco.'

'But she came back, didn't she?'

'Don León fetched her back. He was still obsessed with her. Wanted her to stay with him and star in his movies, with another girl. She refused and there was a big fight here, during a party.' Monica broke off, coughing.

'When was that?'

'Late September, just before she was due to leave.' Monica's face contorted in pain and Petra expected her to stop talking. She was full of admiration when Monica continued, fuelled by her hatred of Emily.

'I was delighted when Olga said she'd overdosed. She was supposed to go back to Morocco for rehab, but she was too sick. Then Olga told me she'd died. We agreed not to tell Don León. If anyone asked, we would say she was in Morocco.'

'Why did Olga tell him tonight?'

'You heard that?' Monica gave a hoarse laugh. 'You were the dancer!'

'Right.'

'Because the police are looking for her, and Don León might say something. Now he knows she's dead, he'll keep his mouth shut.'

'Do you know what Olga did with Emily's body?'

'No idea. Raoul might be able to tell you.'

Petra felt another convulsion rack Monica's body. Despite her toughness, she was weakening rapidly. 'Don't talk anymore, you've been a real help.' Petra cradled her in her arms.

'I knew you weren't a floozy, Minx. You didn't fit the part somehow. I was jealous of you too … your education, the way El Toro looked at you. He's in love with you.'

339

'No, he isn't. I remind him of his sister. He loves you Monica. He wanted your child.' Petra planted a kiss on the girl's platinum hair and with infinite care pulled her closer. With a tiny sigh, she slipped into unconsciousness.

Olga gripped the wheel of the Lamborghini with iron fingers. In the seat beside her, Pablo sat with his arms folded across his chest. She was furious with him for not carrying out her orders. First he had messed about with the girl from Algeciras instead of getting her off the premises as Don León had told him to do. Second, and worse, he had disobeyed her instructions to kill the Mortlake girl and dispose of the body the week after the party, once it became apparent how bad her condition was. He had lied to her, like the scumbag he was, assuring her he had taken care of everything. If she hadn't been so busy training the new steward and making arrangements for the October gala in Puerto Banús, she might have asked him for more details. She should have suspected Pablo might want to keep Emily for himself. He was a loner with no social skills, unable to forge his own relationships. On many occasions, she had caught him studying the girls Don León brought aboard with lascivious intensity and she knew how much time he spent in secret watching pornographic movies.

Now she was following his directions to the place where he said he had kept Emily hidden for over three weeks. The winding, single-track mountain road climbed steeply. Small avalanches of rock littered the left-hand edge of the road. To their right, the land fell away to the coast, the drop at times sheer. Below them, less than a kilometre away as the crow flies, was the villa.

Pablo uncrossed his arms and tapped his window as a police helicopter swept in from the east and circled the villa, its searchlights playing across the property. 'It won't take them long to find out El Toro is a murderer. I saw what he did,' he proclaimed. 'They'll take your precious Don León away and lock him up for good!'

The helicopter passed close to them, illuminating the car in dazzling white, then retreated down the slope towards the villa. Olga's lips were pressed together in a tight line, her face an inscrutable mask. She rounded the next two corners on screaming tyres and brought the Bat to a screeching halt on the inside of a curve where a waterfall hissed down the rock face and passed under the road.

'You're a damn fool!' she shouted. 'You need to know when to keep your foul mouth shut.' Miguel had deserved his punishment. It was a rough lesson that had to be learned. She did not condemn Don León for dispensing the kind of justice he had grown up with on the streets of Bogotá, but she was unprepared for what Pablo said next.

'I'm not talking about Miguel. He fed the fishes a long time ago.' Pablo rubbed his hands. 'I'm talking about Monica. It serves her right for her high-handed attitude.'

With a rapid movement that would have done credit to a much younger, slimmer person, Olga reached into the top of her boot and drew out a silver pistol. She levelled it at Pablo's chest. 'If you're trying to tell me something, say it!' she snarled.

Pablo saw the expression on her face and hesitated.

'Go on, say it!'

'I saw him stab her, right in the stomach, while you were busy with Minx.'

Olga was shocked to the core, but her aim never wavered. She had noticed the haggard look on Don León's face when he entered the bedroom where Minx was tied up. He was building himself a heap of trouble and the police were closing in.

She waved the gun at Pablo. 'Get out of the car, you ungrateful pervert.' The scissor doors slid upwards. 'Go on, get out, out!'

He gave her an uncomprehending look then stepped out onto the road, not taking his eyes off the gun. Slowly he backed away from her blistering gaze.

'I'll take care of Emily,' he offered. 'You rescue Don León.' He started to run away from the car.

'That's exactly what I'm going to do,' Olga cried, 'as soon as I've finished with you.'

Pablo staggered forwards as the first bullet caught him in the shoulder. Olga was already out of the car. She steadied the gun and fired again. This time the bullet slammed into the base of his spine and he fell face down across the concrete slab that marked the edge of the road. With grim determination, Olga lifted his legs and sent his body tumbling down the watercourse to the rocks below.

The police helicopter was circling the estate. She had no time to lose. If it landed and the police found Monica, Don León would be taken into custody. There was also the matter of the girl from Algeciras who was still tied up at the villa, and God only knew what he might have done to Petra Minx.

If only Minx had never come aboard! It had been one incident after another since the beginning of the summer. Olga wished there had been time for things to return to normal. No sooner had she succeeded in counteracting the Mortlake girl's influence over Don León than Petra had taken her place. From the start, Olga had had her suspicions about Minx. Pablo and Monica had agreed that she asked too many questions, was unusually curious about the other Canadian, and far too chummy with Carlo, the new steward. And ever since Petra's arrival, Don León had begun to ignore Olga's advice and make significant errors of judgement. As she sped back down the road to the villa, she prayed she would arrive in time to save him.

With a sinking feeling in her heart, Petra felt Monica's pulse. It was very faint and her skin was clammy. Her breathing was irregular. It was probably too late, but if there was any chance of saving her, she had to try.

Sheik Kamal was astounded when Petra burst through the French doors into the lounge where he and Don León were enjoying a drink. 'You didn't tell me Miss Minx was here,' he exclaimed. 'Where did you find her?'

Don León avoided the question. 'She arrived this evening,' he said. He wondered how she had escaped from her bonds and how long she had been free. He had intended to plead tiredness to get rid of the Sheik as quickly as politeness would allow, then return to Petra and try again to persuade her to stay with him.

'You must help Monica!' Petra shouted. 'Please, Sheik, take her to hospital in the helicopter, she'll die otherwise.' Petra rushed over to where he sat. The urgency in her voice forced him to take notice. He noted too the blood on her wrists and on the front of her clothes.

'Has there been an accident?'

Petra pointed an angry finger at Don León. 'He stabbed Monica instead of giving her the sympathy and understanding she needed.'

'You accuse me of violence when she aborted my child!'

'She only did what Olga told her to do! She loves you, and she wanted that baby.'

Don León groaned as if the world had collapsed around him. 'I don't believe you!'

'Ask Olga then!' Petra whirled round as a stocky figure appeared in the French doors behind her. She had heard the Lamborghini race up the drive and come to a stop a short distance from the terrace.

Olga stood facing them like a pit bull poised to attack. In her hand she held a silver pistol, which she pointed at Petra.

'Is that true? Did you tell Monica to have an abortion? Without consulting me?' Don León's tone was anguished.

When Olga did not reply, he repeated his question.

'Did you, mother? Did you?'

The word "mother" shook Petra to her roots. A few more pieces of the puzzle fell into place. Sheik Kamal looked bewildered. Olga brandished the gun at the two of them.

'Come on, Leonardo! We have to go. The police are here.' As if to confirm her words, the police helicopter passed overhead. She took a few steps into the room and seized the edge of his jacket. He twisted away, tearing the fabric at the seam.

'Why, mother? Why did you do it?'

'For your own good, son. You'd never have been happy with someone like that.'

'You don't know who I would be happy with.' He turned to Petra and Sheik Kamal. 'Let's get Monica to hospital.'

'Don't bother, she's dead.' To emphasize her words, Olga fired three shots in rapid succession at the crystal chandelier that hung in the centre of the room. The lights went out and glass tinkled to the marble floor. She grabbed Don León by the arm and dragged him, with a strength born of desperation, through the French doors.

As soon as she recovered her bearings, Petra chased after them. Don León was running across the terrace after

344

Olga towards the Lamborghini. They passed very close to where Monica lay now in peace on the swing seat. Olga had left the orange scissor doors of the Bat pointing towards the sky. She leapt into the car, pulled Don León into the passenger seat and started the engine. She barely waited for the doors to close before reversing with a screech of tyres and accelerating away down the drive.

As Olga drove out of the main gate of the property at high speed, the police helicopter landed in the courtyard behind the villa. Carlo, accompanied by two policemen, raced up the steps and through the hall into the sitting room where Sheik Kamal stood nonplussed by the turn of events. The light from the hall revealed the debris that covered the floor.

'Where's Petra?' Carlo said urgently.

'Here,' she answered, stepping into the room.

He crossed to meet her and embraced her briefly. 'Are you all right?'

'I'm fine. Monica's on the terrace. She's dead. Don León killed her. Olga has escaped with him in the car. I think we should go after them.'

Carlo and the policemen held a rapid conference.

'The consensus is that we should take Sheik Kamal's helicopter and follow the car. The police will stay here and secure the villa. Several police cars are on their way. They should be able to intercept Olga and Don León before they reach the toll road. Is that all right, Sheik Kamal?'

'My pleasure, Sir. I had no idea Don León was capable of such uncivilized behaviour, nor that his mother had such a hold over him.'

Neither had I, thought Petra.

The Lamborghini barrelled down the hill, jumping the rough spots and potholes. Olga drove with total concentration. Not once did she address Don León or turn to look at him. The first police car, lights flashing, met the Bat on a tight curve where Olga was in the outside lane and so had the advantage of seeing them first. She stood on the accelerator and left them looking for a place to turn round. The second car, also advertising its presence, saw the Lamborghini coming down the hill and positioned itself to block the lane. Olga simply swerved round it on the inside.

Warned by their colleagues, the third group of policemen in the last of the white cars lay in wait at the foot of the giant wind turbines. When the Lamborghini roared past, they tried to follow, but their wheels spun on the sandy terrain. Watching from the helicopter, Carlo and Petra laughed aloud.

'You have to admire her driving. For an old woman, she sure can handle that car!' Carlo grinned.

'She's no old woman. She's a pitiless schemer, determined to exercise control. We all underestimated her and her influence over Don León.' Petra's voice was harsh. 'Did you know she's his mother?'

'Mamma mia!' Carlo raised his eyebrows. 'No, I didn't, but that would explain a lot of things. She seemed out of place on the yacht, and I could never understand why El Toro deferred to her. She wasn't exactly a beauty!'

'Why do you men have to be so shallow?' Petra asked.

'That's not shallow, it's just not deep!'

Petra shook her head in disgust. In a fencing match, Mercutio would always find the correct riposte.

A kilometre further on, the Lamborghini disappeared into a tunnel beyond which the road descended steeply through a gorge until it joined the toll road. Sheik Kamal's helicopter hovered over the tunnel exit, waiting for the car to reappear. When it did, it shot out of the mouth of the tunnel like a cannonball.

'That's odd,' Petra shouted over the din of the helicopter's engine. 'The car's lights are off. Put the searchlights on.'

She craned her neck to see what was happening. The searchlights swept back and forth over the orange roof of the Lamborghini, which seemed to speed up rather than slow down as it reached a dangerous bend. In the instant before the car hit the rock face and ricocheted across the road, Petra knew what she would see next. The Bat crashed through the flimsy metal barrier and rolled over and over down the steep side of the gorge. It had not yet reached the bottom when it ignited in a searing ball of fire. For some, it marked the end of a dream, for others, the end of a nightmare.

CHAPTER TWENTY-EIGHT

Sheik Kamal's pilot alerted the authorities. The search and rescue service, leaving the people smugglers and drug dealers to their own devices, diverted a helicopter from coastal patrol to the site of Olga and Don León's funeral pyre. There was nothing they could do except stand by until the fire services arrived. Petra watched in anguished silence as flames shot up to the sky. Fanned by the rising wind, they spread quickly to the scrub at the bottom of the gorge. However bad the crime, fire was a terrible way to go.

Carlo whistled in awe. 'It's impossible for anyone to survive that inferno, and there won't be anything left of the Lamborghini.'

'A true waste of exquisite engineering,' Sheik Kamal agreed.

'Not to mention human life,' Petra interjected.

'Of course,' Sheik Kamal said. 'Human beings are also exquisitely engineered. As is the new amphibious Quadski. A remarkable machine. Has either of you had the opportunity to experience it?'

Petra had the grace to look ashamed. 'I promise you it will be returned intact, Sheik Kamal.'

'It was all in a good cause. You have enabled me to restore my relationship with my son, for which I thank you,' he said.

Carlo looked uncomprehendingly from one to the other. 'You always were into things up to your neck, Minx.'

'As long as I keep my head above water, I'll be all right,' she retorted.

By the time Sheik Kamal's helicopter landed for the second time at Don León's villa, the forensic team and an ambulance were on the scene along with the Chief of Police, the crew from the police helicopter and the officers from the three police cars. The forensic team was at work on the terrace, which had been sealed off, and officers were conducting an initial search for the murder weapon.

In the formal dining room, which he had commandeered for his temporary headquarters, the Chief of Police listened as Petra, Carlo and Sheik Kamal described what they had seen from the helicopter. He assured them rescue efforts would begin in earnest as soon as the fire could be brought under control, although he entertained little hope of survivors.

'I don't think Olga intended there to be any survivors, Chief,' Petra said. 'She would rather kill her son than have him go to jail. It looked like an accident, but I'm sure it was suicide.' The others nodded their agreement.

'We'll need to take a full statement from you, Miss Minx,' the Chief of Police said. 'You seem to have a very good understanding of the workings of these people's minds. And you were the last person to see the murdered woman alive. I understand that she named her attacker. You also appear to have blood on the front of your T-shirt,' he added.

Petra clenched her fists beneath the cuffs of her jacket. Her wrists were still sore but no longer bleeding. 'Of course, Sir, I'll be happy to make a statement. The blood will be Monica's. I was holding her in my arms,' she said. She had already begun to work out how she could explain her actions at the villa without withholding information, giving only the details that were strictly necessary.

Sheik Kamal stepped in. 'As a business associate of Don León's, I would also be happy to provide a complete statement, Chief, if that would help your enquiries,' he said in his inimitably urbane manner. 'I can attest to the fact that Miss Minx came into the lounge where I was having a drink with my host Don León and asked me to take Monica to hospital in my helicopter. I was astounded to learn that she had been stabbed. And, of course, I was present when Olga appeared armed with a pistol.'

'Thank you both,' the Chief of Police said. 'I'll let you know as soon as one of my men is ready to take your statements.'

'I would appreciate it if you could arrange for me to give mine as quickly as possible, Chief,' Sheik Kamal said. 'I have business to attend to in Morocco this morning. I will wait in the lounge.'

Petra caught Carlo's eye and raised her eyebrows. Sheik Kamal would certainly have to be questioned in connection with the transfer of contraband to *Lady Fatima*, but that was Carlo's baby. The lingerie workshop was a different matter. It was probably quite legal even if some of Zahra's practices bordered on abuse, and Petra was inclined to protect Ahmed if she could. For the time being, though, there were two deaths under investigation, Monica's and Emily Mortlake's. Her priority was to focus on finding Emily's body. And for that, she needed the support of the Chief of Police.

'Thank *you*, Sir,' Petra said, addressing the Chief of Police. 'The arrival of the police helicopter was most opportune. There might have been more carnage if Olga hadn't wanted to escape with Don León before it landed.'

She turned to Carlo. 'I'd no idea whether you would receive my text. Thank you for acting on it so quickly. A pity, though, that we weren't able to save Monica.' It would be a long time before she would be able to forget the extent of the girl's pain, both physical and emotional.

'I had the devil's own job establishing our credentials and convincing the police in Marbella to interrupt the Chief's dinner,' Carlo said.

'You're lucky my staff gave you the benefit of the doubt. We don't like lone operators. It was only because we had an open file on Don León that they thought it advisable to call me,' the Chief answered.

Persuading the local authorities to lend their assistance when undercover activities ceased to be undercover was always difficult. 'Your response is truly appreciated, Chief,' Petra said. 'I'm sure Carlo has told you why I was aboard *Titania*. As I said in my text, I now believe Emily Mortlake, the politician's daughter I was sent to look for, is dead. That's what Olga told Don León in my hearing. Unfortunately, she didn't reveal the location of the body. We need to find Pablo Barcel. He was also here this evening and I believe he knows where it is.' Petra had decided not to divulge her role as the belly dancer, nor the fact that Olga and Pablo had held her captive.

'When was the last time you saw him?' the Chief asked.

Petra looked at her watch. 'About half past midnight. He was sitting in the Lamborghini with Olga, in the courtyard. They were arguing quite vehemently. I heard the car start up and leave the property just after I found Monica asleep, as I thought she was at first.'

351

'We saw the car, Sir,' Carlo interjected. 'From the helicopter before we landed.'

The Chief consulted the sheaf of notes in front of him. 'Right. An orange Lamborghini with two occupants was seen up on the mountain road, about a kilometre north of here. Do you have any idea what they might have been doing?'

'No, Sir,' Petra answered. 'But they could have been going to where Emily is buried. Pablo might be up there now. I think it unlikely that he came back in the Lamborghini with Olga, because she was intent on saving Don León.' She paused to collect her thoughts. 'Olga drove the car up close to the terrace and left the doors open while she came in to get him. And don't forget she was armed.'

'My men are searching the villa and outbuildings now. I'll ask them to look out for Pablo, and I'll send the helicopter up as soon as it's light.'

'Could I join the search, Chief? I'd like to look for anything related to Emily Mortlake, and I know the layout of the villa,' Petra said.

The Chief pursed his lips and looked hard at the young woman. He saw the look of appeal in her bright blue-green eyes and decided not to stick to strict protocol. There was already more than one strange aspect to the whole affair. 'All right, but stay with my men and if you find anything, don't touch it. I'll call for you when we're ready to take your statement.'

One of the officers had drawn a rough floor plan of the villa and its outbuildings and was making notes as the initial search of each area was completed. Petra was keen to know how the police would react to finding cut cords tied to a bed in one of the guest suites and blood on the bedcover. She climbed the grand staircase, taking the left-hand flight of stairs, and joined one of the constables on the upper floor. When they came to the bedroom where she had been held captive, she held her breath. The constable pushed open the door and they entered. It was the same room, but the air was fresh; it had been dusted and swept, and the bedcovers on both beds had been changed. There were no pieces of cord, no bits of tissue, nothing at all to reveal the purposes for which the room had been used just a few hours before. Someone had been at work behind the scenes.

Although Petra was relieved that some of the evidence had been removed, she was also disappointed to find nothing on the upper floor of the villa that might help in her quest for Emily Mortlake. The whole of the upper floor was clean, tidy and as free of any decorative or personal items as it had been on the day Don León had taken her on a guided tour of his domain.

She ran down the other side of the grand staircase, crossed the main hall as she had done earlier in the belly dancer's costume, and joined the team that was searching Don León's entertainment area in the basement of the villa. On entering the wardrobe room, she was not at all surprised to see that the belly dancer's costume and her shoulder-length blonde wig had been picked up and put away. The screening room and the various studios were empty, the lounge and bar in perfect order. When she checked behind the bar, there were no bottles of the Cuvée Ana León, only the usual bar stock and a well known Spanish cava. Everything was as shipshape as Captain Juan had insisted things be aboard *Titania*. She sat down on one of the red and black sofas in front of the giant plasma screen, feeling like a mouse lost in a labyrinth.

Every corner she turned brought her up against a brick wall. The villa was holding on to its secrets.

The Chief of Police took one look at Petra's face and knew she had not found what she might have been looking for. 'Ah, Miss Minx! Right on time. We're ready to take your statement. Sheik Kamal has given his and has just left. I could see no grounds for holding him here.'

Petra silently agreed. Although he had known Emily Mortlake, he had said himself that he had not seen her since mid-September, and Petra was inclined to believe him. The key had been Olga, and now it was Pablo.

Half an hour later, Raoul came into the dining room carrying a tray of coffee and croissants. The first signs of dawn were lightening the sky as Petra signed her statement. She was weary and dispirited. The shock of finding Monica had compounded the anguish she felt on learning that Emily Mortlake was dead. Yet she knew there had to be more and was not ready to give up.

Carlo had discreetly taken himself off while Petra was giving her statement. He found one of the more technical officers on the scene experimenting with the video system in the basement. Replaying the footage of the last thirty-six hours, they made some interesting discoveries. Carlo called the Chief downstairs to show him what they had found.

On Monday night, there had been a copper-haired girl wearing part of a ferry hostess's uniform fondling herself on one of the sofas in the lounge and, later, lying naked on a four-poster bed in a variety of positions. There did not appear to have been any coercion; in fact she seemed to be enjoying herself, but there was enough evidence to implicate Don León in the production of pornographic materials. Switching to another part of the system, the technical officer showed the Chief what had been captured on one of the other cameras.

The Chief of Police returned to the dining room. 'Miss Minx, I'm afraid you have some explaining to do. You may need to add a few details to your statement regarding the sequence of events,' he said. 'And I may want to question you about the death of Axel Rodquist, crewmember of the yacht *Nemesis*,' he added.

'Of course, Sir, no problem.' Petra thought rapidly. The Chief was probably fishing. There was no reason at all for him to link her to Axel. 'I'm sorry,' she said. 'What happened here was rather embarrassing.'

'Actually, my officer thought it was very ingenious,' he said.

'So did I,' Carlo added.

Raoul entered the dining room to enquire if they would like more coffee or croissants. Petra eyed him thoughtfully. Don León's trusty retainer: always on the fringe, keeping an eye on things, clearing up any messes. He seemed to Petra to be shuffling more than he had earlier, making himself appear older. A useful ploy if he wanted to be dismissed as a forgetful old man. He could not fail to be aware of what went on at the villa, and she remembered Monica saying he might know where Emily had been kept after overdosing on whatever drugs she had taken or been given.

'Just a moment, Raoul,' Petra said, as he turned towards the door. 'Chief, I think Raoul too might have some information which could help us. I'd like to ask him a few questions.'

'I suppose you might as well, since you're the reason we're all here today.'

355

'You and your wife have been working for Don León for a while, haven't you?' she asked.

Raoul answered slowly. 'Like I told the constable this morning, five years or thereabouts.'

'And you look after this villa for Don León?'

Raoul nodded.

'So you see a lot of what goes on here – film shoots and parties, for example.'

'Not much goes on here. Most of the time it's closed up.'

'So what do you do? Maintenance? Gardening? General security?'

'Supervision mostly. We use local contractors for maintenance and gardening. And we have electronic security and a guard at the gate. I'm too old to do much myself.'

'What about the recording and video systems?'

'I'm not a technical man.'

If you were, Petra thought, you would no doubt have erased a great deal of the recent footage, to protect yourself if nothing else.

'What about the copper-haired girl who was here yesterday?' the Chief of Police asked. 'What do you know about her?'

Raoul blanched, but recovered himself quickly. 'She left early this morning in the marina car,' he said.

Petra nodded. 'There was a car from the marina in the courtyard when I arrived yesterday evening.' And from Sheik Kamal's helicopter, she had seen a small white car heading towards the toll road, a long way behind the Lamborghini. At the time, it had not seemed significant. Once again, Raoul had succeeded in removing anything incriminating from the scene. 'What about your wife, Bettina isn't it?' she asked him. 'What does she do?'

Raoul gave her a stony look. 'A little cooking and light cleaning. Again, mostly supervision when we have cleaners and caterers in.'

'Quite a nice set-up!' the Chief of Police commented. 'Free board, lodging and transport, a reasonable salary, no doubt, and very little to do for it. Where is your wife?'

'Like I told the constable, she's gone to stay with friends in Ronda. She left after lunch yesterday.'

'What about the film crew that was here on location last night? How come she wasn't here to provide food for them?' the Chief asked.

'We had caterers, so there was no need,' Raoul replied.

'That's right!' Petra exclaimed. 'But I saw an elderly woman crossing the courtyard between six-thirty and seven yesterday evening. I'm sure it was your wife. I recognized her from my first visit here with Don León. So you're lying.'

'Where is she now?' the Chief asked.

Under orders from the Chief of Police, the police helicopter was repeating its circuit of the night before. The officers on board were trying to identify the area where the searchlights had picked up the orange Lamborghini. It had seemed strange at the time for a car of that nature to be on a rough mountain road late at night, yet no one had logged its exact position. After some debate, they zeroed in on a bridge over a waterfall. They had also been instructed to report any unusual activity in the area and, in particular, to look out for an elderly woman weighing about seventy kilogrammes, one hundred and fifty centimetres tall, with grey hair and glasses.

As they flew towards the bridge, the pilot thought he detected movement away to his left. He turned the aircraft to investigate. After a couple of passes, he was sure. A man or a woman in black trousers, green jacket and a hat was climbing slowly but steadily up a track towards the road, carrying a basket. The figure stopped to look up as the helicopter approached and the pilot saw the glint of glasses. He reached for his radio.

The message was phoned through to the Chief of Police in the dining room. 'OK. Keep an eye on whoever it is, we don't want to spook them.' He held the phone away from his ear and turned to the assembled room. 'There's a man or a woman on a path between here and the mountain road. The pilot thinks it's a woman.' He listened again as more information was relayed. 'She's dumped her basket and is moving back down the path, which looks as though it could lead back here.'

Petra jumped up. 'It's probably Raoul's wife! Is that Bettina, Raoul?'

Raoul shrugged. 'It could be, I don't know.'

'Well, I'm going after whoever it is. They need to be brought in.' Petra raced out of the room before the Chief of Police had time to object. She left the villa through the rear door and ran out of the courtyard and round to the right, past where she had parked the motorbike. It was still there next to the stack of eucalyptus logs, but it would be useless on the kind of terrain that lay behind the villa.

Behind the outbuildings was a series of half-covered storage areas and walled pens, which once could have been used for animals. The first area was the wood storage area, then came the gardeners' lay-down area, full of empty flowerpots and sacks of compost and earth. A tractor attached to a cart full of cut branches was proof that they had been at work. In the next area, a pile of rotting vegetation lay in a corner next to a row of refuse bins.

As she ran, Petra kept her eyes peeled for a track or path leading uphill away from the villa. The villa itself had been built on a kind of plateau facing the sea, with its back to the mountain. Petra discovered that the perimeter wall did not go right around the property, only the fence continued in an unbroken line behind the courtyard.

In the wall of the building against which the refuse bins stood was a small door, painted white to blend in with the wall. Following her instincts, Petra continued on into yet another walled area. Facing her was a cattle shed with a wooden manger attached to the wall. To her left, there was only a metre-wide gap between the perimeter fence and the whitewashed wall. Looking down the gap, she saw that a corner of the fence had been cut and bent back to allow passage onto a narrow path. If she wasn't thrown out of the Marine Unit for ignoring police procedure, she would wager her next month's pay that this was the short-cut up to the mountain road.

Petra calculated that it was a good five minutes since she had left the dining room. The woman would be well on her way down the path unless she had changed her mind and begun to climb again. The helicopter was circling not too far away, keeping the road under observation. If it were Raoul's wife, she would likely prefer to return to the relative safety of the villa.

Petra decided the most sensible thing to do would be to wait for the woman to finish her descent. If there were a struggle, it would be easier to overpower her on flat ground than on the rocky path. And if the woman proved not to be Bettina, Petra would have some difficulty explaining why she was taking her in for questioning.

A quick look up the path confirmed that the woman had not yet come into view. Petra stationed herself inside the wall that parallelled the fence. Five minutes later, she heard stones rattling as the woman hurried down the lower part of the path then made her way through the fence.

Petra came up behind her as soon as she emerged from the narrow gap between the fence and the wall. She was certain it was the woman she had seen in the courtyard the previous evening.

'Bettina!' she called. 'I'd like you to come with me. You're wanted for questioning. Your husband is with the police now.'

A frightened look appeared on Bettina's face. She elbowed Petra out of the way. 'I've done nothing wrong,' she said.

'Then you won't mind coming with me. It's better that way.'

The helicopter hovered for a few minutes over the villa then turned to continue its search for Pablo Barcel.

The Chief of Police greeted Petra's reappearance with raised eyebrows and a slight shake of his head. 'Miss Minx, you would do well to remember you are no longer operating alone. However, you do seem to produce results.'

Raoul maintained a stiff silence as Petra steered his wife to the table and pulled out a chair for her. Bettina sat with lowered eyes while the Chief of Police cautioned her to tell the truth, then asked her to explain where she had been going and why her husband had lied about her whereabouts.

'I was just protecting my wife,' Raoul burst out.

'As far as I'm concerned, you were obstructing my enquiry,' the Chief of Police replied. 'Now I'm talking to your wife. What were you doing on the mountain road?'

It was a few seconds before Bettina answered. 'Making a pilgrimage.'

'A pilgrimage?'

'Yes. There's a hermitage up on the mountain.'

'You were carrying a basket. What was in the basket?'

'Food, water.'

'For yourself? How long were you planning to be gone?'

Bettina began to nod her head then changed it to a shake. A tear ran down her wind-roughened cheek. 'Pablo makes me go, at least once a week.'

Petra could no longer contain herself. She grabbed Bettina's shoulder and shook it. 'Why, Bettina? Why does Pablo make you do that?'

'He keeps a girl there. He pays me to take her food, water and clean clothes.'

'How long have you been doing this?' Petra demanded.

'Since the beginning of October. He said it wouldn't be for long,' Bettina whispered. 'I wanted to release her.'

'When did you last see her?'

'On Saturday.'

'So she's not dead?' Petra asked.

'No, unless something has happened to her...' Bettina's voice trailed away.

Petra tensed. Pablo was out there somewhere. She hoped he was dead and not trying to turn what Olga said had already happened into reality.

'Did anyone else know the girl was there besides you and your husband, and Pablo Barcel?' the Chief of Police asked.

'I don't think so. Last night he ordered me to go there today, to check on her and take more food.'

'Do you know where he is now? We're trying to locate him,' the Chief said. His phone rang and he broke off to answer it. 'Can you land nearby to take a closer look?' he asked, raising his hand to ward off any interruption from Petra. 'OK. I'll send up a car to stay on the bridge, and I'll see if the search and rescue guys have finished with the Lamborghini. You can come in when the car gets there.'

He turned to Petra. 'I have good news. The helicopter crew have spotted what looks like a body halfway down a watercourse on this side of the road. What was Pablo wearing when you saw him last night, Miss Minx?'

'A red sweatshirt and jeans.'

'Then it's probably him.'

Petra exhaled with relief and leaned towards Bettina. 'Do you know who the girl at the hermitage is, and why she's being held there?'

Bettina shook her head. 'I was only doing what I was paid to do.'

Petra looked at the Chief of Police. She could hardly bear to hope.

'Let's go,' he said.

The Chief of Police left a deputy in charge at the villa and invited Petra to join him in the car, with Bettina to show his driver the way. Petra's heart was in her mouth as they left Don León's estate and followed the winding mountain road for several kilometres until it became a rough track. There they abandoned the car and continued up the mountain on foot. After a ten-minute climb, they came to a small, whitewashed chapel perched on the hillside. The two slit windows set high in the walls of the hermitage were boarded up. The wooden door was barred and locked with a heavy chain and padlock.

Bettina fumbled in the pocket of her jacket and pulled out a key on a Lamborghini key ring. The Chief took it from her and unlocked the padlock. 'I'll go in first,' he said, knowing that Petra was desperate to find out whether the girl was Emily Mortlake and still alive.

Despite the hermitage's disused air, the door opened with hardly a sound. The Chief pushed it open and held out his arm to prevent Petra from following him in until he had taken a look. The single, square room with its earthen floor was bare except for a cot and a bench. On the bench stood a jug and bowl, and underneath it, a bucket. The stench from the bucket hit him as soon as he entered.

The girl was lying on the cot facing the white wall. She was curled up in the foetal position, one shoulder jutting out from under a rough woollen blanket. Her flaxen hair was a mass of tangles. She appeared to be sleeping. The Chief covered his nose and motioned Petra forward. 'Get that bucket out of here,' he growled to Bettina.

In a few quick steps Petra crossed the room and knelt by the cot. She knew immediately that her search was over. With extreme gentleness, she spoke the girl's name. 'Emily! Don't be afraid. You're quite safe now. Nobody's going to hurt you.' She knelt back on her heels and waited. There was no response. She tried again. 'I'm Petra Minx. Your friend Amy sent me to find you. She wants you to get better. Then you can take that holiday together in Switzerland that you'd planned.'

Again, there was no response and no movement. Petra laid the lightest of touches on Emily's shoulder. Her skin was hot and papery, her breathing shallow. The Chief of Police was already barking into his phone. 'Get me an ambulance and a back-up car – NOW!'

Petra was about to stand up and stretch her legs when there was a convulsive movement from the cot. A hand shot out. It was covered with oozing black blisters in a strange and horrible pattern.

'What have they done to you?' she whispered.

'You cannot imagine,' Emily whispered back. Her face was ashen, her eyes sunk into dark blue circles. Slowly, she lowered the blanket. The whole of her upper chest was a mess of festering blisters and open sores.

The disfigurement was so severe that Petra had to fight back a cry of horror. 'Who would do a thing like that?' She asked the question even though she already knew the answer.

The Chief of Police turned to Bettina and clasped her arm in a firm grip. 'I'll need a statement from you,' he said. 'You'd better have a good explanation.'

CHAPTER TWENTY-NINE

Two days later, Petra and Carlo were sitting amicably together on the roof terrace of their penthouse apartment in the Benabola Hotel overlooking Puerto Banús. The setting sun reflected off La Concha, sending shadows down the steep ridges of the mountainside. Many of the early evening strollers stopped to gape at the blue-hulled megayacht that was now surrounded by police tape and firmly guarded by uncompromising officers. Rumour had been rife in the restaurants, bars, dwellings and boutiques around the marina ever since the party and fireworks that had launched the week in such spectacular style. Break-ins had been a major cause for concern, with several incidents on boats and the theft of a motorbike from outside a café, just after a man was killed in a runaway dinghy.

Petra nursed her glass of champagne, a pink Veuve Cliquot. 'You deserve a medal, Mercutio, for taking those photos of Axel trying to stab me with his knife. If the Chief comes back with more questions about what happened that night and I'm forced to reveal the part I played in Axel's demise, at least I can plead self-defence. For the moment, though, he seems content to treat it as accidental death.'

'I always told you I was prescient.'

Petra gave him a playful nudge. 'Talking about prescience, what about the GPS coordinates I gave you so your people could locate the lagoon where we saw the champagne being unloaded?'

'Most useful, I have to admit. As soon as the Mallorcan police received the results of the analysis on the psychotropic stuff Tom sent in, they were able to make a move. They've found some very interesting laboratories on Theo's property.'

'Theo left on *Nemesis* yesterday, didn't he?'

'Yes. The police found no drugs or funny bubbles on board when they searched her, so they had no grounds for holding him here. I heard they picked him up this morning on his arrival in Palma.'

'I was sorry to hear Captain Juan had been taken into custody,' Petra said. 'He's not a bad person. He was only doing his job as a seaman.'

'He must have known there were drugs on board *Titania*, and you can't tell me that the rendezvous with *Lady Fatima* was normal cruising. I'm sure he can give us a lot of valuable information about Don León's nocturnal activities and regular contacts.'

With criminal activity there was always fallout, as Petra well knew. She held her glass out for a refill. 'I must say this is much better stuff than the Cuvée Ana León, although it doesn't have quite the same aphrodisiac properties.'

'It might if you drink enough of it,' Carlo said.

'You mean I might find you attractive?'

'Alas, probably not as attractive as you found El Toro.'

Petra pictured in her mind the huge head with its shaggy mane of hair, the cascade of earrings and the savage golden eyes. He had radiated a power and a raw sexuality that few men held and had been hard to resist. Yet she condemned him not least for his denigration of women and was ashamed of herself for falling under his spell.

'Wait a minute, what about you and Monica?' she said. 'You told me you were going at it pretty strong when El Toro discovered you!'

Carlo looked sheepish. 'Sometimes, Minx, undercover agents have to do things for the greater good.' Changing the subject, he said: 'How was Emily this afternoon?'

'I was allowed only the briefest of visits. She's responding well to the medication to relieve the itching and combat the infection in the sores, and of course she's sedated. The doctors are amazed that she lasted for so long without becoming delirious and scratching herself to pieces.'

'Strange how little publicity there is about this problem with black henna tattoos,' Carlo said.

'Strictly speaking, they aren't tattoos but skin paintings done with tainted henna paste. Real henna stains reddish brown not black, and it isn't dangerous unless it's mixed with black hair dye – para-phenylenediamine, or PPD. Apparently, PPD seeps through the skin into the blood and is not only toxic but can lead to cancer. It's PPD that caused the chemical burns and awful weals on Emily's hands and chest.'

'Have you any idea where Pablo got it?' Carlo asked.

'There are a number of possible sources: Axel, Zahra, Raoul, for example. But I don't think we'll ever know now that he and Olga are dead. Nor do we know why he began to experiment with black henna. He tattooed without mishap any number of girls with whom Don León had relationships.'

'You were lucky to get away without a tattoo!'

'Mine was a non-tattooable relationship, Mercutio, unlike yours and Monica's! The marks I bear aren't visible from the outside.'

'Perhaps not, but you're wearing *Titania* colours.'

Petra looked down at her blue silk blouse and white trousers. 'I didn't want to stay in student gear any longer, and the job offer did say "uniforms provided", so I helped myself to a few items.'

'I rather liked you in the skimpier ones! Are you staying for the investigation into Monica's death?'

'The Chief of Police said it wasn't necessary. She wasn't dead when I left her and my statement will be enough. Tomorrow I'm going to see Emily again to return her jewellery and try and find out what happened in September. On Monday I'll fly back to London for debriefing, now that I have my passport. What are you going to do, Mercutio?'

'Well, after I've tried to soften you up with more champers, I might sign on with another yacht. Being a steward has its perks – lots of nubile young girls to ogle at.' Carlo pointed to the row of boats closest to the hotel. 'See that three-master down there. All the sails are electronically controlled.'

Petra shook her head. 'Not in the same class as *Titania* or *Nemesis*.'

The following afternoon, Petra took a taxi from Puerto Banús to the private hospital in Marbella where Emily was being treated. She tapped on the door of Room 43. Now that Emily was out of danger, there was no longer a police guard at the door. Petra had read the terse statement Emily had given to the police. In it she accused Olga and Pablo of forcibly restraining her and Pablo of administering the tattoos that had gone so horribly wrong on the night of Friday, September 21st, after a party at the villa. She had also accused Pablo of confining her against her will and of attempted rape. Bettina, she alleged, had provided food unfit for human consumption and had refused to provide medical aid in circumstances where she knew it was required to prevent disfigurement or death. Since Olga and Pablo were dead, there could be no prosecution, but she was raring to testify against Bettina and Raoul if charges were brought. According to the police, she had declined to discuss her summer on board *Titania* and had no comment to make about Don León, Monica or anyone else.

Now Petra was hoping to tie up a few more loose ends in Emily's story, if she could persuade Emily to talk to her. In particular, what had caused the fight at the villa between her and Melanie? What had happened after the fight, and why had Melanie been sent away, but not Emily? Through her conversations with Tom Gilmore in London over the last few days, she had learned a great deal about what had happened to Melanie, but there were still some missing links. Closure would be good, not least for Emily.

Petra knocked again on the door of Room 43, louder this time, and heard Emily answer 'Come in'.

She was sitting up in bed wearing a loose-fitting, blue hospital gown. Her hands were covered in dressings and her fingernails were clean and short, not long, ragged and dirty as they had been when Petra found her at the hermitage. Another day of rest and treatment had made a huge difference to her appearance. Her colour was better, the dark circles were fading, her flaxen hair was recovering its shine.

'You look better today,' Petra said. 'Have your parents arrived from Canada?'

'I don't want them here. They're useless. I'm fine on my own.'

Petra admired Emily's spirit though she deplored her arrogance. It was that spirit and her contempt for her captors that had enabled her to cling to her self-respect and survive, when others would have curled up to die. The

369

arrogance was a shield, a hard shell that she had built around herself. It would be tough to break through.

'I expect you've heard about the accident that killed Don León,' Petra said quietly. 'It was a horrible thing watching the Lamborghini go up in flames.'

'He's no loss to anyone.'

'I thought you liked him.'

'He was almost as old as my father,' Emily said, her voice scathing.

'On the postcard you sent Amy from Cannes, you said he was amazing.'

'Yes, well, things change.'

Petra thought she knew why things had changed. Tom had told her Melanie had been travelling in France and caught Don León's eye in Cannes. Since she had run out of money, she had accepted his offer of a job aboard *Titania*.

'Did they change because of Melanie Tate? Is that why you went off to Morocco with Sheik Kamal?'

Emily gave a small shrug then winced.

'Your friend Sir Henry showed me a photograph of you and Lila after you returned. You looked very thin and unhappy. He thought you'd been taking drugs. Do you want to talk about it?'

'No.'

Petra looked directly into Emily's hard blue eyes. 'You know Sir Henry and Lila were murdered, don't you?' she said, not attempting this time to keep the harshness out of her voice. Sometimes shock tactics were needed.

Emily dropped her chin to her chest. For a long minute, she did not speak. Then she lifted her head. 'Tell me what happened,' she whispered. 'Then I'll tell you what happened.'

'And will you let me call your parents and ask them to come?' Petra asked.

'My mother. Not my father.'

Tom Gilmore found it hard to believe that only a fortnight had elapsed since Petra's departure for Nice. Those two weeks had added more salt than pepper to his prematurely greying hair.

A week ago, he had arrived back in London after his flying visit to Morocco, a disturbed and worried man. Petra's boss had been uninterested in Melanie Tate's plight and had brushed off his concerns for Petra's safety with a breezy "Give it a few days, she'll turn up." Forced to wait, Tom had irritated his co-workers to the point where they had turned and walked in the opposite direction or picked up the telephone to make an urgent call as soon as he came into sight. The old adage "No news is good news" had done nothing to allay his fears.

On Tuesday evening – the day after his return from Morocco – he had been sitting alone, eating a cheese and pickle sandwich and reading an article on the causes and treatment of amnesia, when his blue Ericsson sang a hymn of hope. The arrival of Petra's text both delighted and appalled him. He had contacted Carlo immediately and offered his support if it were needed to persuade the authorities to act on her message.

At noon the following day, he treated his colleagues – at the Government's expense – to lunch and drinks all round to celebrate the news that both Emily and Petra were safe. His final call to Canada on Petra's red phone, at three o'clock that afternoon, had been intensely satisfying. Since then, he had been imitating the Cheshire Cat.

The receptionist buzzed him to say Petra was on her way up. A few minutes later, a tap came on the door. He pulled it open and inclined his body in a short bow, concealing his pleasure with absurd formality.

'Miss Minx! You're back.'

'Indeed I am. I'm difficult to get rid of.'

'I know, you're tough. And, boy, am I glad to see you!' Tom dropped all pretence and lifted her high into the air.

'Mr. Gilmore, Sir! What have I done to deserve this?' Petra looked down at him with laughing blue-green eyes.

'You'll have to write a new chapter for my manual, entitled The Art of Disguise,' he said.

'Dressing-up was one of my favourite pastimes as a child, and the Moroccan costumes hide a lot of sins. I must say I didn't expect you to deliver my passport personally. How did you like the country?' she asked.

'It was too short a visit to make a proper assessment. My old friend the Ambassador is very positive about it. The hospital staff were caring and professional. They looked after Melanie Tate well.'

'Is she still there?'

'No. Her parents flew out yesterday to bring her back to England. She'll continue her treatment here. How is Emily?'

'Much worse off because she insisted she had rejected Don León and didn't want to be tattooed with his logo; instead she wanted twin dolphins and a complicated geometric pattern on her hands. She had a huge allergic reaction to the black henna Pablo used. You know, of course, that the blisters follow the outline of the design.'

Tom nodded. 'The effects are horrific.'

'Emily still has a long and painful road to travel to recover her health and come to terms with her experiences. I hope she'll learn something from them. Her problem was that although she kept stringing Don León along, she didn't want anyone else to have him. When Melanie came aboard and Don León started to pay her some attention, Emily became involved with one of the sailors just to spite him.'

'Let me guess: the one who forgot to lock the coaming and lost his life as a result.'

'That's right. And Melanie stayed aboard *Titania* during the first two weeks of September when Emily was in Morocco. I could hear the jealousy in Emily's voice as she talked about it. After she came back from Morocco, Emily tried to reestablish her dominance, but she still refused to do what Don León wanted.'

'No doubt that had something to do with the kind of movies he was making.'

Petra nodded. 'Carlo and the Chief of Police had a look at a few of them. Mostly girls on girls from what they said. Emily wouldn't be drawn on the subject, although she intimated that Melanie was much more amenable. After their big fight over Don León, Melanie was dispatched to Morocco to cool off. Emily stayed on at the villa in apparent contravention of Don León's orders. Then she had the bad reaction to the black henna.'

'Was she also given drugs?'

'She says not and there's no evidence of it. Olga probably told Don León Emily died of an overdose to cover up her own involvement in the tattooing. The police found a room containing a bed with leather restraints in one of the cellars at the villa, but no tattoo equipment or dyes. I suspect Raoul and his wife Bettina know much more about it than they have admitted to date. They're just trying to save their own hides.'

'I have to say you've done an amazing job, Miss Minx. You had us all on tenterhooks for a while, but you didn't forget what I told you: First in, first out! What are your plans now? Are you leaving London tomorrow?'

'I owe Amy a visit, but there's one thing I need to do before I make the trip to Oxford. I have to talk to my Moroccan friends to see whether Emy wants to leave the workshop and come home or not. I promised I would go back for her. And I won't renege on my promise.'

In the event, Emy told Petra she was content where she was. It was a relief not to have to think about men.

Amy Shire welcomed Petra into her College room in one of the tower staircases. From a small rectangular window in the corner, she had a view of the Dean's garden.

'Emily wanted me to bring you this. It's an apology for standing you up in Switzerland.' Petra handed a blue and gold striped package to Amy, who undid it with pathetic eagerness. Inside were a Spanish fan and an embroidered shawl.

'Just what I need for tonight!' Amy exclaimed. 'How is Emily now? It must have been a terrible experience, being held against her will and in such pain.'

'Emily did try to overpower Bettina when she delivered food for the second time, but she found out Bettina was as tough as nails. Emily ended up with severe bruising and two cracked ribs from being flung to the floor. The weals from the black henna could last for months, and she may need cosmetic surgery. Her hands and chest will never again tan uniformly, so she'll have to keep them out of the sun or they'll look terribly ugly and blotchy. You should alert your friends to the dangers of black henna.'

'I've already had a look at some of the pictures on the Internet. They're gross. Emily sent me an email and told me she has a new Facebook site under her own name. She wants to do some campaigning to raise awareness of the problem. Is she coming back soon?'

'Probably not until next year. She intends to stay in Spain until the treatment is complete, then she's talking about crewing on another yacht.'

Amy shuddered. 'She's mad.'

'She's resilient and I think she's enjoying the attention. The story has created quite a stir on the Costa del Sol.'

Two hours later, after meeting with the Dean to discuss the postponement of Emily's return until the following academic year and the possibility of accepting Ahmed into a post-graduate programme, Petra retraced her steps across the quadrangle to the porter's lodge. The clocks had been turned back the previous weekend and darkness had fallen.

A quartet of students in Hallowe'en costume emerged from the archway on the north side of the quad. The first, a jester in red and gold, reminded her of Mercutio as he danced and pranced, jingling the bells on his cap and rattle. His date was a vamp in a short black dress and a square-cut, psychedelic pink wig. Shades of Monica, Petra thought with a pang. The second couple might have been a figment of her imagination. With a swashbuckler's swagger, a pirate dragged along a pale, blonde girl dressed in a Turkish dancer's costume. He doffed his black skull-and-crossboned hat at Petra, releasing a mane of dark curly hair. They laughed and jostled their way through the Judas gate in the massive oak door. A distant clock struck six as Petra waved to the porter, followed them through the gate and closed it behind her.

There was no more she could do. The last three weeks of dream sequences and nightmare moments were over, her usefulness here at an end. With a despondency that she recognized as the price of disengagement, she began to plan. She would call her sister in Southampton, arrange to pick up her suitcase and book a flight back to Canada – unless she was allowed to take the rest of her curtailed vacation. In which case, if the weather held, she would be able to do some sailing.

As she crossed St. Giles to the Randolph Hotel, the phone in her pocket vibrated. She pulled it out, flipped it open and put it to her ear.

A.K.'s voice crackled through the ether. 'Have you finished there yet?'

'I've just left the College.' Petra heard the disconcerting echo of her words. Tomorrow I'll go back to Southampton…'

'Tomorrow I want you on the first flight to Nassau. Get down to London tonight and see Tom Gilmore. He'll fill you in.'

At once Petra's spirits soared. The boating in the Bahamas would be good.